Praise for *The Chalon Heads*

"One of the best-crafted, best-plotted, and most convincing British thrillers for decades."
—*Daily Mirror*

"The most satisfyingly twisty mystery of the year."
—*Kirkus Reviews* (starred)

"Riveting . . . Maitland's intricate tale never fails to grip." —*Publishers Weekly*

Barry Maitland was born in Scotland and raised in London. He now resides in Australia, where until recently he was dean and professor of architecture at the University of Newcastle, a position he relinquished in order to become a full-time writer. His other Kathy and Brock mysteries include *The Marx Sisters*, which was shortlisted for the John Creasy Award for Best First Mystery and *The Malcontenta*, which won the Ned Kelly Prize for Crime Fiction.

THE
CHALON HEADS

A Kathy and Brock Mystery

Barry Maitland

PENGUIN BOOKS

PENGUIN BOOKS

Published by the Penguin Group

Penguin Putnam Inc., 375 Hudson Street, New York, New York 10014, U.S.A

Penguin Books Ltd, 80 Strand, London WC2R 0RL, England

Penguin Books Australia Ltd, 250 Camberwell Road,

Camberwell, Victoria 3124, Australia

Penguin Books Canada Ltd, 10 Alcorn Avenue, Toronto, Ontario, Canada M4V 3B2

Penguin Books India (P) Ltd, 11 Community Centre,

Panchsheel Park, New Delhi – 110 017, India

Penguin Books (N.Z.) Ltd, Cnr Rosedale and Airborne Roads,

Albany, Auckland, New Zealand

Penguin Books (South Africa) (Pty) Ltd, 24 Sturdee Avenue,

Rosebank, Johannesburg 2196, South Africa

Penguin Books Ltd, Registered Offices: Harmondsworth, Middlesex, England

First published in Great Britain by Orion 1999
First published in the United States of America by Arcade Publishing 2001
Reprinted by arrangement with Arcade Publishing
Published in Penguin Books 2002

10 9 8 7 6 5 4 3 2 1

PUBLISHER'S NOTE
This is a work of fiction. Names, characters, places, and incidents either are the product
of the author's imagination or are used fictitiously, and any resemblance to actual persons,
living or dead, business establishments, events, or locales is entirely coincidental.

THE LIBRARY OF CONGRESS HAS CATALOGED THE HARDCOVER EDITION AS FOLLOWS:
Maitland, Barry.
The Chalon Heads : a Kathy and Brock mystery / Barry Maitland.
—1st U.S. ed.
p. cm.
ISBN 1-55970-570-1 (hc.)
ISBN 0 14 20.0082 5 (pbk.)
1. Brock, David (Fictitious character)—Fiction.
2. Kolla, Kathy (Fictitious character)—Fiction.   3. Police corruption—Fiction.
4. Police—England—Fiction.   5. Stamp collectors—Fiction.   6. Missing persons—
Fiction.   7. Policewomen—Fiction.   I. Title.
PR9619.3.M2635 C47   2001
823'.914—dc21   2001022670

Printed in the United States of America
Set in Bembo

CONTENTS

ACKNOWLEDGEMENTS

I'm grateful to many people for inspiration and help in writing this book, including Detective Chief Superintendent Brian Ridley, Fred Broughton, Tony Judge, Scott and Anna Farrow, Mike and Lily Cloughley, Mic Cheetham, Neil Rees, John Boersig and, above all, Margaret Maitland.

The publishers would also like to express their thanks to Dr Mike Harvey of Stanley Gibbons Ltd on the Strand for his help in creating the cover artwork. Inaccuracies in the reproduction of the envelope are by our design.

The Chalon Head stamps are reproduced courtesy of Canada Post Corporation.

Philately

The term was coined in 1864 by a Frenchman, Georges Herpin, who invented it from the Greek *philos*, 'love', and *ateleia*, 'that which is tax-free'.

Britannica Online, 1997

THE
CHALON HEADS

PROLOGUE

Raphael and The Beast

DC Martin was released from her prison on the dawn of the fifth day. She stepped through the wicket gate in the steel roller door, emptied her lungs of the stale, dead reek of the desolate building, and filled them again with crisp morning air laced with the tang of diesel fumes. Freedom. She stretched her legs, rolled her shoulders and took in the inconsequential sounds of the city stirring all around her. It had been her first real experience of solitary confinement, and she didn't ever want to try it again. Her ears were ringing, her eyes bleary with sleeplessness, her limbs aching. She felt exhausted, grimy and disoriented.

And pissed off. For four days and nights she had squatted in a cupboard in the dark, alone, waiting for a rendezvous that had never happened. It had been a salutary lesson in the effects of sensory deprivation. Her only conversation had been infrequent whispered monosyllabic reports into a radio, her view a dim panorama of cardboard boxes seen through a spyhole. The Hitachi crate had sat prominently in the middle of them, untouched, unapproached. Towards the end, unable to sleep or stay truly awake, she had begun to fixate on that Hitachi sign as an old lag might fixate on a blade of grass or a crack in the wall.

There had been another detective with her inside the building, but they had never met once their positions had been allocated. She knew of his presence only from the toilet, for which from time to time she was grudgingly allowed to leave her hiding place. They had been forbidden to flush that toilet for fear of alerting an intruder, an absurd directive since the evidence of her colleague's presence had become more and more palpable as the days had passed. By the third day the extent of his intestinal problem was becoming overpowering.

The thing had been prolonged far beyond any reasonable use of resources or expectation of a result, becoming in the end simply a monument to McLarren's stubbornness. Mary Martin looked up and down the service lane to see if he might still be lingering, unable to accept defeat, but there was no one, the outside teams called off an hour before. Now that she was in the open air, in the daylight, she could feel ashamed of the resentment she had developed for the outside teams, able to talk freely to each other in their unmarked cars, rotating home to a warm bed and a hot meal. And a bath, and a clean toilet. She had been placed inside because McLarren had developed a particular attachment to the idea that Raphael might be a woman. Mary had had plenty of time to mull over McLarren's attachment to bizarre ideas.

She looked back up at the windows of the second floor, where she had been incarcerated. The dawn sunlight, which was now raking across the rooftops, catching the chimneys and gables in a golden blaze, was visible through the third window from the end, glittering on the interior of the warehouse. Except that the sun was on the other side of the building, and there was no way it could penetrate through the interior to this side.

DC Martin frowned. Perhaps her unseen companion of the toilet had switched on a light on his way out. A buzz of anger went through her. Unreasonably, she told herself. The poor bloke must have been suffering for days, praying for release. And because the thought made her penitent she didn't walk away, as she might have done, but braced herself and turned back towards the wicket gate. Soon she was inside the stairwell, and didn't see the glow in the upper-floor window go off.

At the top of the dark stairs she eased open the door to the second floor and, in the grey light that was filtering through the warehouse, she was astonished to see that the Hitachi box had moved half a dozen yards to the left. The other boxes around it had been disturbed too. She froze, listening for any sound from the cavernous space. But when she finally picked it up it came not from in front of her but from behind, a soft scuffling. She wheeled round and saw a huge dim form bearing down on her across the dark landing. She backed rapidly into the warehouse and it followed her through the doors, materialising into a giant of a man.

They both stopped, examining each other. He was breathing heavily, long black hair tied behind in a pigtail, a thick black beard, tattoos on his bare forearms, a ferocious–looking crowbar dangling from one enormous fist. Behind him was a second man, pale and scrawny, peering round the giant's bulging biceps, eyes widening at the sight of a woman wearing body armour and a police cap.

After a moment's silence, Mary said calmly, 'Police. Don't move. You're under arrest.'

The giant regarded her thoughtfully. The crowbar twitched in his mitt. 'How much you weigh?' he asked ponderously.

'120 pounds,' Mary replied, amazed at her own composure.

'Well, I'm 290. What do they tell you to do, then, in your training, like, when a 120-pound plonk faces up to a 290-pound villain?'

'Get help,' Mary replied.

'That makes sense.'

DC Martin reached a hand to her hip and brought up the Glock, pointing it at the centre of his huge chest. 'Armed police,' she said. 'Did I say that before?'

'No,' he said sadly. 'I don't fink you mentioned that.'

She fumbled with her other hand for the radio, keeping the gun trained on the big man. The other seemed like his frail shadow, moving only when he moved.

'Let me guess,' she said, pointing the muzzle at the skinny anaemic one for a moment. 'You're Raphael, right? The artist?' She returned her aim to the giant. 'And you're The Beast . . . Or is that too obvious? Could it be the other way around?'

The big man shook his head. 'I'm Titch. And this is Marlon.'

'Well,' Mary said. 'And I'll bet you've got the loveliest birth certificates to prove it.'

She had the radio to her mouth when the first blow sent it flying from her hand. Before she could turn, the second hit her, and she crumpled to the floor, all lights extinguished now.

Cabot's

It began innocently enough, in the days before Kathy knew a cottonreel from a woodblock.

The long corridor of the Strand was booming with traffic, dust and petrol fumes hanging in the hot July afternoon air. Half-way along on the shady south side, not far from the set-back entrance of the Savoy Hotel, Brock and Kathy found the shop-front surmounted by the name Cabot's, in ornate raised gold letters on a black ground. Beneath, two small boys had their noses pressed to the glass, mesmerised by a display of old postage stamps.

Inside, in air-conditioned calm, they were confronted by a pyramid of devices, which looked to Kathy as if they belonged in the forensic lab — magnifying glasses both simple and illuminated, watermark detectors, colour indicators, packets of mounts, tweezers, tiny guillotines, short and long wave and ultraviolet lamps for identifying phosphor inks and coatings.

'Nothing stays simple, does it?' Brock said, pointing at the shelves of reference books and albums filling one wall. 'When I was a boy, the complete listing of all the stamps in the world was contained in one small fat volume. Now you need a library.'

He took a pair of half-lens glasses from his jacket pocket and leaned forward to examine a pocket microscope in the display, unconsciously imitating the posture of the small boys at the front window. He might have been their uncle, Kathy thought, or their schoolmaster, a big benign bear of a man in a slightly rumpled suit, grey beard and hair in need of a trim, as unlike the hard young men of Serious Crime as he could be, and therefore dangerous in a different way.

Kathy looked around at the other people in the room. A glass counter circled the space, stools in front, glass shelves and cabinets behind with concealed lighting. A number of customers, office workers in shirt-sleeves by the look of them, were browsing or crouching over the counter, some deep in conversation with studious-looking sales assistants. They were all male, Kathy noticed, and indeed, despite the array of technology at the door, the place had something about it that made her think of an old-fashioned gentlemen's club – an air of ordered calm, of discreetly murmured conversations, of clocks ticking but time standing still.

'Is all this just about postage stamps?' she whispered.

'Mmm . . .' Brock's attention had shifted now to a cabinet of tiny paper fragments. 'Fascinating, isn't it? Another world. Did you ever collect stamps, Kathy?'

'No. I seem to remember collecting things from cornflakes packets, but I can't remember what they were.'

Brock's raised eyebrow told her that that was entirely different, but for the life of her she couldn't see why.

Brock tore himself away from the cabinet and they made their way through a pair of glass doors into a lobby in which another kind of display was mounted, advertising a forthcoming auction. Expensive-looking catalogues were on sale, and posters featured some of the more important sale items. Again Brock delayed, studying a couple of the layouts. 'There's money in it,' he murmured.

Kathy wondered, looking at an old envelope in a glass case. The stamp was crude and scruffy, almost obliterated by a heavy postmark. How much would people pay for such things? Ten pounds? Fifty? A hundred? Surely not the price of a decent camera, or a washing-machine.

They went on past the display to a reception desk standing in front of lift doors.

'Detective Chief Inspector Brock and Detective Sergeant

Kolla to see Mr James Melville,' Brock said. The receptionist considered his identification with interest and made a phone call, then indicated the lift.

A big cheerful man was waiting for them when the doors opened on the second floor, dressed like a banker but with an unruly mop of hair that refused to lie down. He introduced himself, shook their hands warmly and led them into his cramped office, offering them seats. His desk overflowed with papers, a tray of incoming mail threatening a pile of magazines and catalogues, a computer terminal jostling for space in the corner.

'Thank you so much for coming here, Chief Inspector. I do appreciate it. Can I offer you anything? Tea? Coffee?'

They declined. Brock said, 'I was glad to get the opportunity to visit, Mr Melville. I used to be an enthusiast, many years ago, but I never knew where you were.'

'Ah, yes. We and our rivals just along the street.' He indicated the name on the Stanley Gibbons catalogue lying on the desk. Kathy picked it up and began thumbing through it.

'What was your area, Chief Inspector?'

Brock smiled, remembering. 'I had an aunt in Canada so I had plenty of Canadian stamps, as I recall. She used to make a point of sending me first-day covers.'

'Ah, well, they may be worth something now, you never know. We have a particularly outstanding Canadian cover in our coming auction that you'd be interested in. Let me give you both a catalogue . . .' He stooped into the narrow space behind his desk with some difficulty and emerged with copies, which he handed across to them. As he did this he took the opportunity to examine Kathy's hands. No rings, no nail polish, and traces of something – photocopy toner? He nodded approvingly.

'What about you, Sergeant?' Melville asked. 'Were you ever a collector?' He didn't imagine for one moment that she had been, but he wanted to hear her voice. He approved of young women like this, competent and unpretentious, with low heels and little makeup.

'I'm afraid not, sir. I know absolutely nothing about it.'

An intelligent voice, class-neutral, and cautious, like her eyes.

He did like her eyes, and the way her fair hair, cut short, was tucked behind her ears.

'Well, perhaps we'll have the opportunity to show you something of it . . . if you have time.'

What it was that resonated with him about young women like this, James Melville couldn't precisely say, except perhaps that they didn't frighten him the way the others, all legs and lipstick, did. On the other hand, his last attempt to help just such a sensible young woman advance her career in Cabot's had ended in near disaster. He took a deep breath to calm himself and turned to Brock. 'I do hope you won't feel I've wasted your time, Chief Inspector.'

'Not at all,' Brock replied. 'You knew my name, Mr Melville. Have we met?'

'No, I don't believe so, but I know you by reputation from the newspapers.'

'You said you had a problem. Is it to do with the auction? We saw the display downstairs. Looks fascinating.'

'Ah, yes, a major event. But no, that wasn't the reason for my call, Chief Inspector. Rather, it was to do with one of our clients, someone we've known for a number of years, who appears to be in some dreadful trouble. He told me about it only this morning, and I suggested – no, I insisted – that he contact the police.'

'I see,' said Brock slowly. 'But how did you get my name, Mr Melville?'

'It was our client who suggested that if I was to call anyone it should be you. He holds you in very high regard, Chief Inspector.'

'Is that right?'

'Look,' Melville said hurriedly, 'why don't I get him in here and have him explain it all to you himself? He's in the other office at the moment.'

'Sounds like a good idea.'

Kathy watched Melville's departure with interest. He seemed quite anxious, and she wondered who would have chosen to approach Brock in such an indirect way, and have him meet him on ground like this. Royalty, perhaps? The Queen collected stamps, didn't she? Or someone in government, a pop star . . .

8

The door opened, and Melville ushered in a man almost a foot shorter than himself, sturdily built, as formally dressed in dark pinstripe suit, and with a remarkably round, creamy face with Oriental features, jet-black hair swept back from his high forehead. The man was smiling so intently that his eyes were merely horizontal creases in his face.

'Mr Brock!' he cried. 'How are you?' exposing brilliant white teeth, and Kathy was surprised, having quickly adjusted to the idea that this might be a businessman from Hong Kong or Singapore, to hear a cockney accent mildly gentrified to the outer suburbs.

'Good God,' Brock said, sounding astonished and not at all enthusiastic. 'Sammy Starling.'

Undeterred by the coolness in Brock's voice, the man advanced on him, hand outstretched, beaming from ear to ear.

Melville hurriedly drew up another chair. 'I was saying, Mr Starling, that it would be best if you explained the matter yourself.'

The man nodded energetically. 'Yes, yes. But it's good to see you again, Mr Brock! You don't look a day older.'

'Nor you, Sammy,' Brock replied, his good humour evaporated. Kathy could see that Melville was aware of it and was embarrassed. 'What's this all about?' Brock asked.

Starling's face abruptly lost all expression. He hesitated for a moment, then spoke in a low voice, devoid of all the animation it had had before. 'It's my wife, Mr Brock. She's missing.'

'Well, now,' Brock murmured, watching him carefully.

Starling cleared his throat. 'She came up to town at the end of last week. I haven't heard from her since.'

Kathy was trying to fix his age. His smooth face was deceptive, she decided. There was a hoarseness in the voice and creases in the neck and behind the ears that made him much older than he had first appeared. Fifty plus, she guessed. She noticed a pale scar crossing the back of his left hand, slicing across all four fingers above the knuckles. Defence wound, she thought automatically. Starling's appearance, like his accent, had also undergone a process of gentrification, she decided, tailored suits and old scars.

9

Brock frowned as if trying to recall. 'Mrs Starling . . . Brenda?'

'Eva,' Starling said, with quiet force, as if trying to jog his memory. 'Brenda died in 'eighty-seven.'

He drew his wallet from his jacket pocket and took out a photograph, which he passed to Brock, who looked at it for a moment then passed it on to Kathy. It was night, the couple caught in camera flash, he beaming in white tuxedo, she in a short black cocktail dress, hem swinging with her step. No older than thirty, Kathy thought, trying not to appear surprised. More like twenty-five. Black hair swept back from a smiling, vivacious face, long slender neck. Dark, beautiful, Mediterranean looks. Simple but expensive jewellery and dress. You must be rich, Mr Starling, she thought.

'Where was this taken?' she asked.

'Cannes, last year,' Starling said, pleased at the question. 'Film festival.'

'Is she an actress?'

'No,' he said. 'She's my wife.' He blinked at the look Kathy gave him. 'I mean, no, she doesn't work.'

'And you've been married how long now?' Brock asked.

'Three years and seven months,' he said. 'On Saturday.'

'I remember. They called her a princess in the gossip columns, didn't they?'

Starling's mouth gave a hint of a smile and he nodded.

'You said that she came up to town, so you don't live in London?' Kathy asked.

'Our home's in Surrey,' Starling said. 'Near Farnham. And we've got a flat in town, in Canonbury. But she's not there. I've looked everywhere.'

Brock eyed him closely, waiting for more. When none came he said, 'Why this, Sammy?' He gestured at the room. 'What's this all about?'

The other lowered his head and said, 'She's been kidnapped, Mr Brock.'

'Kidnapped?'

Starling sighed. 'I need your help.'

Melville, unable to contain himself further, said, 'Mr Starling came to see me this morning, Chief Inspector, and under the circumstances I couldn't just ignore –'

'Why was that?' Brock asked, keeping his eyes on Starling. 'Why did he come here?'

'Why, on account of the stamps,' Melville said. 'Why don't you show him, Mr Starling?'

Starling reached again into the inside pocket of his suit and brought out two envelopes. Checking the date of the postmarks, he handed one to Brock, who took it from him and carefully drew out a single folded sheet of paper. He read it, then spread it out on the table. A handwritten message had been printed in the centre of the page,

WHERE IS SHE, SAMMY?
IT'LL COST YOU PLENTY
TO FIND OUT.

Above these words was pasted a small faded scarlet rectangle, a tiny picture of a woman's head, surrounded by a decorative frame. It was only when she looked closely at it that Kathy saw that the frame contained lettering, 'Van Diemen's Land', and 'Postage, One Penny'.

'A stamp?' she asked.

Melville nodded.

'It looks old. There's no perforations around the edge.'

'1855,' he said. 'It's a Chalon Head.'

'A what?'

'It's the name of a type of stamp.'

'Is it rare?'

'Quite rare. The catalogue gives this one a value of about one thousand pounds.'

Kathy blinked in astonishment at the grubby little scrap of paper.

'That's an odd way to demand a ransom, isn't it?' Brock said, looking at Starling. 'I thought the general idea was for the kidnapper to get money from the victim, rather than the other way round.'

Starling leaned forward and pointed at the stamp. 'They've glued it to the page with some kind of adhesive, like epoxy or something.' He gazed at Brock with an expression of incomprehension. 'The stamp's worthless now. They've destroyed it. Isn't that right, Mr Melville?'

'That's correct.'

Starling shook his head in disgust, and it struck Kathy that he seemed more upset about this than about the reference to his wife in the message.

Brock examined the envelope. 'Postmark central London, EC1. Address written in hand-printed capitals. Like the note.'

Kathy looked more closely at the tiny portrait. It was of a young woman, presumably the young Queen Victoria, head and naked shoulders, wearing a crown, earrings, a necklace, hair swept back and up. As she examined it, she felt an odd sense of foreboding. She asked Starling if she could have another look at the photograph of his wife, which he had returned to his wallet. He caught her expression and gave it to her without a word. She laid it alongside the stamp. 'It's her, isn't it?' she said to him.

Melville said, 'Sorry?' and she passed them both to him. He too stared in astonishment. 'Good heavens! It is very like her. I had no idea. I've never met Mrs Starling.'

While Brock also made the comparison, Kathy watched Starling. He showed no surprise at her observation, and appeared almost disappointed, as if he had been well aware of this but had been intending to keep it to himself.

'Do you think it significant?' Melville asked, but no one offered a reply. 'I merely assumed that the Chalon Head referred to Mr Starling's area of interest. He has made quite a specialisation out of Chalons, haven't you, Mr Starling?'

Starling nodded. His face was exceedingly difficult to read, its creamy circle creased by his features in what might have been an expression of discreet pleasure, or embarrassment, or pain.

'There were two envelopes? What about the other one?' Brock said.

'That one came in the post yesterday, this one this morning.' Starling handed over the second envelope, posted a day later from the same central London postal district. The format of the message was the same. It read,

DO EXACTLY WHAT YOU'RE TOLD, SAMMY,
IF YOU WANT HER BACK IN ONE PIECE.

There was another, similar stamp pasted above the lines of lettering, this one green, with the value twopence. But this time

12

the stamp was sliced diagonally in two, through the neck of the young queen.

Brock stared at it impassively for a while, then said heavily, without lifting his head, 'You didn't really think that I could conduct some kind of private investigation for you, did you, Sammy?'

Starling tilted his impassive face. 'I'm in your hands, Mr Brock. You know how things stand.'

'Yes.' Brock took a deep breath, as if about to take up a great burden, reluctantly. 'And is there anything else I should know, Sammy?'

Starling lowered his eyes. 'Three months ago . . . they released Keller.'

'Did they, now? I didn't hear that. Well, then, you'd better come back with us and give us a full statement.'

'Ah . . .' Starling looked distinctly anxious now. 'I don't think I should do that, Mr Brock. They may be watching me. That's why I thought we should meet here. And, you know. I could never come to Scotland Yard . . .'

Brock handed him a card. 'Go to this address. Don't worry, no one will know you there.'

He made to get to his feet, but Melville broke in, 'Chief Inspector, the reason why I felt this matter to be so urgent . . .'

'Yes, Mr Melville?'

'I believe it likely that there will be three messages, and three only.'

'Why is that?'

'These Van Diemen's Land stamps, there are just three in that set – the penny red, the twopenny green, and the fourpence blue.'

Brock nodded. 'Yesterday, today, and tomorrow.'

'Quite.'

2

Queen Anne's Gate

They made their way separately to Queen Anne's Gate, Brock and Kathy by taxi, Starling by bus to St James's Park and then on foot by a circuitous route until he had satisfied himself that he wasn't being followed.

As their taxi made its way slowly through the hot afternoon streets, Brock became increasingly preoccupied and sombre. Eventually he rubbed fiercely at the beard on the side of his jaw and said, 'Well, well, and I thought that was going to be a pleasant digression from the usual run of things.'

'You've had dealings with Mr Starling before,' Kathy prompted.

'Very much so,' Brock said heavily. 'Must be eight or nine years ago, the last time I saw him. And I did very much hope it would be the last time, too. Who would have expected Sammy Starling to show his face again, after so long?'

'A villain?'

'He has been. He has a flair for business. Made quite a bit of money for himself.' He stared grimly out of the cab window at the tourists snapping the sentries outside the Horse Guards, broiling inside their breastplates and helmets.

'And who is Keller?'

Brock seemed about to answer her, then changed his mind. 'No, you don't want to know, Kathy. None of us needs this.

This is not a case for us. The first thing is to get it properly assigned. When Sammy arrives at Queen Anne's Gate, we'll hand him over, wash our hands, and get on with our lives.'

He took the photograph of Starling and his wife at Cannes from his pocket. 'Who the hell does he think he is? Aristotle Onassis?' He turned back to the window, brooding.

The offices used by Brock's section of Department SO1, Serious Crime Branch, occupied a row of terraces on the south side of Queen Anne's Gate, several blocks away from the main building of New Scotland Yard, and one of a number of annexes that had overspilled into the surrounding district. For Brock and his team, the independence and relative isolation of the old building from the modern slab office block of the Yard were an asset, illustrated now by the anonymity with which Starling was able to come to them.

The building also had another characteristic, which appealed to its occupants, though not to the asset managers of the Central Property Branch. Originally a row of separate eighteenth-century townhouses, it had long ago been converted to offices, with openings formed through the original party walls to link the staircases and corridors of the former houses into a maze of interconnected passageways serving an eccentric mixture of rooms, whose odd sizes bore no relationship to the standard space allocations for headquarters' staff.

They entered through one of the identical black front doors facing the street, and made their way to the office of Brock's secretary, Dot. She took one look at Brock through her large tortoiseshell glasses and said, 'Problem?'

'Sammy Starling,' he said. 'Remember him?' He seemed as if still not quite able to credit it.

'Oh, no. He hasn't surfaced again, has he?'

'I'm very much afraid so. He'll be arriving here shortly. See if you can get hold of Commander Sharpe for me, will you? Urgent matter.'

Dot picked up the phone, and a minute later transferred the call through to Brock in his office. While he talked behind his closed door, Kathy said, 'Starling seems to have left a big impression, Dot. What did he do? He seemed rather innocuous to look at.'

15

'I never met him in the flesh, but I remember his picture in the papers. Chinese, yes?'

Kathy nodded.

'Yes, a sort of baby face, looked so innocent. Yet he caused so much trouble.'

'How?'

'He gave evidence against three corrupt officers in the Fraud Squad . . .' Dot frowned, thinking. 'But it was more complicated than that. I know it caused Brock a lot of grief. What's he up to now?'

'His wife's been kidnapped, and he wants Brock to take the case on. Brock doesn't want to touch it.'

'I'll bet.' She looked down at the indicator light on her phone, bit her lip and crossed her fingers.

The light kept shining for another ten minutes. When it finally went off, Kathy and Dot waited for Brock to open his door. Instead the phone rang. 'Is Bren in the building, Dot?' Brock asked.

'Yes, I think so.'

'Get him and Kathy in here as quick as you can, will you?'

Kathy waited for DS Bren Gurney, a soft-spoken West Countryman, to appear and they went into Brock's office together. He waved them to seats around a small table.

'Sammy Starling,' he began, face dark. 'Remember his case, Bren?'

'That was to do with the Fraud Squad, wasn't it? Long time ago.'

'Ten years. Sammy's business dealings were being looked into by SO6. Just when it seemed that a case was coming together, Sammy turned the tables by providing evidence of corruption against three senior officers of the Fraud Squad, including the officer investigating him. This effectively undermined the evidence against Starling, and also led to the arrest of the three officers. Of the three, one committed suicide during their trial and one died in prison. The third, former DI Marty Keller, was released from prison three months ago.

'Kathy and I had an unexpected meeting with Sammy earlier this afternoon. He claims that his young wife, Eva Starling, has been kidnapped. He also says that he's afraid to come to the police in the normal way, because of bad feeling over his earlier case.'

Bren looked doubtful. 'Oh, yes?'

'Yes. I've just had a conversation with Commander Sharpe, requesting that he allocate the case to someone else. He disagreed.'

'Were you involved with the earlier case?' Kathy asked.

Brock nodded. 'I was the officer who investigated Starling's allegations against the three SO6 men. I was the one who arrested Keller, and the other two. Sharpe feels that gives me some priority in the present affair. I think . . .' Brock looked away at the window '. . . I think he wants us to quarantine Sammy. Keep him to ourselves. I said I thought that was a mistake. Anyway, that's how it stands. Sammy should be here in a minute. Just don't underestimate him, eh? He has this air of benign innocence, like a child. People have been misled by it. He's tough and he's bright.'

The phone went. Brock listened briefly and replied, 'Bren will pick him up.' He turned to them. 'He's here.'

'I'll send for the files.' Kathy said.

'Yes, do that. Mind you, there'll be nothing on Sammy for years now.' A sudden thought struck him. 'Look, if you want to get to know about Sammy Starling, you should speak to someone who's made a lifetime study of him. Criminal Intelligence did quite a bit of work at one time. Peter White, former DCI. You might speak to him.'

'Former DCI?'

'Yes. Retired a few years ago.'

'Oh. Won't he be a bit out of touch? Perhaps I'd be better to give SO11 a call.'

'It might be best for us to keep this to ourselves at present, Kathy, as far as possible. Sammy's nervousness about contacting us isn't entirely paranoia, especially if this has something to do with Keller. Actually, you'd be doing me a favour talking to old Peter. I'd like to know how he is. Haven't seen him for ages.'

There was something about the way Brock said this that made Kathy pause. 'Wouldn't you rather see him yourself?' she said, probing gently.

Brock turned to gather a file from his desk. 'Maybe another time. We had a slight falling out. Nothing serious.'

Bren introduced himself to Starling at the front desk. As he towered over the visitor, taking his cautious handshake, his impression was of a small, unobtrusive man anxious to avoid trouble, but that meant nothing: Bren had known plenty of diminutive, obliging people who caused untold grief, his wife's mother chief among them. 'They're waiting for you upstairs, Mr Starling. I'll lead the way. It's a bit confusing.'

Starling followed his guide as he disappeared along a corridor, up a flight of stairs, around a corner, down a few steps, up a few more, and round another corner, bringing him eventually to a panelled door. He tapped and opened it, indicating for Starling to enter. Brock, Kathy and Dot were seated at a long conference table. At the far end of the room a tall sash window gave a view into a tiny walled courtyard, in which a few ferns struggled for life.

Brock introduced his secretary, who gave Starling a small smile, examining him with considerable interest.

'It's private here, Sammy,' Brock said. 'We'll conduct a preliminary interview, then see what we can do. Take a seat.'

Starling and Bren took the chairs offered, and Brock pressed the button on a tape-recorder on the table in front of him. 'Dot will set up the paperwork in such a way that the details of the operation are kept as confidential as possible, Sammy. But, clearly, several people will have to know and approve.

'Now, tell me what you know about Keller. Did he write to you from prison? Threaten you in any way?'

Starling shook his head. 'No. All I knew I read in the papers. After Stringer died, it was reported that Keller had been moved up to the maximum security block at Durham, and I heard no more about him. I put him out of my mind, forgot that he existed.'

Brock opened the file in front of him. 'Martin Arthur Keller. Former Detective Inspector in Department SO6, Fraud Squad. Sentenced at the Old Bailey to thirteen years for perjury, conspiracy to pervert the course of justice, the taking of a bribe, assault on a witness, and attempted murder. Released on April the twenty-third this year after serving eight years and six months. Now aged forty-five. He had a wife, who divorced him two years into his sentence. No children. Next of kin given as a brother, Barney Keller, painter and decorator, of Ealing, West London.'

Brock looked closely at Starling. 'The attempted murder charge was what clinched it, wasn't it, Sammy? And you were the intended victim.'

Starling shuddered. 'I still can't take the tube, Mr Brock. Just the thought of those tunnels, turning a corner and seeing him again, standing there waiting for me . . .'

'So it's natural that you'd immediately think of him, especially with him having just been released. But is there anything more than that?'

'A couple of months ago I got this phone call from someone. Male voice, didn't say who he was. Wanted to tell me that Keller was out of jail. Thought I'd like to know.'

'Did the call seem threatening to you? Or could it have been a friend? Someone from the old days, perhaps, who'd heard that Keller was out.'

'I don't know. It was over in a few seconds. But I didn't recognise the voice, and if it had been a friend, why wouldn't they have said who they were? And the call came to my private line at home, which is ex-directory.'

'So you felt threatened by it. What did you do?'

'Nothing at first. I just shrugged it off. Keller had been guilty, and he'd done his time. End of story. What was it to me, now? It had all happened so long ago.'

Starling paused, blank face staring at the blank wall as if trying to picture something, and they waited for him to go on.

'What changed your mind, then?'

'A few days later I woke up in the middle of the night. The way you do . . . do you know what I mean?' He looked at Brock, willing him to understand. Kathy, studying his face, felt she was beginning to read its subtle inflections, catching the swift little shadows, barely detectable, that turned the bland circle from fear to hope, amusement to sadness. 'When you've pushed something you don't want to think about to the back of your mind. And then, suddenly, you wake up, and there it is, big and real, in flashing lights? I thought about the phone call, and I began to think about Keller, and how he'd look at things.

'Ten years ago he was a young, ambitious copper, a favourite with his bosses, Stringer and Harley, obviously heading for the top. He had a lovely wife, nice house, a bit of money in the bank. Whereas I was a man without a future, not long widowed, facing a stretch in gaol.

'Ten years later, it's him that's coming out of prison. It's him that's lost everything, his wife, his house, his money. He has no future. And in the meantime I've been reborn. I'm a successful businessman. I've got a beautiful young wife. I live in a big house.'

Starling took a deep breath, and Kathy picked up a wheeze – a summer cold, perhaps, or hay fever, asthma. His smooth forehead was gleaming with a film of sweat, more than when he'd come in, although it was much cooler in here than outside in the street.

'I lay awake for a long time, thinking about this. It was as if I could see into his mind – as if his thoughts were coming direct to me, through the darkness, thoughts that he'd had more than eight prison years to think. I was responsible, and he would want me to pay, no question of that. And it scared the shit out of me, I tell you.'

'You were always such a cool customer, Sammy,' Brock said quietly. 'Never one to panic.'

'Yeah, well . . .' Starling took a handkerchief from his trouser pocket and wiped the sweat away from his eyelids. 'We get old. And maybe now I got something to panic about.'

Kathy noticed that his hand had a tremor.

'So what did you do?'

'First I spent a lot of money upgrading the security on the house and the flat. Then I arranged to find out what Keller got up to when he came out.'

'How did you do that?'

'There's a bloke I've used before, known him for years. Private investigator. I got him to find Keller and watch him, day and night.'

'And what did he do?'

'He went to Ealing, where his brother lives. Barney had rented a room for him, and given him a job with his firm, painting and decorating.'

'Who's this investigator of yours?' Brock asked.

Starling hesitated. 'He doesn't know about the kidnapping, Mr Brock. And he doesn't need to.'

'Fair enough. What's his name?'

'Sometimes his methods are a bit . . . cost effective.'

'Nice way of putting it, Sammy. We all approve of cost effectiveness. One of the cardinal virtues these days. What's his name?'

'Ronnie Wilkes.'

'So Ronnie Wilkes did what? Searched Keller's room while he was out painting and decorating?' Starling nodded. 'And found what?'

'Nothing,' Starling said.

'No newspaper clippings of your wedding to Eva? No address book with your entry? No prison diary?'

'No.'

'And he followed Keller, and what did that produce?'

Starling shook his head gloomily. 'He works eight or nine hours a day on his brother's jobs, stops on the way home for a pint of beer with the other lads, buys a take-away and goes back to his room. The light goes out at ten o'clock, regular. At the weekend he goes to the football with his brother and his brother's kid – Chelsea supporters. On Sunday he goes to their house for a roast dinner. He sleeps a lot.'

'All very innocent, then.'

'It's not natural. His room is like his prison cell. Worse than that – no radio, no TV, no pictures on the wall, no letters, no mates. He doesn't go anywhere on his own. As far as Ronnie can tell, he's made no contact with anyone he knew in the Met. He shows no interest in women. It's as if, in his head, he's still inside. Or on a mission.'

'Let's not get carried away, Sammy. Anything else?'

'He has a mobile phone, so his brother can keep in touch with him on the jobs,' Starling said cautiously. 'Ronnie came by a record of his calls.'

'Did he indeed? Very cost effective. Anything interesting?'

'Not a thing.'

'How long did Ronnie watch him?'

'Over three weeks, then I called him off. Since then, I get him to do a random tail from time to time, and check Keller's phone calls. There's never been anything.'

'Well, I don't get it then, Sammy. What makes you so convinced . . . ?'

'Men don't behave like that when they get out of prison, Mr Brock. He must have arranged everything while he was inside. He has friends, people he met inside, and before that coppers who thought he got a raw deal. He fixed everything up before he was released, and now he's behaving like a man who assumes he's being watched. He's so well behaved it isn't human. You can see that, can't you?'

Starling was leaning forward stiffly, trying to infect them with his conviction, but all he saw in their faces was scepticism.

'All right,' Brock said, after a moment. 'Tell us about Eva's disappearance. Was there anything, looking back now, to warn you? Any strange cars in your street? Unfamiliar faces in the neighbourhood?'

Starling shook his head. 'They'd have stood out. It's a very quiet spot, where we live.'

'Are you and Eva alone in the house?'

'Marianna lives with us. She was Eva's nanny when she was a girl, and Eva brought her with her when we got married, as her maid.'

'From where?'

'Portugal. They're Portuguese. Marianna doesn't speak much English. Hardly a word, although she's been here over three years now.'

'I see. So when did you last see Eva?'

'Last Thursday, Eva said she was going to go to the flat for the weekend. We had breakfast on the Friday morning, then I took her down to Farnham station and she caught the ten eighteen up to town. I haven't seen or heard from her since.'

Brock looked at him with surprise. 'You let her come up here on her own?'

Starling lowered his eyes. He tried to say something, but the sound came out as a croak. He coughed, clearing his throat, and managed, 'Any chance of a glass of water, Mr Brock?'

Bren nodded and left the room.

'Since I started getting worried about Keller, I hadn't let Eva out of my sight,' Starling said hoarsely. 'I wouldn't let her leave the house to go down to Farnham, or take a walk in the woods round where we live. And it was driving her crazy.'

Bren returned with a glass of water, which Starling gulped awkwardly, almost choking. He brought out his handkerchief again and wiped his mouth and eyes.

'Eva is a fanatic about movies, Mr Brock,' he went on. 'Especially Spanish and South American movies – Brazil, Argentina, Mexico . . . There are certain cinemas in London she's found that show the stuff she likes. At first I used to go with her. Only I couldn't make much sense of it. My Spanish and Portuguese aren't much better than Marianna's English. I'd lose my place with the subtitles, and fall asleep, and Eva would have to wake me up, to stop me snoring.'

He took another sip of water, more cautiously this time.

'So, once she knew her way around, I let her go up to the flat on her own. I opened an account at an Italian restaurant round the corner where she could eat, and she'd have two, three days at a time, doing a bit of shopping, and pigging out on foreign movies. Seriously, she could spend whole days, from waking up in the morning to going to bed at night, sitting in the dark in some movie house, weeping and laughing . . .'

'On her own? No Marianna, or friends?'

'Marianna doesn't like the city, and there's only one bedroom in the flat. Eva's got no friends in town apart from my friends, people my age. I've phoned round them all – none of them have heard from her.'

'What about the phone, Sammy? Don't you keep in touch with her?'

'Yes, of course, normally. But sometimes she gets so wrapped up in the films, and just forgets to answer messages. She's not good with answering-machines, things like that. She doesn't even have a mobile – says she can never remember the buttons to press to turn it on or recover messages. And I never like to make her feel I'm checking on her.

'It wasn't until after the weekend that I started to worry. By Tuesday evening, when I still couldn't raise her, I decided to go up to the flat myself the next day. Then, Wednesday morning, the first letter arrived. Those words, "*Where is she, Sammy?*"' He rubbed his fingers across his mouth. 'It was an accusation. She was missing, and I hadn't known . . . How long had she been gone?'

'The first letter was postmarked Tuesday morning,' Brock said. 'Show them to Bren, will you, Sammy?'

He passed them over to Bren, who took the two letters out of their envelopes, the same questions forming in his mind that Kathy had asked. 'These are old stamps, aren't they?' he began.

Brock said, 'Yes, tell us about the stamps, Sammy. It didn't seem to make much sense earlier.'

'It's quite simple really. I'm a philatelist.'

Kathy saw Bren's face go blank with disbelief.

Starling shrugged. 'I collect postage stamps for a hobby. In my own way, I suppose I'm as fanatical about old stamps as Eva is about movies.'

The others received this with a heavy silence.

'How long have you had this particular hobby, Sammy?' Brock asked finally.

'I started when I was a kid, then I forgot about it for a long time. I suppose I got into it again about the time Brenda died. It gave me something to take my mind off that and other things.'

'It's a tax dodge, is that it?' Bren suggested, a light dawning on his face. 'Some way of investing dodgy cash. Is that right?'

'No.' Starling looked offended. 'It's not a dodge. I suppose you could call it a form of investment.'

'You deal in stamps?' Brock asked.

'I buy, and occasionally I sell, always through reputable dealers, Mr Brock. All above board.'

'You haven't been cheating one of these reputable dealers, have you?'

'No!' Starling said firmly, his hands formed into fists, the thin scars on the fingers of the left hand gleaming pale. 'It's nothing like that.'

'Then what on earth is the point of sending you those stamps?' Brock said, waving a hand at the two notes.

'It's personal, isn't it?' Starling replied. 'It's telling me that whoever sent those notes knows me, knows everything about me – my habits, my interests, my private life. And it's telling me that, whatever they want, the stakes are going to be high, right?'

Brock looked doubtful. 'Who knows about this interest of yours, then? It's not in your police file, as far as I recall.'

'It's not a secret exactly. The dealers, a few friends . . .'

'Not public knowledge, though.'

'Not public, no.'

'All right, now we're going to need to make up a list of all of the people you and Eva come in contact with in the normal run of things. Who does your garden, who services your car, who cleans your windows, everyone. Then we'll start checking them all.'

'Discreetly, please, Mr Brock,' Sammy begged. 'What if one of them is involved, and takes fright?'

'Of course, Sammy. Very discreetly. None of them will know, I promise you.'

Kathy, who had said nothing until this point, spoke. 'Eva knows all about your stamps, of course, Mr Starling. Just as you know about her private interests.'

Starling didn't respond to this, not even looking at Kathy, as if her words had floated by his head without registering.

'Could they be your own stamps?' she went on. 'From your own collection?'

He frowned, as if hearing her for the first time. 'No,' he said softly. 'No, they're not mine.'

'Mr Melville said that you specialise in that particular type – what were they called?'

'Chalon Heads, yes.'

'So you have many Chalon Heads in your collection?'

'Yes.'

'These ones?'

'I have my own versions of them, yes.'

'But these aren't them? You checked that?'

Starling wiped his face again with his handkerchief. 'Yes,' he whispered. 'I did check that.'

3

A Life of Starling

The men were framed in the grid of scaffolding like counters on a snakes-and-ladders board, each working on a different square, transforming the gable of the building from faded green to deep red. Bren gazed at them each in turn through the binoculars. Keller was the one with the shaved head and the least splattered white overalls. He was older than the others, and making slower progress, less fluid in his movements. More single-minded in his labour, too, ignoring them when they shouted comments to each other, or whistled at a girl walking past along the street.

'They've been on this job now for four days,' Ronnie Wilkes said. 'Sammy gave me a bell Wednesday afternoon, but I couldn't get on to it till this morning. I asked at the corner shop over there, and they told me they set the scaffolding up Monday. They had to do a bit of patching first.'

He picked his nose and lit a cigarette. As an afterthought he offered one to Bren, who declined, thinking about what his wife would say about the stink of smoke in his clothes. He wound the window down another inch and blue fumes drifted past his eyes and out into the hot afternoon air. At least it smothered the sour smell of Wilkes's sweat, which had been filling the car. Bren wondered if the other man wasn't getting a bit too old, a bit too flabby for this game.

'Have you got a written record of the times you were watching Keller?' Bren asked.

'Nah,' Wilkes shook his head dismissively. 'I'd just phone up Sammy at the end of each day and give him a verbal report. That's all he needed.'

'Did he give any particular reason for wanting you to watch Keller on Wednesday?'

'Nothing special. But he's been doing that for the last couple of months. He thinks Keller's got it in for him. Is that why you're here?'

'You've seen nothing?'

'Not a bloody thing. It's been the most boring job I've ever had.'

Towards five the painters packed it in. Bren watched them come down the ladders loaded up with their cans and brushes, which they locked away with their overalls in a small shed at the base of the wall. The other three lit up cigarettes, but not Keller, and they all piled into a battered old Capri, Keller folding himself awkwardly into the back.

Bren tailed them to the Red Lion, a utilitarian corner pub half a mile away. They went in at the door facing one street, he through the other, and he watched them between the racks and bottles of the bar. They sat at a table together but, as on the site, Keller seemed detached from them. While they chatted and laughed, he read an *Evening Standard*, less out of interest, it seemed, than as a way of avoiding involvement in their conversations. It was exactly as Starling had told them, except that Keller was drinking fruit juice rather than beer. Bren wondered why he bothered to come to the pub with the others. Starling would say that they were there as background, a camouflage of normality while Keller plotted mayhem. Or perhaps it was the only way he could get a lift home.

From the pub Bren tailed them to the address that Wilkes had told him was Keller's lodging, a large Victorian house with a dozen buzzer buttons at the front door. Keller unwound himself from the back of the Capri with barely a nod to the others and made his way up the front steps of the house. As he reached the door, it opened suddenly and a young woman appeared. She checked herself, startled to see him standing there, then gave a brief smile as she recognised him. He stepped back to let her past, head lowered, then disappeared inside. To Bren it seemed a well-established manoeuvre, two tenants who met occasionally on the stairs and who had tacitly agreed to take no interest in each other.

Kathy wondered at the task she had been given. When Starling left the interview room with Bren and Brock, Dot had given her a sheet from a memo pad with an address and phone number on it.

'This is Peter White's address, Kathy,' she said, as if Kathy should be expecting it. 'I've told him you'll get there about five.'

'Brock wants me to go there now?'

'That's what he told me.' She began to gather up her own and Brock's papers.

'Do you know this White?'

'I met him a few times.'

'Brock said they fell out over something. Do you know the story?'

'Best ask him,' Dot said.

Brock's loyal Dot, Kathy thought.

'Sammy Starling's rather eerie, don't you think?' Dot said. 'Like a big porcelain doll. I'm sure Peter White will be interested to hear what he's up to these days.'

Kathy slowed as she spotted a front garden filled with roses in spectacular bloom. Dot had warned her about the roses. She parked at the kerb opposite and as she made for the front gate a man straightened upright from among the bushes and stared at her. She was immediately struck by how he was dressed, in a crisp white shirt, dark trousers and polished shoes, as if he'd just stepped out from the office, rather than as a retired man pottering in his garden.

'DCI White?'

He stiffened and eyed her darkly. 'Not any more. Come in.'

He had a moustache, as carefully clipped and groomed as his hair, and a healthy, ruddy complexion. In one gloved hand he was holding a magnifying glass, and in the other a pair of secateurs and a stem of leaves.

He saw her looking at what he was holding, and said in an ominous tone, 'I'm in the middle of war . . .' He paused, then added, 'Black spot.' He pointed at the tainted leaves.

'Oh.' Kathy was reminded of the pirate Pugh in *Treasure Island*, who had so frightened her as a child, with his terrifying black spots with which he condemned men to death.

'I'll have a look at this lot inside, under the microscope. I suspect it's coming from the south-west. From there.' He indicated without taking his eyes off Kathy's face. 'I'm pretty sure of it. The warm breezes over the last few days have been coming from that direction. There's a fellow on that corner down there . . .' Kathy turned to follow his pointing finger, towards a distant garden of scruffy rose-bushes. 'Infested. He doesn't spray, you see.'

'Sounds serious,' Kathy said carefully, not sure how to take him. His face was expressionless, as if he were setting her a test, and was only prepared to give so much away.

'It is serious,' he said, and she sensed suddenly that he was angry. 'I went to see him. I offered to spray his plants myself, at the same time as I did mine, but he took offence. He told me to fuck off.'

Kathy heard his particular emphasis on the word, as if this were also part of the test.

'Can you believe that? Why does he grow the bloody things if he's not interested, eh?'

He stared at her for a moment, then turned on his heel and led the way to the kitchen door at the side of the house. He brushed his shoes carefully on a new doormat, placed the rose stalks, glass and secateurs on the draining board, took off his gloves and ran the tap to wash his hands. The kitchen was as immaculate as the man, everything tight in its place.

He led her through to a sitting-room, equally tidy, over-looking a back garden filled, like the front, with rose-beds, burgeoning with blooms. Kathy wondered what he did with all the flowers.

He saw her looking at them and said, briskly, as if it was a business matter, 'New hybrids, David Austins. Put them in two years ago. Coming on well.' And then, without a break, 'Brock sent you, of course. Didn't care to come himself.'

'He's very busy. He did say he intended to buy you a pint when he was next over this way.' It struck Kathy that there was nothing in the room to suggest contact with any other person: no photographs on the mantelpiece, no letters on the empty writing table in the corner, no ornament that might have been another's gift.

'I doubt that, Ms . . .' He looked narrowly at her. 'What did you say your name was?'

'Kathy Kolla. DS.'

'You'll have to excuse me. I've never heard of you.'

She heard the contempt in his voice, and sensed him trying it out for effect, as if not yet certain how far he would punish her for Brock's errors, whatever they might have been.

'I haven't been with SO 1 long – less than a year. When did you retire, Mr White?'

'Five years ago. They say that retirement is dangerous for men – they tend to keel over within a few months. But in my case it didn't go like that. It was Ruth, my wife, who passed away, not two weeks after I left the job.' He stared at Kathy, waiting for her response to this.

She said, 'I'm sorry,' but it didn't seem to be enough.

'Look, I'm very busy right now, Sergeant,' he said. 'I'm not sure I can spare you the time.'

Kathy flushed, becoming tired of this game, whatever it was. 'DCI Brock felt it important to have the benefit of your knowledge of someone.'

'Sammy Starling, yes, his secretary said that when she made the appointment for you. But he didn't consider it important enough to send someone more senior.'

'I –'

'How long have you been in the force?' he interrupted.

'Eight years. I was in Traffic for three, then I got into plain clothes. Serious Crime was what I really wanted.'

'Is that so? You're ambitious, I take it?'

'I suppose so.'

'To climb the career ladder, I mean. One of those women with an eye firmly on the main chance, who rush up through the ranks with plenty of help from the *equal opportunists*.' He made no attempt to keep the sneer out of his voice as he said this.

Kathy wasn't sure whether to laugh or be angry. She said softly, 'You mean that I should know my place.'

'I was eighteen years in CID, learning policing the hard way, before I got to special operations. Oh, I've seen types like you, missy. I've seen 'em using people to get where they want to go. You think you can waltz in here and use me, eh?'

Kathy looked at him, wondering what she had said or done to bring this to the surface. She got to her feet deliberately and made for the door.

'Hang on!' he called sharply after her, but she didn't stop until she had it open, then she looked back over her shoulder at him, half risen out of his chair. He suddenly saw in her eyes that she was angry. 'All right,' he said grudgingly. 'I didn't exactly mean that.'

'Of course you did,' she said calmly, softly, turned away from him and stepped out on to the path to the front gate.

She had reached the gate when his voice came after her: 'Where the fucking hell are you going?'

She paused again and looked back at him standing in the doorway, his face still not quite certain that she was really leaving.

'I'm going back to work, Mr White. I'm wasting my time here.'

His expression changed. 'Hang on! Sergeant! Look . . . look, wait, please.' He hurried towards her. 'I — I was out of line there, yes. But you don't understand . . . how it was . . . the background. I resent the way Brock's done this, but . . . I will help you.'

Kathy hesitated, not sure, as her anger faded, if there was any point in continuing.

'Please . . . *please*.' Now he was begging, and it struck Kathy that he was a very lonely, isolated man whose opportunity for conversation was probably confined to chance encounters in the supermarket or garden centre.

'Might we not start again?' he urged, and with misgivings, because she didn't want to go back to Brock empty-handed, she agreed.

This time he eagerly offered her a cup of tea, which she accepted, and was surprised when he produced a freshly

31

purchased cream cake, as if he had been out specially and had planned this all along.

'Did Brock tell you that we had a bit of a falling out, the last time Sammy Starling came into our lives?' White said, when they had established themselves in the sitting-room once more.

'He wasn't specific.'

'I'm not blaming Brock for what happened,' he said, in a conciliatory tone. 'But I do blame Sammy, and Brock relied on Sammy, too much, I thought at the time . . . I'm sorry, you probably don't know what I'm talking about.'

'Brock said that Starling was being investigated by the Fraud Squad when he produced evidence of corruption against three of their officers.'

'Keller, Stringer and Harley, but most importantly Tom Harley. You heard what happened to him, did you? Did Brock tell you about that?'

'He didn't say much.'

'No, that doesn't surprise me.' A touch of acid returned to his voice. 'Superintendent Tom Harley, one of the finest police officers I knew. Accused of taking bribes. We all knew that was garbage, and we all admired the way he coped with it, the indignity of it, him a superintendent accused by slime like Starling.'

Kathy noticed a fleck of white in the corner of his mouth, beneath the neatly clipped moustache, as he paused for effect.

'We all thought Tom was managing all right. He was a very dignified feller. Never let on for one second, to us or to his family, that it was getting to him. But inside it ate him hollow. One afternoon he went home, swallowed two packets of paracetamol and half a pint of whisky and lay down to die. At a particularly low ebb, you see. The trial was looking bad. But his wife found him, and they took him to hospital and pumped him out, and a week later he was feeling much better. New evidence had been found, and he wanted to live after all. Only his liver had been destroyed by the pills. They couldn't do a damn thing to save him. It took him three months of agony to die.'

'I'm sorry,' Kathy said. 'That was tragic. But he should have known better.'

She saw White bristle, and she added quickly, 'Brock didn't mention that.'

'Did he not? I do wonder why.' The bitterness in White's voice was strong. 'It was a matter of trust, of knowing whom to trust. Brock chose to believe little Sammy China, until it was too late.'

Kathy noted the nickname, which she hadn't heard before. 'What about the other two, Keller and Stringer?'

'Oh . . .' White made a gesture of dismissal with his hand . . . they were guilty all right, no doubt about that.'

'And Brock was the investigating officer?'

'That's right. He went after them like the blessed furies, Keller and Stringer and Harley, all on the word of Sammy Starling. Harley was innocent, but by the time Brock realised that Tom had done himself in.' White jerked himself to his feet and went over to the window, staring moodily out at his garden.

'Keller is out of jail now,' Kathy said, and began the story that Starling had told them. At first White seemed not to hear, but then his face cleared and he gazed intently at her until she had finished.

'So Sammy thinks young Keller has taken his princess, does he?' he said, with fierce relish. 'And Starling really does care, does he? Has it really hit him hard?'

'Don't you think it would?'

'You never knew with Sammy what he felt or cared about, but funny things happen to old men.'

'He's not old.'

'Same age as me. Sixty-three.'

Kathy tried to hide her surprise. 'You made a study of him, when you were with Criminal Intelligence, didn't you? Brock thought you might have . . . I don't know, some recollections . . .' What had he expected her to get from White, she wondered.

White looked away, then seemed to make up his mind. 'Some recollections, eh? You just come with me, Sergeant.'

Puzzled, Kathy followed him out into the narrow hall and across to one of the front rooms. He opened the door, switched on a light and waved her in.

It was as if she had stepped straight from a suburban semi into the basement of some bureaucratic archive. Industrial shelving completely lined the walls, including the window, which had been boarded up, and contained row upon row of neatly labelled file boxes, classified by number and letter codes. In the centre of the room stood a table with some carefully stacked items of office stationery, a desk lamp, a computer, printer and photocopier. It was like a transplant of a bay from the old Criminal Records Office.

It seemed that DCI White had left the Yard with copies of a great deal of material. 'I was afraid they'd throw it out after a while, Kathy, you see, then regret it later.'

He smiled conspiratorially, and Kathy noted this first use of her first name, as if he wanted to draw her into some form of collusion.

'I may be mad to show you this, Kathy,' he said. 'You could go right back to the Yard and get me into serious trouble for having all this. Well?' He leaned forward intently. 'Have I made a big mistake, confiding in you, Kathy? Have I?'

Kathy drew back a little, uncomfortable. The room was claustrophobic, and White's manner, ingratiating now, seemed not much better than his earlier rudeness.

'The only thing on our minds at present is the whereabouts of Eva Starling . . .' she said, deciding that she'd better show some encouragement '. . . Peter. This is very impressive.'

But this wasn't quite enough for White. 'Yes, Kathy, but can I *trust* you? Can I really confide in you?'

'I think so, yes.'

He said nothing for a moment, staring fixedly at her as if to read her thoughts, to see whether she deserved his trust. Then he nodded, and said, 'Very well. Sit down at the table, and we'll see what we can find for you.'

He didn't seem to need an index, but went straight to one shelf and brought an armful of files across to Kathy, sitting down beside her at the table. One contained old photocopies of police documents, another court records, a third newspaper reports of the trial, already turned musty and yellow with age, their creases fixed and brittle, although it had been only ten years before.

'He was a cocky young bastard, no question of that,' White said, showing her a cutting from the Metropolitan Police magazine the *Job*. It showed a grinning Keller wearing the broad shoulder-pads of an American footballer over the title 'Top Rusher for London Mets'. 'All the self-confidence in the world. But we never thought he was bad. Not until Starling dumped on him.'

'Is there any question about his guilt? Could Starling have framed him?'

'I don't think so. Not in the case of Keller and Stringer. In the months after Tom Harley tried to take his own life, their defence collapsed. At the end, no one seriously believed they hadn't done what they were accused of. There were some, though, who thought it was excusable, and thought their sentences too harsh. Exemplary, was the judge's word.'

'You? Did you think it excusable?'

White hesitated. 'Compared to —' Then he stopped himself. 'No, no. It wasn't excusable.'

'Compared to what?' Kathy said. 'Compared to Sammy Starling?'

White lowered his eyes. 'You're a bright one, aren't you, Kathy?'

For a moment Kathy thought his tone was almost flirtatious.

'Yes, that's right. Compared to Starling. But that was my fault, see.'

'How was it your fault?'

'Oh . . . he was my personal target, if you like. Is that the right word? No, a target is too passive a thing. Sammy was never passive. My nemesis, is that it?'

He frowned and stood up and went to a shelf containing reference works, where he pulled down the *Shorter Oxford*. 'Yes . . . not the first meaning, see, the agent of retribution, but the second meaning of nemesis, "a persistent tormentor; a long-standing rival or enemy". That was Sammy Starling to me. And it was my fault because I could never find the means to bring him down.'

He returned to his seat and opened the first of the Starling files.

'Born 'thirty-four in Maudsley Hospital, Denmark Hill, South London. His mother, Mary Pang, died in childbirth. Her husband, and Sammy's father, was Charlie Pang. The Pangs

35

arrived in London in 1931, God knows where they came from. They had barely a penny, and they changed their name just before Sammy was born. The story is that they had intended to take the name Sterling, as in sterling silver, but somehow it got muddled to Starling.

'Whether that's true or not, I don't know. What was true was that old Charlie Starling didn't live much longer than his wife, and the little orphan Sammy was taken in by a family called Hubbard in the same housing scheme, off the Brixton Road. He was never formally adopted, just taken in, the way people did in those days. Sammy China, the kids called him, a bit of a novelty. Later on, two of the Hubbard boys ended up working for Sammy, and the youngest girl, Sally, became housekeeper to him and Brenda. You met Sally? No? Quite a character, she is.

'Sammy was a bright little kid by all accounts, and the Hubbards did their best for him. They were a good, solid, working-class family, and it wasn't them taught him to be a villain. I used to think he was more a cuckoo than a starling, a cuckoo in the Hubbards' nest. If anyone did the teaching, it was Sammy, who began to make a bit of a name for himself in the black market after the war. I think it's in their blood, don't you? Dodgy trading . . .' He saw the look on Kathy's face and realised he was on shaky ground again.

'Anyway,' he went on hurriedly, 'for a few years he operated on his own in a small way, supplying the market for goods in short supply — forged petrol coupons, unlicensed building materials, scarce car components recycled from proud new car-owners who hadn't intended to part with them — small stuff, but enough to maintain a certain lifestyle for a young fellow on his own. He had one or two frights from the law, but he was nimble on his feet, and operating on his own, it was difficult to pin him down without actually catching him in the act. And then, all of a sudden, he met and married Brenda.

'Now Brenda was something special — not a beauty, but a character, and sharp as a needle. Her family had well-established criminal connections, see — there's a whole special shelf of the NRO devoted to that family tree. And it was then that Sammy's criminal career began to become altogether more serious, and more ambitious.

'That was the time when the Kray twins were beginning to make a name for themselves, the late fifties, and Sammy got drawn into the edge of their circle. He would have been a couple of years younger than Ronnie and Reggie Kray, and for the sake of moving into a bigger game he made himself into a good and useful servant, the way Brenda told him. Sammy knew them all – the Krays, Frank Mitchell the mad axe man, Jack "the Hat" McVitie, the Richardson gang – all crazy, violent bastards.'

'Was Sammy violent?' Kathy found it difficult to imagine, yet she had misread that bland childlike face several times already.

White shook his head scornfully. 'Never. Just being in the same room with Ronnie Kray made some men wet themselves, but Sammy Starling never had the bottle to frighten a mouse. He was more devious, sneaky. He'd fix you with that smiling moon face of his and slit your wallet, not your throat. Money was what he was good at. Where they were wild and greedy and impulsive, he was sly and cautious, and kept out of the limelight. They frightened him, and after a bit he wanted out. There was an incident . . . You've noticed the back of his left hand, have you? Yes, well, he decided to change the company he kept. And I suppose you could say that he had a certain vision.'

'What was that?'

'You've got to remember what it was like then, Kathy. In 1960 there were no more than two or three hundred drug addicts known to the Home Office in the whole of England and Wales. Think of that! Today there's probably more than that in Budleigh Salterton. And those addicts were mostly old folks who had become dependent on their pain-killers. The number had been steady for years. Ten years later there were thousands, almost all of them under the age of thirty. Sammy spotted that. He saw what was coming, a new and lucrative market that was barred to legitimate businessmen. So he got to know the new people, made new friends, and made himself useful to them by finding ways to recycle all that fresh new cash they were suddenly awash in. I have to admit that it took us a while to figure out what he was doing – he was way ahead of us, see.'

White put the first volume of his Starling file to one side and opened the second.

'Then we had a stroke of luck. In 1972 a teenager named Carole Sykes died in a road accident on the M6.' White began thumbing through the oldest pages of the file to find the reports of the case. He had recovered his spirit, Kathy saw, like an old retriever, hunting through the documents. 'Here. She was travelling with two boys from the same part of South London to a party in Manchester. Their cylinder head gasket blew near Stoke, and they had to pull on to the hard shoulder. Next thing, the two lads saw Carole wandering off into the traffic lanes, waving at the pretty trucks. She was run over by at least eight heavy goods vehicles before the traffic came to a stop and they managed to attract the attention of a patrol car in the southbound lanes. The post-mortem established that Carole had been high on LSD at the time of her death, and for once we were able to establish a clear trail back to the supplier, and from there to the supplier's banker – Sammy Starling. We actually found the cash that Carole had paid in Sammy's possession. Even so, and despite the publicity surrounding the case, he got away with just three months inside. That's what I mean, you see, when you ask if Marty Keller's actions were excusable. Keller didn't kill anybody, did he? And yet he did nearly nine years.'

'He did try to kill Sammy, though, didn't he?' Kathy said, recalling Brock's summary of the case. 'He was found guilty of attempted murder.'

White snorted dismissively. 'On Sammy's evidence, mainly.'

'Is there anything else on Sammy's record?'

'No. To this day, that's his only conviction, apart from a couple of minor misdemeanours when he was a teenager. The effect of his conviction was only to make Sammy more careful. When he came out he restructured his business, as any businessman might do after a setback, and went on as before. No matter what we did, we couldn't corner him after that. His great strength was that he was never too greedy. As more and more money and profits drew more and more greedy people into the drugs game, Sammy's profile seemed relatively insignificant by comparison.'

'You don't sound convinced, Peter.'

'No, I was never convinced. I knew our man. But when it came to allocating priorities for Criminal Intelligence, Sammy became less and less important. Then, in 1983, something happened that changed things for Sammy.' White turned the pages until he came to a series of newspaper articles from that year. 'He had a son, Gordon, sporting type, good-looking lad. In July that year he drowned, water-skiing in the Mediterranean. Brenda was devastated. What made it worse was a report in *Paris Match* a couple of weeks after the accident. I've got it here somewhere . . . Yes, here it is. Written by their top crime reporter. It refers to Sammy's career and conviction after the Carole Sykes death, and it claims that the autopsy on Gordon had revealed that he had been taking cocaine before his fatal accident. The parallels are discussed at length. "Divine retribution" is one of the phrases used, as I recall.

'The revelation was especially telling to those of us who had followed Sammy's career, see, because he had made it an iron rule that the people around him should never touch the merchandise. The people he worked for might supply anyone, from the richest to the poorest, the oldest to the youngest. But if they touched it themselves he'd drop them flat.'

'What did he do?'

'Immediately after the funeral, he and Brenda went on a world cruise for three months. When they came back, he put out the word that he was retiring from the business. They bought a house out in the country, and sold up everything in town. Sammy even sent me an invitation to his retirement party, cheeky bastard.'

White turned to a page on to which was stapled a silver-printed invitation to "Detective Chief Inspector and Mrs Peter White" to "celebrate the retirement of Sammy and Brenda Starling", at their home at the Crow's Nest, Poacher's Ease, Farnham, Surrey.

'Did you go?'

'Certainly not.'

All the same, Kathy thought White showed a certain pride in showing her the invitation.

'Tom Harley got one of these, too. He'd been trying to get Sammy on his financial dealings – foreign-currency transactions and the like. He showed me his invitation. He was outraged. I remember him saying that the day he accepted a drink from

Sammy Starling would be his last. One day, he said, Sammy was going to pay.'

He stared grimly at the invitation for a moment, then whispered, 'Only he was wrong. He was the one who paid.'

'Did Starling really retire, do you believe?'

'Yes, yes, I do, in point of fact. If it hadn't been for Gordon I would have had my doubts, but I saw them when they came back from their cruise, and I could see there had been a change in both of them. That didn't stop me hoping we could still find a way to punish him. By that stage I'd been following Sammy Starling's career for twenty-five years. It wasn't easy to break the habit of a professional lifetime. And I knew Tom Harley was still investigating the fraud angle, and from time to time I was able to give him a bit of help and advice.'

White stopped and stretched and looked around the room as if returning from some other place. 'You didn't realise what you were letting yourself in for, Kathy, getting me to open all this up again. Your tea's cold. All this talk . . . Maybe you'd join me in something stronger?'

'I'm fine, thanks, Peter. But you go ahead. You're the one doing the talking.'

He went out of the room briefly, returning with a very large tumbler of whisky. He took a deep swallow, put it down beside his files and cleared his throat. 'Where had we got to?'

'You were saying that the Fraud Squad were still interested in Starling.'

'Tom Harley, yes. By 1986 he reckoned he was getting close, too. That's when Sammy realised that Tom wasn't going to leave him alone, retired or not.' White took another gulp of the whisky. 'I have to say, Kathy, that he did a very professional job – Sammy, I mean. It was a lesson to us all. After a couple of decades as an active detective in the force, you've lived through plenty of rough patches. You've upset people, made errors of judgement, said things in anger that were better left unsaid. That was as true of Tom as of any of us. It could have been me, or Brock, or the Commissioner himself. But it was Tom that Starling set his sights on. Like any businessman faced with a dangerous rival, he set about gathering the knowledge that would give him the advantage. He focused on Tom's rough patches from five, ten, twenty years before. Where he couldn't reach the information himself, he hired consultants, ex-coppers or civil staff who could access the files and the gossip that has that peculiar edge of truth about it, that irresistible authenticity. And then he hired other people, more imaginative than himself, scriptwriters and professional story-tellers, to weave the inno-cent facts of Tom Harley's life in with the less innocent dealings of Marty Keller and Jerry Stringer – both men whom Tom distrusted instinctively, but had to work with, day on day. And so Sammy fabricated a story of such *corrosive* plausibility and corruption that nobody could dare gainsay it, see.'

With each gulp of whisky, White was becoming more animated and loquacious.

'But you blame Brock, especially, do you, Peter? For giving credit to Starling's plot?'

'Yes! I warned him, didn't I? He didn't know Sammy the way I did. He thought he was small beer. He accepted everything, hook, line and sinker, because he knew that Keller and Stringer were suspect, and Sammy's story was so good. I warned him, but he didn't listen – thought I was a boring old fart, didn't he? Until it was too late, and Tom was dead and gone, and Keller and Stringer were doomed, and Sammy was free as the birds in spring . . .' Another bitter pull at the whisky.

'Is that where your files stop, Peter?' Kathy asked. 'In 1987?'

White gave her a conspiratorial look. 'Oh, no, Kathy. An old Starling watcher like me can't help himself, see.' And he pushed aside the second file and opened volume three.

'This one is much more speculative,' he said slowly. 'There are no official police reports here, see, 'cos Sammy stopped being an official subject of Criminal Intelligence in 1987. This file is all cuttings from magazines, and company reports, and travel records, and the like.'

'No *official* police reports, you say.'

White grinned. 'Tom Harley's old mates in the Fraud Squad were always willing to pass me the odd note when it seemed relevant. Nothing wrong with that.'

'And after you retired?'

White waved airily.

'So, how does the story continue?'

'The eighties weren't kind to Sammy, despite his managing to wriggle out from under the Fraud Squad investigation. The year before Tom Harley decided to go for him, his wife died. She'd never got over their son, and now Sammy had lost them both. He still had Sally Malone looking after the house for him – that was the Hubbard girl I mentioned before. She'd been with them for years, started out babysitting for them, and then, when she was widowed young, she moved in with them and became their housekeeper.

'So Sammy wasn't left alone, as a widower . . .' White continued, unconsciously stressing the word 'alone', '. . . but it hit him hard all the same. He realised, I suppose, how much he'd relied on Brenda. Then in 'eighty-seven, in the thick of the trial, there was the stock-market crash, and he did badly out of that. So for several years after that he became reclusive, see. Hardly got out at all.' He turned pages until he found a copy of a passport-renewal photograph of Starling from that period. The face scowled into space beyond the camera, grey and unfocused, the hair lank.

'Would that be when he started collecting stamps?'

'Stamps?'

'Yes. He claims to be a philatelist.'

'Does he now?' White screwed up his nose, thinking. 'Do you know . . . I do recall something about stamps . . .' He started thumbing through the file until he found a photocopy of a computer printout. 'Yes, this is it. A request from Cabot's Ltd of the Strand, London, for a credit check on Sammy. Four years ago.' White beamed at Kathy, pleased with himself. 'Cabot's are auctioneers and dealers in rare stamps.'

'How did you get hold of that?'

White said nothing, looking smug.

'How much did he want to spend with them?'

White pointed to the figure. 'Forty thousand.'

'He must have been serious. Doesn't that seem unlikely to you? Sammy Starling a stamp collector?'

White shrugged. 'Old men . . .' he began, then stopped himself. 'I suppose it was a form of investment. People do that. He had other business investments on the go.'

'Yes, that's what he called it.' Kathy didn't mention the

stamps on the ransom notes. 'All right, Sammy went into a decline. Go on.'

'Ah . . . then the *miracle* happened.' White's tone was heavy sarcasm, but his eyes lit up as he used the word.

'Eva?'

'Eva.'

'How did that come about?'

'Sammy and Brenda had been friends with a couple called Cooper, living in Uxbridge. A year or two after Brenda died, they got Sammy to invest in a time-share development on the Algarve, in southern Portugal. They persuaded him to go out there to look at the place in the spring of 'ninety-three. While he was there he met their Portuguese partner, Dom Arnaldo de Vasconcellos, and his eighteen-year-old daughter Eva. Sammy and Eva were married less than six months later.'

'A whirlwind romance,' Kathy said.

'That's right.' White turned to several pages of cuttings from newspapers and magazines showing pictures of the wedding.

'Posh,' Kathy said. 'What kind of people are they?'

'Old money. Portuguese aristocracy. About as far from Sammy Starling's bloodline as you could get, I'd say.'

'A very odd match, then.'

'Like I say, Kathy, a miracle . . . for Sammy that is.'

'Most of these reports are Portuguese, Peter,' Kathy remarked. 'You have been busy.'

'We asked Interpol to do us a favour.'

'But you'd retired by then, hadn't you?' She smiled at him reassuringly.

He grinned back and finished his whisky. 'Are you sure you wouldn't like . . . ?'

She shook her head and he left the room again for a refill. While he was away, Kathy examined the pictures, the bride in white, somehow managing to look spontaneous and effervescent despite the burden of the traditional wedding gown in which she was wrapped. Sammy looked transformed from the nadir of his passport picture, tanned, ten years younger, unable to stop beaming.

White resumed his seat beside Kathy. 'The happy couple!' he said, his breath heavy with the Scotch. 'Well, now. You tell me,

Kathy, as an attractive young woman yourself, how the bloody hell did he do it, eh? What did she see in him? What did her old dad see in him, eh?'

'He has got a certain . . . style,' Kathy said.

'Bollocks!' White snorted. 'The Alsatian next door has got a certain style, and she didn't marry him!'

'Money, then.'

White nodded with grim satisfaction, his eyes fixed on a picture of Eva lifting the skirts of her full white gown with both hands to negotiate the church steps. His expression suggested, Maybe if I'd had money . . .

'How much is he worth, have you any idea?'

'Any idea?' White scoffed. 'I could give you an estimate of his net worth that's within ten per cent, guaranteed.'

'I'm impressed. How much, then?'

Like a magician coming to his star turn, White turned the pages until he reached a section of financial data. There were copies of credit checks, photocopies of bank statements, property valuations and share transactions.

'God!' Kathy breathed. 'How did you get all this, Peter?'

He smirked. 'Grand total, one point eight million, sterling. That's *sterling*, not *starling* . . .' White guffawed at this witticism. His speech was becoming slightly slurred now.

'I'd have thought it might have been more.'

'It was, at the time Brenda died, but as I said, he got burned in the 'eighty-seven crash. Panicked, didn't he? Didn't have her steady head to save him. But it's been building up again since then, see.'

'So that's what Marty Keller is after, do you think?'

White thought about it. 'Not Keller . . . No. The poor bastard has just finished eight years inside. Had a hard time of it, I heard. He'd have to be crazy to start all that again. Risk going back. No, he's not your man.'

Kathy looked at her watch. 'I'll have to get going, Peter. Is there anything else you can tell me?'

White began turning the pages of the reports again. 'You saw this one, did you? And what about this?' He was searching for something of interest to her, not wanting to let her go. She watched him politely for a while longer, asked him to give her photocopies of some of the key documents, then got to her feet.

'What's he like now, then?' he said quickly, following after her. 'In the flesh. How is he holding up?'

'Starling? Worried, panic-stricken, I suppose, lack of sleep, but physically in pretty good shape.'

White ignored the last bit. 'Panic-stricken, eh? My God, yes, he will be. How much will he pay for her? Half a million? One million? Everything?'

As they reached the door, he said, 'Have you anything to implicate Marty Keller, apart from motive and Sammy's imagination?'

'Early days,' Kathy said, evasive.

'You sure it isn't Sammy done her in, making it look like a kidnapping?'

'That's always a possibility.'

He followed her out to the front gate. 'Now, Kathy,' he said, 'I want you to promise me something.'

'It's all right, Peter.' She turned and met a gust of whisky breath up close. 'I won't tell anyone about your files.'

'Not just that. I want you to promise to get back to me if you think of anything you need to know, day or night. Promise?'

Kathy smiled, feeling sorry for this sad, obnoxious old bloke.

'What if I think of something?' he said, suddenly worried. 'How can I get in touch?'

'Do you know Brock's office number?'

'Not Brock! I'm not going to contact him. What about you?'

Kathy gave him a card, writing her mobile number on the back for him.

'Good, good. And one last thing, Kathy,' he said.

'Yes?'

'If I were Marty Keller after revenge,' he whispered, as if the roses might have ears, 'I wouldn't just want Sammy Starling to suffer.'

'No?'

'Oh, no. I'd want to bring Brock down, too. *Very* much.'

Kathy blinked, thanked him, and hurried to her car.

Kathy sensed that the examination of the flat was coming to an end. Among the décor of black and silver and white, Brock, with his grey hair and beard and white nylon overalls, looked like an incongruous designer item. He sprawled in the white Italian hide settee, scratching his chin with a latex-gloved hand, looking deeply dissatisfied.

'Nothing interesting?' she said, picking up an overall pack for herself.

'Puzzling. She's been here, sure enough – there's some dirty clothes in the laundry basket and a used towel in the bathroom. But I'd swear the bed hasn't been slept in since the sheets were changed, which according to Sammy would normally have been last Thursday, when the cleaner comes in.'

He got stiffly to his feet and went on, 'No signs of a struggle, but look at this . . .'

He led her into the kitchen, where two men were examining the worktop beside the sink, a polished grey granite surface lit by hidden low-voltage spots. Compared to her own modest facilities, Kathy thought the place resembled an art gallery more than a kitchen. One was holding a camera with large flash attachment, the other a fingerprint powder brush. The one with the brush, an Indian, looked round, and Kathy recognised Leon Desai, their liaison with the forensic science lab. Brock was taking this seriously, she thought.

'Hello, Kathy.' He nodded to her, with his cool smile. No matter what mayhem his job took him into, Desai was always cool, a source of irritation to Bren and some of the others.

Kathy said hello and followed Brock over to a corner of the kitchen floor.

'What do you make of that?' he asked her.

At first she saw nothing, then made out a faint trace of brown against the cream ceramic tile. 'A footprint?'

'Could be. And possibly blood. The rest of the floor's been washed clean, by the looks of it.'

'What about the neighbours?'

'We're being discreet so we haven't made a big production of it yet, but we've spoken to a few. Most use the place as she did – hardly any permanent residents. This being a ground-floor flat, facing the back, tucked away, it wouldn't be difficult for someone to come and go unobserved, if they knew their way around. There's a door to the residents' car park just along the corridor from the front door to this flat.'

Kathy looked around. 'It's very tasteful . . .'

'Oh, very. Classic, simple, expensive . . . tasteful.'

'Is that Sammy Starling?'

'Not unless he's changed in that too. Sammy wouldn't feel the need to acquire any taste himself. He'd just hire someone who already had some. It would mean nothing.'

He led her back into the living-room. 'You saw Peter White?'

'Yes.'

'How did you get on?'

'We nearly didn't. He tried to put me in my place early on. I walked out.'

Brock grinned. 'That's the way. He buckled after that, did he?'

'We started again. He's still keeping a file on Sammy Starling, you know. He seems haunted by him, and by Keller and Harley . . .'

Kathy saw the shadow cross Brock's face. She went on, 'It was useful background, I suppose, for me. He told me Starling's life story. But nothing directly relevant to this.'

'Bitter, is he?'

Kathy nodded. 'He tries to lose himself in his roses.'

'His wife, Ruth, started growing them a year before his retirement, to give him something to do. He had no other interests than police work before then. Does he have any thoughts about Keller?'

'He doubts Keller would have the stomach for it after all that time inside.'

'We're finished, Brock.' Leon Desai stood at the doorway. The SOCO photographer came past him carrying his big aluminium equipment case. He peeled off his gloves and overalls and Desai let him out of the front door.

'Yes . . .' Brock sighed. 'We're all finished. *Kaput. Finito.*' He glanced at his watch. 'I'm hungry. Mrs Starling was known at a little Italian place around the corner, La Fortuna. Fancy giving it a go?'

The stark décor, unusual modern chairs and cutlery, lush white

47

tablecloths, all signalled *expensive* to Kathy. For the first time she felt personally confronted by Eva Starling's lifestyle. She was pretty certain she couldn't afford to eat anywhere where Eva was known.

The menu confirmed this. Kathy's heart sank as she searched in vain for a modestly priced plate of spaghetti Bolognese.

She looked at the reaction of the other two. Desai was frowning intently. He caught the look on her face and silently mouthed the word *help*. Brock bore an expression of mild surprise as his eyes scanned the large but sparsely printed document through his glasses. 'Now I understand why this place is called La Fortuna. This is on me, by the way,' he murmured, and waved aside their brief, unconvincing protests.

When the wine waiter visited their table Brock asked what Mrs Starling might have chosen, and barely blanched as he ordered a bottle of the same.

'She had very good taste, didn't she?' Desai said. 'The flat, I mean.'

'Is that her?' Kathy asked. 'I mean, rather than some interior designer that Starling might have hired.'

'Yes, I think so. Because of her clothes. Kryzia suits, La Perla underwear, Xenia shoes. All spot on.'

'*La Perla underwear?*' Brock echoed. 'What do you know about things like that, Leon?'

Desai smiled, unfazed. 'It's my job to be observant, Brock,' he said smoothly.

Kathy looked at him with interest. She'd never heard of Xenia shoes.

'Yes, well, you're absolutely right,' Brock said. 'Sammy Starling wouldn't have a clue about La Whatsit underwear. Brenda was strictly Marks and Sparks, no matter how much money she had.'

'Maybe Eva educated him,' Kathy said.

'Yes, maybe.' He returned to studying the menu. 'Anything else you found to be observant about, Leon, apart from the lady's underwear?'

'The videos.'

'Go on.'

'The titles.' He pulled out a notebook and read from it. '*The*

Young and the Damned, The Criminal Life of Archibaldo de la Cruz, The Exterminating Angel, The Discreet Charm of the Bourgeoisie, That Obscure Object of Desire . . .'

'So?'

'They seemed kind of evocative, belonging to a beautiful young woman who's just disappeared.'

'They're all Buñuel titles,' Brock said. 'He liked stories about sex and death and obsession.'

The waiter appeared at his elbow, and Brock returned the glasses to his nose. He lifted the impressive menu.

'And Signora Starling is coming to join you?' the man said hopefully. 'Shall I lay another place?'

'Unfortunately not,' Brock said. 'You know her well? What's your name?'

'Tomaso.' The man looked smoulderingly at Kathy. 'You are friends?'

'Yes,' Brock said. 'I think we can claim to be that. You could say that we may be the only friends she has left.'

'The only friends?' The waiter looked puzzled.

'Yes. It seems she may have been betrayed by her other friends, Tomaso.'

'Is so?' He now looked vaguely troubled.

'Is so. Did she bring her other friends here?'

'No, here she eats alone. Sometimes with Mr Starling, when he is in London.'

'When was the last time you saw her, Tomaso? Last weekend?'

'No. She hasn't been here for three weeks, a month.'

'Are you sure? Mr Starling keeps an account here, doesn't he? Would you mind checking it for us?'

The waiter looked at him disdainfully. 'I'm sorry, sir, I couldn't possibly —'

Brock showed him his warrant card. 'Eva is missing, Tomaso. This is important.'

The man looked startled.

Brock said, 'And keep this to yourself, please, Tomaso. That's important too. Now, our order . . .'

Later, after he had served their meals, Tomaso returned with a printout of the Starlings' account. 'As I said, the last time she was here was the fifteenth of June.'

Brock looked at the document. 'Fine, thanks.'

Tomaso hesitated. 'There was one time she came here with someone, a man.'

'Oh, yes?'

He saw he had their full attention. 'Not a young man. Middle-aged. Not very . . . smart.'

'When was this?'

'Maybe a year ago.'

'Did she say anything to you about him? It must have seemed odd.'

'She was joyful, I remember. Very happy. He seemed very uncomfortable. He didn't belong in a place like this, I can tell you.'

'She didn't introduce you? Mention a name?'

'I don't think so.'

At the end of the meal, as he served them their coffee, Tomaso spoke again to Brock. 'Is right? Eva is really missing?'

'Yes, Tomaso. She really is. Is there something else you can tell us?'

The waiter looked unhappy. 'Do you know about her phone?'

'Her phone?'

'Her mobile. She leaves it with us, when she is away from London. Yesterday a man called to collect it. He said he was her friend.'

'When was this, Tomaso?' Brock said quietly.

'Yesterday lunch-time. I wasn't here. One of the other guys gave it to him.'

'Is he here now?'

Tomaso nodded.

'All right,' Brock said. 'We'd like to talk to him.'

When the waiter had gone, Kathy said, 'Starling said she doesn't have a mobile.'

'I know,' Brock said. 'But can you imagine a girl like Eva without a phone in her bag?'

Tomaso returned with a younger man, the same dark southern-Italian looks. He spoke little English, and Tomaso acted as interpreter.

'This is Massimiliano. He works in the kitchen. He says the

man was middle-aged, English. He was coming out of the toilet at the back, and he stopped by the door to the kitchen and spoke directly to Massimiliano. He had a little Italian, and used sign language as well. Massimiliano told him he must talk to one of the others, but the man was in a hurry, and the restaurant was busy. He knew where Signora Starling's phone was, behind the little bar in the corner there, and he said he would help himself. Massimiliano didn't object.'

Tomaso stared balefully at the other man, who looked sulky and unrepentant.

'Could it have been Mr Starling, Tomaso?' Brock asked.

'I don't think so, sir.' Tomaso looked very uneasy. 'Mr Starling doesn't know about the phone. Eva says it's her little secret. That's why she leaves it here. She says he doesn't like her to have a mobile, because of her health.'

'Her health?'

'Yes, you know . . . the electric waves.'

'All the same, describe Mr Starling to Massimiliano, will you? Just to be sure.'

They watched him talking rapidly to the cook. Massimiliano's eyes widened and he shook his head and said something.

'Not Chinese,' Tomaso said. He spoke some more to the cook, then again to Brock, lips pursed with frustration. 'He has no description besides this. He didn't take notice. He was too busy. His mind was full with his sauces.'

When they had gone, Desai suggested, 'A boyfriend?'

'Maybe,' Brock grunted. 'It certainly seems she had her little secrets. The question is, were they lethal?'

'Lethal?'

'If she was being a bad girl, and Sammy couldn't cope with it . . .'

'You think he's killed her?' Desai was fascinated. 'And staged the kidnapping business?'

'Well, it is very stagy, isn't it? That business of contacting us through Cabot's, and the way we're brought in when two out of three messages have been delivered. All seems a bit like a script someone's prepared for us. I've already experienced one of Sammy's surprising little scripts, and I don't fancy taking part in another.'

'That's what White suggested to me,' Kathy said. 'That Sammy might be behind it.'

'Did he? Well – but you have other ideas, Kathy? From your questions to Sammy about the stamps on the notes?'

'It was the business of these valuable stamps being ruined. What was the point? Then I thought that they must have been sent by someone who knew Sammy was obsessed by stamps, but didn't themselves know or care about them. It was like a gesture designed to get under his skin. I thought it might be the sort of thing that an angry wife might do.'

'Oh, I like that.' Desai smiled. Brock conceded a nod.

'And Sammy had thought of this too,' Kathy went on. 'When I pressed him, he acknowledged that he'd checked to see if they were his own stamps.'

'Well,' Brock said, 'if you're right she's alive, if I'm right she's dead. Let's hope you're right, Kathy. Ah, the bill . . .'

4

The Canada Cover

They had arranged for Sammy Starling's mail to be intercepted. He drove up from Farnham early the following morning, Friday the eleventh, and was sitting in the conference room at Queen Anne's Gate at six a.m. when a messenger arrived with an envelope addressed identically to the first two. Apart from Brock and Kathy, Leon Desai was there with an expert from the Questioned Documents Section of the Physical Sciences Division of the Metropolitan Police Forensic Science Laboratory, which deals with counterfeiting, handwriting analysis, typewriter identification and other matters relating to the analysis of documents. The expert, Bert Freedman, took charge of the letter, briefly examining the exterior with a magnifying lens before carefully slicing open the envelope and drawing out the note from inside.

There was the expected fourpence blue head of the young Queen Victoria, the stamp this time cut into four pieces. Beneath it, the message read,

EVA'S PRICE IS LOT 15
CABOT'S COMMONWEALTH AUCTION.
BUY IT.
HAND-OVER INSTRUCTIONS
ON YOUR MOBILE 4.00 P.M. SATURDAY

Starling was very pale as he read and reread it. Then he nodded to himself, as if this was to be expected, and raised a glass of water to his lips, hand trembling.

'That's the auction we saw advertised yesterday at Cabot's, is it, Sammy?' Brock asked softly, and Starling swallowed and nodded.

'We've got the catalogue somewhere. Do you know what lot fifteen is?'

Starling gave a little shake of his head, still speechless.

Kathy got to her feet. 'I've got it in the office.'

A minute later she returned and placed the book in front of Brock. He had barely glanced at it since Melville had presented it to him. Now he looked at the illustration on the front cover to which Kathy was pointing. It was a photograph of a small envelope addressed in looping copperplate letters, with a black stamp of a Chalon Head design in the corner. Beneath the photograph was printed 'Lot 15'.

He picked up the catalogue and turned over the pages until he found a description of the item, which he began to read out: ' "Canada Cover, 4 June 1851. Unique pre-issue 12d 1851, SG 4, on env. addressed to Mrs Sandford Fleming, 185 Bloor Street, Toronto; one neat strike scarce franking . . ." '

He stopped reading aloud as his eyes scanned on down the page until he said, 'There's an estimated value here . . .' He hesitated then said, '£450,000. Can that be right?'

They all turned to Sammy Starling, who stared back at them, impassive.

'Let's get Melville here,' Brock said. 'We've got his home address. Get a car to pick him up.'

James Melville arrived an hour later in a state of some excitement – it wasn't every day that one was roused from one's bed and whisked off in a police car, waving like royalty at the people in number seventy-three who had observed it all from their bedroom window. He shook everyone's hand effusively.

'We're getting breakfast sent in,' Brock said. 'What can we get you? Croissants? Coffee?'

They settled down to business.

'I really didn't expect to hear from you again so soon, Chief

54

Inspector,' Melville said. 'Have things come to a head?' He looked with concern at Starling, who gave no reaction, his attention seemingly turned in upon himself.

'The third note has arrived, and it involves your company, Mr Melville. I'd like to record your comments, if you don't mind?'

'Oh, no, certainly.'

'Let's just establish who you are.' Brock reached forward, pressed the switch on the recorder and made some introductory remarks. 'Now, you are the general manager of Cabot's, is that right?'

'Not quite. I am Cabot's manager, Early British and Colonies.'

'Are you in charge of the auction that starts tomorrow?'

'Our senior auctioneer, Christopher Conway, will be conducting the auctions, but much of the material will come through my department. The event is spread over three days, Saturday, Monday and Tuesday, with British Commonwealth stamps on Saturday, British only on Monday, and foreign on Tuesday. It is predominantly an auction of rare and classic stamps, so the first two days are essentially my responsibility. Our manager, Foreign, is running the third day.'

'I see. Well, we have a problem that we would like to discuss with you, in confidence, of course.'

'Of course.' Melville took out a pair of glasses as Brock showed him the third note, read it quickly and then exploded, 'But that's utterly preposterous! Good heavens, Mr Starling, what can I say? I'm devastated!'

'There are a number of things I don't understand about this, Mr Melville,' Brock went on. 'Perhaps you could help us. First, tell us about lot fifteen.'

'Oh, my goodness! Lot fifteen!' Melville stared at him wide-eyed, then gazed in sympathy at Starling. 'Lot fifteen, indeed!'

'We've found the entry in the auction catalogue you gave us yesterday,' Brock said. 'What's so special about it?'

'You remember we spoke yesterday about the Chalon Head stamps, Chief Inspector? Such as the ones on the ransom notes. Well, this is the very first Chalon Head, from 1851. It is simply unique. Until nine months ago we didn't even know it existed.'

'And that's significant?'

'Oh, exceedingly.'

'Could you give us a very brief summary of why that is? For the record?'

'Well, now . . .' Melville frowned, marshalling his thoughts. 'The first adhesive postage stamp was issued eleven years before, in 1840. That was the famous British penny black, and it's hard to imagine now what a radical invention it was, a uniform rate national postal system, prepaid by means of an adhesive token, which was cut off a sheet with scissors – later they added perforations for ease of tearing – and stuck to the letter. Since no other country had such a system, there was no need to put the name of the country on the stamp, which is why British stamps to this day are the only ones without the country's name on them. But they do have the monarch's head, and that goes right back to the penny black. The design of that stamp was based on a side-profile portrait of Queen Victoria, which was engraved by William Wyon for a medallion struck when Victoria came to the throne in 1837.

'Now in that same year the artist Alfred Edward Chalon also made a portrait of the young Queen. He sketched her standing in her robes of state on the grand staircase of the House of Lords on the occasion of her first visit there, and from this sketch he painted three versions of a full-length portrait. One went to the Queen herself, another to the King of Prussia, and the third to the King of Portugal.'

'Portugal?' Brock said, glancing at Starling, who appeared not to hear. 'That's interesting. And that portrait was the basis of the Chalon Head stamps?'

'That's right. Instead of a profile portrait like the Wyon penny black design, it shows, as you know, the Queen's head and shoulders almost frontally as she turns to view something off to her right. It was never used for a British stamp, but as colonies around the Empire began to bring out their own stamp designs, the Chalon portrait proved to be a favourite with a number of them. In all, eleven colonies produced Chalon stamps, beginning with Canada and Nova Scotia in 1851.

'The Canadian post offices were part of the British system until that year, when they first issued their own stamps – the threepence beaver design, sixpence portrait of Prince Albert, and twelvepence Chalon Head of Queen Victoria. These new stamps were designed by a young Scotsman who had emigrated to Canada a few years before. He went on to become chief engineer to the Dominion government, and responsible for the construction of the Canadian Pacific Railway. And his name was Sandford Fleming.

'And so now we arrive at lot fifteen. Here is our young Sandford Fleming, temporarily separated from his wife, he in Montreal, she in Toronto. It is her birthday. He decides to send her a letter, using a first print from the first plate of his new high-value stamp. We have the letter, dated the fourth of June 1851. But note this . . .' Melville leaned forward to emphasise his point. 'The twelvepence black was not released for public use until the fourteenth of June. And, moreover, the stamp that was then released was different from the one Fleming had sent to his wife ten days before. The principal difference was in the corner numbers, which in his version, as you can see in the catalogue picture, were black figures on a white ground, like the corner letters in the British penny black. But in the final version, which came into general circulation on the fourteenth of June, they were reversed to white figures on black ground.' Melville sat back, eyes bright with enthusiasm. 'So there you have it, the sole example of a stamp which no one knew existed *and* on a cover addressed by its designer, himself a notable historical figure. The first Chalon Head!'

There was a moment's silence as they waited to see if he had finished. Then the document expert, Bert Freedman, rubbed his hand across his bald head and said, 'Fascinating.'

'Have I misread this bit here in the catalogue, Mr Melville?' Brock asked. 'The estimated value. It looks like £450,000.'

'That's right, though really it's impossible for us to put an accurate figure on it because it is absolutely unique. Ever since its discovery there has been tremendous interest – from Canadian collectors especially, of course, but also right around the globe. Undoubtedly it will attract keen bidding, possibly a record sum.'

'Do stamps fetch that kind of figure?'

'Oh, indeed, yes. The highest sum paid so far for a philatelic item was for a cover rather like this –'

'A cover being an envelope?' Brock queried.

'An envelope with the original stamp on it – that's the term we use. It was for a cover of 1847 bearing both the penny red and the twopenny blue stamps issued by the British colony of Mauritius in that year. Neither stamp is unique, but they are both very rare, and this was the only known cover to have both of those stamps on it. It was auctioned in Zurich in 1993, and it fetched almost six million Swiss francs – that's two and a half million pounds sterling.'

'Oh . . .' Brock said. 'I see.'

'We don't expect the twelvepence black cover to reach that figure, but it's not impossible that it could go over a million.'

There was silence, then Melville whispered, 'I really am most sorry, Mr Starling.'

Starling seemed to rouse himself, as if he'd been contemplating some entirely different matter all this time. He turned to Melville and said quietly, 'You can't allow anyone else to buy it, Mr Melville. It would be my wife's death warrant.'

Melville looked deeply troubled. 'I understand, Mr Starling. I do understand that, and yet . . . I'm not sure how we can prevent it . . .'

'What about the seller? Will they deal with me direct before the auction?'

Melville shook his head. 'Several people have already tried that, but the owners are determined to test the market at auction. They sense that there is a strong field, and I have to say that they are right.'

'But if I explained to them what was at stake? A woman's life?'

Melville looked anguished. 'We will try that, of course, yes. But you must understand that the cover was found among the effects of a descendant of the original sender, Sir Sandford Fleming, with the instructions that the estate was to be realised to the fullest possible extent, in order to establish a trust for medical research. From my dealings with the trustees, I believe you will find them to be absolutely resolved to carry out their instructions to the letter. We have already experienced that determination, when we negotiated our terms for the auction, and again when several of our clients asked us, like you, to negotiate a sale before auction.'

Sammy's face became immobile once again.

'I do wish I could advise you otherwise, Mr Starling,' Melville went on.

Brock said, 'Maybe you could clear up one or two other difficulties I'm having with all this, Mr Melville. I'm puzzled why anyone would consider this a suitable ransom demand. Surely such a thing would be highly traceable and difficult to turn into cash.'

'Yes . . . that is interesting, isn't it?' Cabot's manager said, bringing his fingers together as if in prayer while he considered this. 'It's the same as stealing works of art. There are unscrupulous collectors who so covet particular items that they will buy them, stolen, even though they can never admit they own them, or show them to anyone else.'

'Yes, but that isn't exactly the case here,' Brock said. 'If such a collector wanted this item they could bid for it. So presumably they would only buy it later at a substantial discount, considering the disadvantages of so doing. But what is the point of that to the kidnapper? If he wants, say, a million pounds from Mr Starling, why not ask for a million pounds, rather than a stamp that can only be sold on at a discount?'

Melville thought about this, then said, 'Two suggestions. First, the kidnapper may not intend to sell it on. He himself may be the collector who doesn't care whether the item is stolen or not, so long as he can possess it.'

Brock considered that. 'Yes, all right. That's a possibility we can follow up with you, Mr Melville. You must have some ideas about such people. The second suggestion?'

'Portability. The one really distinctive thing about valuable stamps is how small and portable they are. More than gold, more than Impressionist paintings, a rare stamp is the most compressed example of portable value. You must have heard the stories of refugees escaping from Germany before the last war with a fortune in rare stamps in their pockets? Your man can put this twelvepence black in his wallet and go anywhere in the world with it, undetected. No metal detector will pick him up, no bank computer will identify him when he sells it.'

Breakfast arrived, and they fell silent as they ate, each pondering the implications of what Melville had said. Finally

Starling wiped his mouth with a paper napkin, cleared his throat and said, 'Well, there's no alternative, is there? I'll just have to buy the Canada Cover on Saturday. What's your top figure, Mr Melville? One million? One and a quarter?'

Melville spread his hands. 'I suppose that's just conceivable, Mr Starling. I wish I could be more helpful. The catalogue value for a copy of the normal Canada twelvepence black, the fourteenth of June issue, is £45,000, but that doesn't provide any guide for this unique version, with its direct association with Sandford Fleming.'

Starling nodded. 'One and a quarter then. Let's aim for that. I shall need you to value my collection. Will you do that? Give me a price?'

'Of course.'

Starling looked at his watch. 'I've got a lot to do if I'm going to raise that much by tomorrow. The market's low at the moment. It'll be a fire sale. Anyone interested in a nice house on the North Downs? A three-year-old Merc?' He gave them all a mirthless smile.

'It isn't our policy to pay ransom demands to kidnappers,' Brock said heavily. The words sounded hollow as he spoke them.

'No?' Starling said. 'Well, you catch the bastards by lunch-time tomorrow, Mr Brock, and there'll be no need, will there?'

'Is there no alternative, Chief Inspector?' Melville asked.

'What about . . .' Starling hesitated. 'A copy?'

'Exactly what I was thinking,' Bert Freedman jumped in.

'A copy?'

'Yes!' The document expert nodded vigorously. 'I mean, Mr Melville's point about how a stamp is much more portable than a suitcase of banknotes – much easier to replicate too, I'd have thought.'

'You want to make a forgery, Bert?' Brock said.

He gave a sly smile. 'Just a thought. Mind you, this isn't my area. We'd need expert advice. But I suppose you'd have that at Cabot's, Mr Melville?'

'Not really,' Melville said slowly. 'We rely on technical specialists to provide authentication for clients. We could

60

certainly recommend someone. For this type of stamp, this period . . .'

He looked at Starling, who said, 'Dr Waverley?'

'Yes, Tim Waverley. Mr Starling has used him in the past. Very sound.'

'I'd only consider something like that if Waverley thought it was feasible,' Starling said.

'Well,' Brock said reluctantly, 'perhaps we should get his advice.'

'Anyway,' Starling rose to his feet, 'I've got work to do.' He drew himself up to his full five foot six and said to Brock, voice exhausted, 'Find her for me soon, please, Mr Brock. She must be going through hell.'

Brock got up and walked with him out of the room.

Melville watched them go, then murmured, 'This is really a nightmare, isn't it? It could turn out very bad for us, too, couldn't it? If things went wrong, and anything happened to Mrs Starling . . .'

'You've got to know Mr Starling quite well, have you?' Kathy asked.

'I couldn't really say that. He's a rather enigmatic person, don't you agree? I still find it quite difficult to make out what he's thinking.'

'As if he's playing poker all the time.'

Melville gave a little smile. 'Exactly. But then he suddenly says something, like just now, and you realise he feels everything the way you or I . . . I'm sorry, I didn't intend that to sound racist. It's just that he is a rather complex character, I think, quite surprising in a number of ways, and yet it's hard not to think of him in terms of stereotypes like "inscrutable".'

'Yes.'

'The thing that I find utterly bewildering about all this, really quite deeply disturbing, is the way it's being done.'

'How do you mean?'

Brock came back into the room. 'Won't see a doctor. Says he hasn't slept since Monday night. Not the best way to see about selling off everything you own. Sorry, I interrupted. You were saying something, Mr Melville?'

'Oh, we were just talking generally. I was saying that I

61

found the way Mr Starling is being threatened quite . . . well, chilling.'

'How do you mean?'

'The use of the Chalon stamps, in the notes, and then again in the ransom demand itself, the Canada Cover. It's so very personal, you see, as if the whole thing has been carefully contrived to touch him in the most personal way.'

'I'm not sure I follow,' Kathy said. 'You mean, because he collects that particular type of stamp?'

Melville gave a pale smile. 'I'm sorry, Sergeant. I know you're not interested in postage stamps, and it must all seem a little weird to you. But it isn't just that he collects Chalons, they are his special field. He is the expert, the authority. He wrote the book.'

'The book?'

'Yes: *The Chalon Heads: A Chronology*. It came out two or three years ago.'

'Mr Melville, I am astonished,' Brock said slowly. 'I was surprised to learn that Sammy Starling was a collector of stamps, but to imagine that he's written a book . . .' He shook his head. 'A *chronology* . . . Since when did he use words like that?'

Melville nodded. 'I must say that that was my initial reaction too. And yet it is a very worthy little piece of work. It isn't by any means an exhaustive study, and it relies heavily on other sources, but it is intelligently presented, with some quite imaginative speculations. There is an excellent analysis of the symbolism of the portrait itself, for example, and of the image of the young queen, vulnerable and beautiful.'

Melville pointed to the illustration of the Canada Cover on the catalogue, with its twelvepence black Chalon stamp. 'I must say I'd never thought about it before, but you note the naked throat and shoulders, compared for example with the portrait of Prince Albert, which came out at the same time on the Canadian sixpenny stamp, in his formal uniform with heavy collar and epaulettes. A rather intriguing argument is developed concerning the use of this feminine image in projecting the global power of a patriarchal British Empire during the nineteenth century. I showed it to my wife, and she thought it was written by a feminist.'

Brock stared at him in disbelief. 'Sammy Starling a feminist? I thought I'd heard everything, Mr Melville.'

Melville smiled, sucked in his cheeks. 'I suppose it wouldn't be too disloyal to let on that he had a little help. A rather bright young woman, who worked here with us for a while – not unlike yourself, Sergeant, in style – I mean, you remind me a little of her . . .' He felt himself beginning to flounder, and hurriedly went on, 'On my recommendation, Mr Starling employed her for a couple of months as a research assistant for his book. He was in a great hurry to get it done, and she was a very organised person, just what he needed. And I wouldn't be too surprised if she might not have helped with the writing of it too.'

'That sounds more like our Sammy,' Brock said. 'I'll bet he never wrote a word.'

'Have you any idea why he would have wanted to write such a book?' Kathy asked.

'Vanity, I suppose. It was self-published, I understand. The publisher's name – Philatelic Speciality Press, or something like that – was his own invention, I believe.'

'So other collectors would have known of his interest in this type of stamp through his book. Might one of them have kidnapped Mrs Starling as a means of acquiring this unique stamp? Is that feasible?' Brock asked. 'I must say I find it pretty implausible.'

'Yes,' Melville agreed. 'It's unthinkable. And yet . . . I have remarked to my colleagues in the past that one or two of our customers would willingly sell their mothers for some item they particularly desire. There are as many types and characters of philatelists as of any other group of human beings, Chief Inspector, and among them are certainly a few obsessive ones. For them, collecting becomes a compulsion, and I have, on occasions, found something almost frightening about their absolute need to acquire some variation or fault of great rarity, or a specimen that will complete a classic set.'

'But of all the collectors who would be interested in the Canada Cover, Mr Starling himself would be the most obsessive, wouldn't he?' Kathy came in. 'If that's his special field, then the first Chalon of all, on a cover handwritten and posted by the man who designed it, would be pretty much a cult object, wouldn't it?'

'*An obscure object of desire*,' Brock murmured. 'Yes, Kathy. You're absolutely right.'

Dr Waverley, the forgery expert recommended by Melville, arrived shortly after ten a.m., and was soon deep in discussion with Bert Freedman and Leon Desai. A lanky, slender man, with wire-framed glasses and long fair hair that kept falling forward over his forehead, he affected a kind of scholarly foppishness in complete contrast to Freedman's air of the stubby-fingered mechanic. Despite this, the two experts quickly took to each other, and became enthusiastically embroiled in the technical problems of convincingly reproducing the Canada Cover.

After a while Brock asked how things were going.

Waverley replied. 'Time . . .' he said, pinching the bridge of his thin nose, 'that's your main problem. The original plate was engraved by a man called Alfred Jones, using the recess printing or direct-plate printing method. It's hardly used today, partly because it relies on highly skilled engravers, and it can take weeks of effort to produce a single die. There's no possibility it could be done in that way in twenty-four hours.'

'Aren't there more rapid methods of achieving the same effect?'

'That's what we've been trying to work out,' Freedman said, his face lit up with the challenge. 'Recess printing produces quite a distinctive effect of raised ink surfaces, which an expert would be able to spot with just a magnifying glass. I reckon we could get something very close using the right kind of ink. What I'd like to do is get the original under the scanning electron microscope down at our Chemistry Division, but Mr Melville's understandably reluctant.'

Melville did look uneasy. 'It would mean removing it from the exhibition in our foyer. So many people are coming especially to view it, and then there's the insurance aspect, and the approval of the owners . . .'

'I think we should do whatever's possible, Mr Melville,' Brock said.

'Yes, yes, of course. I'm just waiting for a return call from the insurers, then I'll make a call to Canada.'

'We're going to have to photograph it anyway, Mr Melville,' Freedman said. 'No way we can do this without taking the original to Lambeth for a couple of hours.'

'Anyway,' Waverley continued, 'paper shouldn't be a problem. It's what's called laid paper, which has a distinctive pattern to it, but I have some original samples that could be used, and thankfully the original has no watermark. Similarly the envelope. The ink, now, that's another problem . . .'

He gave a brief dissertation on the issues raised by fugitive and non-fugitive inks, went on to the manufacture from potato starch of the gum required as adhesive for the stamp, and concluded with a few remarks about the artificial ageing of dyes and papers. Freedman was captivated.

'All right,' Brock said. 'Let's do it. If nothing else, it may give us some leeway if Sammy fails to get the cover at the auction. Tell us what you need, Bert, and I'll sign the requisitions. What about you, Dr Waverley? Can you spare us some of your time?'

'I wouldn't miss it for anything, Chief Inspector. Forgery is my field. I'm fascinated to see just what we can come up with.'

'Thank you. You might keep an eye on Bert here, too. The idea of crossing to the other side seems to be exercising an unhealthy appeal.'

Freedman chuckled. 'That's where the money is, Brock. What do you say we make an extra couple, eh, Tim? One each.' He rubbed his bald pate in gleeful anticipation.

5

An Auction

'There's a season of Brazilian films showing at a little fleapit in Camden Town, called the Cinema Hollywood.' Brock passed round a sheet with information on performance times at that and several other cinemas which featured foreign-language films.

'They knew her at the Cinema Hollywood – quite a regular, apparently. But we can't find anyone who remembers seeing her there during the past week. We're checking all the cafés and shops between Canonbury and Camden Town. What else? Bookstores that sell books on cinema, stores that sell foreign videos, credit-card checks, hairdressers, clothes shops that sell La Perla underwear . . . Nothing so far. Well, Bren, what have you got?'

'About as little as everyone else, by the sound of it. We've been watching both Marty and Barney Keller since Friday afternoon, and neither has given the slightest indication that they're up to anything.'

'Nothing at all?'

'Not a thing.' Bren frowned unhappily. 'More than that, Brock . . .'

'Yes?'

'Well, to be honest, Marty Keller just doesn't look like he's got it in him any more.'

'How do you mean?'

'I remember seeing him once. He played for the London Mets, in the days when people thought it a bit weird playing the American game. It was a novelty, and I went along one afternoon to see what it was all about. I remember him because he was such a showman. He scored a touchdown, and started jumping and whooping like he was doing a war dance or something. The crowd loved it.' Bren sighed and ran a hand through the short crop of his hair. 'This guy we've been following isn't the same bloke. This one doesn't look as if he could scare a kitten. He's turned in on himself, doesn't meet anybody's eyes, only speaks when he's spoken to. To me, he looks like a man who's had the shit kicked out of him, and just wants to be left alone. That's my impression.'

Brock considered this sombrely. 'Could be just an act.'

'Yes, I know. Does it bloody well, though. What I thought was that we could get one or two guys from the old days, who knew him well, to bump into him by accident, chat him up, tell us what they think.'

'Could look a bit obvious.'

'And at the same time we should find out how he was behaving inside. I mean, if he was throwing his weight around in there, then this is more likely to be an act.'

'We have something on that. There's a report from the prison psychiatrist at Durham. Keller went through a period of depression just over a year ago. He was on medication for four months, and his behaviour is described as "subdued" after that.'

Bren sat back. 'Well, then, that's it. I reckon they broke him. I reckon he's all washed up.'

Kathy walked from Trafalgar Square the length of the Strand, enjoying the sun on the northern pavement. The street was quiet compared to a weekday, and she spotted the huddle of people on the other side from some way away. As she got closer, she again noticed that the crowd drawn to Cabot's auction rooms was uniformly male. Whiskery old men in corduroy and tweed struggled past eager schoolboys dragging at their fathers' hands. Tourists in jeans tried to see what the fuss was all about while men in suits slipped past and made for the lifts. Apart from the occasional tourist, the only females visible were a couple of women selling catalogues at the desk in the foyer, and what looked like a journalist, with notebook and ballpoint, talking to one of them as she served the impatient horde thrusting money at her. Kathy worked her way inside and made for the stairs.

There was a bigger crowd on the first floor, milling around the display of lots to be auctioned that afternoon. Kathy noted the closed-circuit cameras, the uniformed security hovering in the background, and the number of staff answering queries at the counters. She positioned herself near the door in the line of one of the cameras, and examined the catalogue she had brought with her. At over two hundred pages it was a substantial document. Almost two thousand lots were to be sold over the three days, and the catalogue cover was titled 'Major International Stamp Auction' above the illustration of lot fifteen. On the rear cover another illustration showed lot six, a roughly cut circle of paper with the words 'Hamilton Bermuda 1849' printed with crude lettering, which Kathy thought might as well have been done with a child's toy printing set. Checking inside, she discovered that this scrap, described as a 'Perot', was expected to fetch £80,000.

'Ms Kolla?' A man's voice murmured in her ear.

'That's me.'

'Follow me, please.' The young man, trimly suited, insinuated himself through the crush coming through the door and led her out to the stairs and up to the second floor. He look briefly over her shoulder as if to see if they were being observed, tapped on the door and led her in.

The room had the crowded, expectant atmosphere of a crime operations room. She nodded to Leon Desai, standing against the opposite wall with Dr Waverley, who was clutching a battered old briefcase to his chest. Brock was sitting at the far end, beneath the windows, talking earnestly with James Melville and another man in a pinstripe suit. Sammy Starling was sitting at the central table flanked by two heavily built men. He appeared dazed, his eyes unseeing, and he seemed to have grown smaller, probably due to the size of the two beefy men on each side of him. From time to time one or other of them would speak softly to him; he seemed barely to hear, and they repeated their comments until he gave a little nod or frown in acknowledgement. They seemed quite relaxed. It looked to Kathy as if at least one of them was armed.

In a moment the trim young man returned with two more people, a man and a woman, and Brock, seeing that everyone was now present, indicated that they should all sit. Despite the crowd in the room and the heat outside, the air-conditioning was fiercely efficient and the men all kept their jackets on, giving the gathering an air of formality, like a funeral party, Kathy thought. She found herself sitting next to Melville, who placed a small pile of books in front of her.

'You said yesterday you wanted to do some reading up on stamps, so I took you at your word.'

'Thanks.' She smiled, checking the titles.

'Don't mention it. Always looking for converts. I should start with the Watson.'

Brock cleared his throat and began with introductions. The man to whom he and Melville had been talking was the senior auctioneer for the afternoon's business, Christopher Conway. The man and woman who had come in last were also from Cabot's, he in charge of security, and she to act as liaison between the police and the company staff. The two men sitting with Starling were police officers, hostage and kidnap specialists from SO10 Crime Operations Group, ominously named Gallows and Heath.

'I must emphasise at the outset,' Brock went on, 'how essential it is that everything proceeds as normal this afternoon. The very last thing we want is to alert Mrs Starling's kidnappers to the possibility that anyone in this building, apart from Mr Starling, knows that something is amiss.'

Starling gave a jerky, emphatic nod that betrayed the state of tension in his body.

'We must assume that they, the kidnappers, will be present at the auction this afternoon, and are probably already here in the building. We are monitoring the closed-circuit cameras from the room next door, and we have other people outside the building, but we will not be making any attempt to detain anyone here.' Brock turned gravely to the auctioneer, 'Even if we have an armed hold-up here this afternoon, Mr Conway, we will have to let your people call for assistance in the normal way, just as if we weren't here. Our first concern is Mrs Starling's safety.'

Melville said, 'Chief Inspector, you will have our full co-operation. Cabot's are horrified that criminals should have chosen this way to extort money from one of our most valued clients. If it helped, we would be willing to postpone or cancel the sale of lot fifteen, but under the circumstances I believe you feel we should continue . . .'

'That's right. I understand you've had no success with the sellers, Mr Melville?'

Melville shook his head. 'I put Mr Starling's final offer to them a short time ago. They turned it down, I'm afraid. As I anticipated, they're not interested in a private sale before the auction. They scent a seller's market this afternoon.'

'And you feel they're right?'

Melville turned to the auctioneer at his side. Conway nodded. 'Demand has been hardening these past six months, especially for these very special high-value pieces.' He had a rich, polished voice that demanded attention. 'Lot six, the Bermuda Perot issue, which you can see on the back of the catalogue, should give us the first real indication of how things will go today. Apart from its general rarity and quality, lot fifteen also has a particular significance for Canadian collectors. We have six overseas bidders who have made arrangements for telephone bidding, three of them from Canada, and we know them all to be serious collectors.'

'How will the auction work, Mr Conway?'

The auctioneer described how the afternoon would run. At midday the public viewing of the pieces to be sold would close, and the hall would be set out with furniture and facilities for the auction. Tables would be set up for Cabot's staff taking telephone bids from other parts of the country and from overseas. Other staff would represent postal bids, which had been streaming in over the previous weeks, by mail and fax. All buyers attending the auction in person would be given a numbered card, which they would raise to indicate a bid to the auctioneer.

'You and your colleagues will be able to watch the proceed-ings on the closed-circuit television sets in the next room, Chief

Inspector. You could make your bids anonymously by phone from up here as well, Mr Starling, if you wished.'

'No,' Starling said, voice hoarse. 'I want to be seen. I want them to know that I get it.'

Kathy saw Conway's mouth begin to form the response, 'But what if you don't?' Then he changed his mind. 'Very well. In that case I suggest we place you at a seat on the centre aisle, perhaps towards the front, so that you can be seen and so that you can leave as soon as lot fifteen is sold. I take it you want to do that?'

'Yes.' Brock agreed. 'I'd like Mr Starling to come back up here to wait for the phone call.'

'One of our staff will stay with him throughout. I anticipate that we'll get to lot fifteen by two forty-five.'

'Will you have the names and addresses of everyone who attends the auction?'

'Yes. Everyone provides details as they register, and postal and telephone buyers provide bank or credit-card information in advance.'

'We'd like to have those names and addresses as they become available.'

Melville and Conway conferred, then Melville confirmed his agreement to this.

'Well, now,' Brock sat back, 'I think that's all we need at the moment. We have one or two things to go over with Mr Starling, and I'd appreciate it if you could stay with us for a while longer, Mr Melville.'

The other Cabot's people filed out of the room, and Brock turned to Desai. 'Leon, how did things go at the lab?'

'Very well, I think. Bert Freedman sends his apologies – he didn't get any sleep last night, and went home for a couple of hours. Dr Waverley has more stamina. He worked all through the night with the lab boys, and he'd be best to describe the result.'

'Fine. We very much appreciate your help, Dr Waverley. Please tell us.'

Waverley looked pale, his eyes bright and rimmed in pink. He stood the briefcase on his knee, opened the flap and groped inside. After a moment he found a pair of white cotton gloves, which he put on before reaching back into the briefcase again, this time lifting out a plain white envelope. Setting the briefcase aside, he drew a piece of cardboard packing out of the envelope, unfolded it and slid the contents out on to the table. There was a murmur of appreciation as everyone saw the envelope with copperplate handwriting and the black stamp.

Melville said, 'The Canada Cover!'

'As close as we could get in the time available,' Waverley said.

Melville took a small magnifier from his pocket and went over to the envelope, peering closely at it, nodding as his eye moved from one part to another. Finally he straightened. 'Astonishing. Really very good. Have a look, Mr Starling.'

Starling got to his feet, came round the table and took the magnifying glass from Melville. When he'd made his examination he looked at Waverley anxiously, biting his lip with tension. 'I can't tell the difference,' he said.

'Nor I,' Melville concurred. 'It really is quite astonishing. Congratulations, Tim. Well done.'

'The question is,' Desai said, 'can we use it? *Should* we use it?'

They looked at Brock, who in turn faced Waverley. 'Will it fool an expert?'

'I've been giving that some thought, Chief Inspector.' Waverley pushed the unruly lock of hair back from his eyebrows and straightened his glasses. He looked sombre. 'It's really a matter of how much time and equipment they'll have access to.' He looked apologetic. 'I'm sure you've thought all this through, but presumably your opponents will be just as conscious as you of the possibilities of substituting a fake.'

Brock nodded.

'Well, then they're hardly likely to do an exchange on the spot. If it were me, I'd want some time – an hour or more – and access to a microscope and perhaps other equipment to check what I'd been given before I went through with the deal.'

Starling became agitated. 'You mean I have to trust them? Hand over the stamp, then walk away and wait for them to decide whether to honour their part?'

No one answered him. They could imagine the ending he had pictured in his mind, a scene from an old movie, him leaving the envelope in a specified place, a car squealing into view, the rear door thrown open and Eva jumping out into his arms . . .

'Sammy,' Brock said softly, 'I'm afraid Dr Waverley is right. They will surely want to check what they're given.'

'And if that's the case . . .' Waverley automatically swept at the lock of hair '. . . as James says, it's really quite astonishing that we were able to get so far in just twenty-four hours. It would certainly fool someone without access to technical tests. But an expert, with a portable microscope, that's much more problematic.'

The room was silent for a moment, then Brock said, 'Your professional opinion, Dr Waverley. Is it worth trying?'

Waverley hesitated, then shook his head regretfully. 'If it were my wife, I wouldn't risk it. I wish very much I could say otherwise, but I think there's at least a fifty per cent chance they'd smell a rat.'

Starling's face dropped. Waverley looked sadly at him. 'I'm sorry, Mr Starling. We did our very best.'

Starling looked round the room at each face in turn, then lowered his eyes. 'No, you're right, Tim. I can't risk it either.' He sounded tired and defeated.

Reluctantly Waverley folded the false cover back into its cardboard packing, slid it into the envelope and returned the envelope to his briefcase. He began to take off the gloves. Starling rose to his feet and said he had to go to the toilet. At the table, Waverley paused and reached back into the briefcase. 'I think it would be best, Chief Inspector,' he said, holding up the white envelope, 'if you kept this in your possession. It is, after all, a very good copy, and we don't want any mistakes.' He smiled ruefully and handed it over to Brock, who put it into the inside pocket of his jacket.

They waited for Starling to return, his shoulders bowed. 'OK, Sammy?' Brock asked, and he nodded. 'All right.' Brock turned to the SO10 men. 'What will they do, at four, when they ring?'

'Step one, try to separate Mr Starling from us. Step two, separate the stamp from Mr Starling. Our priority is to prevent the first happening. Everything flows from that. You got your mobile, Mr Starling? Batteries charged up?'

Starling produced it from his hip pocket. The other man took it from him and began opening it up.

'Encouraging they want to use this,' Gallows went on placidly. He had an unruffled calm about him that seemed to soothe Starling.

'You'll be able to trace their call?' he asked.

'I doubt that will help, Mr Starling,' Gallows said. 'But we'll be able to hear all your conversations. And if all else fails and you need to talk to us, just dial a number, any number, and we'll be connected to you.'

'Won't they be able to tell?' Starling asked doubtfully.

Gallows shook his head. 'OK, Tony?'

The other man had the phone in pieces now on the table in front of him. 'Yeah.'

Gallows reached into his jacket pocket and brought out a plastic pouch from which he emptied a coil of wires and attachments on to the table. 'Member of Rotary, are we, sir?'

'No.'

'Well, we are now.' He picked out a lapel pin and attached it to Starling's jacket, then slipped a piece of equipment into Starling's inside pocket. 'And this is so you can listen to us.' He offered a small pink plug and showed him how to insert it into his ear. 'Make it the side you don't use for the phone. OK?'

As they fussed over him, Kathy wondered if, in some other part of the city, Eva was also being prepared for that moment.

Heath had reassembled the mobile phone, and handed it back to Starling, who took it gingerly, as if it might explode.

'What do I do now?' he asked.

'What would you do if we weren't here?' Gallows replied.

He considered that. 'Go downstairs and look at the lots until they closed the room, I suppose. Then go for a walk or something, till it's time for the auction.'

'Then that's exactly what you should do.'

Brock agreed. 'You can give this electronic stuff a trial as you go, Sammy,' he said. 'You'll soon get used to it.'

Sammy Starling straightened upright and began to walk slowly to the door, then stopped and turned to face them all. 'I just want to say . . .' his voice was little more than a whisper, and

74

they had to strain to hear him '. . . that I'm very grateful for what you're all doing. When Eva and I are reunited . . . I hope we can find a way to express our thanks properly.' He turned and walked out of the room, poking at his ear.

'Nice to see some manners these days,' Gallows murmured to Heath.

'Yeah,' the other replied, getting heavily to his feet. 'Touching.'

When they had gone, Brock turned to Melville. 'How did his fundraising go?' he asked quietly.

'Remarkably smoothly, considering the shortage of time. It's really rather frightening, how rapidly the assets which have taken a lifetime to accumulate can be valued and disposed of, if people put their minds to it. It was easier than – No, I'm sorry, that's a macabre thought.'

'What is?'

'I was about to say that it was easier than dealing with a deceased estate. Mr Starling's bank has transferred the sum of 1.15 million pounds sterling into a special Cabot's account, against the properties in Surrey and London, including contents, his two cars, and various securities and investments held by the bank. I think they got an astonishing bargain, incidentally, but the poor chap had no choice, within the time constraints. A further two hundred thousand has been guaranteed against some investments he holds, we will purchase his entire stamp collection for one hundred thousand, and we're currently waiting for written confirmation from his partner in a Portuguese property venture that he will deposit one hundred and fifty thousand against Mr Starling's share. Total one point six million. The buyer's premium and VAT add twenty-five per cent to the bid price, so that gives him a top bid of one million, two hundred and eighty thousand pounds. That should be enough.'

'Let's hope so.'

Soon after one thirty people began to take their seats for the auction, and by ten to two the room was full. On the floor above, Kathy watched their faces on the TV monitors, picking up the atmosphere of increasing anticipation. Desai came over and sat beside her.

'I went down to have another look at lot fifteen in the flesh,' he said.

'Does it look like a million pounds?'

'No, not at all. It's absurdly primitive, like something from a child's toy post office, imitating the real thing. When I was looking at it, I thought, The people who made this had built a world empire but they hadn't even invented a proper bicycle, let alone the telegraph.'

James Melville joined them. 'Nearly time,' he said. 'Did you get a chance to view the real lot fifteen, Sergeant?'

Desai nodded. 'We were just talking about it. I don't know if it was just my imagination, but I thought perhaps it did look different from the thing the lab made up.'

'Forging stamps isn't as easy as you'd think, although plenty of people have tried.'

On the screens a stir went through the people in the auction room as Cabot's staff took their seats at the telephone and postal-bid tables. There were four cameras within the hall, one focused on the auctioneer's dais, one on the front of the audience where Sammy Starling and the young man from Cabot's were seated, and the other two panning slowly around the room, guided by an operator sitting at a console in front of Kathy.

Melville pointed out some of the people who were known to him, collectors and their agents, regulars at Cabot's auctions, and clients who had expressed an interest in particular lots. He identified someone who was there to bid on behalf of a well-known newspaper proprietor, another representing the German philatelic museum in Frankfurt, who were interested in a valuable set of 1914 German New Guinea stamps overprinted by Australian occupying forces.

The camera moved on, and they watched the faces on the screens, expectant now, sensing the approaching hour. Sammy Starling's face came into focus.

He had spent an hour walking slowly along the Victoria Embankment, stopping frequently to stare at the river flowing darkly by. A couple of minders had trailed him at a discreet distance, and he had spoken to no one except for a desultory conversation with Gallows on his transmitter.

He was now the most immobile person in the hall, staring

fixedly ahead while the rest of the room shifted and whispered, flicking the pages of catalogues, trying to identify interesting-looking buyers, speculating on the big items.

'Mr Conway's taking his place,' Kathy called, watching the attention of the audience riveting on the auctioneer. Brock and the others took their seats in front of the screens.

'Good afternoon, ladies and gentlemen,' Conway's voice came over the loudspeaker, clear, suave, authoritative. 'Welcome to day one of Cabot's Summer Stamp Auction. The lots today are British Commonwealth, excluding Great Britain. Lots one to fourteen are an exceptionally fine group from Bermuda, beginning with lot one.'

An appreciative murmur came from the floor as an assistant brought lot one forward to the platform and held it up; the show had begun.

The first five lots, though rare, were an overture, allowing Conway to get into his stride, the audience to become entirely focused. After twenty minutes they reached the first major item, lot six. Conway's voice seemed to take on a greater firmness as he introduced it.

'Lot six, the first Perot issue of 1849. This is a one penny black on bluish grey, Stanley Gibbons catalogue number zero two, with clear to large margins, some suspicion of thinning, but nevertheless a superb example and the finest of the two known Perots of 1849. It is illustrated on the back cover of your catalogue. Only eleven Perots are known to exist, five in black and six in red of which one dated 1848 in black, and two in red of 1853 and 1854, are in the Royal Collection. This example was discovered in 1904 and is listed in Ludington's. A fuller history of the Perots is provided on page eighteen of your catalogues.'

Conway paused, the introduction over. 'Now, ladies and gentlemen, who will open the bidding at forty thousand pounds sterling?'

After two hectic minutes, in which telephone bids vied furiously with bids from the floor, lot six, estimated to fetch £80,000, was sold for £113,000.

'Poor Sammy!' Kathy murmured. On the screen, his image remained immobile as he stared unblinkingly straight ahead, oblivious to all the excitement around him.

After forty-five minutes, lot fifteen was brought to the front of the room. A murmur from the audience was audible over the loudspeaker. This was potentially the biggest item of the day, and Conway rose to the occasion, summarising the history of the Canadian Cover in the most dramatic terms. He opened the bidding at the reserve. 'Three hundred thousand pounds, ladies and gentlemen. Do I have a bid?'

There was a satisfied murmur, a silence, and then a gesture from the postal-bids tables. They were off.

At six hundred thousand, an increasingly fraught competition between the postal bids and several bidders in the audience reached a kind of impasse. Conway sensed a shift of mood and tried to revitalise the flagging pace. 'At six hundred thousand . . .' he said, frowning. 'Number forty-eight.'

On the second monitor they saw Starling raise his card for the first time.

'Six ten.' Conway, relieved, pointing briefly at Starling. 'Number twenty-two.'

There was a silence, then one of the telephone bidders made a sign.

'Six twenty!'

Another telephone operator signalled.

'Six thirty,' and they were away again, several other cards in the room joining in. By seven hundred and forty thousand they had dropped out and Starling was left as the sole bidder within the room, pitted against the two telephone bidders. All three made their bids slowly, letting the tension rise at each new step, Conway skilfully filling the gaps with comment and encouraging banter while the two telephone operators consulted with their unseen customers. At eight hundred and fifty thousand, one of the two looked up to Conway and shook his head slowly and deliberately.

'Eight fifty I am bid,' Conway said, indicating the other telephone operator. 'Am I bid eight sixty?' He looked expectantly at Starling. The whole hall did the same, staring with fascination towards the stiff-faced man, who gave no sign that he had heard or was in any way involved with this. Watching him on the screen, it seemed to Kathy that there was something heroic in Starling's composure. In that situation, knowing how much more was at stake than his fascinated audience suspected, Kathy doubted that she could have retained such control over the timing of every gesture. Unless, of course, he didn't care.

'Eight fifty-five?' Conway prompted, playing to Starling's reluctance.

'Eight fifty-five?'

Finally Starling's card lifted, and a sound of people taking a deep collective breath came over the loudspeaker in the upstairs room.

'He was quite a poker player, I believe,' Brock said.

The man at the telephone whispered and raised his hand almost immediately.

Once again Starling dragged out his own counterbid, which, when it finally came, was accompanied by another great sigh from the room.

'They're on his side,' Brock said. 'Willing him on. One of *us* against some faceless tycoon in Tokyo or Toronto.'

The bidding dragged on in five-thousand-pound steps, each painfully attenuated by the stoic figure at the front of the hall, until they reached nine hundred thousand pounds. This time it really did seem as if Starling had reached his limit. Conway urged, he teased, he created silences against which the whole room strained, but Starling moved not a muscle. Finally, reluctantly, Conway moved into his final patter.

'Nine hundred thousand pounds I am bid, for lot fifteen, the telephone bid, going once . . . going twice . . .'

Starling lifted his card majestically above his head and said, in a clear voice that his opponent might well have heard over the telephone line, 'One million pounds.'

There was a stunned silence, and then a wave of applause swept round the room.

As it died away, all attention turned to the telephone operator. He sat hunched over his instrument, free hand covering his forehead as he spoke urgently with his customer, repeating, waiting. He looked up at Conway, who was repeating the bid. He shrugged, he spoke again into the phone. Then, finally, he lifted his head, eyes bright, and gave a nod to the stage. The audience drew in its breath. For a moment the auctioneer seemed at a loss. He blinked, then recovered and said calmly, 'One million and five thousand, ladies and gentlemen.' He turned towards Sammy and repeated, more firmly, 'One million and five, I am bid.'

Starling responded immediately, as if he had fully expected this. He lifted his number card. From those close enough to see, scattered applause broke out.

'One million and ten,' Conway said.

Again the telephone bidder took an age to respond. He seemed to be interrogating the operator about his opponent, and the man was tugging at his hair as he whispered rapidly into the mouthpiece. Then he nodded again to Conway.

'One million and fifteen.'

Sammy's hand came straight up again. On the TV monitor his face had taken on a pugnacious expression, lower lip thrust forward. He didn't flinch when his bid was topped once again, and immediately brought up his numbered card.

Yet the unseen telephone bidder was equally tenacious, and slowly, still in five-thousand-pound steps, the bidding reached one million one hundred thousand, then one million two hundred thousand.

When Sammy reached one and a quarter million, someone in the audience, unable to contain themselves, let out a whoop of excitement. Conway paused, and the expression on his face, one eyebrow somewhat raised, sent a ripple of laughter round the room, which turned into a roar. It seemed to break the tension, which had become almost intolerable. Perhaps, too, it broke the heart of the man hanging on the other end of the phone line. He heard it quite clearly over the satellite link, sighed and quietly told the Cabot's operator that enough was enough. He picked up the renewed roar of applause that greeted this, and sadly put down the phone.

'Quite a performance,' Brock said, watching Starling on the monitor, rising to his feet to the cheers of the room. He stepped out into the central aisle and stood for a moment, letting them all see his face. There was no sign of excitement or triumph there, and its impassivity startled those close enough to see, so that their clapping faltered. He began to walk unhurriedly up the aisle to the door. Brock glanced at his watch. 'Two minutes to three.

Better tell our people outside the building. We want photographs of everyone who leaves between now and four.'

A few minutes later Sammy Starling appeared at the doorway to the upstairs room. At close range he looked more stunned than composed, his eyes unblinking, breathing shallow. At his shoulder the young man who had sat beside him in the auction was grinning with excitement. Behind him, two security men in uniform brought in a plastic pouch, which they laid reverentially on the table in the middle of the room.

Starling stared down at the tiny envelope. 'It is very strange,' he said, 'to see everything you possess boiled down to just that.' He looked at Brock. 'They've cleaned me out. They couldn't have got any closer to what I was worth if they'd been my fucking accountant.'

Another man had appeared at the doorway, solemn-faced and bearing a sheaf of documents. He gave a respectful little cough. Sammy turned to him and said wearily, 'I hope you're not expecting a tip, sunshine.'

The man gave a wan smile. 'Of course not, Mr Starling,' he murmured. 'The total damage is the bottom figure, here . . .'

Sammy looked, shrugged. 'Not a problem, old son.' He flashed his brilliant white teeth.

Fresh coffee was brought up, the Cabot's people retired, and the room settled into a tense wait. While Brock and the SO10 officers conferred on possible contingencies, Kathy sat down beside Starling.

'How do you think she's coping?' she asked, stirring her cup.

She sensed that he didn't welcome the approach. 'With blind terror, if she's got any sense,' he said softly. 'How do you think?' Any euphoria from his auction triumph had evaporated.

'Sorry. I just meant, is she the calm type or is she likely to panic if there's a crisis?'

'Christ . . .' He rubbed a hand across his face. 'No, she isn't the calm type. Yes, she'll jump out of her skin with panic, especially after five or six days and nights with them.'

'I just have no idea what she's like as a person. She's obviously very beautiful.'

'She's beautiful . . . She's bright, she's wilful, she's proud, she's got fantastic taste, a terrific imagination. And none of that's going to be the slightest use to her. I don't know if she's very brave . . . I don't suppose she's ever had to be. Having something like this happen to you . . . How brave would you be?' He looked at Kathy, appraising. 'How much experience have you had, eh? How much experience have you had of the kind of bastards who've done this to Eva?'

'We don't know who —'

'Oh, yes, we do. *I* know.' He turned and stared out of the window at the luminous blue sky high above the Strand. 'I lived among them for years, people like this. And it scares the fucking shit out of me, Kathy, believe you me.'

Kathy felt a hollow feeling in the pit of her stomach, which the sight of Gallows and Health calmly checking schedules on a clipboard didn't allay.

Then Starling added, the tone of his voice low now, confiding, 'If anything goes wrong, get in touch with Sally for me, will you? Sally Malone.' He pulled out a business card and wrote the name on the back, and a London phone number. 'Tell her I said . . .'

When he didn't finish the sentence, Kathy prompted, 'Yes?'

He shrugged. 'That I'm sorry.'

The phone call came at four precisely. They were all sitting expectantly round the table, staring at Starling's mobile lying in front of him, and watched him flinch as it began to ring. The exchange was brief.

'Did you get the stamp, Sammy?' A disguised voice. Probably male.

'Yes, yes. I have it here.'

'Have you told the coppers?'

'No I swear!' Starling's brow was glistening with sweat.

'Get a taxi, now, fast. Head west. Brentford. Take the M4. I'll ring again in twenty minutes. Got that?'

'West, Brentford, M4. Let me talk to —' But the line had clicked off.

And then a rush of activity, Starling flustered, grabbing his phone and the brown envelope in which was sealed the Canada

Cover, the others bunching around him.

'The earpiece, Mr Starling!' Gallows yelled, as he bundled out of the door.

The room emptied, leaving Brock, Kathy and a couple of radio operators. Brock and Kathy went to the window and watched a taxi slide to the kerb just as Starling ran out of the front door. He jumped in, unaware that the driver was one of Gallows's men, and they heard his hoarse instructions over the loudspeaker: 'Take us to the M4, quick as you can.'

The taxi pulled out into the traffic, and after a minute they heard the driver's voice, 'M4, guv? You going to Heathrow?'

Brock turned to the others. 'That's a possibility.'

Starling's voice said, 'I'll let you know when we get on the motorway. I'm expecting a phone call.'

'Fair enough.'

The driver kept up a muttered commentary on their journey, 'Usual traffic in Trafalgar Square . . . getting clear now . . . no problem in the Mall . . . past Buck House now . . . I'm taking the Cromwell Road route — OK with everyone?' His radio squawked an affirmative.

Brock and Kathy sat down at the table with London street maps and waited, watching the time.

'We've traced the call, sir,' one of the operators said. 'It came from a mobile phone. From a West London location. The phone is registered in the name of Eva de . . .' She made the person at the other end repeat the name '. . . de Vasconcellos.'

'Eva's maiden name,' Brock said. 'What address do they have?'

There was a delay, then the operator repeated a Canonbury address.

'That's not the flat,' Kathy said.

'No.' Brock had a *Yellow Pages* directory open in front of him, searching. 'Here it is. La Fortuna. She's given the restaurant as her address.'

The taxi was on the M4, passing through Osterley Park, when the phone, which Starling was gripping in his right fist, rang again.

'Heathrow, Terminal One,' the voice said. 'Have him drop you at the arrivals level and then you stand outside the main exit doors, under the canopy, beneath the sign for the Terminal Four transfer bus, and wait for my next call.'

Starling passed on the instructions to the taxi driver, who played dumb. 'Going on a trip, guv? Somewhere exotic, I hope. Nice little Greek island, maybe?'

'I bloody hope not,' Starling muttered. 'I haven't brought my passport.'

'You did say the arrivals level, though, guv?'

'That's right.'

Back in the Strand, Brock and Kathy listened to the reports from SO10 cars converging on Heathrow. The consensus seemed to be that Terminal One would only be a transit stop. 'There's every kind of transport there,' Gallows's voice droned reassuringly, 'taxis, coaches, car rentals, transfer buses, the underground, the fast train . . .'

'Should we join them, Brock?' Kathy asked, but he shook his head.

'This is what Gallows and his crew are supposed to be good at. We'll keep out of their way – we can hear what goes on better from here, anyway.'

Knowing their destination, Gallows overtook the taxi on the M4 and reached Terminal One some minutes ahead of it, positioning his car fifty yards beyond the exit doors and in sight of them. He switched on the emergency lights and his partner got out and made a play of searching in the boot.

'Taxi's arriving now,' he said. 'Starling's taken up position . . . OK, his phone's ringing! They must have seen him arrive. They must be in sight of him.'

The message on Starling's phone was relayed to those waiting in the Strand.

'Go in the doors, Sammy. There's an information desk straight ahead. There's a package waiting for you there, addressed to Mr S. Starling, for collection. Do what it says inside. Don't question it or think about it. Just do exactly what it says, and everything will be all right. Eva's waiting for you, Sammy. Don't screw this up.'

The phone clicked off, and Brock and Kathy heard Gallows

come on. 'We heard everything, Sammy. Just do what he says. Read the instructions, then tell us what they say, the way we showed you.'

He got a snuffling grunt by way of reply.

After a couple of minutes, Gallows came on the air, talking softly, slightly out of breath. 'I'm inside the building. He's reading his instructions. It's quite a big package . . . several bits of paper . . . I can't see exactly . . . There's a hell of a crowd of people here. Looks like several planes have just arrived, and there's building work going on . . .'

An unfamiliar voice came on. 'Sonny boy,' it said, 'we're approaching now. Shall we join you inside?'

'Stay outside for now,' Gallows replied. 'Keep your eyes peeled. For the moment . . . Sammy, talk to me! What do the instructions say?'

The line went silent as everyone waited for his reply. It came finally, two words, almost indistinct in the middle of a burst of muffled sniffing, as if Starling were disguising the movements of his mouth behind a handkerchief. 'Left luggage.'

'OK.' Gallows sounded relieved. 'Go ahead. I'm not far behind. Tony, get in here, will you?'

Gallows tracked the small figure of Starling through the crowd, past the foot of the escalator leading to the departures level overhead, towards a sign for left luggage. It pointed the way to a staircase, which Starling took, climbing above the heads of the crowd, then passing out of sight when he reached the landing. Gallows followed barely ten yards behind, reaching the landing a few seconds later and seeing the counter of the left-luggage office beyond. Several people were queuing there, but Starling wasn't one of them. Gallows double-checked, then turned to the stairs continuing upward. No Starling.

'Sammy, you're not at the left luggage. Where are you?'

There was no reply. Gallows ran up the flight of stairs and found himself, with several thousand others, at the western end of the huge departures floor of Terminal One.

'Sammy . . . Mr Starling, *sir*!' Gallows whispered into the ether. 'Where are you?'

At Cabot's, Brock, Kathy and the others strained forward in

their seats, hearing the change in Gallows's voice as he ordered units up from the floor below.

Then, like a message from deep space, came the snuffling and almost incomprehensible whisper from Starling. Two more words. 'Gate thirteen.'

'Good!' Gallows breathed. 'Slow down now, Sammy. Take your time. Let me catch up with you. Let me find gate thirteen . . .'

It took several minutes of confused exchanges between the police team and the airport police, who had now been brought into the operation, before it was established that there is no gate thirteen at Heathrow's Terminal One.

'One to twelve and sixty to ninety are domestic gates, accessed through the departure gate in zone east,' an unfamiliar voice intoned. 'Fourteen to fifty-six are international, opposite check-in zone H.'

'I've got him!' Heath's voice broke in, excited and breathless. 'At least, I think I have . . .'

Running up the escalator from the lower level, Heath had jostled his way through the crowded departures concourse ahead of his partner. Beyond a block of duty-free shops he had spotted a small figure of Oriental appearance, dressed in a dark business suit as Starling had been, hurrying through the crowd. The man was carrying a bright yellow plastic carrier bag, with 'duty free' in large black letters across its sides, and was making his way towards the security checkpoint in zone east, giving access to the domestic gates. It seemed to Heath that his air was one of resolution, chin up, like a soldier advancing bravely towards the front line. Heath watched him drop the carrier bag in a rubbish bin near the doorway, then proceed beneath the large sign PASSENGERS ONLY BEYOND THIS POINT. He disappeared behind the screen wall beyond, empty-handed apart from a white boarding card clutched in his right hand.

'Shall I try to talk my way through the gate, chief?' Heath said. 'Might be a problem.'

Gallows told him to stay where he was. 'We'll get airport security to take you through. Where the hell are they?'

After a short pause, Gallows came on again, bursting with

frustration. 'Sonny boy? Get up here. I want you to keep watch on a rubbish bin.'

'He could have dropped the envelope in the bin,' Brock said. 'Why isn't Sammy talking to us?' he growled. 'He's up to something.'

By the time the SO10 men had been met and escorted through to the departures area, it had been established that a Mr S. Starling was booked on a British Midland flight to Glasgow, due to be called from gate eighteen in half an hour's time. The computer showed that he had checked in forty minutes previously, using the self-service check-in machine in the Terminal One departures concourse. Trying to appear unhurried, though filled now with the same foreboding as Brock, Gallows and his colleagues searched the domestic departures area from end to end. They went through all the gate lounges, the bars and cafés, the book and souvenir shops, the toilets and executive lounges, without success. They watched the final travellers queuing through gate eighteen, and ten minutes later stared gloomily through the observation windows as the Glasgow flight lifted slowly into the late-afternoon sky, without passenger S. Starling.

Out in the general concourse, no one had been seen making any attempt to remove anything from the waste bin. Finally Gallows asked airport security to arrange for a cleaner to rummage through the bin and report on what was inside the duty-free bag. The answer came back after an interminable wait: one mobile phone, one Rotary lapel badge, one pink plastic earplug, and a small transmitter.

Sammy Starling had vanished.

6

A Feminist Theory of Stamp Collecting

When he became reconciled to the fact that Starling had given them the slip, Brock's first reaction was that the missing Eva had been a blind, and that it had been Starling's intention all along to steal a million-pound rare stamp. Yet when he questioned Melville and the Cabot's finance expert again about Starling's arrangements for payment, he was assured that his houses, cars and all other assets were now inescapably in the hands of Cabot's bankers.

After he'd gone, Brock turned to Kathy and drew up his shoulders in a great shrug, turning up his palms. 'Well, what the hell do we do now?' It was the first time Kathy could remember seeing him so completely at a loss. For some reason that no one could fathom, Starling had apparently run them all round in circles, and as far as anyone could tell, the only one worse off was himself. Unless Eva really was missing, of course.

'We'll wait for another hour,' Brock said, without much conviction. 'He may have hidden somewhere in the terminal and be planning to leave on a later flight under an assumed name.'

By six fifteen they had picked up all their gear and were on the point of leaving, when Kathy's phone rang. She heard Desai's voice.

'Hello,' he said, and hesitated a moment as if he weren't quite sure which of several openings he might use. Then he said, 'Are you looking for Sammy Starling?'

'Yes. It's a strange story . . .'

'He's here, with me. Do you want me to put him on?'

Kathy stared at the instrument in her hand, astounded. 'Where are you?'

'At the Canonbury flat. I came back here to have another look round, and Mr Starling just walked in the door.'

He was sitting on the white hide sofa with a glass of brandy in his hand, looking pale and puffy. Brock burst in and glared down at him, Kathy following.

'This had better be good, Sammy,' he barked.

'I can't stop long,' Starling said. He had the unhealthy sheen to his skin that Kathy had noticed before, and the asthmatic wheeze back in his voice. 'I only called in here to pick up my car. I left it here this morning. I have to get back to Farnham. They've told me to wait there.'

Brock sat down facing him. 'What happened?'

Starling took a deep, laboured breath. 'They told me to go to Heathrow . . .'

'Yes. I know that. Terminal One. You were to go inside and pick up instructions at the information desk. What then?'

'There was a big envelope waiting for me. Inside were three smaller envelopes, each with a number, one, two and three, and a note, hand-printed, like the others. It told me to open envelope number one, and do what it said inside.'

He took a gulp at his brandy, choked and broke into a coughing fit. Desai, standing by the door to the kitchen, disappeared briefly and came back with a glass of water. Starling waved it away and continued hoarsely. 'Inside was a plane ticket, a boarding pass, an empty duty-free carrier bag, and another note telling me to go to the stairway marked for the left-luggage office. When I got to it I was to continue up the stairs to the departures level and head for the domestic departures area. I was to go through the passengers-only checkpoint, and make my way to the lounge at gate eighteen, where I was to open envelope number two.'

'You told us gate thirteen,' Brock growled, leaning forward as if he might be about to grab Starling and shake the truth out of him.

'Did I? Yes, that's right, I remember. I misread it the first time. It looked like it could have been thirteen, only it was eighteen. I was in a state, Mr Brock, believe me.'

Brock glared at him. 'Go on.'

'The note also said that the metal detectors at the security checkpoint would pick up any electronic devices about my person, and that, if I wanted to see Eva alive again, I should put any such equipment, together with my mobile phone, into the carrier bag, and deposit it in the waste bin near the entry to the departures area.'

'That's nonsense, about the detectors,' Brock said.

'Is it? But how was I to know? If I walked through that gate and the alarms went off, where would Eva be then? I couldn't risk that. I did what I was told.'

'Go on.'

'I reached gate eighteen. There was a big crowd around and I couldn't sit down. I opened the second envelope, and it said I was to keep going along the departures concourse and then follow the signs for the flight connections centre. It said I had to hurry. When I reached it, I was to open the third envelope. I did that. Envelope three told me how to go through the security gate there and take the escalator down to the Terminal Two link, and follow it until I came out in the Terminal Two concourse. Honestly, it's like a maze, that place. I was completely lost. I just followed the instructions.'

He took another deep breath and reached forward for the glass of water. At the same time there was an urgent buzz from the doorbell. Desai went over to the intercom and they heard Gallows's voice. In a few moments he was inside, facing Starling, who avoided his glare.

'We're in Terminal Two,' Brock said softly. 'From domestic departures in Terminal One he walked to the flight connections centre, and from there to Terminal Two.'

Gallows swore softly.

Brock nodded at Starling.

'So I came out on to the main concourse of Terminal Two, just opposite international arrivals. And there's this big notice-board there for people to leave messages for people coming in. It's got like tapes across it to stick your messages behind, with the name showing. There were a dozen or more messages already there. My note told me to address the envelope with the Canada Cover to Mr Chalon, and put it on to the board, dump all the envelopes and messages they'd given me into the rubbish bin next to it, then walk out of the building, get a cab and head straight home to Farnham. It said they would contact me there once they'd checked the cover to make sure it was genuine. Sometime within the next twenty-four hours, it said.' He looked around, eyes wide. 'That's exactly what I did.'

Gallows pulled out a phone and walked over to the window. He spoke rapidly for a couple of minutes, then returned to the others. He took a notebook from his pocket.

'How long did it take you to walk from Terminal One to Terminal Two, you reckon, Mr Starling?'

'I don't know. Ten minutes? Quarter of an hour?'

'You went through the departures checkpoint at Terminal One at four thirty-two. So you would have caught your cab from Terminal Two by five, yes? And you arrived here at what time?' He looked at Brock and Desai.

'Six eleven,' Desai said.

'Traffic on the M4 and into the city is light this afternoon. I made it here in eighteen minutes with the sirens going. Your taxi would have done it in twenty-five, thirty minutes, no problem.' He made some calculations. 'That leaves three-quarters of an hour unexplained.'

Starling looked confused. 'I must have been inside the terminals longer. The taxi was slow.'

'We'll get you to retrace your movements, and time you, but I would have thought ten or fifteen minutes would have been long enough for what you described.'

'Look, I —' Starling's protest was interrupted by Gallows's phone. The policeman turned away and listened, then rang off.

'Sergeant Heath. He says there's no envelope addressed to Mr

Chalon on the noticeboard at Terminal Two now, and no notes or envelopes in the rubbish bin next to it.'

'Look,' Starling spoke with a low intensity, 'I don't give a fuck whether you believe me or not. I've just given away everything I own, and all I want to do is get back to Farnham and wait for the message. Are you going to stop me?'

Brock said, 'No, Sammy. But we're coming with you.'

'No! Not until Eva's free! I've played it by the book this far. If they want me in Farnham, it must be because they're going to release Eva near there. I'm not having them frightened off by coppers crawling over the place.'

Brock thought about that. 'All right. But Sergeant Kolla goes back with you, and stays with you until we hear something.'

They agreed on that, Gallows insisting on searching Starling anyway. He had no Canada Cover about his person, nor any evidence of the afternoon's events to confirm his version.

Kathy had some difficulty finding the way. She drove fast to Farnham and made the double left turns out of the main street as she'd been told, the road climbing into the wooded slopes of the North Downs. Commuterland came to an end, and she found herself in forest country, suburban gardens giving way to stands of woodland conifers. She wound down the window and breathed in the pungent smells of pinewoods baking at the end of a fine summer day. In the golden glow of the late afternoon, the landscape seemed entirely unspoiled, dappled sunlight on trunks and foliage playing against the deep dark shadows of the woods. But from time to time, at the edge of the gravel road, a discreet sign would advise the presence of secluded homes with rustic names – Timber Glades, Oak Rood, Still Ponds.

She realised eventually that she must have gone wrong, and drew in at the side of the road. She was beyond the limits of the London *A–Z*, and the Surrey road map she had didn't show enough detail. A man approached over the crest of the rise ahead, a retired resident of the forest community by the look of him, jauntily swinging a walking stick and heralded by two enthusiastic Labradors.

'Lost?' he said cheerfully as he drew alongside. The smell of pinewoods was very strong.

'I'm looking for a road called Poacher's Ease,' Kathy said. 'At least, I think it's a road.'

'Ah! Looking for Sammy Starling, are you?' he said, in a clipped public-school accent.

'That's it,' Kathy said. 'You know the place, then?'

'Prime spot. I'm a neighbour. You're quite close.'

He gave her directions and made her repeat them before he and his dogs would let her go. She watched him in the rear-view mirror, striding off down the track, whistling, the dogs competing to find the most interesting smells along the way.

She did as instructed, continuing on over the crest of the hill until she came upon the high rhododendron hedge he'd mentioned, and beyond it the turning into a side lane with its name, Poacher's Ease, carved into a wooden sign. Lined with hedges, the lane twisted up the ridge, deeper into pinewoods, an occasional set of gates identifying hidden house lots, the last and most private of all being marked with brick gate-posts and a wrought-iron sign, The Crow's Nest, and the figure of a flying black metal bird. Beyond the iron gates Kathy saw the gravel forecourt of a substantial house, brick and half-timbering, forming one side of a clearing in the woods.

There was no sign of Sammy's Mercedes in the drive, and Kathy realised that, despite her delay, she had arrived ahead of him. She parked near the front door, got out, stretched and waited, listening to the sounds of bird calls coming from the woods rising towards the ridge. There was a small track just outside the gates, she noticed, winding up through the trees, and when Sammy still didn't appear she thought it would do no harm to get a sense of the surroundings of the house. She followed it through the bracken that bordered the lane and began to climb up the hillside, catching glimpses back down through the dark foliage of the weathered tile roof of the house.

At the summit she found a cairn of old sandstone rocks with a metal plate on which were inscribed radiating lines with the names of the distant places that might be seen from this vantage-point – landmarks in Hampshire towards the lowering sun to the west, in Surrey to east and south, and beyond, in the hazy southerly distance, the swell of the South Downs in West Sussex. Kathy stood there for a while, gazing out at a column of pale smoke rising in the still air beyond Haslemere, a solitary glider catching the last thermals above Petersfield. Eva would have come up here, she thought, on her own perhaps, and she wondered what an eighteen-year-old Portuguese girl had made of this, and of the sixty-year-old man she had so impulsively married.

Kathy turned back along the trail, then struck off over the ridge and across the reverse slope, treading silently on carpets of pine needles. A cuckoo called from the depths of the woods, the falling second note of its call sounding forlorn and lonely.

She had worked her way round in a wide circle, expecting to come upon Poacher's Ease again, but instead found herself approaching a small cottage through the trees. She was coming on it from behind, she saw, noticing a neat little vegetable garden, a washing-line with a couple of tea-towels drying, roses climbing profusely up a trellis.

She stood for a moment, admiring this domestic nest in the forest, relishing the pungent smells of the deep woods at the end of a hot summer day, the faint buzzing of insects, cooing of birds, when something — a soft noise, perhaps, or a foreign smell — made her stiffen, the hair stand on the back of her neck. She turned, wondering what on earth it was, saw nothing, stepped forward a pace and found herself face to face with a man, not three yards away, standing motionless close against the trunk of a huge horse-chestnut tree.

'Hello again,' he said, voice casual but eyes wary.

'Oh . . .' Now she recognised him as the man who had directed her on the road to Starling's house.

'Not still lost, I hope?'

'Just taking a walk.'

'Staying here, are you? With the Starlings?'

'That's right. Where are your dogs?'

'They're inside with my wife.' He indicated the cottage. 'Why don't you come in and meet her? Toby Fitzpatrick.' He held out a hand.

The Labradors heard the click of the back gate and came hurtling out of the kitchen door, barking enthusiastically.

'Down!' Fitzpatrick called. 'Henrietta, shut up!'

They circled Kathy, bodies oscillating with the thrashing of their tails, and she offered them a hand each to sniff. Satisfied, they formed an escort to the kitchen door.

'Darling!' Fitzpatrick called into the interior. 'You about?' He led Kathy through a busy little kitchen into a small living-room, at the same time as a woman came down an open timber staircase set against the opposite wall.

'This is a friend of the Starlings, Helen. I just found her prowling in the woods.' Fitzpatrick gave a half-hearted laugh, as if he knew, even as he said it, that his banter was off-key.

Helen Fitzpatrick was of an age with her husband, late forties, and looked fresh and pink from a bath taken after a day working in the garden. She was wearing slacks and a gingham shirt, her hair drawn back in a band, and she smiled at Kathy with her mouth, but not her eyes. Close-to, her features looked tired beneath the flush of the bath, as if she might recently have been ill.

'Really? A friend of Eva's?' The mouth kept smiling, but the eyes narrowed cautiously.

'That must be Poacher's Ease,' Kathy said, looking out of the window to the lane at the front of the cottage. 'I thought I must be in the right area. I went for a walk.'

'You're only about fifty yards from the Crow's Nest, though you wouldn't know it,' Toby Fitzpatrick said, making an effort now to sound sociable. 'Let me get you a drink. Sherry all right? About all we've got at the moment. Bit low on supplies.'

For some reason this seemed to irritate his wife. Kathy noticed her mouth tighten, and she thought, Oho, I've arrived in the middle of a row – that's probably why he was skulking outside in the woods. 'No, I won't, thanks. Thanks all the same.'

'Is Eva back, then?' Helen Fitzpatrick went on.

'Not yet, no. Sammy's expecting her any time. But you know what she's like.'

'Oh yes,' Toby Fitzpatrick said. 'Free as a bird, old Eva . . .' This time his wife definitely flinched. He noticed it too, and added hurriedly, 'I think I may have a sherry. You, darling?'

His wife gave an abrupt shake of her head.

'You sure, er, Kathy?'

'No, I'd better get back. Sammy will be wondering where I've got to. They're lovely.' She pointed to a pair of vases holding an assortment of flowers from the garden, white cosmos and pink daphne spilling around spikes of lemon yellow digitalis.

'Helen's a marvel in the garden,' Toby said appeasingly, in his wife's direction.

Kathy paused at the front door, with its view of the lane, and said, 'You didn't see Eva by any chance, did you, when she left for London?'

'No, we didn't,' Mrs Fitzpatrick said. 'I went with a couple of friends to play tennis there last Sunday, and Sammy said she'd already gone. I thought she'd be back by now. Why do you ask?'

'Doesn't matter.' Kathy smiled. 'Thanks for showing me your home. It's idyllic.'

Helen Fitzpatrick smiled back without warmth. 'Yes,' she said. 'It is.'

When she returned to the house Kathy saw the dark-blue Mercedes parked at the front door. Starling answered her ring, checking over her shoulder as he let her in. He looked limp and pale.

'No word?' she asked.

He shook his head. 'Just been trying to get one of the vultures off the phone,' he said. 'My financial adviser. Thinks I'm selling up and moving to the Caribbean.'

He led her into a generous hall, a staircase curving up to a first-floor gallery.

'This place was built for a movie producer,' he said automatically, as he had said a hundred times before.

'That must appeal to Eva,' Kathy said.

'What?' He didn't seem to follow.

'With her interest in movies.'

'Oh, I see . . . No. English movies weren't of any interest to her.'

Weren't? Kathy thought.

As they passed a panelled door Starling stopped and opened it on to the kitchen. A small dark woman was working at a central table, tears streaming down her lined brown face. It took Kathy a moment to realise that she was peeling onions.

'Marianna,' Starling called to her. 'This is Ms Kolla, a visitor.

She stays the night.' He spoke slowly and distinctly. 'In the guest room. OK?'

Marianna stared at them stonily through her watery eyes. 'OK.'

As they turned away, Starling said, 'Speaks almost no English. Won't be much point in trying to ask her anything.'

He showed her upstairs to a large bedroom, comfortably furnished, like the rest of the house, in a traditional cottage style completely unlike the stark modern furnishings of the London flat. Much of the long side of the room opposite the doorway was filled by a range of casement windows, framed in bunched, flowery curtains. Kathy went over to them and looked across a broad lawn towards the spectacular panorama she had seen from the cairn, extending out over forested hills rolling away to a distant hazy horizon. The layout of the house and its approaches had been contrived to hide this spectacle, the whole point of the siting on top of the Hog's Back, until the visitor reached the public rooms on this, the south-facing side of the house. Kathy opened a window and leaned out on the sill, savouring the view and the evening woodland smells, and wondering how anyone would rather spend their days locked up in the darkness with Buñuel.

'Make yourself at home,' Starling said behind her. He turned away abruptly and would have left if she hadn't called out.

'Mr Starling, I'd like to see Eva's room.'

He seemed about to object, but then turned and she followed him to the opposite end of the house, and into another bright room with the same spectacular view to the south. There was a large four-poster double bed at one end, two armchairs by the windows, and a connecting door into a dressing-room and bathroom area at the other end. Starling led Kathy briskly through a further connecting door to a small sitting-room beyond. There was a sofa and a TV, a pile of videos alongside it.

'I'd like to have a look around here and in the bedroom, if that's all right, Mr Starling.'

Starling hesitated, then said, 'No.'

'Pardon?'

'No, it's not all right. I'm sorry, but if the time comes . . .

Until then I don't want any of her things disturbed. There's no need. You won't find anything useful.'

'Mr Starling, I think –'

'No. End of story.' He put an arm out to the door and closed it firmly on her.

'Dinner should be about eight,' he said, leading her to the corridor. 'There's booze in the lounge, and the TV. Help yourself.'

'Where will you be?'

'I'll wait by the phone in my study, downstairs.'

She nodded. 'I'll just have a wash, then I'll come down. You will let me know if the phone goes, won't you, Mr Starling? Before you answer it?'

'Of course.' He turned and walked away stiffly.

There were fresh towels in the *en suite* bathroom, with little touches – a cluster of exotic sea-shells around the soap dish, a bunch of dried flowers in an elegant wicker basket, an unopened bottle of unusual bath oil – that someone had gone to a lot of trouble to find and to lay out. Not Sammy Starling, but who? Marianna, perhaps? Eva? They had an air of having been there for a long time, like dried offerings discovered in an Egyptian tomb. Perhaps they were the work of Sammy's first wife, Brenda, remaining undisturbed in the guest room. Certainly the majority of furnishings in the house must have been her choice. The carpets and curtains dated from the five years she had had here before her death, and there were few signs that anyone had tried to supplant her style of plump, comfortable, traditional domesticity. The interiors of this house and of the flat in London were two opposite poles, each complete and uncontaminated by the other.

Kathy went out on to the landing and back down the curving staircase, her footsteps silent in the thick pile carpets. From behind the closed kitchen door she heard the sound of chopping, but otherwise the house was silent. The door to the lounge was half open, and she went into a long room with french windows opening out to the southerly lawns. Opposite was a large fireplace with logs piled beside it, ready for the autumn. A mixture of sofas and armchairs were arranged companionably around it, and old oil paintings of rural scenes decorated the

98

walls. Among them, looking slightly incongruous, was a studio portrait photograph of the head and shoulders of an elderly man. Taken in black and white, Kathy assumed at first that it was old, for the man looked like a nineteenth-century patriarch, with thick white hair and moustache, peering imperiously at the camera through *pince-nez*. But at the foot she saw the stamp of a Lisbon photographic studio and the date, 1987.

Kathy noted the drinks cabinet of which Starling had spoken, and at the other end of the room a TV and a writing desk. There were a couple of videos in the cabinet with the TV, Kathy discovered, old Disney films for young kids. Relics of a Christmas party, perhaps. Surely not Eva's choice. She could find nothing at all in the room that might have been Eva's choice, apart from the photograph, presumably of her father.

She opened the french windows and went out on to a terrace of warm York stone. Beyond the lawn to the right she could see the corner of a crystal blue swimming-pool sheltered by a yew hedge, and beyond it a tennis court. All looked well maintained, hedges clipped, weeds suppressed. Below the tennis court lay an ornamental pool and next to it a rose garden, enclosed by a bank of shrubs.

A clock chimed seven as she went back into the lounge. Although it wasn't yet nearly dusk, the circling trees were casting lengthening shadows across the lawn, and the house interior was becoming dark and sombre. She went through to the hall and saw a passageway beyond the stairs. The door at the far end was half open, light reflected along the wallpaper of the passage. She walked silently towards it and saw Starling seated at a green-baize-topped table, concentrating on some sheets of paper spread across the surface, his nose only inches away from the pages, which were lit by a bright spot of light from the illuminated magnifying instrument he held in his hand. She stepped into the room and looked around at his den, a desk and one high-backed leather chair beside the fireplace, a small bookcase and a wine rack against one wall.

He was wearing a white shirt, and for a moment she thought of a surgeon, or a dentist, intent on some delicate surgical procedure. But she knew that the focus of his attention was a postage stamp, one of a number on the white page in front of him. There was a multitude of colours, she saw, dull, faded colours, oranges, greens, sepias and blues, but all of the same unvarying design.

He looked up at her.

'Chalon Heads,' she said, then noticed with a shock that he was crying, tears glistening on his cheeks.

He stared at her, his round face absurdly expressionless, given the tears.

'Sorry. I didn't mean to disturb you. I saw the light . . .'

She turned to go but he called after her, 'No . . . It's all right. Come back, if you want.'

His voice was hoarse and also rather plaintive, as if he had a need to say something.

'You think this is mad,' he said, and she wasn't sure at first what he was referring to.

'This,' he said, pointing to the sheets of stamps.

'Oh. Actually I'm trying to get the hang of it. Mr Melville lent me some books. I'm still on primitives – postmaster provisionals, Sydney views, cottonreels and woodblocks. There's a lot more to it than I realised.'

He dipped his head in a little bow. 'Very conscientious of you, Sergeant, trying to understand the mind of the deranged philatelist.'

'Are you deranged?'

'Just at the moment it feels very much like that.'

'He said that you'd written a book on the Chalon Heads.'

Starling nodded.

'I'd like to read it, if I may.'

'There's a copy in the bookcase in the living room. Help yourself.'

'Thank you. He said it was very well regarded.'

'Mr Melville is a kind man. He arranged for this.' He indicated the sheets of paper in front of him, and Kathy saw for the first time that they were coloured photocopies. 'My collection belongs to Cabot's now. But James had these copies made for me. He realised that these are my favourites.' He turned his head sadly to the pages. Kathy stepped closer to the table and stood at his shoulder looking down at them.

'This one, for instance . . .' Starling lifted a page with a single block of twenty identical brown Chalon Heads, four rows each of five stamps. 'Nova Scotia, 1853, one penny brown, block of twenty, mint. Beautiful, beautiful . . .' he whispered, lost in admiration. 'It was a present – from Eva.'

'From Eva? So she knew about stamps too? She knew what to buy for you?'

'No, no . . .' Starling sighed. 'It was chance, and yet, like the innocent she was, she hit the jackpot first time. She found me these for my birthday, a couple of years ago, from some little hole of a stamp shop. I was knocked out.'

Kathy looked at the block of pristine stamps, Eva's present, twenty tiny self-portraits. She wondered if Eva was aware of the striking resemblance. But how could she not be?

Starling turned the page, sighing at the treasures that were no longer his.

'I'll go and find your book,' Kathy said softly.

He didn't respond and she turned to leave. Then he said, 'They're not going to call, you know,' and he gave a little sob.

'Of course they will,' she said.

'No, no. You were right, you see.'

'How do you mean?'

'The stamps on the ransom notes. You asked if they could be my own.' He turned and looked directly up at Kathy, tears brimming from his eyes. 'You suspected that she was behind it, didn't you? Well, you were right, they were mine.'

'What?' Kathy was stunned. 'But you said . . .'

'You asked me if I'd checked to see if mine were missing, and I said I had, because I thought if I didn't then you would insist that we look. But I hadn't checked, because it would have been like doubting her, and also . . . because I was afraid to find out the answer.'

'And now you have checked?'

'No. I have . . . I had many thousands of stamps, not all properly mounted and catalogued. It was always possible that I might overlook some. But Cabot's have been very thorough.' He lifted a document from the table and handed it to Kathy.

'Over the past couple of days they have listed and valued all of my stamps. The Chalons are listed separately, Van Diemen's Land stamps under Tasmania.'

Kathy turned to the Tasmania pages and found about fifty entries, each identified by a number code.

'That's the number given in the Stanley Gibbons catalogue, which is the standard reference. You see that the numbers begin at SG 19, of 1856.'

'Yes, I see.'

'The stamps on the notes were from the year before, SG 14, 15 and 17, which I also used to own. But they are not on Cabot's list.'

'Are you quite sure you had them? There are so many, and they all look the same.'

'I'm sure. You see, 14, 15 and 17 are the first Van Diemen's Land stamps to use the Chalon design, and I made a great point about getting the first ones from each of the countries which issued it.'

He slumped in his seat, shoulders sagging. 'You were right, Sergeant Kolla. She took them.'

'Someone took them.'

He shook his head hopelessly. 'Who else?'

'How long have you realised this?'

'Just now. I was going through the list. She's not alone, of course. The voice that told me to go to the airport, it was a man's voice . . .'

Kathy felt a great flood of relief. She had been right, Eva was safe. The whole thing had been nothing but a bizarre domestic dispute, carried to absurd, hysterical lengths. Brock could sleep easy again, and they could all get on with more pressing, more mundane, more real crimes. But for Sammy Starling, moving on would be much more difficult. She looked at him in his devastation, and said gently, 'I'll have to tell Brock about this, Sammy. Will you speak to him?'

He groaned. 'Please,' he whispered, 'I . . . I won't talk to him right now. Tell him I'm sorry.'

There was a single french window from the study on to the end of the stone terrace, and Kathy stepped outside to make her call to Brock. From there she could watch Starling through the window, head in hands, motionless.

'He what?' Kathy heard the same progression in Brock's voice that she had gone through, from consternation to annoyance to relief. 'Well, so you were right, Kathy! Thank God for that.'

'It was very cruel, wasn't it? Putting him through all that. She must really hate him.'

'Putting us *all* through all that! Presumably the pair of them took off from Heathrow some time this afternoon while we were all running around in circles. Bloody nerve!'

'Yes. I'm kind of worried about Sammy. He's shattered.'

'No doubt he's reflecting on the fact that if he'd paid more attention to you he could have saved himself well over a million quid. You want to stay there tonight?'

'I think I should.'

'OK. Does he have any malt?'

'Could be.'

'Pour yourself a big one. I can't pretend I'm not relieved. Forensic were coming up with the damnedest things . . . Night.'

He rang off before she could ask him what they had come up with. She shrugged and returned to the study. Starling looked up. 'Was he angry?' he asked.

'Not really.'

'Will you be leaving now?'

'I thought I might stay. After all, we can't be sure . . .'

He smiled sadly at her and said, 'I'll see how Marianna's getting on with dinner.'

In the lounge Kathy turned on a couple of table lamps, then went over to the drinks cabinet and poured herself a small Scotch. There was a shelf of books above the cabinet, the only books in the room, and all slim volumes. There was a guide to contract bridge, a compendium of games of patience, an English–Portuguese phrase book, and a copy of *The Chalon Heads: A Chronology*, by Samuel Starling. Kathy picked it out and went back to the armchair. Touchingly, she thought, the book was dedicated to Eva's father, Dom Arnaldo de Vasconcellos. The introduction was titled, 'A Female Head of the Greatest Beauty'.

When a thing has never existed before in the world, what should it look like? The first aeroplanes were designed to look like birds, the first motor cars like horseless carriages, and the first postage stamp like a coin or medallion. When Rowland Hill invented the adhesive postage stamp, he took the advice of Benjamin Cheverton that its design should incorporate 'a female head of the greatest beauty, to be executed by Mr Wyon', and based on William Wyon's commemorative medal of 1837, showing the head of the newly crowned Queen Victoria in profile.

This established a model for almost all future British stamps, and seems an inevitable and natural reference to the practice, dating back to ancient Roman times, of showing the sovereign's head, in profile, on the currency of the realm. It gave a classical legitimacy to the new device, and a respectability which a piece of gummed paper otherwise sorely lacked.

Kathy shook her head, thinking that this could never have come from Sammy Starling.

But was it so inevitable? It is interesting to reflect that, as other countries clamoured to take up the British invention, few followed the British design. The Tsar of Russia's head does not appear on the nineteenth-century stamps of that country, which instead bear the Romanov coat of arms. Neither do we find the German Kaiser's head, nor that of the King of Greece.

Yet we do find the head of Queen Isabella of Spain on her country's stamps, as well as a variety of mythical female figures – Ceres, Germania and Britannia, for example – on those of other countries. What is the reason for this preference for female heads? Whence comes this reluctance . . .

Whence, Sammy? she thought, raising her eyebrows. Whence?

Whence comes this reluctance (except in the stamps of the United States, where the Presidents' heads parade blithely through the nineteenth century like a succession of Roman Emperors) to portray male rulers? And why did Cheverton ask, not for, say, 'a fine head of the sovereign', which would have been a natural way of putting it, but instead for, 'a female head of the greatest beauty'?

Perhaps the French Revolution had made the European mon-archs somewhat nervous of portraying themselves as detached heads: it might give the people ideas. Yet this does not account for the gender-specific nature of this reticence. Perhaps, rather, there was something offensive, to both male rulers and their subjects, in the association of their image and a paper token which was both disposable and worthless after a single use, and which entailed a kiss, an oral assault to the reverse of the image, in order to use it?

Kathy's eyes widened and she took another sip of her drink. No wonder Mr Melville had had kittens. As for Sammy, she doubted he had ever read his book, let alone written it.

Clearly this unease did not apply to the female image – on the contrary, there was something compelling about performing these actions with 'a female head of the greatest beauty'. And in 1851 the most ravishing, the most erotic of these female images appeared: the Chalon Head.

The original portrait of Queen Victoria by Alfred Edward Chalon shows a rather bemused young woman of eighteen years of age, who has just acceded to the throne. Her full-length figure is overwhelmed by the surrounding architecture and by the heavy drapery and clothes with which it is encumbered. The overall effect is ponderous, formal, and intended to give authority and respect to someone who must have seemed an exceedingly fragile holder of great office.

But when the first Chalon Head postage stamp appeared fourteen years later, this image had been subverted in numerous ways. Unlike the Wyon profile portrait, remote and conventional, we now see her fully rounded, in three dimensions, staring wistfully out at us. Only the head and naked shoulders of the woman in the Chalon painting are now shown and, with the heavy robes of state edited away, we have no reason to believe that she may not be posing for us entirely naked, apart from the crown and jewellery she wears.

And in more subtle ways, too, the original portrait was changed, to greater or lesser degrees, in the various versions of the Chalon stamp. Where the painting had her mouth tightly, primly closed, many of the stamps now show her lips parted invitingly; her eyes are enlarged, her rather plain features prettified, and the teenage puppy fat of the original takes on a more voluptuous womanly form. In every respect, the sexual potency of the image has been enhanced and made more graphic.

The Chalon image was never used on British stamps; perhaps it was too explicit too close to home. But in the Empire it was a smash success. It ran and ran, and as late as the 1880s, when the real Queen Victoria was in her sixties, the citizens of the Australian and West Indian colonies were still licking the image of the eighteen-year-old virgin girl every time they put a stamp on a letter.

There was a small noise at Kathy's back. Startled, she turned and saw Marianna standing behind her.

'Dinner,' she growled disapprovingly.

'Thank you.' Kathy got to her feet and followed the little woman to the door. In the hall she was pointed to another open doorway, through which Kathy found a dining-room with a long mahogany table and a dozen chairs, and two places set at the most distant opposite ends.

It was an uncomfortable meal. Marianna's spicy *cataplana* stew was excellent, but the silence of both Starling and the house-keeper was oppressive. Kathy attempted to break it at first, but met with so little success that she soon gave up.

Starling waited until she had finished, hardly touching his own plate, then rose to his feet and said, 'I really feel quite done in. I think I'll go to bed now, if you don't mind. It's been such a very long week.'

When Starling had gone, Kathy took the plates through to the kitchen and tried without success to talk to Marianna, who snatched the dishes from her, clucking with annoyance, and ignored Kathy's attempts to make conversation.

Kathy went back up to her room and locked the door. She had brought nothing with her, but she needed nothing that wasn't available in the little *en suite* bathroom. She showered, washed her underwear in the basin, and sat naked for a while, watching a huge golden moon rise over the dark forest. She had never been involved in a kidnapping before, and had had no idea how it would develop. She pictured Eva at Heathrow, with dark glasses, headscarf and boyfriend, plucking Sammy's million-pound stamp from the messages board and disappearing into the blue, and felt sad that it could end like that.

Some slight movement caught her eye, beyond the far edge of the lawn, where the woodland curled around the rose garden. She stared hard and saw first one, and then another cautious figure emerge from the twilight gloom of the woods. Deer.

They moved delicately forward to the edge of the ornamental pool, and lowered their heads to drink.

Later, in bed, drifting off to sleep, Kathy became aware of the murmur of distant voices. It was a warm night, her windows open, and it was hard to judge how far away they might be. She got out of bed and leaned out of the window, hearing them more distinctly, from the east side of the house, the kitchen end, where she could just make out the glow of a light reflected on the shrubbery. A man and a woman, she thought, arguing, or at least disagreeing. She tried to match them in her mind with the sounds of Starling and Marianna's voices, but couldn't be certain. After a few minutes they stopped abruptly, and she heard nothing more.

7

A Female Head of the Greatest Beauty

The next morning, Marianna presented them with a huge breakfast of bacon and sausages, tomatoes and eggs, all served on an enormous platter in the centre of the dining table. Starling eyed this banquet – enough for a dozen people – balefully.

'I had to tell her, last night,' he said to Kathy. 'She thought you . . .' He scowled at the heaped food. 'She thought I'd brought you here while Eva was away.'

'She thought I was your bit on the side?' Kathy tried helpfully.

'Yes. So I told her about Eva having disappeared. I had to. And I told her you're with the police.'

'And this is her reaction?'

'It's her way of coping. She's baking loaves of bread now. It's crazy.'

'Well, it seems a shame to waste this. Do you mind if I eat? I'm hungry.'

'Go ahead.'

'How about you?'

He shook his head and turned away to the french windows. He pushed them open, but didn't go outside. Instead he pulled a packet of cigarettes from his pocket and lit up, his actions awkward, a tremble in his hand.

'I didn't know you smoked,' Kathy said, pouring a cup of coffee from a huge jug.

'Gave up, eleven years ago.'

'Did you buy those on the way back from the airport?'

Starling didn't answer, blowing a stream of pale smoke out towards the cloudless morning sky. He didn't explain, and Kathy let it go. From the kitchen came a sound of banging, as if Marianna were attacking a side of beef with a cleaver.

At ten fifteen, when Kathy was on the point of leaving, there was the sound of a motorbike in the gravel forecourt of the house. The front doorbell rang, and Starling went to answer it, Kathy close behind. A messenger in black leathers and a bright-yellow helmet was pulling an envelope from the pouch on his chest. He presented it and a clipboard to Starling, who signed. The messenger made to restart his bike, but Kathy stopped him.

'Hang on,' she said. 'Who's the sender?'

'It's all right.' Starling's voice came dully from the hall behind her. 'It's from Cabot's. This is their address label. Must be more papers to sign.'

'Got the dogs tied up somewhere, have you?' the messenger said, looking around cautiously.

'Dogs? We don't have any.'

'Really? Looks like a pack of wolves has gone for that parcel at the gate.'

Kathy looked beyond him and saw the trail of torn paper leading from the gates away down the lane. 'That's odd,' she said.

Behind her, Sammy said, 'Jesus Christ . . . What's this?'

She turned and saw that he had torn open the outer envelope of the express courier service, and also an inner envelope. He had discarded these on the floor, and was holding the contents, in one hand several slivers of paper, and in the other a sheet with printed writing like the ransom notes.

' "THIS MADE ME VERY ANGRY, SAMMY," ' he intoned.

He looked from one hand to the other in horror, then turned to Kathy. 'What does it mean?' She went to him, took the pieces of paper from his other hand and realised that they were the precious Canada Cover, cut to bits.

*

Helen Fitzpatrick is in her kitchen, preparing a lamb roast for Sunday lunch. She has removed most of the fat from the small joint, a treat, and stuck sliced cloves of garlic into the flesh. Now she is preparing the potatoes. She hears the Labradors outside the kitchen door, excited by something, not a visitor but some game they are having between themselves.

'What are you up to, girls?' she calls, and smiles to herself.

She has peeled the potatoes, cut them into largish pieces, and is now mixing them in a bowl with olive oil and crushed garlic.

One of the dogs, Henrietta, comes thumping through the back door, growling and dragging something by the sound of it. She doesn't look up. This happens every now and then. The girls find something in the woods, a half-rotten hedgehog one time, a dead crow another, and they proudly bring it back to the cottage for her approval.

'Very nice, dear,' she says, keeping her eyes fixed on the potatoes as she spreads them on to a roasting tray and reaches for the sprigs of rosemary. 'Now, be a good girl and take it away again, will you? Whatever it is.'

Henrietta obliges. Helen hears the dog and its burden thumping back out through the door, and the excited yelp of the other dog waiting outside. She looks down at the floor and sees a trail of slime sweeping across the tiles and out again.

Down below the cottage, on Poachers' Ease, Kathy is following the trail of the torn parcel from the gates along the lane. First there is the outer wrapping, with a label addressed to S. Starling Esq., then the torn pieces of a grey cardboard box. She is followed by the courier, who is still anxious about encountering a pack of savage dogs, and behind him Sammy, looking bewildered, and then Marianna.

At the open cottage gate, Kathy is met by a burst of excited barking from one of the Labradors. The other one, the older and darker of the two, Henrietta, isn't barking. She is on all fours, nuzzling something under a bush.

'What have you got there, girl?' Kathy asks, approaching her, and then stops as the dog bares its teeth at her and growls a warning. 'Come on, girl. Show me what you've got.'

The dog flattens itself against the path, pretending to be

invisible, but when this doesn't seem to deter Kathy she suddenly snatches at her prize and leaps forward towards the lane, dragging it clumsily with her. Kathy has a glimpse of black hair, then the dog careers into the path of the courier, drops its burden at his feet and jumps back, tail thrashing. He looks down, sees a human head, and passes out cold.

Marianna's shrill, piercing scream echoes through the woods, bringing Helen Fitzpatrick running down her front path. She stops dead at the gate, taking in the astonishing, frightful tableau in front of her, a man stretched out flat on the road, Kathy shouting into a phone, Sammy frozen, Marianna holding something in her hands, something waxen yellow with long flowing black hair, the head of Eva.

Given that it was the part of his wife's anatomy Sammy Starling found most troubling, he is thinking how telling it is that he should end up with just her head.

It had been that way from the beginning, her face the thing that first knocked the breath out of him, standing on a blazing hot beach, muttering curses after the departing taxi, the dazzling sunlight bouncing up from the white sand like stage lighting. He looked round and was confronted by a pair of almond eyes, dark as a desert Arab's, in a perfect golden-brown oval face, framed by jet-black hair centre-parted and drawn back across the ears. It was a face he had never seen before, and yet one he seemed to have known for ever. The sublime eyes blinked, held his stunned gaze for a moment, and turned away. Only then, as she floated off across the baking dune, did he appreciate the beauty of the long golden limbs, the bottom exquisitely highlighted by a startling yellow bikini, the curve of the shoulder, the fluid swing of the walk, the sheer bloody *class* of the whole corporeal production.

Later, even after he came to know that body in more intimate and compelling detail, the face never lost its ability to stop him in his tracks, to reduce his harshest voice to a hoarse mumble, though with time the nature of its power changed. The magic of its features, their innocent perfection, wasn't diminished as they became more familiar. Rather they became more disturbing as he learned to recognise their variations and effects – a cool sideways look, the angle of an eyebrow, a wrinkle of the nose – and to invest them with his own shadows of meaning. *Why are you so old, Sammy?* he believed them to say. *Why can't you keep up with the young men jogging along the edge of the shore? Why can't you ravish me all night long, as they would surely do, given half a chance?*

Her body told him that he might be young again, live for ever in a state of grace. Her face said, *Who are you kidding, Sammy?* And now, all that is left is her face, ruined, staring up at him reproachfully from the gravel. *Why am I in this state, Sammy? How did it come to this?*

Helen Fitzpatrick has taken charge of Marianna, rocking the sobbing woman in her arms. Two patrol cars have arrived, securing the lane. The distant wail of police sirens sounds through the morning woodlands, a new species of sad cuckoo disturbing the Sunday peace.

'How do I know you're with the police?' she demands of Kathy over Marianna's sobs.

Kathy shows her identification. 'A doctor will be here soon. Will you be all right for a few minutes?'

'I want to know what's happened!' Mrs Fitzpatrick's eyes are bright and sharp with shock and what could have been anger or distress. 'Please!' She reaches forward with her free hand and grabs the sleeve of Kathy's shirt. 'Is that really –? Tell me!'

'Mrs Starling, yes.'

'Where did it come from? I don't understand. The dogs . . .'

'It appears to have been in that box over there.'

And Helen Fitzpatrick's eyes light up again with renewed dismay as she takes in the torn box, as if the container has taken on the horror of its contents.

'Look, would you take Marianna back to the Starlings' house for me, and wait for the doctor?'

'But what's been happening? Why are you here?' She is almost hysterical.

Kathy sighs. 'Mr Starling received a ransom note concerning his wife a few days ago, Mrs Fitzpatrick.'

'She was kidnapped?' The woman looks horrified.

'Apparently. We didn't want the kidnappers to know that Mr Starling was in touch with the police, which is why I couldn't say anything to you last night. But now this has happened we will want to talk to you.'

'What about? Surely you don't think I . . .' Helen Fitzpatrick stops herself and flushes deeply. 'I mean . . .'

Marianna suddenly cries out, 'Cold! So cold!' She is rubbing the palms of her hands together.

'Are you, dear?' Helen says, her voice steadying in response to the other woman's distress. 'We'll find you something to keep you warm.'

'No!' Marianna cries, her face contorted with despair. 'Eva! My poor Eva is freezing!'

They seem immobilised in an unnatural silence, waiting for something to happen, local men, brought in by Kathy's call.

'DS Kolla,' she says. 'Serious Crime.'

Kathy is struck by the way their eyes keep flitting back to the thing lying between them, then away again, searching for something less disturbing to settle on.

The head of a young woman, grotesquely discarded in the middle of the roadway, impossibly out of place. The right side strikingly attractive, even after this has been done to her, her large dark eye disconcertingly open, plaintively staring up at the averted faces of the men. The left a mess, where Henrietta has been eating her.

Kathy approaches to within a couple of feet and gets down on her hands and knees, so as to see more clearly. The hair is long, very black, drawn back to a clasp on the crown of the head, some strands loose and spread across the right eye and nose; Kathy resists an urge to reach forward and draw them clear. Looking more closely, she can see that the woman's beauty is an illusion held together by a darkly tanned complexion. Beneath it the flesh has become waxy yellow. She can tell nothing from the raw cut across her neck, although she notices that there has been little leakage of fluids on to the gravel surface. There is a faint smell of something organic, not yet bad but nauseating all the same when taken with its source.

They are observing her, she knows, as she crouches there in the middle of the lane, and she begins to find their silence irritating.

One of the men clears his throat. 'We're expecting SOCO any minute,' he says, feeling the need to explain their inactivity.

They are speaking with hushed voices. Kathy has never seen men behaving like this at a murder scene. Is it because the woman was so beautiful? If it were the head of an old man would they be talking as if they were in church?

'When DCI Brock arrives,' Kathy says loudly, 'tell him I'm in the house with Mr Starling. When the doctor arrives, ask him or her to get the temperature of the head first, then come to the house. OK?'

8

Severed Heads and Penny Reds

Kathy went up the curving staircase and along the upstairs corridor, picking up the sound of quiet sobbing as she approached the last door, to Marianna's room. A bright, sunny bedroom like the others, it enjoyed the same panoramic view to the south. Helen Fitzpatrick was standing at the window, absorbed in it, the doctor sitting on the bed beside the older woman, patting her now motionless hands.

'She's calmer now,' she said to Kathy. 'I've given her something.'

A soft breeze ruffled the bunches of flower-print curtains.

'I'd like to take her into Farnham and interview her as soon as an interpreter arrives,' Kathy said. 'See any problem with that?'

The doctor frowned. 'She's had quite a shock. It would be kinder to wait.'

Marianna looked up at Kathy. 'No,' she said, voice cracking. 'I speak now.'

Surprised that the woman had understood her words, Kathy said, 'If you feel up to it, Marianna. It could help us.'

Mrs Fitzpatrick said, 'Perhaps it would be best if I came with you, and afterwards Marianna can come home with me, if she doesn't want to come back here straight away.'

Marianna gave a little shrug, as if it was all too much for her, then said that she wanted to change from her work clothes before going anywhere. While she did this, Kathy went along the upstairs gallery to the master bedroom. There was the large four-poster bed, extravagantly decked out in swags of several kinds of fabric. The bedding was neatly made, a pair of men's pyjamas under the pillows on one side, a woman's silk night-gown on the other. Kathy drew on a pair of latex gloves and worked her way round the room, examining everything. From the bedroom she moved on to the dressing-room, and was admiring the labels in Eva Starling's wardrobe – Armani jacket and slacks, Valentino satin dress, Jill Sander coatdress, Gucci navy cotton pinstripe shirt, Balenciaga and Issey Miyake – when she heard someone else come into the bedroom. She looked out and recognised Leon Desai in the silver overalls and overshoes and gloves.

She hadn't realised he had arrived. Brock would have sent for him, of course, because he was always the most reliable and meticulous. She watched him silently as he homed in on the woman's dressing-table. So cool, arching his superior Indian eyebrow at something.

'The lipstick isn't here,' Kathy said, glad that she made him jump.

He recovered quickly, giving her a little smile. 'Hi, Kathy. I wondered where you were.'

She felt pleased that he had been wondering that.

'I should have known you'd be somewhere around, stuffing up my crime scene,' he added, turning back to the dressing-table. 'You had the same idea, did you?'

'Her makeup looked fresh, as if she'd been getting ready to go out, or to meet someone. But the lipstick is different from the ones here.'

'I'd better take it all.' He took a fold of plastic bags from his pocket and began collecting Eva's jars and tubes, pencils and sticks.

'Anything from the head?' Kathy asked, watching the neat, economical way he moved. She now felt slightly un-comfortable being alone in a bedroom with him, with such an absurd, frothy meringue of a bed flaunting itself at the far end.

'The bed's a bit over the top, don't you think?' Desai murmured.

'I hadn't particularly noticed,' Kathy said. 'Yes, I suppose it is.'

'Trying to make a statement, do you think?' he said.

She didn't reply to that. She felt odd, light-headed, and she was aware of a slight shake in her hand. Reaction to the adrenaline rush, of course, the shock of seeing Eva like that.

'The doc reckons at least twenty-four hours. Probably severed with a long-bladed knife. And she was probably dead before they took her head off.'

'I should hope so,' Kathy breathed. She looked at Eva's dressing-table, so elegant and well stocked, and imagined her here not many days ago, glancing carelessly out at the view she probably took for granted, trying to decide which of all her lovely clothes to wear.

'I'd better go,' Kathy said. 'Got to take the housekeeper in to Farnham.'

'Hang on,' he said.

He came towards her, somehow managing to look elegant and purposeful in the silver overalls that made the other SOCOs look like a cross between astronauts and circus clowns, and dropped to his knees at her feet. The bizarre thought came into Kathy's head that he was going to propose to her.

'Give me your foot,' he said, and she dumbly obeyed, lifting the left one. He took off the shoe and examined the sole. Then he replaced it and did the same with the right.

'That's OK,' he said. 'I just wanted to know what manner of crap you'd brought in here.'

She took a deep breath. 'Do you do that with all the detectives, Leon?' she asked.

'Just the women,' he said, with the faintest smile. 'I have a thing about women's feet.'

'And women's underwear.'

'I'm trying to do something about my image, Kathy,' he said, straightening up and meeting her eyes. 'Become more human. I'm told people think I'm distant.'

'I don't think this is what they have in mind, Leon. They probably want to see you playing rugby and drinking beer.'

'Ah. *That* human . . .'

He had compelling dark eyes, she thought, and they were testing her in some way.

'DS Kolla!' They heard a call in the distance.

'Underwear's in there.' Kathy pointed over her shoulder and left.

They arrived at Farnham police station at the same time as the interpreter, a grey-haired woman who worked part-time for the overseas service of the BBC. Helen Fitzpatrick remained in the front waiting area, while the others were shown into a small interview room where Marianna accepted a glass of water. She seemed somewhat restored, with fresh makeup and clothes; a cardigan over her shoulders, navy slacks tapering to very small feet in gold slippers. But her expression was dull and withdrawn, and her responses at first hesitant.

Kathy began by asking her about herself. Her full name was Marianna Pimental, and she was fifty-three, she said, speaking so softly and tentatively that the interpreter had to lean forward in her chair. She was unmarried, and had been with the de Vasconcellos family since she was seventeen, at first in Vila Real, then later, after Donna Beatriz died, when they moved to the south coast. When Eva married in 1993, and this first reference to Eva brought a pause for the sharp intake of breath and several suppressed sobs, she had not accompanied her to England. However, Eva had sent for her in the following year, and despite Dom Arnaldo's increasing ill-health and her own reluctance to go abroad, he had insisted she must go.

It was true that she had learned very little English, despite having now lived in England for several years. Neither Eva nor Senhor Starling required it of her, and she had no friends here. She was extremely homesick, and had been since she arrived. Were it not for Eva, her only wish would be to return to Portugal and to Dom Arnaldo.

'Does Mr Starling then speak in Portuguese to you?' Kathy asked.

He tried, though his command of the language was extremely limited – he had learned it from playing tapes in his car. Eva thought her husband's attempts to speak her language were comical, and did not encourage them.

'Apart from being homesick,' Kathy said, 'are the arrangements at the Crow's Nest satisfactory? Is Mr Starling a good employer?'

Donna Eva was her employer, Marianna corrected. Senhor Starling was proper. He would customarily address her through Eva, rarely directly. She had no complaints to make about him.

She had now referred several times to Eva without tears, and Kathy tried to move more directly to discussion of her. 'You must have known her better than almost anyone,' she said.

Marianna nodded gravely. That was true.

'What was she really like?'

Marianna proceeded to deliver a precise eulogy. Her mistress had been the most beautiful baby, the most intelligent child, the most considerate young woman that God had yet managed to create. She was in every way perfect. There was nothing more that could be said.

'Who on earth would want to harm her?'

Marianna's face darkened. She had seen the barbarians, on the television, from the taxi window in London, even once in Farnham itself – boys without hair, skinheads, monsters allowed to roam loose in the streets of England.

'Have you ever seen anyone in particular, either at the Farnham house, or in the London flat?'

She had only once been to the London flat.

'Really? I'm surprised that you didn't go there with Eva. Why was that?'

Senhor Starling needed to have his meals prepared, the house maintained. Eva always considered his needs first. In London she ate out, and the flat had a cleaning woman once a week. It was inconveniently small, and it wasn't necessary for Marianna to be there. She certainly had no wish to go to London.

'How often did Eva go there?'

It varied. Perhaps twice a month.

'Did she have many friends there?'

Marianna turned from the interpreter and stared suspiciously at Kathy as she heard the question in Portuguese. Eva made many friends, because she was so charming. But she did not go to London to meet friends. She was a perfect wife in every way.

'I can understand, then, why Mr Starling would have wanted

her to be his wife, Marianna,' Kathy said, feeling the frustration of this indirect dialogue, 'but, really, why did she wish to marry him? Surely she could have had her pick of fine young men, Portuguese men?'

That was true, she could have, and many had tried to woo her, although she was still so young. Perhaps, after so many young suitors, Senhor Starling's maturity had appealed.

'Perhaps? Didn't she tell you, you being so close to her?'

Marianna hesitated. Yes, that was what she had told her. And Senhor Starling was a man of substance.

'Rich, you mean? But I thought that Eva's family was already rich?'

The woman swelled up with umbrage. She could not possibly speak of Dom Arnaldo's affairs. That would be intolerable. It was enough to say that his family was of the House of Aviz, and related to the de Souza Holsteins, the dukes of Palmela. They had been cushioned from the consequences of the revolution of 1910 by Dom Arnaldo's grandfather's estates in Brazil, and it would be insufferable to suggest that Donna Eva had married for money.

'She really was a princess, then, was she?'

Marianna deflated slowly. It was true, though Eva was far too unostentatious to parade her superb lineage generally, that she was of royal blood. Through the de Souza Holsteins, Eva was related by blood to the Princess Helena, wife of Prince Christian of Schleswig-Holstein, and daughter of no less a person than Queen Victoria of England herself.

They stopped for a cup of tea. They had heard the authorised version of Eva, Kathy knew, a portrait of perfection painted by a loyal and doting companion. It explained nothing — why Eva had married Starling, why she went up to London, why someone might have hated her so much that they could mutilate her in that way.

'She has beautiful clothes, Marianna. Do you help her to buy her clothes?'

Marianna pursed her lips in disapproval at the question.

'No? But, then, who does? Surely not Mr Starling?' Kathy gave a little smile of incredulity.

Senhor Starling was a very generous husband, Marianna said stoutly. Why not Senhor Starling?

'I don't doubt he's generous. But he has no idea about good taste, Marianna. Come, now. The house in Surrey is very comfortable, but it doesn't have the style of Eva's clothes, or of the London flat.'

Eva bought her own clothes, on her own, Marianna maintained. She bought them because Senhor Starling wanted her to be happy and to look nice.

'Do they go out together much? You know, to functions where she needs to dress so smartly?'

Certainly, they went out, with friends. But, when pressed, Marianna could name only one couple, Mr and Mrs Cooper, who had visited and stayed with them in Farnham, and with whom Eva and Starling had stayed in some other part of London.

Kathy sighed and waited a moment before going on. 'It wasn't the clothes that they quarrelled about, then?'

Marianna started at the word 'quarrelled', even before it was translated for her, and once again Kathy had the suspicion that her lack of English might be a matter of convenience.

What did she mean? What was she implying? Eva and Senhor Starling *never* quarrelled.

'Oh, Marianna,' Kathy shook her head sadly, 'I think we both know that isn't true.'

The woman bristled, and Kathy was afraid that she would simply refuse to go on. But then she fixed Kathy with a fierce eye and said, in English, 'You must say nothing against Senhor Starling. He gives her everything, more than everything. He spoils her. Sometimes she is too extravagant. Too much. She is . . .' and her face crumpled as she finished '. . . so young. Sometimes she is lost. No life, no home.'

She dabbed at her eyes, mouth trembling on the brink of sobs.

The phrase struck Kathy, as if it were the first truthful thing Marianna had uttered. 'Yes, of course,' she said gently. 'And this time, before she left, did she give you any idea at all of what she intended to do? Where she might be going?'

Marianna shook her head.

'A name, perhaps, of a shop? Or a movie?' Kathy brought out

the list of films showing at the Cinema Hollywood. 'Have a look at these titles. Maybe she mentioned one to you?'

Marianna took the list out of politeness, dubiously. She ran her eye down the page, stiffened and looked up in horror at Kathy. And then the grief, which had been so strangely numbed by the processes of officials, of doctors and police, all in their strange clothes, welled up again in an overwhelming rush, and she began to wail inconsolably.

It took several minutes before she calmed sufficiently for the interpreter to be able to make herself understood to Kathy. She, too, had read the list, and was looking pale.

'What's the matter?' Kathy said, her arm round Marianna, seeing the expression on the interpreter's face. The woman pointed to a section of the list setting out a programme of the films of the Brazilian director Glauber Rocha, her finger resting on the title of the 1970 film *Cabeças Cortadas*.

'What?' Kathy said, vainly trying to follow this as a woman constable tried to help her with Marianna.

'*Cabeças Cortadas*,' the woman gasped. 'It means *Severed Heads*.'

Helen Fitzpatrick was on her feet when they reached the waiting room, and hurried forward to put an arm round the sobbing Marianna. She looked searchingly at Kathy.

'I think it's best that she lies down for a while,' Kathy said softly. 'I'll get a car to take you home, if you don't mind looking after her.'

Helen agreed. 'I'll take her back to the cottage until we can get something organised. How's Sammy?'

'Not good. I've got some business here, and then I'll call on you.'

After they'd gone, Kathy returned to the area of the interview rooms, in the corridor meeting Bren clutching a plastic cup of thin frothy coffee in his big fist.

'How's it going with Sammy?' she asked.

'Brock called in the doc again to look at him. Can hardly get a word out of him, as if he's just turned in on himself.'

'I think he and Eva quarrelled over money. Marianna admitted she was extravagant.'

'Any idea when this was?'

'No. She's fallen apart again. I don't think we'll get anything more from her today. I'm going to talk to the neighbours now. I just wanted to let you know.'

'Brock wants me to pick up Keller, just to make absolutely sure he's not involved. My money's on the guys working on the Heathrow passenger lists.'

'How do they know what to look for?'

'A couple ticketed but only one checks in, someone with a record, I don't know. But I'll bet he's there somewhere. Why else take us out to the airport?'

'Why do that to Eva? Why destroy the stamp?'

'Fury, contempt. Someone who hated Sammy so much that he wanted to take everything Sammy owned and tear it up in front of his eyes, rather than keep any of it himself. Who would hate that much?'

'Sammy did time for being involved in selling drugs to a girl who died. But that was years ago. Surely it would have to be something more recent?'

'Maybe that's where Keller comes in – the killer waited until Keller was released so that the finger would point at him.'

Helen Fitzpatrick was in her living-room alone with the two dogs, Marianna resting upstairs in bed, Toby Fitzpatrick out. 'He still doesn't know what's happened,' she said distractedly. 'He has a friend he usually meets on a Sunday morning, and they walk down to the local for a pint. I tried phoning the pub, but they said he'd just left.' She ran a hand through her hair as if to wipe away her anxiety. 'Would you like a coffee?'

The Labradors followed them into the kitchen, keeping a close eye on Kathy.

'I suppose you see things like that all the time, do you?' Helen said, filling the kettle, keeping her eyes away from the area of freshly mopped floor. Now that Marianna was taken care of, she was suffering her own reaction. 'That – that head.'

'Not quite like that.'

'It's so bloody unsettling. When you've known someone, to see them like that . . . There's something so, I don't know, *uncanny* about it. Horrible.'

Kathy nodded. 'You're not a nurse are you, by any chance?'

'Me? No. Whatever gave you that idea?'

'The way you took care of Marianna. You seemed to know what you were doing.'

'Oh.' She gave a tight smile. 'I suppose that's always been my role. Eldest child of a big family or something. I get to take charge in the emergencies. Then fall apart on my own later.' She reached up into a cupboard for a bowl of sugar and knocked the spoon on the way down, sending it flying to the floor, white crystals spraying across the worktop. 'Damn!'

'Don't worry.' Kathy knelt to pick up the spoon while Helen got a cloth to wipe away the sugar. 'Did you know Eva well?'

'I don't know about "well". Some friends and I play tennis with her from time to time, and I suppose we saw as much of her as anyone else around here.'

'But you weren't close friends with her? Or Mr Starling?'

'To be honest, they don't have anyone you'd call *close* friends in this area. Most of the people living up here are retired, their families gone, and she was much too young and lively to be interested in them, while he just seemed content to be with her.'

'He really doted on her, did he?'

Helen looked sharply at Kathy. 'You're wondering . . . Actually, yes, he did dote on her. I remember how he was when she first arrived. It was . . .' Helen Fitzpatrick pursed her lips '. . . touching, I suppose, or, at least, it would have been . . .'

'You mean the difference in their ages?'

'Yes, I did find that rather hard to accept, I must admit. I'm sorry, that's not fair, especially now. It probably just shows my age, I suppose. But I did actually find it rather nauseating, a man like that fawning over an eighteen-year-old girl. I mean, what if it had been your daughter?' She turned away and began spooning coffee into a pot.

'That was when she first arrived, you said. Did that change?'

'Oh, I don't know, really. I mean, after people have been married a while, their relationship becomes more settled. You know what I mean. But he was still very attentive.'

'Did they argue?'

'I – I don't know.'

'Helen, it's really important we understand the background to all this. It isn't being disloyal to tell us what the real situation was. It may be irrelevant, but we do need to know.'

She met Kathy's eye. 'I'm not . . . I'm not trying to hide anything. I just don't know. We really didn't know them that well. I always felt him to be . . . well, I'm not being snobby, but a bit socially unsure of himself, even though he had all that money. When he brought home his new wife, they were invited everywhere, of course – everyone was fascinated, them being such an unlikely couple. But she just seemed rather bored, and he said almost nothing, and people gave up.

'We saw more of Eva because of their tennis court. There are three of us who play, and we'd had our eyes on it for years, but we never dared bring it up when Sammy was on his own, before Eva came. But when Eva arrived, we thought this was our chance. We asked if she played, and then suggested we all had a game, so she practically had to invite us to use the court. I'm sure she saw through us, but she didn't seem to mind.'

'Was she keen on tennis?'

'She was good when she wanted to be, but she wasn't much interested, really. More the pool. She loved the pool, whereas I never saw Sammy go near it.'

'So you knew Sammy before Eva?'

'Yes, but not well. He'd already lost his first wife when we moved here.'

'When was that?'

'Five years, no, six years ago now. Yes, it was 'ninety-one when they made Toby take the *package* – terrible euphemism that, isn't it? Like a poisoned Christmas gift.' She spoke bitterly.

'Nasty, was it?' Kathy said.

'Yes, it was actually. Hit us at the worst time. Anyway, in the end it worked out because we found this place. I used to come to the Hog's Back when I was a small girl. I had an aunt who lived out here, and I had these wonderful memories of hot summer days with her. So when Toby lost his job, and there was no particular reason to stay where we were, I thought back to those days and started to look for something in this area. It took a lot of time and searching to find something we could afford and still leave enough to –' She stopped, embarrassed. 'I'm sorry, you don't want to hear all this. You want to know about Sammy and Eva.'

'So you first met him six years ago.'

'Yes. He'd been living up here for some time by then, him and the dreaded Sally, his housekeeper. I remember thinking how funny it was, Mr Starling living in the Crow's Nest. Later I thought it rather appropriate. Anyway, we hardly saw him at first. He was like a hermit. It was probably a year before we did more than nod as he drove past in the lane.'

The two dogs, who had settled into a watchful sprawl, jumped suddenly to their feet, ears straining. 'Is that Daddy?' Helen asked, and opened the back door for them. They hurtled out, returning a few moments later with Toby Fitz-patrick.

'Oh, hello.' He hesitated in the doorway. 'Didn't realise we had visitors.'

'Something dreadful has happened, Toby,' his wife said, rising to her feet. 'This is Kathy Kolla — you remember, from last night? It turns out she's a policewoman. A detective.'

His mouth opened, but before he could speak Helen went on rapidly, 'It's about Eva, darling, Eva Starling.'

'Eva?'

'Yes, Eva.' She was talking very deliberately to him, holding him with her eyes. 'The most awful thing. She's been mur-dered.'

'Eva . . . murdered? That's not possible . . .'

Their conversation was oddly stilted and one-sided, like a nursery teacher talking to a child in front of a stranger. The dogs reinforced this, moving to Helen's heels and examining her husband's face as if they knew very well which of them was top dog. Fitzpatrick fiddled with his left ear, worried, frowning with concentration.

'I saw her, darling,' Helen went on. 'I actually saw her — her head.'

'What?'

'She's been decapitated. Her head was lying there in the lane. I saw it.'

Toby Fitzpatrick's eyes widened, his mouth opened and the colour drained from his face as abruptly as if a plug had been pulled. Kathy moved forward quickly, thinking he might pass out, but he reeled back from her against the kitchen sink, turned, ducked his head into it and threw up. It was almost, Kathy thought, as if his wife had done it deliberately, the brutal phrasing, to shock him, or shut him up. She wondered if he wasn't very bright. Or was there something else, something about Eva, perhaps, that Helen didn't want him to blurt out?

He straightened, gasping, and turned on a tap, tugging some sheets from a roll of paper towel and wiping his mouth and face. 'Sorry . . . Sorry . . .'

'Poor darling,' Helen said, going to his side and putting an arm round his shoulder. The dogs moved in too, trying to get between the two of them, and Helen had to shoo them away.

'That's appalling,' he whispered. He stared at Kathy, his face grey. 'Really? Her head?'

'Marianna's upstairs, resting,' Helen said. 'She went to pieces. We'll look after her until she's herself again.'

'Who? Oh, yes, I see.'

'Well,' Helen went on, brisk now, 'the coffee's ready. Let's go and sit down, if there are other things you want to ask us, Sergeant?'

They sat in the living-room, a coffee table between Kathy and the Fitzpatricks, and on it a fresh bunch of flowers from the garden arranged expertly in one of the glass vases. Kathy recognised it now as an Iittala design, like one the office staff had given a retiring secretary earlier in the year. It seemed to be the only recent thing in the room, everything else comfortably worn and scuffed, twenty-year-old Habitat and Scandinavian beech.

'When did you last see Eva?' Kathy said.

'Two weeks ago,' Helen said promptly. 'We had our regular game of tennis with her on that Sunday morning. I'm pretty sure I didn't see her during the following week, and then last Sunday, when we called again, Sammy answered the door and told us that Eva had gone up to town for a few days. He said we could use the court anyway, which we did.'

'Was that not surprising, that she hadn't told you she wouldn't be home for your game?'

'Oh, no. That was the way she was. She'd get an idea in her head and just do it. I told you, we weren't close.'

'Sammy told you she was at their London flat?'

'That's right, in Canonbury.'

'Have you ever been there?'

'No! We weren't friends like that. I never went with Eva on her London trips.' Helen slid her hand into her husband's. 'All right now, darling?'

He nodded and reached forward for his coffee cup, still looking dazed. He stopped before his hand reached the cup and said, 'But why? Why would anyone do a thing like that?'

'We don't know, Mr Fitzpatrick,' Kathy said. 'Do you have any ideas?'

'Me?' He looked horrified.

'I mean, are you aware of anyone who had a grudge against the Starlings?'

'Oh . . . Oh, I see. God, no, no. We don't, do we, darling?' He looked to his wife for help. She shook her head.

Kathy said to her, 'Did Sammy say how long she'd be away?'

'I don't think so. He said something about this Sunday, I think, that she'd be back for her game this weekend.'

'Did she discuss her London trips with you? What she did?'

'She said she went shopping and watched foreign movies.' Helen shrugged.

'Did you believe her?'

'Well, we had no reason not to. I mean, she never gave any hint that there might be a boyfriend or anything like that.'

'That idea did occur to you, though.'

'Oh, only as a thought to brighten up our boring lives, Sergeant. I mean, she was very pretty, and young . . . So it's something you're considering?'

Kathy didn't respond to that. 'And she would disappear for three or four days at a time.'

'Yes.'

'Did she never mention a name, someone she bumped into in London, someone who went shopping with her?'

'No, no one. We tried to pump her, but she didn't chat with us like that. It's hard to describe. We were never intimate in that way. She was totally uninterested in the kind of things we talked about, and didn't share with us what she did.'

'Sounds frustrating.'

'It was, actually. Hard work, wasn't it, darling?'

Fitzpatrick nodded obediently.

'Do you mean that she didn't settle here, like Marianna? Was she homesick?'

'I don't think it was that. It was more a generation thing. We were all old enough to be her parents. She just didn't open up with us.'

'Weren't there any younger people around that she could talk to?'

'Not really, no.'

'What about you, Mr Fitzpatrick?'

'Me?' He looked startled.

'When did you last see her?'

'Oh . . . I don't know, really. Not for ages.'

'It would have been at the Randolphs', wouldn't it, darling? Their cocktail party at Easter? The Starlings were there.'

'Yes, yes, you're probably right.'

Kathy looked at her watch. It occurred to her that Helen Fitzpatrick might be getting more out of this than she was – grist for the tennis-club rumour mill. 'The thing we're most interested in at the moment,' she said, 'apart from Eva's recent movements, is any sightings of strangers in the area in the last few months.'

'Yes, I was thinking about that,' Helen said. 'We do get people walking in the woods up here, up to the cairn on the hilltop, especially at this time of year, although usually they take the bridle path up the ridge rather than coming along Poacher's Ease. We have our regulars – an elderly couple from Guildford, the scouts from Aldershot . . .'

'The bird-watcher chap we kept seeing last year, with the moustache,' Fitzpatrick offered.

'I don't remember, darling.'

'Yes, you do! He talked to you about the roses on the front trellis. Said the soil was too acid or something.'

'I'm interested in anyone like that,' Kathy said. 'I'd really appreciate it if the two of you could think about this and write down notes of anyone you can recall — descriptions, times, conversations, and so on. I'll call back tomorrow and go over it with you.'

Kathy got to her feet to leave. The front door opened directly into the living-room, and just inside it were a row of coat pegs on the wall, a walking-stick stand, and a small table covered with the Sunday papers. Kathy stopped dead when she noticed among them the title of a magazine, partly obscured by junk mail. *The Philatelist*.

'You collect stamps, Mr Fitzpatrick?' she asked, picking it up and studying it.

Again that startled, vaguely confused look came over his face, and his wife answered for him. 'Yes, he does. It's your hobby, isn't it, Toby? Like the garden is mine.'

'I'm interested in stamps,' Kathy said.

'Are you?' He looked incredulous.

'Yes. Why not?'

'Well, you're . . .'

'You're far too sensible!' his wife broke in. 'It's the most boring hobby devised by man.'

Kathy looked at her, seeing the alertness in her expression. Helen caught her look and immediately backed off, smiling blandly.

'You must know that Sammy Starling is a big collector,' Kathy said to Fitzpatrick.

'Er . . .'

'Yes, of course we know.' Helen again, firm. 'Look, you wanted me to be frank with you about Sammy Starling, Sergeant, right?'

'Yes?'

'Well, tell her, Toby!'

'Tell her?'

'Yes, about what he did to you. The penny reds!'

'Oh . . .' He grinned doubtfully and looked, somewhat embarrassed, at Kathy. 'Are you sure you want to know?'

'I'd be fascinated.'

He blushed. 'You would? But why? I mean, is it relevant?'

'It was a dinner party at the Randolphs',' his wife said. 'You were talking to Dennis, telling him about your penny blacks, or something, and Sammy was listening to you. He was on his own, before Eva appeared on the scene. The next day he phoned up and said he wanted to see your stamps. We were both astonished.'

'Yes, that's right,' Fitzpatrick said. 'Very surprised.'

'We thought he was just lonely,' Helen said, 'and wanted something to do.'

'Yes, so I invited him up for lunch, and I showed him my albums and so on. I thought he was interested in starting the hobby himself and I talked about how he could go about it. He never gave the slightest indication that he was a collector already.

'He seemed to have no idea about stamps at all, which surprised me, really. I mean, I thought most boys would have tried it at some stage – it doesn't cost anything to cut the stamps off your mum's letters, and collect sets and swap with your friends, and so on. I thought everybody did that. I suppose it appeals to some instinct to organise and classify.'

'And acquire!' his wife added. 'That's what interested him. He liked to acquire things – do you remember that story we heard about the shares in Marcus's company? He wouldn't stop until he had them all.'

'Yes, well, it may have been that, but I wasn't sure. He just sat there quietly and I explained how it works – philately, I mean.'

'And how does it work, Mr Fitzpatrick?'

'Do you really want to know?' he said doubtfully.

'Maybe just an outline.'

'Well, once you get past the initial schoolboy stage, you realise that there are so many postage stamps produced that you can't possibly hope to collect them all. So you begin to specialise. Maybe your father's office has a branch in Germany, say, and he keeps the envelopes from correspondence for you, so you specialise in the stamps of that country. Or you may collect a theme, like stamps which have pictures of butterflies or astronauts, or something. I've never seen the point of that myself, but it's very popular these days. My collection was started by my father, and he concentrated on Queen Victoria, and I've continued that. I . . .' He paused. 'I'll have to show you, to explain about the penny reds.' He got to his feet and disappeared for a moment, returning with a thick volume.

He rested the book on the window-sill and opened it to the first page of faintly gridded paper on which were mounted six identical plain black stamps.

'Penny blacks?' Kathy asked.

'You do know something, then. This one belonged to my father, and that one he gave me for my eleventh birthday. I can still remember that moment, owning my own penny black . . .'

'It's a sort of cult object, is it?' Kathy asked. 'The penny black?'

'That's right. Because it was the first. They printed about seventy million altogether during 1840, until early 1841, when they changed the colour to red, but most got lost or destroyed. It was some time before people thought about collecting them.'

'Why would you want more than one?' Kathy asked. 'If they're all the same stamp.'

'Because he's addicted,' Helen said tightly. 'He can't help himself.'

He shook his head earnestly. 'They actually aren't the same. They printed the stamps using a number of engraved steel plates and there are slight differences between the plates. This one came from plate 6, and this from plate 1A, for instance.' Toby Fitzpatrick was becoming articulate and animated.

'But they're all still penny blacks?'

'Yes. That becomes another way of specialising, you see. To get into all the variations and types of just one stamp or group of stamps.'

'And some people think flower arrangement is boring,' Helen said, the attempt at humour defeated by the strain in her voice.

He turned over the thick leaves of the book, showing Kathy three pages full of stamps of the same design as before, but now a deep reddish brown. Every stamp looked identical, except for their postmarks.

'This is the penny red, which was used between 1858 and 1879. They're much easier to find.'

'How many have you got?'

'One hundred and fifty.' He pulled a magnifying glass out of his pocket and gave it to her. 'Have a look at that scrollwork on the right-hand side.'

She looked, and eventually managed to distinguish the numerals 1, 7 and 1, hidden in the decorative edging along one of the red stamps.

'Plate 171. Each one is different.'

'You've got one gap.' Kathy pointed to a space on the first page of the reds.

'Yes. I've managed to find a copy of every plate except 77.'

'It's rare, is it?'

'Extremely. I go to stamp fairs and so on, hoping to come across a copy that everyone's missed, but there's not much chance of it.'

'And valuable?'

'Yes. Most of these would have a catalogue value of anything from a few pence to a few pounds. You could probably pick up the lot in an auction for a couple of hundred. But an example of plate 77 could be worth up to twenty thousand if it had been used, twice that unused.'

'Ah!'

'Yes, that's what Sammy Starling said, as I remember.'

'That impressed him?'

'Definitely.'

'Just tell the story, darling!' Helen broke in impatiently.

'Sorry. Well, anyway, he went home, and then, about a week later, he called in again. Said he had something to show me. It was a brand new album, crisp new pages, empty, I thought. Then he showed me the first page. In the centre of it was a single stamp, a penny red. And I thought, Well, that's a nice start, he's been down to the stamp and coin shop in Farnham and got himself going with a nice little album and he's bought his very first stamp, a penny red, fifty pence worth. I said, "It's got a nice neat postmark, Sammy. What's the plate number?" He didn't say a word, and I got the glass and had a look, and there it was, plate 77.'

'I thought Toby had had a stroke,' Helen said. 'I came into the room at that moment, and he was standing over there, gawping at nothing, looking like he'd just seen God.'

'It was a bit of a shock,' Fitzpatrick conceded.

'Actually, it was cruel,' she said, turning to Kathy. 'The way he did that to Toby. Like the school swank, showing off. Toby had been collecting those penny reds for years. He'd got them all – all except the one that he knew he'd never own. And Sammy just waltzes off and buys *the* one, worth far more than the whole of the collection that Toby and his dad had built up over fifty years. It was very cruel.'

'I don't think he really meant it like that, Helen. You read that into it. He was just a bit out of my league, that's all, when it came to resources. He admitted to me then that he'd been collecting for years. He'd been having me on. It was his idea of a joke.'

'Well, it certainly took the shine out of stamp collecting for you for a while, darling, didn't it?'

He hung his head. 'Yes, it did rather.' He met Kathy's eyes and added, 'He gave it to me.'

'Plate 77?'

Fitzpatrick nodded. 'He just handed the album to me, and said, "Go on, you have it," and I was so embarrassed I didn't know what to say. He said that wasn't his area of interest, and it had been worth it just to see my face.'

'An expensive joke,' Kathy said, and thought, Like sticking valuable stamps on ransom notes.

'I suppose I should have felt incredibly grateful, but somehow it felt all wrong – I just felt humiliated.'

'And did he show you his collection after that?' Kathy asked.

'Oh, yes. It's fantastic. Makes mine look pathetic. I still squirm every time I think of that day, showing it off to him.'

'For him it was like buying stocks and shares,' his wife said dismissively. 'An investment. He didn't do it for love. You *grew* your collection, darling. He just bought his.'

Toby Fitzpatrick sighed. 'I suppose so.'

Helen walked with Kathy to the gate. The smell of the pinewoods was heavy in the warm sunlight, the murmur of bees coming from her cottage garden. 'It's pretty sad, really,' she said. 'Sammy Starling had all that money, and a lovely wife, and that fabulous house with the stunning view, and I don't think I've ever seen him smile once. Even when he was showing Toby his latest philatelic triumph, he just looked . . . impassive. As if he couldn't afford to show pleasure. How could you not be happy in a place like this?'

Although the sun shone brilliantly through the high tree canopy, there was a growing heaviness in the air, and a rim of clouds towards the west that hinted at an approaching change.

As they reached the gate a car swerved fast around the bend in the lane to their left, and sped on towards the Starlings' house, over the spot where Eva's head had lain.

'Idiots!' Helen glared after them.

'It might be ours,' Kathy said, 'or it could be the press. They'll be here soon enough. This story is nasty enough to get a lot of interest, Helen. You'd better be prepared.'

9

Approaching Thunder

Kathy followed the route of the car up the fifty yards of lane that separated the Fitzpatricks' cottage from the Crow's Nest. She rounded the last curve of rhododendron bushes and saw the vehicle halted at the wrought-iron gates, behind two others standing there under the eye of a uniformed man. It was the press, she saw, and hurried past the loose knot of people forming by the lead car.

Inside the house, Kathy put on the nylon suit that one of the SOCO team offered her and went up the stairs to the master bedroom, and from there through the dressing-room to Eva's sitting-room. Leon Desai was still there, working on hands and knees in a corner of the room with another man holding an ultraviolet lamp. The man was red-faced and sweating inside his overalls, unlike Desai, who rose gracefully to his feet on seeing Kathy and came over to her.

'I'm on my way to see Brock in Farnham,' she said. 'I wondered if there was anything here I could pass on.'

'Nothing definite,' he said briskly.

'So there was nothing in here that Sammy was trying to hide from me?'

'No bloodstains, if that's what you mean. But take a look at this.' She followed him to the window, seeing the clouds in the far distance creeping forward from the western horizon. The glider was up again, a tiny pale cross against their darkness, working its way up a thermal, apparently oblivious to their threat.

Desai pointed to the security bolts, which had been drilled into each timber window-frame. 'Sammy is very security conscious, of course,' he said.

'So?'

'Only that we can't find the key that opens them. It's certainly not in this room. Same in the bedroom next door. That's odd, don't you think? You'd normally keep it somewhere handy. All the other rooms do.'

He pointed to a door that connected the sitting-room with the corridor. 'That door is locked, no key. And that one . . .' he led her through the dressing-room and pointed to the door leading from the master bedroom to the corridor '. . . has a key, which we found in the lock, but on the outside.'

'The outside?'

'Right.'

'You're saying that this suite of rooms is like a prison.'

He shrugged. 'The windows are double glazed, sealed, the house heated and cooled by ducted air. All very snug and tight.'

Kathy looked round the room, thinking. 'Anything else? Any signs of violence?'

'Just one.' He went over to the door connecting the bedroom with the corridor, and pointed out a shallow depression in the timber panelling on the bedroom side. 'Recent, we think, and there were slivers of porcelain in the carpet beneath it.'

'Somebody threw an ornament at the closed door?'

'Or at somebody standing in front of the closed door, yes.' He turned away, brisk. 'Nothing much, really. We'll keep looking.'

Farnham divisional police station was experiencing its busiest Sunday lunch-time in years. More uniforms had been called in to secure the grounds of the Crow's Nest from the photographers and camera crews who were now roaming through the surrounding woods, attracted by the first reports of the sensational nature of Eva's death. The small canteen was filled with sweating men and women, hips loaded with equipment, trays loaded with chips, exchanging cheerful banter. Kathy went down to the interview rooms in the basement. She found the recording-room and went inside to watch the interviews in progress on the monitors.

Brock was on the left of the screen, sitting forward in his chair, contemplating the man in front of him in silence, rubbing the side of his beard with the index finger of his right hand. Starling faced him across the table, stiffly upright, features expressionless. Only his slender fingers, clenching and unclenching on his lap, gave any clue to his internal state.

'You're sure you're up to this, Sammy?' Brock said, with what sounded like genuine concern.

Starling gave a little nod. 'I'm all right, Mr Brock, really.'

'You look very calm, Sammy, all things considered,' Brock said quietly. 'If I may say so.'

Starling took a little time to reply. Eventually he tilted the sphere of his head back and said, 'That is the way we are, Mr Brock. We hide our feelings. We remain inscrutable.'

'We?'

'We English.' If he meant it as a joke, there was no indication from the set of his face.

Looking at the two of them, it struck Kathy that their appearances were reversed, Starling calm and distant, Brock slightly dishevelled, as if he'd left home in a hurry when he'd heard the news. But more than that, Brock seemed the more troubled of the two, the more uneasy.

'Why don't we clear up the business of the time you took to return from Heathrow?' he suggested.

'Yes, of course. That was stupid of me. I see that now,' Starling conceded calmly. 'I caught a taxi outside the terminal. I told him to take me to Canonbury. At about the Hammersmith flyover I changed my mind. I told him to go instead to Camden Town, which he did. He dropped me at Camden Town tube station.'

'Why did you change your mind?'

'I decided to go to the Cinema Hollywood, where Eva often used to go.'

Brock stared at Starling, making no comment on this.

'I went to the Cinema Hollywood,' Starling finally said, 'to see – to see if Eva was there.'

'Explain that for me, Sammy,' Brock said softly.

'I thought, if Eva was behind this, if she was hiding out somewhere, it might be there, in the dark, watching those films.' Starling looked at him sadly. 'It was a stupid idea. She wasn't there, of course. And then I felt ashamed of myself, doubting her like that. So I didn't tell you.'

'But of all the places you thought she might be, that was the most likely?'

'I thought so.'

'Do you think she met somebody there?'

The brief crease in Starling's eyes might have been a wince. 'If anywhere, I thought there. But I might be quite wrong.'

'We'll take a closer look at that place. Anything else?'

'*Anything else?*' Starling tilted his face back and let out a deep sigh. 'Oh, Mr Brock, why? Why did they have to do that? To Eva? To the cover? Did they just have to destroy beautiful things?'

Brock lowered his head and didn't reply. Again Kathy thought how uneasy he looked, as if he knew more than Starling and could see no good in it.

There was a knock at the door and a man in shirt-sleeves came in with a message for Brock, who read it, and got slowly to his feet. 'That's enough for now, Sammy,' he said with a sigh. 'I'm terminating this interview at . . .' he looked up at the clock above the table '. . . one eight. Time for lunch, Sammy. Sunday lunch. Where are you going?'

Starling looked at him in surprise. He began to say, 'Home,' then hesitated.

'I wouldn't advise you going home. The place is crawling with press reporters and cameras.' Starling's body sagged slightly as he took this in.

'What about Mr and Mrs Cooper?' Brock suggested.

Starling thought. 'Yes, I suppose . . .'

'Want to phone? We can take you there, and someone can collect some things for you from your home. What about Marianna? She's with your neighbours, but the press will soon sniff her out. Shall we get her to the Coopers too?'

'I — I don't think so. No, no. There's some Portuguese people, attached to the embassy, friends of Eva's family. They might . . .'

Brock led Starling towards the door. He towered over the other man, whose shoulders had now slumped. When they reached the door, Brock stood aside to let him through. Starling looked at him and said, 'It can happen to anyone at any time, Mr Brock. Don't forget that.'

'What can, Sammy?'

'That you lose everything. We're just sacks of potatoes brought to life for a short while. We have no hold on anything.'

Brock stared at him but didn't reply.

'It could happen to you, Mr Brock. This afternoon, maybe. Or tomorrow. Or next week.'

He turned and walked through the door.

On the other monitor, Bren was making little headway with an uncommunicative Marty Keller. There was no overt aggression or even resistance in the former police inspector's responses. In his body posture, his facial expressions and tone of voice, he maintained that air of withdrawal and passivity that Bren had described from his earlier observations of him. But his eyes had a surreptitious life of their own. They darted around the room, exploring the little differences from when he himself would have conducted such an interview as this, over ten years before. The one place they didn't look was at Bren.

'Have you got a problem, Mr Keller?' Bren said, provoked into irritation.

'Sorry?'

'You won't look at me. Is there a problem?'

'A problem? No.' But he kept his eyes on the table in front of him.

Bren took a deep breath. 'Have you had any form of contact with Mr Samuel Starling or any member of his family in the past six months?'

Keller shook his head.

'Please give an answer.'

'No. None whatsoever.'

'You haven't seen him, or written to him, or visited his properties, or seen his wife during that period?'

'No.'

'Has any person known to you had contact with Mr and Mrs Starling during that period?'

Keller thought about that for a moment. 'No.' He seemed to have no curiosity about the reason for these questions.

'Are you sure about that?'

'Yes.'

'Have you ever asked anybody, at any time during the past nine years, since June of 1988, when you were found guilty of certain criminal charges, to report to you on the whereabouts, activities or affairs of Mr or Mrs Starling?'

Keller's eyes rose to the ceiling. 'That's a broad question.' The break in the monosyllabic responses was a relief to Bren, Kathy saw.

'Yes, it is a broad question. Answer it, please.'

'I may well have asked my brother what Starling was up to, especially in the early stages. Before I lost interest.'

'How long ago would that have been, that you lost interest?'

'Four years . . . five.'

'Why did that happen?'

'You realise, after a while, what's important, that's all. Sammy Starling isn't important. Not to me.'

'What is important to you, Mr Keller?'

The eyes drifted down from the ceiling, avoiding Bren, and considered the floor. 'Getting through today.'

'You went through a bad patch about a year ago.'

'Did I?'

'It's on your prison record.'

'Is it?'

'Answer my question, please.'

'What was your question?'

'Did you undergo a period of mental depression in July to September of last year?'

Keller said nothing for a while, then, 'Yes.'

'What was the cause of that?'

Keller shook his head in mid irritation, his eyes turning up to the camera mounted in the corner of the ceiling, so that he seemed to be looking directly at Kathy. 'It can happen like that, when you get towards the end of a long stretch. It sometimes gets harder instead of easier. Because you know the end is within reach, every day becomes longer, more difficult to take. You begin to wonder if you can hang on that long. You wonder if you might just give up, with the finish almost in sight.' He spoke clinically, without self-pity.

'Was your brother concerned about you?'

'You'd have to ask him.'

'Did he try to think of some way to give you strength again? Something to look forward to, perhaps?'

'I don't remember.'

'Perhaps he thought that it would be good for you if you could get angry with Sammy Starling again? Give you something to live for?'

Keller lowered his eyes from the camera and considered the table once more, then gave a soft laugh. 'Been on a course, have you? Well, go on then, tell me.'

'Tell you what?'

'What you're dying for me to ask. Starling, Starling, Starling. What's happened to him, then? Why am I here?'

'Mrs Starling has been kidnapped, Mr Keller. And murdered.'

Keller stared unblinkingly at the table for a long time before speaking again, in a quiet, neutral voice. 'Oh . . . Well, I don't know anything about that.' He turned his head away towards a corner of the room and seemed to address some invisible person there. 'Who's leading the inquiry, may I ask? Not you, I take it?'

'DCI Brock is in charge of the investigation.'

'Is he still around, then? And still a DCI? Well, well.' Keller looked abruptly up at the camera again, a faint smile on his mouth, and with a start Kathy realised that Brock was now standing silently by her shoulder. She hadn't heard him enter the room.

'I'm surprised he isn't here in person, conducting this interview,' Keller went on, peering up at the lens. 'But, then, I suppose, under the circumstances, it would have been difficult for him.'

'What circumstances are those?' Bren asked.

'Oh . . . it's a long story. And an old one. Too old.' Keller gave a wan smile, returning his attention to the far corner of the room. 'Sammy's wife, eh? Blimey, Sammy's wives do have it tough. That's a high-risk occupation, that is, being married to Sammy Starling.'

'Wives?' Bren said, frowning.

'Well, you'll know more about that than me.' Keller gave a humourless laugh. 'You're the copper, after all.'

'Kathy.'

Kathy turned to the sound of Brock's voice, low and intent.

'I've got Dr Mehta lined up to do an autopsy on the head. I'm going back up to town now. Will you let Bren know?'

Kathy nodded. 'I'll help make arrangements for Marianna,' she said. 'Then I want to talk to Sally Malone, if we can find her.'

'Malone?'

'She was Starling's housekeeper for ages, until a couple of years ago. He asked me, just before the auction, to contact her if anything went wrong. Maybe she knows something about Eva.'

'Yes . . .' Brock frowned in thought. 'I remember her. I think that's a good idea. Tell you what, sort out Marianna, then pick me up in two hours at the morgue. If you've found Sally we'll go to see her together.'

'Shall I bring her in?'

'No.' Brock rubbed his face, weary. 'Let's see her in her natural habitat, without prior warning.'

The dark thunderclouds were filling half the the sky by the time Brock reached central London. The forensic pathology unit was attached to the coroner's office and court, and he was stopped at the security desk in the front hall and made to wait for Mehta to come up and collect him. Sundeep Mehta was Brock's first choice for the difficult autopsies, and he'd had no qualms about bringing the little Indian in on a Sunday. A dapper man with large eager eyes and a professionally perverse sense of humour, he had discovered his talent for interpreting the remains of the dead early in his medical training in Bombay. He now proclaimed loudly at dinner parties that medicine would be a wonderful occupation if it were not for the live patients, and that it was the absence of these which made pathology his inevitable career path, but this was merely his way of putting people at ease when they discovered, somewhere during the main course, what it was that he did. The truth was that, just as the subject of a biography remains alive to its biographer, so his subjects were alive to him, their whole life stories compressed into the final moment of their existence.

He led Brock through the barrier, protesting at the hopelessness of reaching a proper conclusion on the basis of just one major organ.

'You really must find me more, Brock! Otherwise I shall very probably disappoint you. Mind you,' he went on, as they waited for the lift, 'this is becoming very fashionable, so I suppose I must forgive you.'

'What is?'

The lift doors opened on a startled clerk as Dr Mehta cried, 'Decapitation!'

'Really?'

'Yes, yes! Don't you go to the movies? Or read the newspapers? Everyone is doing it, it seems, although this is the first I've had on my table so I should thank you for that. I have a theory about it, you know.'

'That doesn't surprise me, Sundeep,' Brock said drily.

'Now, now. My theory is that it is symptomatic and expressive of a widespread perception of the breakdown of social order. Think of the French Revolution! Heads rolling around absolutely everywhere!'

'I see.'

'In my study at home I have an etching which I found years ago in an antique shop in Inverness. It shows a rather corpulent, jolly man sitting in a frock coat and wig and knee breeches, explaining something to the artist. It is a portrait of Simon, Lord Lovat, as the inscription at the foot says, "Drawn from the Life and Etched in Aquafortis by William Hogarth, Published According to Act of Parliament, August 25th, 1746".'

'You've lost me, Sundeep.' They stepped out of the lift and began the walk down the long, bare, underground corridor.

'Lovat was a Highland chieftain, captured by the English during the Scottish rebellion of 1745. He was taken to the Tower of London, where he was drawn by Hogarth before they took him out and chopped his head off. He was the last person in the UK to be executed by the Crown by beheading.'

'I still don't see . . .'

'Well, look, the last official beheading coincides exactly with the Act of Union and the formation of the UK! And this current taste for decapitation is thus a reflection of the fact that everyone knows that your precious United Kingdom is falling apart at the seams!' Dr Mehta gave a great hoot of triumph and swept through the door into the anteroom of the large dissecting room.

'Very convincing, Sundeep,' Brock muttered, suspecting that he'd got his history confused and taking the overalls, gloves and other protective clothing he was offered. 'I'll bear it in mind as a possible motive. No doubt the defence will find that useful.'

'You have a suspect, then?'

'Not really. A lover, the husband . . .'

'Oh dear.' Mehta rolled his eyes with disappointment. 'Always the lover or the husband.'

Brock followed him through the plastic swing doors into the large, brightly lit chamber.

Sixteen stainless-steel dissecting tables are set out in two long rows, flanked along the walls by continuous ranges of stainless steel benches and sinks. Tomorrow, Monday, the busiest day of the week, every one of the tables will be occupied by a corpse, but today only one is in operation. On the big table, Eva's head, lying pathetically on its side, looks forlorn and lost.

Mehta introduces Brock to his assistant, Annie, a young woman with thick, shoulder-length hair. Annie gives Brock a quick, toothy smile and gets on with her preparations, setting out instruments and sample jars on the worktop. She has heard Mehta's patter a hundred times before.

'We're just waiting for the results of the Hep C and HIV tests. Shouldn't be long now,' Mehta explains, and almost immediately a woman in a white lab coat appears at the plastic doors, and nods to Mehta. Annie watches as he examines the paper the woman offers him. He nods and asks a question or two, then returns to Brock's side. 'All clear,' he says.

Annie has already interpreted the results from his body language, and has put on a white face mask and plastic goggles. She stands at the end of the table, takes Eva's head firmly between her raw pink rubber-gloved hands, and holds it upright, face up to the ceiling. Mehta moves round to the far side of the table, pulling on his gloves, and waves Brock forward.

'Now, I did mean what I said about needing more, Brock,' Mehta says. 'You see, they've cut through the neck high up, so we're missing both the hyoid bone and the thyroid cartilage, which, if we'd found them to be damaged, could have been indicative of manual strangulation. In fact, one of the things I'm sure you've already considered, Brock, is that the reason we're being given only this much of her could be to establish her death and identity without revealing something else.'

Brock grunts. 'Like?'

'Like the cause of death, or·maybe something else entirely – perhaps she was raped, or was pregnant, for example. But all may not be entirely lost. Although we are missing the thyroid gland itself, pressure on it during an assault can result in abnormally high levels of thyroid hormone in the blood, so we can test for that. However, as you can see, there's no great congestion of the face, nor swelling of the conjunctiva of the eyes, which would have indicated occlusion of the air passages and obstruction of the veins from the head.'

'Isn't the obvious cause of death having her head cut off?' Brock asks bluntly.

Mehta chuckles. 'Actually, that's the one cause we can rule out. She was already dead, probably for several hours, when the head was separated. Look, you see, no lividity. But if we turn her over . . .'

Annie rotates the head face down against the steel table, and Mehta lifts the long black hair away from the scalp, revealing a darker purplish discoloration on this side.

'After she died, she lay on her back and the blood drained to that lower side, becoming a permanent lividity stain after a few hours. Now, if the neck had been cut initially, the lividity pattern would taper away towards the open wound, where the blood could drain away. But as you see, there's no sign of that. The severing of the head took place after lividity had established itself, and was carried out using a broad-bladed weapon of some kind . . .'

He points to the flesh of the throat. 'You see the length of the strokes. Heavier than a carving knife, I would imagine, lighter than an axe. A cleaver perhaps. And the spinal cord severed with a single heavy anterior blow with the same instrument.'

The pathologist pauses while Brock looks closely at the exposed white bone.

'All right,' he says, straightening up. 'And the time of death?'

The pathologist shakes his head sadly. 'Rigor has disappeared from the facial muscles, and there is no sign of the onset of putrefaction. But the temperature that the doctor who attended the scene took from the inside of the mouth was only five degrees centigrade, on a warm summer's morning, so it's quite possible that the head was frozen or chilled, and if that was the case, I couldn't hazard a guess. Sorry,' Mehta continues. 'We've taken swabs of the cosmetics, to see if we can match them to those found in the house and the apartment.'

'Could you say how long they might have been applied before death?'

'That would be clever, now wouldn't it? But I'm afraid not. I can tell you that her eye makeup hadn't been disturbed by tears, and her lipstick could have been smudged by a kiss, but I couldn't add any scientific substance to what you can observe for yourself.

'Shall we proceed?' Mehta asks, and takes hold of the head while Annie turns away for a scalpel. While Mehta holds Eva steady, Annie plants the tip of the knife firmly into her scalp above the left ear, and draws it slowly across the top of her head until she reaches the right ear. Then she works back across the cut, easing the scalp away from the skull with the blade, until the whole forward half is loosened. She puts the scalpel aside and takes hold of the flap of scalp with both hands and folds it neatly forward, until it lies, inside out, over Eva's face. She picks up the scalpel again and detaches the back half of the scalp similarly, pulling it away so that the top of the skull is entirely exposed.

Annie turns back to the bench and lifts a power tool from a wall bracket. It has a circular saw blade at one end, and a heavy waterproofed cable extending from the other to the wall. Mehta nods to Brock to step back, while he continues to hold the head still for his assistant.

Brock turns away. He has known young officers to become fascinated, even obsessed, with this place and others like it, taking every opportunity to attend autopsies, not because they were ghoulish but because they thought that they sensed, in the calm efficiency and control of the procedures, and the lurid reality of the evidence, that such places contained some great truth about their own mortality. But this is an illusion, Brock thinks. The only truths here are the little ones, commonplace and sordid, that Mehta and his colleagues can tease out of the fabric of broken bodies.

Annie's bone saw is screaming as it cuts two clean arcs across the top of Eva's skull. At last it stops, and Annie sets it aside. She prises a steel tool into the cut, turns it, and the top of the skull cracks open like a coconut shell. She lifts away the separated piece, and looks inside to the brain.

Brock is thinking of Starling's final comments, about people being merely sacks of potatoes. The sentiment is undeniable in here. Yesterday, perhaps, this beautiful young woman was a personality, changing other people's lives; today she is being taken apart with cool precision on a stainless-steel disassembly line for failed human machines. The miracle isn't that these human contraptions stop functioning all of a sudden, but that they somehow keep going for as long as they do.

Which is Keller's modest aim in life, apparently: to keep going until tomorrow. It seems a reasonable ambition.

Annie has removed Eva's brain from the skull, and turns to lay it in the pan of a weighing machine on the side bench. Dr Mehta releases his grip on Eva's head and flexes his arms as Annie puts her hands under a running tap, then takes up a marker pen and writes on the white board fixed to the wall above the bench:

    name : Starling
    brain : 1386

Meanwhile Mehta has begun work on Eva's brain. He holds a long, straight-bladed, square-ended carving knife, which he uses first to separate the brain into its component parts – cerebrum, cerebellum and stem – and then to cut them neatly into quarter-inch slices. He spreads them out on the steel worktop, with the expertise of a chef on a TV cooking programme. Each slice has

148

the pattern of a spreading tree, like a sectioned floret from a cauliflower. Mehta lifts three pieces and drops them into a jar of fluid in front of him. The rest he leaves for Annie to scoop into a small plastic bag while he runs his gloved hands under the tap and returns to the head on the table.

'All looks normal. But I was wondering earlier about her nose . . .'

'What about it?'

'Let's take a look, shall we?'

Gently he folds Eva's scalp back over her missing section of skull, and considers her face. 'Dear, dear.' He chuckles. 'Those naughty dogs! Didn't leave us much of the left side, did they? Labradors, you say? I'll be a bit more respectful next time I meet one. But the right nostril is quite intact.' He lifts a scalpel and slices into it. 'Ahaa! Have a close look, Brock!' Mehta beams.

'If I must. What am I looking at?'

Annie stands impassive in the background while the two men peer at Eva's nostril. She removes her protective glasses and watches unblinking as her boss clowns around. Brock is aware of this, thinking that she looks like every efficient female assistant contemplating an older male supervisor, silently willing him to stop wasting time so that she can get on with her next job. He wonders if Kathy ever looks at him in that way.

'The membranes in the lining of her nose. They're damaged, see? In fact . . .' Mehta delicately scrapes the flesh with the tip of his scalpel '. . . there's been so much tissue damage that the cartilage dividing the nostrils has been eaten into. And it looks as if she may have an abscess in the bone of the sinus.'

'Cocaine?' Brock suggests.

He nods. 'She had quite a habit.'

'So, she wasn't such a good girl, after all. A heavy user, you say?'

'A gram-a-day girl,' the pathologist pronounces decisively. 'Probably been on the stuff for at least a year.'

'Really?' Brock says. 'That is interesting.'

'Didn't you expect it?' Mehta asks.

'We haven't found any drugs so far.'

'What about signs of bleeding?'

'Nosebleeds?'

'Yes. Especially at night, while she slept. Cocaine shrinks the blood vessels on contact when it's inhaled. The circulation to the membranes would be impeded, and tissue would die and become detached. A girl this dedicated, her pillow would very likely have blood on it in the morning.'

'Interesting. Something to look for. Many thanks.'

'Not to mention the money,' the pathologist goes on. 'A gram would set her back – what? A hundred quid? That's forty thousand a year. Strictly cash. Good grief, that's more than my kids demand for their pocket money!'

Five minutes later Dr Mehta is still chuckling about that as Annie puts the plastic bag of Eva's brain back inside her head, packs out the cavity firmly with shredded cotton waste, replaces the skull top and sews up her scalp with twine. By the time she's finished, and has hosed down the head and table, Eva's right profile looks almost herself again, wet from a swim in her pool, apart from the nasty damage to her nose.

10

Sew Sally

Kathy spotted Brock on the far side of the reception area, talking into his phone. From the set of his shoulders and the look on his face she thought he was having an argument, and waited for several minutes while his conversation continued. Eventually he snapped the instrument off and turned towards her, frowning deeply. He hardly acknowledged her as they went out into the street, and continued to be preoccupied as they walked to the car.

'Been raining, has it?' he asked suddenly when they reached it, as if he'd only just noticed the wet pavements and tarmac shiny black.

'Yes, we had a thunderstorm. More on the way. Didn't you hear it?'

'You can't hear anything down there. Did you track down Sally Malone?'

'I've got two addresses, both in South London. One her home in Peckham, and the other a business address, Sew Sally.'

Kathy got behind the wheel, conscious of him watching her as she put the car into gear and moved off. She continued to have the unsettling impression that he was examining her as she drove south towards Vauxhall Bridge.

'I called at the Cinema Hollywood on the way. They were

taking the manager in to make a statement. She says that she knows Eva well, but insists that they never saw her accompanied by a man.'

Brock said nothing.

'Anything useful from Dr Mehta?' she asked eventually, when his silence showed no sign of breaking.

Brock grunted and turned to stare gloomily out of the window at the post-modernist office building that MI6 flaunted at the south end of the bridge. 'It seems that Eva used cocaine.'

'Really?'

'As much as a gram a day.'

'Hell. Surely Sammy must have known.'

'One would think so. We'll have to search the house and the flat again. Leon and his pals need to come up with more than they have so far.'

Kathy wasn't sure if there was criticism in this. The old man definitely seemed out of sorts. 'That reminds me, Leon phoned. He wants to meet us after we've seen Malone,' she said. 'He suggested six o'clock at Queen Anne's Gate. He said it's important, but he wouldn't let on what it was.'

Brock grunted again. He was wiping the side of his face with a handkerchief, then examining the white cloth. He caught her sideways glance at him as she drove.

'I thought . . . Stupid question, but I haven't got any spots of blood on me by any chance, have I?' he asked.

'No. No, there's nothing.'

He put the handkerchief away. 'I always feel I need a shower when I come out of that place.'

'Doesn't he give you a face mask?'

'He doesn't bother when they're HIV negative. But the test is a quick one, and not a hundred per cent reliable.'

'He seems to know what he's doing.'

'Hmm. His assistant is good. Annie. Have you met her?'

Kathy shook her head. Large dollops of rain were beginning to smack the windscreen again, the tyres swishing as they hit puddles on the road surface.

'Very efficient. Don't know how she puts up with old Sundeep.'

'No choice, I expect,' Kathy said, and immediately became aware again of Brock's glance in her direction.

Sally Malone's home was one of a curving terrace of small late-Victorian houses, each with its own rather absurdly grand portico sheltering its front door. There was a builder's skip at the kerb in front of hers, and several of the houses appeared to be in the process of restoration. Estate agents' boards cluttered the silent street. There was no reply to their knock, so they returned to the car and drove west along Peckham High Street towards Camberwell.

They found the sign Sew Sally in a side-street over a grimy shop-front behind which a chaotic variety of refurbished over-lockers, blind hemmers, sewing-machines jostled for attention. There seemed to be the hint of an electric light in the depths behind, despite a Closed sign on the door. The rain was streaming down now, warm as soup. Brock got out of the car, strode over to the doorway and hammered with his fist. Kathy used an old newspaper abandoned on the back seat to cover her head as she ran after him. As they waited, him knocking again, she watched the shoulders of his grey suit turn dark as the water saturated the material.

'No luck,' he growled in disgust, and was about to turn away when the blind covering the inside of the glass door twitched, and a sharp little nose peeked around its edge, at about waist height. Suspicious eyes examined them up and down, then the door clicked open on a chain.

'What's the matter?' a female voice complained. 'Can't you see the flippin' sign? We're closed.'

Kathy flicked her warrant card in front of her eyes. 'Let us in, will you, love? We're getting soaked.'

The face disappeared and the door banged shut. Then a chain rattled and the door swung open for them. They pushed inside and stood dripping on a grubby strip of carpet, confronted by a small elderly woman armed with a large carving knife.

When Peter White had described Sally Malone as a 'character', he'd had in mind one of those tough little cockney women portrayed in films about the Blitz, a sparrow who could take any amount of punishment without complaint, and whose indomitable spirit more than made up for her diminutive size.

This was somewhat fanciful, for although she had begun life in poverty, Sally had experienced enough years of comfort to have developed an irritating whine when things didn't go her way. But her toughness was beyond question, as was her combativeness where her own interests, and those of her friends, were concerned.

'I know you, don't I?' She peered up at Brock's face.

There were no lights on in the interior of the shop, and the daylight filtering through the rain-drenched shop-front gave the place an eerie underwater atmosphere, like a submarine graveyard for old sewing-machines. Brock, with water dripping from his grey hair and beard, looked the part of King Neptune.

'Hello, Sally. It's been a long time.' He waited for her to register his face.

'Gawd,' she muttered finally, her eyes widening in alarm. 'What do *you* want?'

'We've come to talk to you about Eva. When was the last time you saw her?' Brock stooped towards her, peering down at her upturned face.

'Eva? Sammy's Eva?'

'That's the one. When did you last see her, then?' Brock insisted quietly.

'Months . . . years ago. I don't know.'

Brock frowned at her, looking unhappy. 'How about last week?'

'Last week? No, no!' The suggestion seemed to alarm her more. 'Why are you asking?' she countered, trying to get some of the initial truculence back into her voice. 'Why do you want to know? Are you looking for her? Is she missing or something?'

'She's dead, Sally. Eva's dead,' he said flatly.

Sally froze. 'No. How?' Her whisper was barely audible above the swish of the rain against the window of the shop and the rumble of distant thunder. 'Has there been an accident?'

'She's been murdered.'

Sally's little fist rose to her mouth, muffling her cry. 'Oh, Gawd! Sammy?'

She looked from one to the other of her visitors, aware of them both studying her reactions.

'Sammy?' Brock prompted.

'Is Sammy all right?' she asked, forcing firmness into her voice.

Brock nodded.

'When did this happen? I didn't see nothing in the papers.'

'You will tomorrow.' Brock looked around them in the gloom. 'What about a cup of your famous extra-strength tea, Sally? I think we could all do with one.'

She seemed reluctant but when Brock showed no sign of relenting she led them down a short corridor, jammed with cardboard boxes and drums of fluids, to a small room at the back lit by a fluorescent ceiling baton. There was a table in the centre of the room, and seated at it a man even smaller and more wizened than Sally, with grizzled grey hair and a pair of thick-lensed glasses perched on the end of his nose. He looked up from the machine he was repairing, a tiny screwdriver in his hand.

'This is my partner, Rudi Trakl,' Sally announced, and to him she added in a mutter, 'Old Bill.'

The little man raised his eyebrows. 'Trouble?' he asked, in a quavering voice.

'You remember Sammy Starling, what I used to work for, Rudi? His wife's been murdered.'

'No!' His eyes followed Sally over to the kitchen sink, where she returned the carving knife to a drawer and filled a kettle with water. Outside the window a small cat spotted her and began plaintively scratching the frame. Bedraggled, it was pressed against the glass to avoid a cascade of rainwater from a broken gutter overhead, which drowned its cries. Sally ignored it. 'Go on, then,' she said. 'Sit down.'

'I'd like to wash my hands, Sally,' Brock said. 'Kathy'll fill you in.'

He followed her directions back along the corridor, and they heard a door close and the sound of a tap. Kathy sat down and gave Sally a short account of Eva's kidnapping. The little woman sat motionless on the other side of the table, hands clenched on her lap, from time to time exchanging glances with Rudi, until Kathy came to the discovery of Eva's head, when Sally's hands shot to her mouth again, smothering her cry.

'That's horrible!' she moaned, voice quavering. 'Who could do a thing like that?'

'Yes,' Kathy said. 'Who?'

The kettle began to whistle. Sally got shakily to her feet, unplugged it and began the automatic actions of making a pot of tea. 'I still don't see why you should come to me,' she muttered. 'It's three years since I've seen Sammy. I haven't seen either of them since I moved out.'

Kathy noted that this wasn't quite what she'd said when Brock had asked her how long it had been since she'd seen Eva. 'How long did you live with the Starlings?' she asked.

Sally sniffed. 'Since 1964.' She swore softly at the cat, which was still scratching the window-frame, and reached across the sink to open the window for it. It slid in quickly, and stalked, still mewing, to the fridge. Sally followed it and reached inside for a bottle of milk. She poured some into a saucer for the cat and the rest into a small jug, which she placed on the table with the pot of tea.

'What's he doing?' she complained to Kathy, perking her head towards the sounds of a running tap.

Kathy shrugged. 'What made you go and live with Sammy and his wife in 1964?' she asked.

Sally put some mugs on the table and sat down with a sigh. 'My Colin was killed in an accident on the buses. Brenda and Sammy had just moved north of the river, to a big house in Tottenham. Brenda felt sorry for me, being left on my own, and asked if I'd like to do their cleaning, and soon I was living there, doing their cooking an' all. That would have been when I first met Mr Brock, too,' she added.

'Really?'

'Yes. That was his beat then, Tottenham.'

'He came to Sammy's house?' Kathy was intrigued. She knew almost nothing about Brock's early career.

'I suppose. I didn't get out much, bringing up the little kid.'

'Your kid?'

'No, no. Sammy and Brenda's boy, Gordon. He was just a toddler.'

'Ah. So you were really close to the family.'

'Of course. Brenda was a good mother, but she was kept busy, looking after Sammy's affairs. She always got herself involved in whatever he was doing. That's why they had such a good marriage, a proper partnership.'

'Unlike Sammy and Eva, do you mean?'

'I never said that,' Sally said stiffly. Kathy thought of the parallel with Marianna, both women's lives spent rearing other women's solitary children.

'It must have been hard for you when Gordon died, then.'

'Brock told you about that, did he?'

Kathy didn't correct her, although she wondered why Brock had told her so little. She felt herself groping for the right questions.

'It was hard all right. Brenda took it specially badly. I watched her go downhill from that year.'

'Do you think that had something to do with her death?' Kathy improvised.

'Of course it did. That's when the depression started. It was terrible watching it taking hold of her, for two long years, until she finally — Oh, at last! I thought you'd got lost, Mr Brock.'

Kathy looked up as Brock came back into the room. He slung his damp jacket on the back of the spare chair and sat down, ignoring Sally's attempt to tease him.

'Since when have you been in sewing-machines, Sally?' he said, drawing a mug of black tea towards him and pouring in some milk.

'There's plenty around here makes their own clothes and curtains, and need a good second-hand machine, or their old one fixing up. We do a nice little business, Rudi and I, keeps us out of mischief.'

'Rudi . . .' Brock looked thoughtful. 'Have we met before, Rudi? Name's familiar.'

'Everyone I've ever known was known to you, Mr Brock.' Sally gave a little cackle.

'Well, you always kept such interesting company. And the two of you own this business, do you?'

She nodded. 'We make a good partnership. Rudi's good at the mechanical side, fixing up the machines, and I do marketing and the books.'

'Marketing?' Brock gave a little smile, and she scowled and thrust a handbill at him, advertising their services.

'Did Sammy help you get started – financially, I mean?'

'No. We did it on our own.'

'Has Sammy ever been here?'

'No.'

'Sally was telling me that she hasn't seen Sammy since she left three years ago,' Kathy added.

Brock looked as if he didn't appreciate her interruption. 'I see. After you'd lived under his roof for thirty years.'

'Haven't been invited back, have I?' Sally sniffed.

'Eva kicked you out, did she?'

Sally bristled. 'I decided it was time to retire from being Sammy's housekeeper,' she said stiffly.

'To take up a career in marketing.' Brock sipped his tea. 'That must have been a big wrench for you. After all those years.'

Sally Malone said nothing.

'She was headstrong, was she, Sally? Wilful?'

'Used to getting her way, yes. Well, she was a princess, wasn't she?'

'Sammy likes to get his own way, too. That must have led to a few arguments, eh?'

'I never heard a cross word between them,' Sally said carefully. 'Not one.'

'He was generous to her, I believe.'

'Very. Clothes, jewellery, as much spending money as she wanted.'

'Cash?'

'I'd say so. Why? You think that's what got her into trouble? Flashing it around?'

'And you never saw them quarrel?'

'Never. It was all lovey-dovey.'

'What about the flat in London? Why did she go there?'

'You'll have to ask Sammy that,' she replied primly. 'They didn't consult me. And it wasn't long after that that I left.'

'So when did you see her last, Sally?'

'I told you, three years ago, when I left the Crow's Nest. I ain't seen either of them since.'

'What about Marty Keller? Seen him?'

'Gawd.' She lowered her mug to the table, and Kathy noticed the tremble in her hand. 'Is he involved in this?'

'Sammy believes so.'

'But Keller's still inside, ain't he?'

Brock shook his head, and Sally pressed her lips tight, face pale.

'Then that must be it. After all this time! Can't they leave us alone? Poor Sammy . . .'

'Poor Eva,' Brock said. He turned to Kathy. 'Anything else?'

'I'd like to hear how Sammy and Eva got together,' she said.

Brock glanced at his watch.

'How did that happen, Sally?' Kathy prompted.

'I think he was as surprised as anyone.' The little woman bit her lip. 'Well, like I said, he'd lost Gordon, then Brenda, and that had changed him. He'd depended on her so much, see, all those years. He didn't say much, but I could tell he was lost. He was a great one for believing in luck, and I think he'd decided that his luck had run out. He closed himself off, all stiff and hard. Hard as ice.

'Then one spring, 1993 it was, he went off on business to the Continent, Portugal, all stiff-faced, complaining of his indigestion as usual. A week later he came back, and he was a different man. He'd got a bit of a tan, and there wasn't no more talk of his tummy no more. I said, "What's come over you, then?" And he gave me a hug, and said, "Sally, I feel as if I've just woken up after a long sleep. For the first time in years I can smell the roses." Then he went out into the garden, which he'd hardly set foot in since Brenda passed away, and he wandered round, looking at the flowers. That evening I remember he cut up some apples for the deer that come down from the woods.'

'Did he tell you it was a woman?'

She snorted. 'He didn't need to tell me that. He went up to town and bought himself a whole new wardrobe, and had his hair trimmed. He went to see his doctor, and joined the fitness club. Two weeks later he was off again, back to sunny Portugal, with a new set of travel luggage full of mysterious, expensive-looking little packages that he didn't discuss with me.'

'Just like that? And the romance went according to plan?'

'I don't know that it did, not at first. He came back after that second trip looking out of sorts. He didn't seem miserable exactly, more serious, like, and determined, as if he'd realised that what he had in mind wasn't going to be so easy as he'd first thought.'

'But he didn't talk to you about it? He knew, I suppose, that you wouldn't approve, her being a teenager . . .'

Sally took a sip of her tea and pointedly didn't reply.

'So what did he do then?'

She pondered. 'He went back . . . No, hang on. First he sent Ronnie Wilkes over.'

'Wilkes?' Kathy said.

'Yes, you probably know him, Mr Brock. Sammy uses him to do odd jobs.'

'What odd job did he do in Portugal?'

'I've no idea. I just remember him at the house. He was around a lot then, planning things with Sammy. Then Sammy went over himself a couple of times, and next thing he told me was that he was getting married to a Portuguese princess, and I had to sound surprised – well, I was surprised about the princess bit.'

'And you hadn't met her? She hadn't come over to see him here, to see his house?'

'No. I never saw 'er until October, when they came back from their honeymoon.'

'Did you realise that she was going to be quite so young?'

'He'd kept good and quiet about that. When she stepped out the car I thought at first she must be a stepdaughter or something. I was looking past her, looking for the wife, until Sammy told me this was her.'

Kathy smiled. 'What was she like?'

Sally considered, then spoke carefully. 'She was fresh and excited, like a kid. Well, she *was* a kid. Sammy looked embarrassed and ecstatic both at the same time. She gave me a kiss, I remember, and some presents because I hadn't been invited to the wedding.' Kathy noticed the way Sally's eyes narrowed as she said this. 'French perfume, and some small pieces of jewellery. Modern, like. Not really my taste, but the thought was there.'

'She was young enough to be his granddaughter, Sally. It must have been very awkward for you.'

She conceded a nod. 'We were careful with each other, so as

not to cause offence. She could see, when she changed things – the curtains in the dining room that Brenda had chosen – she could see that I . . .'

'Didn't approve?'

'Felt sad. It wasn't for me to *approve*. But I did find it difficult. Some of the things she tossed out we'd 'ad for thirty years.'

We'd had, Kathy thought. She sensed Brock becoming impatient, and she told him that she was finished. She wondered what they could have hoped to get from Sally. An admission that Eva visited her on her trips up to London? It seemed unlikely.

They returned to the front of the shop. The rain had subsided to a light shower, the sun struggling to glimmer through breaks in the cloud cover.

'Let us know if you see any sign of Keller, or anything else unusual, Sally.'

'I'll keep the carving knife handy, Mr Brock.'

'A security alarm would be better. And a mobile phone.'

'I've got those too, don't you worry.'

They drove for a while in silence, then Kathy said, 'What did Brenda Starling die of, Brock? Keller said something about Sammy's wives being accident-prone? What did he mean?'

Brock didn't reply for a whole block. Then he stirred in his seat and sat more upright, as if he'd come to a decision about something.

'She killed herself, Kathy,' he growled. Another block passed before he went on. 'She walked down to Farnham station one summer evening, while Sammy was playing with his stamps, and laid her head on the track.'

'God . . .' A woman with a pram stepped out on to a pedestrian crossing ahead of them and Kathy forced her concentration back to the road, so that at first she didn't register what he said next. Then she pulled to a stop and asked him to repeat it.

'I said, her head was destroyed.'

Five minutes later he stunned her a second time. She had crossed Westminster Bridge and manoeuvred through the traffic streams gyrating around Parliament Square, and then spotted a likely parking space on the approach to Queen Anne's Gate when he said, 'I think it would be best if you came off this case, Kathy.'

'What?' She was so surprised that she responded as if it were a joke. 'I thought you needed my unique blend of female rationality . . .'

'I made a mistake,' he interrupted quietly, and she realised that he wasn't joking.

She gripped the wheel tightly as she reverse parked, waiting for more, but none came. 'Have I done something wrong?'

He frowned at his hands, balled into fists on his lap. 'Nothing like that. It's just a matter of judgement. I haven't been . . .' he searched for the right word '. . . comfortable, about you working on this case, from the beginning. Let's just leave it at that. I think you'd be more suited to some other area.' He turned away from her, looking out of the side window.

She flushed. More suited to some other area? She repeated his words in her head a couple of times, trying to extract some additional meaning from them. 'You have another case you want me to switch to?'

'Another area,' he repeated. 'SO6 have been looking for bright young women.'

'Fraud Squad! Brock, I –'

'It's not a debate, Kathy;' he said, opening the door. 'I've already arranged it. You're to report to Superintendent Mc-Larren in the morning.'

11

A Parting of Ways

As she followed him along the twisting corridor through the offices at Queen Anne's Gate Kathy felt numb. She'd never been sacked before, and the building heightened her sense of displacement. It was so unlike the usual police office building, so particular to Brock and his team, that its eccentricity emphasised the sudden fact that apparently she no longer had a place here. She knew Brock meant it when he had said it wasn't a matter for debate – she'd seen him do this once before, to another DS who'd let him down. The man had vanished without a word to anyone, his desk swept clear of its neat rows of family photographs. But he had deserved it: he had made a mistake. What mistake had she made?

Bren and Leon Desai were waiting outside Brock's room, talking quietly together. They continued their conversation as Brock unlocked his door, strode in and threw his wet jacket aside over a chair. They hardly acknowledged Kathy hanging back.

'What's the story, then, Leon?' Brock said, sitting heavily behind his desk and waving them to chairs. He rubbed a hand across his face, as if trying to wipe something away. 'You've got some results already?'

Desai seemed even calmer and more collected than usual. Kathy envied him his composure as she tried to decide, as feeling returned gradually to her, whether she felt more anger or despair.

'We're hopeful that the cardboard box will tell us something. It seems to be a distinctive type. They're looking into that now.'

'Yes? That all? What about the courier envelope?'

Desai hesitated. He drew himself more upright in his chair, an attaché case across his knee, and said, 'Yes, the envelope. It was brought into the company's dispatch centre at Lambeth at eight this morning by a man, but we can't get a useful description. As you know, the envelope contained the Canada Cover and a note, cut into four pieces – the former, not the latter.'

The latter, Kathy thought, feeling a niggle of resentment now against Desai and his immaculate English. My career just collapsed without warning, and he's distinguishing between the former and the latter.

Desai opened the case and took out two photographs, which he handed to Brock.

'As you can see, the note is like the others.'

Brock read its message out loud:

"THIS MADE ME VERY ANGRY SAMMY."

'What's that supposed to mean?' he asked.

'We think he's referring to the Canada Cover.'

Brock frowned, staring at the second photograph. 'Yes, but why? He's making a protest against money? I don't understand. Why does a million-pound stamp make him very angry?'

Desai cleared his throat. 'It seems that it isn't the right stamp.'

'Eh?'

'The fellows in the lab believe that that cover isn't the one that was auctioned yesterday.'

'A forgery, you mean? Sammy gave them a copy?'

Desai nodded. 'Actually, they believe that cover is the copy that the lab made for us.'

Brock sat forward in his chair and stared intently at him for a moment before he said, very deliberately, 'That's not possible, is it, Leon?'

Desai lowered his eyes but didn't reply. The room was very silent.

Eventually Bren said, 'Hang on. I thought you blokes told me yesterday that we didn't use that lab copy?'

Desai stayed silent. He sat apparently unperturbed, eyes lowered. Then Kathy noticed the tip of a pink tongue appear briefly between his brown lips, and for the first time wondered how composed he really was.

'Kathy? You were there, weren't you?' Bren asked her, but she continued watching Desai and said nothing. She remembered clearly Brock putting the envelope containing the laboratory copy cover into his jacket pocket after they had decided not to use it. It was the same jacket now lying, wet, across the chair in the corner. She wondered where Desai was going with this.

'Leon,' Brock said at last, an edge to his voice, 'why don't you tell Bren what's on your mind? You're the one playing detective.'

Kathy noticed Desai give the slightest flinch at the word 'playing'. As laboratory liaison officer, he wasn't really one of them, a 'real' detective.

'The lab fellows are quite convinced that this is their copy,' he replied, voice calm and evenly modulated. 'They have a list of fifteen points of identification. If necessary we could get Dr Waverley, Cabot's expert, to confirm it. He worked on the copy too.' He met Brock's eyes. 'That's really all that I have, Brock. How it could have happened . . . I've no idea. But I thought you should know.'

'In front of witnesses, Leon?' Brock asked softly.

Desai met his eyes and said carefully, 'The two fellows from SO10 were at the lab when the document people came up with this. They seemed extremely interested. I thought we . . . you should be careful.'

Brock considered him thoughtfully. 'I see. Thank you, Leon. Gallows and Heath, eh? Who invited them, I wonder? I thought they'd packed up and moved on.'

'I don't know that anyone invited them,' Desai said. 'I have the impression that they are very unhappy about what happened yesterday. They seem to be digging around.'

'I can confirm that,' Bren added. 'Central File Office were on to us this morning for a file on Sammy Starling that we're holding. SO10 had requested it, apparently.'

'And they asked me more questions this morning about how I came to be at the Canonbury flat when Starling returned there from Heathrow,' Desai said. 'At the lab I got the impression they weren't too impressed that I was working on a Sunday. They seemed to expect to have the place to themselves.'

Brock scratched his beard, thinking, then got slowly to his feet and walked over to the window. The rainclouds had cleared, leaving the city sodden under the low evening sun. 'I came back here after Sammy and Kathy left for Farnham yesterday afternoon,' he said softly, as if to himself. 'I took the envelope with the copy cover out of my jacket pocket and put it in the safe over there.' He pointed to a dark-green government-issue safe standing in a corner of the room. It was the size of a small two-drawer filing cabinet, and an unstable-looking heap of documents stood on top of it. 'As far as I know, it's still there.'

He went over to the safe and crouched in front of it, turned the combination lock on the front and swung the door open. He reached inside and straightened up again, holding a white envelope which he handed to Desai without a word. Then he went back behind his desk and sat down, passing a hand across his eyes as if he had many other things on his mind.

Desai opened the envelope slowly, his reluctance apparent. And now Kathy felt sorry for him. It was as if Brock were forcing him into the role of Judas Iscariot. It seemed that she might not be the only one heading for the outer darkness.

From inside the envelope Desai brought out the fold of protective cardboard and opened it cautiously. There was nothing inside.

'All right, Detective Desai,' Brock's voice seemed a long way away. 'What do you make of that? Give us the benefit of your deductive powers, why don't you?'

Desai cleared his throat again and the pink tongue made a brief reappearance before he spoke. 'The inference is that Sammy Starling handed over the copy cover for his wife's ransom, and the kidnappers realised that what they'd been given wasn't the real thing. So they cut off her head as punishment.'

'Go on.'

'If that was the case, there are two possibilities.' His voice had hardened imperceptibly in response to Brock's needling. 'The first is that Starling knew what he was doing, and did it deliberately.'

'How?' Brock insisted. 'How could he have done it?'

'He was in the upstairs room at Cabot's with you for about half an hour from the time you pocketed the envelope to when he went out with Gallows and Heath. Then after he left the auction room he came back upstairs and was again in the same room with you until he left to catch the taxi to Heathrow.'

'The room had that overactive air-conditioning, remember?' Brock said quietly. 'Even with everyone there it was cool. I kept my jacket on all the time, didn't I?'

Desai nodded.

'Sammy Starling has been many things,' Brock continued, 'but never a pickpocket, to my knowledge. Is it credible that he could have lifted that envelope from my inside pocket, removed the cover from the cardboard sleeve, then replaced the envelope in my pocket, without me or anyone else noticing?'

Desai hesitated, then said, 'Probably not.'

'What's the alternative?'

'Someone else did it, and gave him the cover to substitute later, in the taxi maybe.'

'The same objection applies,' Brock insisted. 'Only one other person in that room really had the opportunity to do what you're describing, Leon. Me.'

Desai lowered his eyes and said nothing.

'Well? Am I right?'

He nodded.

'But you said there were two possibilities. One, that Sammy knew what he was doing. What was the second?'

'That he didn't.' Leon looked at Brock unhappily. 'I'm only putting forward a train of logic, sir.'

'Don't call me sir. This isn't the bloody Army, Leon. So where does this train of impeccable logic take us?'

'Someone might have switched the two covers during the half-hour or so that they were both in the same room, between the time the authentic auction cover was brought upstairs after Sammy had successfully bid for it, and the time he left for Heathrow. He then went ahead with the ransom handover, not realising that what he had was the copy.'

'And again, who was this someone?' Brock demanded.

But Desai had had enough. He shook his head and shot a glance at Bren, seeking support. Bren looked deeply worried.

'I wasn't there,' he began cautiously, 'but isn't it possible that someone could have lifted that cover from your jacket somewhere else, Brock? Did you go somewhere that wasn't air-conditioned, perhaps? I don't know, the gents or something.' He saw the look on Brock's face, and the suggestion died on his lips. 'Well,' he said instead. 'What do we do, then?'

'*We* go home and get a bath and a drink and something to eat,' Brock said wearily. '*Detective Desai* writes a report of the conversation we've just had, and in the morning he gives it to Commander Sharpe.' He got to his feet and walked round his desk, picked up his jacket and made for the door. He stopped as he passed Desai and said, 'Do you want to search me, Leon? Make sure it isn't about my person?'

Desai looked at the floor.

'Don't worry, old son,' Brock said, gazing down at his bowed head sadly. 'It's been a bad day for us all.' He slung the jacket over his shoulder and walked out, leaving the three of them sitting in silence in his office.

Bren was the first to move. He stood up, went to the door and looked down the empty corridor. Then he let out his breath in a long sigh. 'What the bloody hell's got into the old man? I've never seen him like that before.'

Desai looked up and said in a low voice, 'He shouldn't have said that, about me wanting to search him.'

'No,' Kathy said. 'He shouldn't have said that.'

They both looked at her, almost as if they hadn't been conscious of her being there before.

'Well, what do you reckon, Kathy?' Bren said, with a hint of accusation in his voice. 'You were there yesterday, right alongside him. You didn't seem to have much to say.'

'No, I didn't. I was still in shock, actually, Bren. Just as we arrived here he suddenly told me he wanted me out of the team. He said he was transferring me to Jock McLarren in Fraud, as of first thing tomorrow.'

'What?' A look of dismay filled Bren's face. 'Jesus! Why?'

'I think the term he used was "a matter of judgement".

Apparently he hasn't been happy with me being on this case from the beginning.'

'What the hell's got into him?' Bren's face expressed appalled incomprehension, as if something absolutely dependable, like Christmas or the BBC *Six o'Clock News*, had failed to occur.

Desai, who'd had longer to think about this, said quietly, 'Maybe it's exactly what he said to Kathy – a question of his judgement. Perhaps he's lost it.'

Bren stared at him in disbelief. 'I don't buy that.'

'A breakdown, then.'

'Breakdown? Brock?' Bren looked scandalised.

'It can happen to anyone,' Desai said. 'It's just a matter of applying enough pressure for long enough. Everyone buckles eventually.'

'What form, exactly, do you think this breakdown may have taken, Leon?' Kathy asked.

He avoided her eye. 'There are some parallels between Brock and Starling, one could say. I mean, their careers have run in parallel to an extent. On the one hand Starling, a man who's been a thief and a parasite all his life, and on the other Brock, a faithful servant of the public good. It would be very hard – impossible, I would say – for Brock not to think that Starling has no moral right to all that money he's putting up for his wife's ransom, no more than the kidnappers have a right to it.'

'You're saying you believe he *did* steal the cover?' Bren's outrage was apparent in his eyes, although he kept his voice even.

'I think it's possible, yes,' Desai said.

'That, Leon old chum, is the most preposterous thing I've heard coming from you yet.' Bren's voice was low and dangerous. 'And if I hear you spreading it about, I'll rip your bloody tongue out. Have you understood so little in the time you've been working with us?'

'What's your solution, then, Bren?' Desai said coolly.

'Someone picked his pocket.'

'That just isn't credible, Bren. Brock said it. What about you, Kathy?'

Kathy was looking around the room, as if she might spot some clue as to what was going on inside Brock's head. It was simply furnished, yet chaotically untidy within confined areas, as if someone who yearned for clean and Spartan surroundings was constantly battling with inundations of paper. There appeared to be no personal mementoes from his years in the force – no group photographs, no framed certificates, no souvenirs or trophies. No evidence at all of the journey from Tottenham to here that she could see.

'Bren's right,' she said at last. 'It's unthinkable that Brock would steal the stamp . . . And if he had, we wouldn't have known about it.'

Bren gave a short laugh, his anger fading as quickly as it had come.

Desai looked unconvinced. 'So?'

'I don't know,' Kathy said. 'And it doesn't look as if I'm going to be able to help you find out either.'

'I'll talk to him in the morning,' Bren said. 'I'll get him to change his mind abut transferring you.'

'Thanks,' Kathy said, without conviction.

On her way out, she stopped at her pigeonhole in the general office. There was the latest copy of the *Job*, an invitation from the Christian Police Association to attend their next meeting, a call for nominations for the Equal Opportunities Committee, and a typed note from Brock's secretary Dot.

Kathy,

   DCI Brock has asked me to pass on to you the following. You are to be reassigned to Department SO6 as from midnight Sunday 13 July. Please report at 9.00 a.m. on Monday to the office of Superintendent McLarren, level 5, Cobalt Square.
   Paperwork will follow.
   Best wishes and good luck,
   Dot.

Kathy walked slowly through the deserted Westminster streets, under a sky darkening once more beneath a new belt of thunderclouds. She tried to shake off the numbness that she had felt in Queen Anne's Gate. It was the numbness of reality suspended, of watching the familiar going haywire all around her, and she tried to ease it off carefully, for it could easily be replaced with anger or self-pity. She could feel both working just beneath the surface, growing on the painful knowledge that she had been discarded, without proper reason or explanation, on the judgement of the one person whose judgement she had most trusted. But neither anger nor self-pity would help her understand what was going on.

The thought of finding food, of returning to her empty room, made her heart sink. She imagined Helen Fitzpatrick in her snug cottage deep in the woods, cooking something for her dogs, perhaps, discussing with her husband the awful events of the day for the tenth or twentieth time, each debriefing the other companionably over a glass of sherry.

She stopped, feeling the spit of the first fat raindrops, and frowned at her pale reflection in the glass of a darkened shop window.

'No life, no home,' she said out loud. It took her a moment to recall that the words were Marianna's, describing Eva.

She wondered vaguely if she was only now reacting to Eva's shocking death. Delayed shock. She turned the idea over slowly, without enthusiasm.

Paperwork will follow.

It didn't make her angry. Just depressed. She recalled the odd way Brock had looked at her in the car. Had he really lost confidence in her?

She was conscious of a car approaching down the deserted street. She heard it slowing as it drew near, and saw the out-line of its reflection gliding to a halt in the shop window, but didn't turn round. It wasn't Brock's car. What now? she thought. A mugging would round off a perfect day. The car door clicked open. A dark figure slowly approached her in the reflection, the face dark, as if masked, but still she didn't turn round.

'Kathy?'

She took a deep breath and turned. 'Hello, Leon,' she said brightly.

'You all right?'

'Of course.'

'Since when have you been interested in surgical appliances?'

She turned and looked back at the shop window, seeing its

contents dimly for the first time. She smiled at him. 'I was just thinking. Something struck me.'

'Anything that'll help us?'

She realised that he must be feeling as exposed as herself, and felt guilty at being so self-engrossed. 'Probably not. You off home?'

'Not really. Couldn't face it right away, not after that.'

She was interested that he was reacting in the same way as herself.

'I thought I might get a drink somewhere,' he said. 'You don't fancy one, do you?'

Yes, she thought, and heard herself say, 'No, I don't think so.'

'Can I run you anywhere, then?'

'I'm just going to the tube station.'

'Well . . .' Her manner made him uncertain. 'Get in, if you like.'

She got in.

'Which station?' he asked.

She didn't answer at first, then said, 'Can I change my mind about the drink?'

He drove across the river. They were somewhere in Lambeth, she realised, but she had never been in the street before, lined with seedy commercial and light-industrial premises with high-rise flats looming behind. She'd never seen the little corner pub before either.

'It has the advantage that coppers don't use it,' Desai said, as he opened the door into a small, quiet and comfortingly subdued bar, and later, when he had bought them drinks, he explained that he sometimes came here from the forensic science labs, which weren't far away in Lambeth Road.

They drank in silence for a while, then Desai said, 'Do you want to talk about it?'

Kathy roused herself. 'If you like.'

'You look worn out. Are you sure?' He sounded calm and concerned, the way she would like to sound. She thought how very black and sleek his hair was, like a cat's, and wondered what it would feel like to stroke.

'No, no. I'm fine.' She took another sip of the brandy and nodded emphatically.

'So Brock really did fire you, did he?'

She took the note from Dot from her jacket pocket and handed it to him without a word.

'Well, well.' Desai seemed impressed.

'Didn't you believe me?' she asked.

'I . . .' He hesitated. 'All sorts of possibilities have been going through my mind in the last couple of hours, Kathy. Sorry.'

'Like what?'

'Like you were part of whatever game Brock's playing.'

Kathy frowned deeply at her glass.

'I'm sorry,' Desai repeated. 'I'm completely in the dark. And I thought, well . . .'

Again he hesitated, and again Kathy prodded him. 'You thought what?'

'Well, it's been suggested . . . that you and he have something going.'

Kathy looked at him in astonishment. 'Suggested by whom?'

He looked embarrassed. 'No one important.' He waved a hand. 'Forget it.'

'Not by Bren . . . or Dot?'

'No, no. No one like that. No one at Queen Anne's Gate. But you just seemed very close, the two of you, and I suppose people speculate, more out of mischief than anything, and it isn't as if I know you that well.'

'I thought we knew each other, Leon,' Kathy said.

She met his eyes: they were disconcertingly mesmeric, dark, intent and unblinking. Then, finally, he smiled, ruefully perhaps, regretfully. 'Not really,' he said quietly, and turned his attention to his drink. 'It's been a rough day,' he went on. 'For you especially. Did you get any lunch?'

'No.' She realised that that was probably why the brandy seemed to be working so fast.

'We could get some food here. It isn't too bad.' He offered the idea cautiously, then half withdrew it. 'Sorry. You've probably got plans.'

'No, that sounds fine. Maybe just a sandwich or something.'

He went back to the bar. He returned with two more brandies, which he set down on the table, and then took a mobile phone from the pocket of his black leather jacket. 'Excuse me a moment.'

He walked over to the open door of the bar and stood there with his back to her, making a call. Her heart sank as she watched him. He's cancelling some other arrangement, she thought, and had a vivid picture of a pretty Indian wife and several children, beautiful girls perhaps, dark-eyed like their father, waiting patiently for him to come home.

When he returned to his seat facing her she said, hearing the edge in her voice, 'I hope you're not cancelling something on my account, Leon. I'd just as soon get back.'

'No, it's OK,' he said. 'I really couldn't face the family hearth right now. I'd much rather talk things over with you.'

His coolness shocked her. 'Don't they mind you being away all weekend?'

'They're used to it. Sometimes, if I'm working late at the lab, or just don't want to go home, I stay here. There's a couple of rooms upstairs here. I'm one of their regulars – they give me a good rate.'

'I see. Very convenient.'

'Yes.'

She studied him as he reached for his drink. This was a side of Desai she hadn't seen before. She was half-way through her second brandy, and was beginning to feel less fragile, able to take a more detached and expansive view of the world. 'Tell me, if you don't mind me asking, what exactly do you say to her? Do you actually tell her that you can't face coming home?'

He smiled. 'No. She wouldn't appreciate that. And I didn't say I'm having a drink with an attractive blonde from work, either. That would give her ideas.'

'I'm sure it would.' She tossed back the end of the drink and clenched her teeth. 'What's her name?'

'Her name?' He looked at her as if this was an odd question. 'Indira,' he said, off-hand.

'And how many children does Indira have?'

'Two,' he said. He looked as if he didn't want to pursue this and made to get up. 'I'll get you another brandy.'

'No, you won't,' she said firmly. 'My round.' She got to her

174

feet and had to make an effort to steady herself as she walked to the bar.

When she returned she said, 'Is she very pretty?'

'Who?'

'Who? Indira, of course.'

He looked perplexed, then said, 'I suppose she was once. Now you'd call her, what? Homely, I suppose.'

Kathy's eyes widened. 'God, Leon!' she breathed. 'That's a hell of a way to talk about your wife.'

Desai looked at her without expression, then said, 'Indira is my mother, Kathy. I spoke to my mother.'

For a moment Kathy imagined an extended Indian family, three generations or more, and thought, This is getting worse. Then he added cautiously, 'I live in Barnet, with my mum and dad. I don't have a wife.'

Kathy was saved from making a reply by a large plate of sandwiches which appeared in front of her in the centre of the table.

'Do you want mustard, dear?' the woman asked. She had a rich, hoarse, smoker's voice. An actress's voice.

'Er . . .' Desai looked at Kathy, who shook her head.

'Well, yes.' He sat back with one of the sandwiches in his hand and regarded Kathy gravely. 'It's been a sod of a day. I'm just the messenger, so I suppose it's understandable him giving me a hard time. But that doesn't explain his dropping you, does it?'

Kathy was grateful for his change of subject. 'No.' She reached for a sandwich.

'You were working closely with him. Didn't you notice a change in his manner at some point?'

She thought about that. 'After the autopsy, I think. He seemed quite preoccupied after that . . . didn't seem to want to talk about it. I thought he was upset by seeing her like that.'

She met his eyes again. 'It was upsetting, Leon. Even when you've seen it all a hundred times before. I felt we almost knew her. And the beheading. It's so . . .' She searched for the word. 'Abrupt?' That wasn't quite it. Not strong enough. 'Brutal.'

'But the autopsy was only this afternoon, wasn't it? And yet when you got back to the office your transfer had already been arranged.'

'Yes, you're right. Before that we watched Bren interviewing Keller, and I thought then that Brock seemed off-colour.'

'You mean because of what had happened to Eva? Wasn't he concentrating on the interview?'

'No, no, he seemed completely focused on Keller. I think that was what seemed to disturb him. He seemed shocked at how much Keller had changed.'

'And he was the one who put Keller away in the first place.'

'Yes.'

'Well, what do you think it was? Guilt?'

'I don't think so,' Kathy said slowly. 'Why should he feel guilty about putting Keller away?'

'Do you think Brock believes Keller killed Eva?'

'I don't know.'

'What about Sammy?'

'I don't think Sammy killed her.'

'I'm not asking what *you* think,' Desai said quietly. 'I'm asking what *Brock* thinks.'

'I said I don't know,' Kathy said, beginning to feel exasperated with his persistence. She really didn't want to go on talking and thinking about this. 'He interviewed Sammy this morning. I watched part of it. Sammy seemed very calm, I thought, considering what he'd just seen. He admitted to stopping on the way back from the airport, to look for Eva at the Cinema Hollywood.'

'Is that plausible?'

'I don't know. Brock seemed to accept it.'

'Anything else?'

Kathy frowned as she tried to remember. 'Sammy said an odd thing at the end, as he was leaving. Something about how this sort of thing could strike anyone, at any time, even Brock.'

'Was it a threat?'

'It didn't seem like that.'

'But that could be it.'

'What?'

'Well . . . suppose Sammy said something — that, or something else — something that jarred with Brock. He had relied on Sammy's evidence to nail Keller, hadn't he? Suppose he heard something that made him doubt Sammy. And then he watched

Keller being interviewed and realised how much he'd damaged Keller, putting him away.'

Kathy looked sharply at him. 'That's a bit fanciful, Leon. Totally fanciful.'

'He's already been through one traumatic case with Sammy, and now it's happening again. If he begins to think that Sammy is unreliable in this one, then what does that say about the earlier one?'

Kathy remembered Brock's words in the taxi right at the beginning, after they'd first met Sammy: 'This is not a case for us.'

She sighed, 'I don't know, and right now I don't really want to think about it.'

'I think you must,' he persisted.

She glared at him over her sandwich. 'Leon, having a quiet conversation with you sometimes feels pretty much like being dissected.'

He considered her, calmly and sympathetically. 'Interesting choice of words. Do you identify very much with Eva?'

'What? No! Of course not.' The sudden juxtaposition of Eva's severed head with her ham sandwich made Kathy choke. 'Anyway, where does this take us?'

'I don't know. I'm just trying to see it from Brock's point of view. Maybe he's trying to protect you. That's what you'd like to think, isn't it?'

Kathy turned away, trying to summon up something really scathing to silence him with, and was struck by a figure standing at the bar, a girl in a tight black leather skirt and long matching boots, with a spectacular shock of red hair. 'Is she on the game?' she said.

He turned and looked. 'No. She's a bloke, actually. They like to come here.' He jerked his head towards the adjoining bar, at a group in stiletto heels and extravagant hairstyles.

'They're all blokes, are they?' she said, a smile spreading over her face. 'That's interesting.'

'What is?'

'Nothing.'

'What do you mean?'

Kathy looked at him nonchalantly, lifting her glass to her lips.

'I suppose that's what you meant earlier, about us not knowing much about each other.'

'Eh?'

'Well, come on, Leon. You're very knowledgeable about women's underwear, you hang out in transvestite bars, and you live with your mum. I mean, that's interesting.'

She admired his composure. 'Circumstantial evidence,' he murmured, smiling at her as if what she'd said was rather endearing.

When they'd finished the sandwiches, he offered to drive her home on his way back to Barnet. The rain was coming down hard now, and they ran to the car. Along the way he told her about his family, forced out of Uganda during Idi Amin's expulsion of Asians in 1972. 'We got out with two suitcases and a kind of woven bag,' he said. 'Everything else was left behind. I have this very clear picture in my mind of my parents sitting on the bags on a dusty street in the blazing sun, waiting for a taxi to the airport. They are small people, you see, and they were sitting on these bulging bags to try to make sure that nobody stole them. Despite the humiliation of their situation, they were very calm and dignified, and somehow managed to look as if they weren't in the least troubled.'

'That's where you get it from, then,' Kathy said. 'You're very calm.'

'I didn't feel it this afternoon. You've lost both your parents, haven't you?'

'How did you know that?'

'It came up during the Angela Hannaford case.'

For a second the name took Kathy back to the place where she had first met Desai, in Angela Hannaford's bedroom, the girl's blood sprayed across the walls, and him ordering her to clear out before she contaminated his crime scene.

'How did it come up?' she said.

'I think it was Alex Nicholson who mentioned it. You remember her?'

'The forensic psychologist, yes. How come I find out from you that everyone's talking about my private life behind my back?' She heard herself sounding snappy, and realised it was because she'd imagined at the time that Desai was interested in

Dr Nicholson. She took a deep breath and tried to clear her head, feeling stupid.

'Because you're interesting,' she heard him say, above the noise of the wipers and tyres in the heavy rain.

He pulled in as close as he could to the front door of her block in Finchley. The evening was prematurely dark and sodden and miserable, and Kathy paused before getting out of the car. Then she felt his hand on her arm. She turned to face him.

'You OK?' he asked softly.

She had a sudden overwhelming urge to ask him to come in with her, and keep her company. And for the second time that evening her mouth said the opposite of what she wanted. 'I'm just fine, Leon,' she said, with a smile. 'Take care.' She reached across quickly and brushed a kiss across his cheek, then turned and ran.

Later, lying alone in her bed, she worked out why she had done this. The image of Helen Fitzpatrick in her cottage had returned to her, and she decided that she had wanted Leon Desai as a comfort, like Helen's dogs or Sammy's stamps, something absorbing and sympathetic and, above all, distracting from the bleak, dark night on the other side of the window-pane. But Eva had gone out into that dark night and never returned, and she depended on Kathy to find out what had happened to her.

That made no sense, of course, for Brock had forestalled that possibility.

Soon after dusk, around 10.30 p.m., a car drove along Matcham High Street in South London and came to a stop fifty yards short of an archway leading into a cobbled service courtyard behind the shops. Two men got out and walked into this courtyard. A horse-chestnut tree loomed dark and heavy with foliage on the far side, and they made their way past it to a small lane, on one side of which stood a terrace of two- and three-storey houses. They stopped at the first front door and knocked. The house was in darkness, and the sound of the brass door knocker echoed inside without response. They tried again, then returned across the courtyard to the archway and back to their car, where they waited for a further hour, watching. No one went through the archway during this period. Finally one of the watchers made a call on the car radio. The driver restarted the engine and they drove away. When their tail lights had disappeared, a bulky shadow emerged from the bus shelter, which stood twenty yards beyond where they had parked, walked to the archway and through into the courtyard.

Brock waited for some minutes in the darkness beneath the horse-chestnut, watching for other visitors, before going to his front door and letting himself in. He didn't put on any lights when he got inside, but went upstairs and ran a bath, poured a large glass of whisky, and took the remains of a gourmet steak and kidney pie from the fridge. When he had finished all three in the darkness, he went to bed and fell asleep. Later he started awake, sweating, with a dream vivid in his mind of being smothered by someone else's scalp and hair, pulled forward over his face.

12

Cobalt Square

Cobalt Square had been intended as the doom of Queen Anne's Gate and all the other scruffy little outposts in the bureaucratic diaspora of Scotland Yard. When it was completed in 1995, it had brought a thousand civilian and police staff together within the one block, emptying Drummond Gate, Bessborough Street, Jubilee House, Mandela Way and a dozen smaller headquarters buildings and annexes in the force's biggest move since New Scotland Yard vacated Norman Shaw's buildings in Westminster. Located not far from the south end of Vauxhall Bridge, where the MI6 building stands, it is naturally seen as part of some sort of nexus of the forces of law and order. Less flashy in its post-modernism than the MI6 building, more sober in its brick-framed glass curtain walling, Sally Malone would have pointed out that this was the two-bob side of the block, as against the half-crown riverbank site of the other building. Taken with its size, this more sombre expression of the Met complex makes the security services building seem almost frivolous. Approaching the front door of Cobalt Square, Kathy wondered what bureaucratic amnesia had allowed Brock's team to remain free at Queen Anne's Gate for so long.

Superintendent McLarren was not available when Kathy arrived at level five. After half an hour, she was told to get herself a cup of coffee and return at ten. This was repeated several times. Towards noon, just as she was wondering if she was doomed to spend the rest of her life like this, wandering the corridors of Cobalt Square, she was told that Superintendent McLarren had returned and would see her immediately.

A tall, wiry Scotsman with a sharp beak of a nose and unexpectedly luxuriant eyebrows, McLarren was in good spirits. 'Come in, lassie, come in!' He waved her into his office and told her to sit.

'We'll go through and join the others in a minute, but I wanted a wee word with you first, Kathy. Welcome aboard!' He thrust his hand at her. It was bony and the grip hard.

'Thank you, sir.' She knew that he liked to be referred to as Old Jock in his absence, and sir to his face.

'You only just made it, you know.' He gave her a grim smile and perched himself on the edge of his desk.

'Really?'

'Oh, yes. So . . .' He stared at her with a gleam in his eye, as if he were expecting her to say something heartfelt.

'Thank you for having me, sir,' she said, dutifully.

'Yes, yes.' He continued fixing her with the enigmatic gleam. He wanted more. 'Do you know what I'm thinking, Kathy?'

'No, sir.'

'I'm thinking, Kathy, that I'm looking at a shipwrecked sailor who's been pulled into the lifeboat from the stormy seas, but who doesn't yet understand what a near thing it was.'

Kathy tried not to look surprised. 'Really, sir?'

'Aye, really. Is there anything you regret, tell me, about coming aboard?'

Kathy found it hard to find something appropriate to say. 'Er . . . Well, I suppose I regret coming off the Starling case, sir. It was . . . interesting.'

'Oh, fascinating indeed! Kidnapping, decapitation and philately! What could be more fascinating!' He chuckled. 'Well, then, if that's all, then you regret nothing.'

'I'm sorry, I don't follow.'

He leaned forward. 'I am now the investigating officer in the Starling case, lass. That is what we shall be working on together.' He peered closely at her reaction from under his lush eyebrows, and when her face showed none, he added, 'Brock is off the case, and his team likewise. That's what I meant about you being only just in time. Twenty-four hours later and you wouldn't have been allowed within missile range of the Starling case.'

'Brock is off the case, sir?'

'DCI Brock is suspended from duty, Kathy, as of midnight, last night. The rest of his team is to have nothing further to do with the case. But, by good fortune, you have scrambled on board to provide us with some measure of continuity. Now do you understand my metaphor, Kathy, of the shipwrecked sailor?'

'Yes, thank you, sir. I do understand.'

He mistook her smile as a sign of her gratitude at having been saved, rather than relief that Brock's actions might, after all, have been explicable.

'But why is DCI Brock suspended, sir? Surely no one believes . . . Is it the missing stamp?'

'It's not really for me to comment, lassie, except to say that it was more than one thing.'

'More than one?'

McLarren tapped his fingers on the edge of the desk. 'I'm talking about the whole bungled kidnapping and ransom operation. Our friends in Crime Operations Group are taking a very dim view of it all.'

'SO10 are going to be working with you now, sir?'

McLarren looked particularly pleased with himself at this question. 'Indeed not. Crime Operations Group have gracefully conceded that this one is entirely ours.'

'But surely, extortion, kidnapping, that's their field, isn't it?'

'I was able to convince them that the Starling case is not, essentially, about extortion, kidnapping, decapitation or murder. It is about postage stamps.'

'Postage stamps?'

'More particularly about the forgery of rare postage stamps, which is fraud, our bailiwick.'

Kathy looked astounded.

'You doubt it, Kathy?'

'Well, I had no idea . . .'

'Really?' He looked carefully at her. 'Brock didn't mention the forged Chalon Heads to you?'

'No.' Once again Kathy felt the ground giving way under her, just when she thought she had found some basis for understanding Brock's actions.

'The ransom notes, three Tasmanian Chalon Heads, you remember? Van Diemen's Land?'

'Yes, they were valuable stamps . . . forgeries?'

'Aye, forgeries, lassie! The forensic laboratory discovered this towards the end of last week, and I was informed straight away, as was DCI Brock.' He saw the question forming in her eyes, and laughed. 'Why was I informed? I'll be talking about that in our briefing.' He checked his watch. 'Aye, best be getting on with it. I just wanted to give you that introduction before we started, Kathy. Establish where we stand.'

Establish my indebtedness, Kathy thought.

As McLarren turned to gather up documents from his desk, he said casually, 'That young Indian laddie Desai, forensic liaison, seemed pretty bright to me. What's your opinion?'

'He's good,' Kathy said cautiously. 'Very thorough.'

'You'd recommend him, would you? Only we need a good liaison man on the team now, and he isn't really part of Brock's immediate team, as I see it. I thought I'd bring him on board.'

There was something about the disingenuous way McLarren said this that alerted Kathy. 'Yes, I'd recommend him, sir,' she said.

'Good, excellent! Now, let's go and meet the others.'

She followed him out of his room and along a short corridor to an open-plan office area, which served as the main base for his team. A dozen men and one woman were there, some drinking coffee, talking in undertones, clearly waiting for his arrival. Kathy was startled to see Leon Desai among them. She had thought, from McLarren's comments, that he hadn't made up his mind about bringing Desai in, but there he was, looking quite at home among the others. She stared at him for a moment, and a horrible thought came into her head. *Surely to God he hasn't been working for McLarren all along?* At that moment Desai noticed her at the door and gave her a smile. She grinned back and banished the nasty idea. Next to him Kathy recognised Dr Waverley, the forgery expert. He looked like a tourist, politely interested in what was going on around him, and gave Kathy a small smile of recognition.

McLarren introduced Waverley, Desai and Kathy before beginning his briefing. She recognised a couple of faces in the room, and paid particular attention to McLarren's deputy, a detective inspector called Tony Hewitt. He was a younger model of McLarren, tall, fair-haired and lean, and he reminded Kathy of the saying that owners choose dogs that look like themselves. Being rawer and less established, Hewitt was not yet able to afford the air of benign patronage which his boss liked to affect. He looked mean and sceptical, the way Kathy imagined McLarren must once have looked, and he regarded her carefully, without enthusiasm.

'Several of you are new to this particular corner of our activities,' McLarren began, 'so I'll begin with a wee historical perspective. Just so you understand that this is a particular *obsession* of mine,' he grinned ferociously from beneath his eyebrows, 'and that I will be very upset by any *lapses* on our part.'

He cleared his throat and turned to a white board, took up a blue marker and wrote *Mary Martin*.

'One year ago, almost to the day, a young DC of ours, Mary Martin, was brutally murdered in a warehouse in Kilburn. You may remember the case. No one has been arrested for her murder. For those of us who knew Mary, this remains an *open wound*.' He glared at Mary Martin's name on the board. 'She was at the end of a stake-out that had gone on, fruitlessly, for several days. Everyone had cleared the building and left the scene, but it seems she was lured back inside, to one of the upper floors, without calling for assistance. There, she was attacked with some kind of cleaver or axe, so savagely that her head was almost separated from her body.'

Kathy was aware of the deep silence in the room, and of a tightening in her throat.

McLarren turned back to the white board and wrote a second name. *Picasso*.

'As the more culturally aware of you will know,' he went on, lightening his tone disconcertingly, 'Pablo Picasso is one of this century's greatest artists. Now, three years ago a merchant bank in the City bought a very rare set of Picasso etchings for its board-room. They were delighted with them, not least because they portrayed a mythical beastie, half man, half bull, in various stages of ravishing a beautiful young maiden, a scenario with which merchant banks no doubt closely identify.'

He paused for jocular appreciation, then continued, 'However, a year later the art dealer from whom they had acquired these works committed suicide, and rumours began to circulate that some of his products had not been what they seemed. So the bank invited an expert, a Picasso specialist, to check their drawings. He said they were fine Picassos, all right – he couldn't find any fault with their execution or technical specification. The only trouble was that they couldn't possibly exist. The number of copies made from the original plates had been very carefully controlled in order to maintain their high value, and these were not among them.

'What made it worse was that the bank had bought two sets of these valuable etchings, and had given the second to their retiring chairman as a token of their esteem. After some discreet and embarrassed enquiries, it transpired that the second set could not be authenticated either.

'At this point, we were brought in, and after a while our enquiries turned up a name . . .'

McLarren wrote it on the board. *Raphael.* 'Like the great master. According to an informant, these amazingly good forgeries had been done by someone new, someone we hadn't come across before. It was rumoured that he was a brilliant art student, nickname Raphael, using his talent to forge masterpieces in order to maintain an expensive habit he'd acquired, and with the bent dealer to feed the work into the art market. The proof of this lay in the signature, our snout said. Look closely at it, and we would see that there was a small feature which doesn't correspond with the legitimate Picasso signatures. We checked and, sure enough, there it was. The point was, said our snout, that there were at least two more sets out there.

'It took us some time to track them down, but the information proved absolutely correct – we found four sets of Picasso forgeries in all. But, despite our success in this, Raphael himself was remarkably elusive. We began to get reports from other sources. Raphael had moved on from art works, it was said, now that his dealer was dead. Now he was creating papers for undocumented asylum seekers and illegal immigrants. No sooner had the Home Office got itself involved than he had shifted to tickets for pop concerts and World Cup football matches. And the Raphael *myth* just grew and grew. Raphael, it was now suggested, was actually two people. Being himself unworldly, interested only in creating his perfect forgeries, the artist had a partner who negotiated the mechanics of getting them into the marketplace. This person, by contrast with Raphael, was extremely practical, violent and ruthless, nicknamed *The Beast . . .*' McLarren paused to write this up. '. . . although, like his partner, he has no criminal record and exists nowhere within police files. Both of them, we might say, in their own way, are extreme talents.'

Kathy had heard of McLarren's legendary obsession with the forger Raphael. It was one of those colourful stories that brightened up the conversation of weary detectives over a pint of beer after a long and boring day. Because of this, the story had been embellished and improved upon over time, a process that McLarren did nothing to discourage. They had checked every graduate and drop-out from art schools in the UK for the past ten years, it was said, and come up with nothing. Then it was rumoured that Raphael was a young Central European, or an Arab, and had manufactured his own entry and identity papers so that he was in effect invisible to official eyes. Kathy found it interesting to hear the authentic McLarren version.

'Then again,' he went on, 'it has been suggested that Raphael may be a woman, an idea which greatly appeals to my sense of gender equity and equal opportunity among the criminal classes.' McLarren bared his teeth in a silent laugh which was given voice by a couple of people in the room, but not, Kathy noticed, by the sole other female member of the team.

'Meanwhile, however, as time passed and Raphael continued to elude arrest, some people came to doubt even his very existence.' This was said with sudden bitterness and a hooded glance in Kathy's direction, an accusation against Brock, she guessed.

'The great thing about a master forger is that, if he's really good, no one will know anything about him – it's only the failed forgeries that get discovered. After months of abortive investigation, we still only had the Picasso etchings as proof of Raphael's existence, and our lords and masters were becoming infected with this scepticism. And then Mary Martin was murdered.'

He added more writing to the board: *RIP 8.7.96.*

'A new kind of printing machine had come on to the market in Japan. A kind of copier of holographic images, as on credit cards. We thought that Raphael might be interested in getting hold of it. A UK company that makes security passes and the like was the first to import one, and we made arrangements to encourage Raphael to steal it while it was in transit in London. Unfortunately, Raphael's timing was faulty, and when he finally made his move, only Mary Martin was there to take him on. She was armed, but she stood no chance against them, Raphael and The Beast, poor lassie. Her gun was drawn – we found it later beneath her where she fell – and we may imagine her, facing Raphael alone, perhaps, the first copper to set eyes upon the mystery forger, unaware that his frightful companion, The Beast, was coming upon her from behind, the fatal blows being struck from the rear.'

McLarren's voice was thick with regret as he described this tragedy, but Kathy thought she detected a certain relish about the way he lingered over an event that had revitalised his case. From that moment, the pursuit of Raphael had become a top priority.

'Six months ago our informant warned us of another area of Raphael's expertise – rare stamps. It was thought he may have been secretly active in this field for some time. We advised dealers, and heard nothing more for a while, until now.'

McLarren paused for effect, his gaze sweeping round the room like the beam of a lighthouse. 'On Friday last, ladies and gentlemen, our forensic lab came to the fascinating conclusion that three rare postage stamps attached to a series of very strange ransom notes in a kidnapping case in Surrey, were expert forgeries.' He smiled grimly as the room stirred with interest at this. 'Aye, aye. Well, now, perhaps you would tell us about the stamps, Dr Waverley, if you would be so kind.' McLarren said this with exaggerated politeness, and a little sweeping bow as the other man stepped tentatively forward.

He pushed the long lock of his hair back from his forehead, and it promptly flopped forward again as he stooped to take a folder of photographs out of his briefcase. 'Would it be useful to pin these up, do you think?' he asked McLarren, who gestured briskly to one of the others.

'Er . . .' Waverley gazed at the pictures as the man pinned them to a noticeboard on the wall beside the white board. Kathy recognised the stamps from the ransom notes, enlarged to fill the page. 'Well, these three stamps were released in August 1855 in Tasmania in Australia. The design was engraved by W. Humphrys after a watercolour sketch by E. Corbould, and the stamps were recess printed in London by Perkins Bacon Limited. They have been used and cancelled, as you can see, in two cases with a pen, and, in the case of the fourpence blue, with a postmark which is recognisable as the pattern used by the Launceston post office.

'They are fine examples – or were, before someone got to work with the scissors and glue – otherwise undamaged, clean but not unnaturally fresh, good margins . . .'

Waverley touched his hair absently again, staring at the pictures as if trying to remember something. 'Yes. Value probably around nine hundred for the penny carmine, five for the twopence green, and one hundred for the blue. Say fifteen hundred all up. You might be lucky and get them for a thousand.

'They were all printed on a white wove paper, with a watermark of a large, six-pointed star.' He indicated a print of a ghostly white image on a grey background. 'That's quite interesting, because there was another issue of these three stamps in the following year, 1856, printed locally by H. and C. Best of Hobart, on paper without a watermark, and with current values almost the same as the 1855 issue. You see my point . . .' He turned and looked doubtfully at his audience, who showed no indication whatsoever of seeing his point.

'If you were going to forge these three particular stamps, why go to the trouble of forging the 1855 issue, and have to make the watermark, when you could forge the 1856 issue instead? Well, the answer is that he didn't make the watermark paper — that's perfectly genuine. The large star watermark was used in a number of stamps of Crown colonies of that early period, and what our man appears to have done is to take a genuine stamp of low value, completely erase the printing on it, and then reprint it with his own engraved high-value design. And that is quite beautiful, I must say. He has done it superbly well, using precisely the same recess-printing method and the same inks that Perkins Bacon would have used a hundred and forty-two years ago. It really is most impressive.'

Dr Waverley became lost in admiration for a moment before McLarren spoke sharply. 'Not readily detectable, then, Doctor?'

'Well, quite. To be perfectly honest, if you presented me with one of these, I would have the greatest difficulty in identifying it as a forgery. What gave the game away was your laboratory analysis. With your mass spectrometers you were able to pick up faint traces of the modern solvent that had been used to remove the earlier inks. Having found that, it was possible, using your scanning electron microscope, to find traces of the earlier dye, which appeared to be a light yellow-green. My guess is that he used the one penny green of 1856 from the colony of Victoria, which is worth only a few pounds, as his base. It was very bad luck for your forger — without that kind of laboratory equipment and analysis his work really would have been undetectable.'

'A master forger, then, Dr Waverley!' McLarren cried.

'Indeed, yes. Absolutely. Quite the best I've seen.'

'And where there's one, or three . . .?' McLarren continued to prompt.

'Yes, well, as you know, Superintendent, after you spoke to Cabot's about this, they agreed to us looking at the collection of stamps which Mr Starling has deposited with them, towards payment for the Canada Cover, which was used as the kidnap ransom.'

'And what have you found?'

'Well, we've only just made a start. We selected a dozen stamps at random, all Chalon Heads. Seven of the twelve showed spectroscopic traces of the solvent.'

Kathy wondered at how fast McLarren had moved. Cabot's must be in a panic, she imagined.

'So, Mr Starling's collection is possibly riddled with forgeries, is that right?'

'Well, we don't know yet . . .'

'You yourself advised Mr Starling on his stamp purchases in the past, did you not?'

Dr Waverley reddened. 'I was recommended to Mr Starling by Cabot's to authenticate a set of rare stamps he was thinking of buying a couple of years ago. After that he occasionally had me check a particularly expensive item for him.'

'You'll no doubt be keen to establish whether any of those were the work of our master forger, eh, Doctor?' McLarren grinned at the other man's discomfort. 'At any rate, we know that Mr Starling was one collector who was the victim of this forger. And if there's one, there'll be others. Not much point going to all that trouble just to make one or two copies.'

'I'm afraid so.' Waverley agreed. 'One thing I hope we'll establish is whether the forger has stuck to Chalon Heads or whether other rare stamps have been copied.'

'Aye. These Chalon Heads were a particular speciality of Mr Starling, I believe?'

'That's correct.'

'Which brings us back to the kidnapping of Mrs Starling, and the unusual kidnap notes. Anyway, Dr Waverley, that's our problem, not yours. If you've nothing further to tell us just now, we'll let you get back to the laboratory. Eric here will take you down to the street and arrange some transport for you. Many thanks.'

They shook hands, and one of the detectives led him away.

'Well, now,' McLarren rubbed his hands and began pacing back and forward in front of the board, 'what do we make of this?'

'Sir.' Inspector Hewitt spoke.

'Tony! Have you any thoughts to enlighten us?'

'If Starling was a victim of Raphael, why would Raphael kidnap his wife?'

It was a rhetorical question, and McLarren nodded encouragingly. 'Aye, aye . . .'

'Maybe Starling had twigged to Raphael's racket, eh? Maybe he'd figured out what was going on. He realised that Raphael had ripped him off for thousands of quid for dud stamps, and he was threatening Raphael in some way. So Raphael's partner started to get rough with Starling, to shut him up, teach him a lesson. Leaving his wife's head at the garden gate was a tough lesson, yes? Right in line with what we know of The Beast.'

'Ye-es . . .' McLarren flapped his hand like a conductor, wanting more.

'Well, the point is, Starling must know who Raphael is.'

'Yes!' McLarren clapped his hands delightedly. 'Well done, Tony. That is indeed the point. And now we must persuade him to tell us.' A general murmur of enthusiasm broke out around the room. McLarren beamed, then noticed Kathy. 'DS Kolla? You look troubled?' The room went quiet again.

'Have you had the forensic report on Eva Starling's head, sir?'

'No, not yet. Who's the pathologist?'

'Dr Mehta. I expect they're waiting for the toxicology reports. But apparently she had a heavy cocaine habit.'

'I see.' He rubbed his jaw with a bony hand as he took this in. 'And how does that help us, would you say?'

'I . . . I don't know, sir.' Kathy felt dumb, a party-pooper.

McLarren let this hang on the air for a moment. 'Well, we'll await Dr Mehta's report with interest,' he said, with a faint sarcasm that provoked a chuckle from someone, and turned to the tasks awaiting his team. A list of active, large-scale stamp collectors was being compiled from Cabot's and other major dealers; they were to be interviewed and arrangements made for their recent acquisitions to be sampled by the laboratory.

As the meeting broke up, the other woman in the room came up to Kathy and introduced herself as DC Colleen Murchison. 'Don't let the old man bother you,' she said cheerfully. 'It used to upset me until I watched one of those nature programmes on TV, about dominance rituals among gorillas, and I suddenly realised I was watching old Jock. Now whenever he puts on one of his performances I just imagine him eating bananas and thumping his chest.'

Kathy smiled, then Colleen glanced towards Desai. 'What about him?' she asked. 'He looks tasty.'

'Do you think so?' Kathy said, as if she'd never considered the matter.

'Oh, yes. I like the smouldering Eastern type. I wouldn't mind sharing a banana with him.'

'Well, give it a try. Why not?'

'Can't, unfortunately. My betrothed would play up. What about you?'

'Hmm . . .' Kathy looked thoughtful. 'Is this the first time he's worked with you lot?'

'Yeah. This is the first time I've seen him around.'

'You're sure?'

'Absolutely. I'd have remembered him.'

On her way out, Kathy found a quiet corner to make a phone call to Queen Anne's Gate. She got through to Dot.

'What's going on, Dot?' she asked. 'Can I talk to the boss?'

'Oh . . .' Dot, usually so brisk and businesslike, seemed lost for words. 'Kathy, it's just terrible.' She was speaking in a whisper, as if she might be overheard, and Kathy thought she heard a catch in her voice, like tears.

'Are you all right, Dot?'

'I'm all right, but they're taking the place apart.'

'Who are?'

'You know . . .' she whispered. 'The Internal Bureau.'

'Is Brock there?'

'He's gone, Kathy. I don't know where.'

'Bren?'

'I – I'll have to go . . .'

'Get him to phone me, will you? If you can –' The line went dead.

Kathy was not assigned to the group seeking out stamp collectors. Instead she accompanied McLarren and Hewitt to their interview with Sammy Starling. She didn't understand why she had been so favoured, until she saw Starling's reaction to her presence, which was to ask immediately where Brock was.

'DCI Brock has been taken off this case, Mr Starling,' McLarren said carelessly, turning over the pages of the file in front of him.

'Taken off? What do you mean, taken off?' Starling insisted, in a tone of contained panic.

'I mean exactly what I say, Mr Starling. You will not be seeing him again.'

'What?' Starling yelped. 'But I – I insist on seeing –'

McLarren looked slowly up from his papers and fixed him with a withering look that killed his demand in mid-sentence.

'You and DCI Brock go back a long way, I understand, Mr Starling,' he said, in a soft, dangerous tone. 'How would you describe your relationship?'

'What?' Starling bit his lip anxiously, his eyes disappeared into the narrowest of creases and his round face took on an aspect of doll-like innocence.

'Friendship, would you say?'

'Oh,' Starling said cautiously, after a pause. 'I wouldn't presume to say that, Mr . . . Mr . . .?'

'Did money ever change hands between you, Mr Starling?'

Now it was Kathy who bit her lip, to stifle the objection that she almost shouted at McLarren.

'Money?'

'Money, yes.'

'I think that's a matter between Mr Brock and me.'

'I take that to mean yes.' McLarren's voice became almost a purr. 'What did you give him money for, Mr Starling?'

'Eh?' The folds of flesh around Starling's eyes parted until his eyes appeared about to pop out of his head. 'No, no. You've got it wrong! In the beginning, when I was starting out, I sometimes gave him a bit of information, like, in exchange for cash. He gave me cash.'

'Yes? And the reciprocal, Mr Starling, the *reciprocal*?'

'What? I don't follow.'

'*You* also gave *him* cash in exchange for information, am I not right?'

'No! Absolutely not. No way!'

'Stamps, then? You gave him valuable stamps?'

'What? No, no! You've got this all wrong. What's this all about?'

'He's interested in stamps, isn't he?'

'He never told me if he is. We never talked about stamps, until this thing with Eva happened.'

McLarren glared with deep displeasure. 'You are not being helpful, Mr Starling. If you want our unstinting assistance you must give us yours. *Reciprocity* is what this is all about. A token of good faith.'

'I want to help you, of course I do, but I can't tell you what isn't so, can I?'

'I wonder if you would be so loyal to DCI Brock if you realised . . .' McLarren left the sentence dangling, then shook his head and muttered, 'No matter.'

'What? If I realised what?'

McLarren sighed. 'It's hard to deal with you, Mr Starling, hard to help you, when you're so uncooperative.'

'Please,' Starling said desperately. 'What should I realise? Maybe this is all some terrible misunderstanding. If you'd just tell me –'

'A misunderstanding!' McLarren turned to Hewitt at his side with a look of incredulity. The other man snorted. 'A very tragic misunderstanding, if that's what it was, Mr Starling. Very tragic. Let me put it to you then, very simply.'

He watched Starling carefully as he continued. 'The stamp which you gave to the kidnappers by way of the ransom was not the authentic stamp which you had bought and they had demanded. It was a copy, which they detected, and naturally were exceedingly unhappy about. So unhappy, in fact, that they killed your wife and cut off her head to teach you a lesson.'

Starling might himself have been dead, so immobile had he become as he listened to this. Finally, his lips parted enough to whisper, 'No.'

'Oh, yes. And it wasn't just any copy that you gave them. Our laboratory has confirmed that it was the copy they had made the night before the auction, which *DCI Brock* instructed them to make.' He held up a sheaf of official order forms. 'These are his requisition sheets . . . in order to substitute for the real stamp, but which in the end it was decided not to use. You remember?'

Another long, immobile pause before a whispered 'Yes.'

'Yes. And now the intriguing question. After your refusal, DCI Brock put the copy into his jacket pocket, do you remember that? Never mind – several witnesses confirm it, including DS Kolla here. So the question is, how? How was it possible that the copy in DCI Brock's pocket, and the real stamp which came up from the auction, became, shall we say, confused? Have you got an answer to that?'

Starling gazed at McLarren for a long while, his eyes screwed up so tight that Kathy thought he might be about to cry. Then he said, 'Who are you?'

'I told you my name at the beginning, Mr Starling,' McLarren said, with laboured patience. 'Jock McLarren — Superintendent Jock McLarren.'

'Yes, but *who* are you? I mean, who are you *with*?'

'Fraud Squad, Mr Starling. You've had dealings with us before, I believe, ten years or so ago.'

Starling whispered some oath or prayer, and the last of the colour faded from his cheeks. 'Why?' he croaked. 'This is a murder inquiry. My wife has been murdered.'

'Yes, yes.' McLarren said dismissively, as if that were the least of his concerns. 'Now, in the light of what I've just told you, is there anything you would like to tell me about your relationship with DCI Brock, eh? Come along, man, we haven't got all day.'

Starling's pale moon face remained deadly still, eyes invisible. Then the three police officers saw a glistening drop of water form in the outer corner of each crease, and tumble simultaneously down each cheek, followed by another, and another, though Starling remained perfectly still and silent as he wept.

McLarren turned away with a look of disgust on his face. 'I am interrupting this interview for a five-minute break for Mr Starling to compose himself,' he said fiercely towards the tape-recorder, got to his feet and strode out of the room.

Hewitt followed him out, leaving Kathy to supervise Starling's recovery. After a while he wiped his face with a handkerchief, and sipped at a plastic cup of water, but otherwise said and did nothing to give Kathy any clue as to what was going on inside his head. She had felt her stomach knot with alarm after listening to McLarren's accusations against Brock, and wondered what had made him so convinced and confident that he could spell them out to Starling. She wanted to tell Starling that she was sure there was some other explanation for what had happened, but she was acutely aware of the video camera and the one-way mirror, on the other side of which McLarren and Hewitt were probably watching her.

After ten minutes of silence, the door opened and the other two detectives returned. McLarren was talking intently to his assistant, and Kathy picked up the last words of his sentence, '. . . by the balls, Tony.'

Hewitt nodded and took the central seat facing Starling, who showed no sign of having heard McLarren's words.

'Let's talk about fraud, Mr Starling,' Hewitt began coldly. 'On Saturday you handed over a substantial collection of postage stamps to the dealers Cabot's in exchange for credit towards the purchase price of an item bought that day at auction.'

Starling blinked uncertainly, then nodded.

'A number of those stamps have now been shown to be forgeries.'

Kathy recognised Starling's now familiar reaction to shock: his features switched off and went into a state of immobility. To Hewitt, this reaction appeared simply obstructive.

'That's fraud, Mr Starling,' he said harshly, his voice louder. 'Passing forgeries off as the genuine article. You've been guilty of serious fraud.'

'No,' Starling muttered.

'Well, what's your explanation?'

'I didn't know . . . Are you sure?'

'How could you not know? You're an expert, aren't you? You get advice from experts. Of course you would know.'

'No. It's impossible.'

'That's right, it's impossible you couldn't have known. That's the view the court will take, before they put you away.'

Starling stiffened at this, and McLarren broke in, speaking almost caressingly after Hewitt's harshness. 'Aye, Mr Starling, fraud on this scale can only lead to prison.'

'Scale? How – how many stamps?'

'Oh dear, oh dear, our lab people'll be busy for weeks before we know the full extent of it. And the longer you keep us in the dark, Mr Starling, and the more you make us work it out for ourselves, the harder will be the penalty of the court, believe you me. But, then, you know how hard the court can be with cases of serious fraud, don't you? Not that your earlier assistance to the court in providing damning evidence against some of our former colleagues will help you now.'

Hewitt seemed to lose patience. Out of a folder he snatched the enlarged photographs of the three Tasmanian stamps and threw them down in front of Starling. 'Recognise these?'

Starling focused on them, then nodded slowly. 'The ransom notes. The stamps . . . probably came from my collection.'

'Forged!' Hewitt barked angrily. 'How did you acquire them?'

'I – I don't know. From Cabot's . . .'

Hewitt shook his head. 'Their records show not.'

'Well, Gibbons, perhaps, or Christie's . . . I don't know. You say these ones are forged?'

'You must keep a record of your purchases, don't you?'

Starling stammered, 'I'm afraid not.'

Hewitt threw back his head in disbelief. 'Oh, spare us!'

'Truly.'

'When did you buy them?'

The silence stretched longer this time, before Starling said, 'I have no idea. I can't remember.'

Hewitt glared at him. 'Mr Starling,' he said, voice full of menace, 'you know where these forgeries come from – you must.'

'No.'

'It's sometimes claimed,' McLarren said, musing, 'that the courts are harder on crimes against property than those against the person. Your case should provide an interesting test of that, Mr Starling. It'll be fascinating to see whether your sentence for fraud is longer or shorter than that for obstructing the course of a murder inquiry.'

'You think the forger murdered Eva?' Starling whispered, brow wrinkled in concentration.

McLarren pointed a bony finger at him. 'And you know who he is, don't you, Mr Starling?'

Starling looked from McLarren to Hewitt and back again, as if just now realising what they were saying. 'I want a lawyer,' he said. 'I won't say any more without a lawyer.'

They broke for lunch and to give Starling time to call his

lawyer. When the detectives were alone, McLarren said, 'A pathetic figure.'

'A bloody irritating one,' Hewitt said angrily. 'You can't tell what's going on inside that balloon of a bloody head. Can't see his eyes.'

'He's a *starling*,' McLarren said. 'A greedy wee scavenger. But he's been hit by a real predator, a hawk. When he's had time to absorb that, I'm sure he'll understand that he has no choice but to lead us to him. But I'd like something to convince him that he should be more frightened of us than of Raphael. I have no doubt that his lawyer will advise him that we would need a great deal more incriminating evidence than we presently have to charge him with intent to defraud Cabot's.'

'The idea of prison seemed to put the wind up him,' Hewitt offered.

'Aye, that's true.' McLarren nodded thoughtfully. 'Kathy, that information you had about his wife's drug habit, were his properties thoroughly searched for drugs?'

'We didn't know about the drugs when the searches were done, sir.'

'Well, why don't you organise another, more thorough search? You know what to look for now.'

'Sir, if I may say . . .'

'Aye, lassie. Go on.'

'Sir, you're wrong about Brock and Starling. I'm quite sure DCI Brock wouldn't have done anything wrong.'

McLarren smiled at her. 'Very loyal, Kathy. I like that. But, in any event, it's others that'll be pursuing that one — I was only shaking the tree to see what might drop out, and sowing one or two seeds of doubt, to mix my metaphors. Oh, and there's something else apart from drugs that you should be looking for — the records of his stamp purchases. I have little doubt that he did keep records of some kind, and he would have had no reason to destroy them up until now. Paperwork is the thing, you see, Kathy, that trips most of us up in the end. That's why you should be very wary of the kind of methods that DCI Brock no doubt insisted upon.'

'Sir?'

'Aye, the focus, I mean, on understanding the subtleties of

human nature and motivation, and so on. Was that not his way of it? Well, in my experience, human nature is depressingly predictable and uniform, Kathy. What is amazingly various are the means we find to disguise it. And it's usually the paperwork that exposes our fraud. You should concentrate on that. Get a degree – statistics, something like that, or information science. That's the way of the future for policing.'

13

The Yellow Bikini

There was some relief from the heat of the city up on the North Downs, where a light breeze stirred the heavy foliage along the woodland lanes as the two cars made their way towards the house. Another car was already there in the forecourt, empty, but as they came to a stop Leon Desai appeared at the far corner of the house and walked towards them. Kathy had the key, and as the others unpacked their gear, she opened the front door. The interior was still and airless, the silence heavy as if the place had been brooding on its owners' fate. Another vehicle arrived in the driveway, and a dog-handler got out with a beagle on a lead. They moved to the front of the group, the dog perky, wagging its tail happily.

'We'll start at the top and work down,' Desai said, and the team of SOCOs, dressed up in their nylon overalls, shuffled forward to the stairs.

'This is the bit I don't like,' Kathy said, hanging back.

'How do you mean?' Desai was pulling on his latex gloves with a look of purposeful detachment.

'I don't mind so much searching a place with the owners there,' she said. 'It's in the open, everyone knows what's going on. But coming into an empty house I feel like a thief, or a spy, prying. I don't like it.'

'That's a bit of a fine distinction for someone in our line of work, isn't it?' he said.

His calmness, his indifference to the atmosphere in the house, niggled her. 'Don't you know what I mean? Don't you feel anything?'

'Shame? Is that what you mean? No, of course not. I'm doing my job, Kathy. So are you.'

'I just sat in on McLarren interviewing Sammy Starling. He told him everything that you told us last night, about the forged Canada Cover. He seemed so confident that Brock is guilty.'

Desai nodded but said nothing.

'We've got to do something, Leon. They've really got the knives out for Brock.'

'I think it may be too late for that, Kathy,' he said quietly. 'My advice is to look out for yourself.'

She froze as he reached forward and took hold of her arm.

'Really,' he said softly, his mouth coming closer to her ear. 'I mean it, Kathy. Let it go. Start again.'

She met his eyes, trying to read what was going on in his mind. He turned away and went up the stairs, two at a time.

They began in the roof space, beneath the clay tiles baking in the afternoon sun. It was hot, slow and uncomfortable work, checking the hidden corners around rafters and trusses with flashlights, wearing face masks as they groped through the fibreglass insulation quilts laid between the joists. By the time they clambered down the loft ladder and pulled off their masks they were red-faced and soaking in sweat inside their overalls. The overalls themselves were filthy with dust and debris from the roof space, and they peeled them off and put on fresh ones. Then they spread out through the upper rooms. The only disconcerting find was something that Desai pointed out to Kathy in the dressing-room attached to the Starlings' bedroom. He opened a wardrobe door and pointed to a steel cabinet inside. Its door was open, several umbrellas inside.

'Did you notice this before?' he asked her.

'No. What about it?'

'I've just realised what it is.'

Kathy still didn't get it. 'What?'

'It's a security cabinet. For guns.'

He swung the door closed, showing her the heavy lock.

'Sammy has a gun?'

'If he does it isn't there now.'

After a fruitless search of the first floor they moved on downstairs, gradually, imperceptibly, becoming resigned to failure as their search yielded nothing. The final straw was the safe that they discovered set into the floor beneath a corner of the carpet in the room Sammy Starling used as an office and den. Its door was unlocked and wedged open with a fold of paper, as if to tell them that they needn't waste time damaging the door trying to open it. There was nothing inside.

When they had finished in the cellar, they spent a further hour in a search of the outbuildings and grounds. Then Desai told the SOCO team and dog-handler to go home.

Kathy found him standing by the side of the swimming-pool, between the house and the tennis court, screened by hedges and shrubbery. It was just after six, the western sun still hot, its light glittering on the motionless surface of the blue water. He looked defeated, and she realised how much he'd wanted to get a result.

'Eva probably kept it all in London,' she said. 'That's what the flat was for, wasn't it?'

'She was here for weeks at a time. She would have needed to keep some here too.'

'Well,' Kathy said, 'Sammy must have taken it. He must have known.'

Desai shook his head doubtfully, then roused himself and said, 'I told your lot to go home.'

'Yes, I know. Can I get a lift back with you?'

'Sure.'

'What about the forensic evidence? Is there nothing new?'

'Nothing that helps.' He squinted against the glitter from the surface of the pool. 'The toxicology results have come back, confirming Eva's use of cocaine, but nothing that helps with cause or time of death. The cardboard box was manufactured in Finland, probably within the last year, and there were traces of raspberry jam on the inside. God knows what that's supposed to mean.'

He stretched his arms over his head and sighed. 'Great-looking pool.'

'Looks very tempting.' Kathy was feeling soiled and exhausted.

'There's a costume in the hut . . .' He indicated a small rustic changing hut that stood at one end of the pool. 'Why don't you have a swim?'

'You're the swimmer.' She smiled, remembering when she'd once come across him in the pool at Pimlico that the Yard staff used.

'There's only a woman's costume.'

'No, I couldn't do that,' Kathy said. 'Not wear her things.'

'They're probably there for visitors. Go on. I'm in charge. I order you to search the pool.'

She laughed and he smiled, a lovely smile, she thought, with beautiful even white teeth, all the nicer for being so rare.

'All right. Why not.'

There were a couple of towels hanging from pegs inside the hut, some very old flippers, a deflated pool mattress, and a yellow bikini. While she changed and stood under the shower head that stood beside the pool, Desai wandered off to the rose garden that fringed this end of the lawn. Kathy's reservations about using the pool disappeared when she dived in. The shock of cool water stripped away the disappointments of the day, and by the time she'd swum a dozen fast lengths she felt renewed. She climbed out and was standing dripping on the stone surround, a towel round her hair, when she heard something behind her, rustling among the bushes that formed a screen against the woods. Turning, she was surprised to see a Labrador at the far edge of the pool, Toby Fitzpatrick behind it. His face was an image of shock, the look of horror so intense that Kathy thought briefly that he must be having a heart-attack. She removed the towel, shook out her blonde hair and said, 'Hello, Mr Fitzpatrick. It's Sergeant Kolla, remember?'

'Oh . . . Good Lord, yes . . . I didn't recognise . . .' He flushed scarlet, coughed and blinked rapidly. 'Sorry. I thought I heard voices . . . thought I'd better investigate – Henrietta!'

The dog was on the point of diving into the tempting water.

'Stay! Sit!' he cried. It settled reluctantly on its haunches, tongue lolling, eyes pleading. The second dog had now appeared out of the bushes.

'I'd better get them away,' he said, turned on his heel and disappeared as abruptly as he had come, calling sharply to them to follow.

'Who was that?' Desai had returned to the other end of the pool.

'A neighbour,' Kathy said. 'He looked as if he'd seen a ghost – Eva, perhaps. Now I really am embarrassed.'

Desai smiled and Kathy, feeling her embarrassment grow rather than diminish, threw herself back into the water, diving deep. Fitzpatrick had seen her body in the yellow bikini, not her head, and for a second it had been written all over his face that he thought he was seeing Eva.

Kathy swam hard to the bottom of the deepest part, until her hand touched the grating on the bottom outlet. Desai had said that she should search the pool, and that, she thought, was what she had better do. She tugged at the grating, which lifted surprisingly easily. Beneath it, standing inside the sump, she saw a green tube. She took hold of it, replaced the grating, and returned to the surface. Taking her time, she swam to the steps. Desai was sitting on an oak bench, watching her. 'I'm very jealous,' he said.

She shook back her hair, water dripping all around her on to the warm stone paving. 'What do you reckon this is?' She gave him the tube, two inches in diameter, nine inches long, with a metallic green finish. 'It was in the sump below the grating in the centre of the pool floor. Is it something to do with the chlorination?'

He turned it in his hands and read a tiny inscription on the bottom. 'Made in Italy'. He turned the top and it began to unscrew. 'It's a small vacuum flask. Neat.' He looked up at her, then beyond her towards the bushes where Toby Fitzpatrick had appeared. 'Let's take it inside.'

'OK,' she said, and picked up her towel.

When they got to the kitchen he laid a sheet of plastic on the table and set out a small stack of sample bags. He drew on a pair of latex gloves and finished unscrewing the lid of the canister. It was an elegant little container, a designer item, something to store a chilled cocktail for a warm day at the races, perhaps. But in this case it contained three small plastic bags. The first contained a little black pipe and a disposable butane lighter, the second a few crumbs of what looked like gravel, and the third a smear of white powder.

'What are the little rocks?' Kathy asked.

'Looks like freebase,' he replied. 'They treat the powder with solvents to get rid of impurities, and it ends up like this. It's very pure, and it can be smoked, which would save her nose.'

Kathy sat back and thought, then she reached for her notebook and the phone. She found the number she was after and pressed the buttons.

'Hello? Is that Sally Malone? . . . This is DS Kolla, Sally, from the Met. I saw you yesterday, with Chief Inspector Brock, remember? . . . Yes, look, this sounds a bit odd, but I wanted to check something with you. The thing that brought Sammy and Eva together, was it the swimming? . . . No, *swimming*. Only, why I ask, I understand Eva was a great one for the water, and I thought maybe that was something they had in common? . . . Really? Are you sure?'

Kathy listened for a while to Sally's voice then said goodbye. She snapped the phone off and smiled at Desai. 'The man you saw out there by the pool, the neighbour.'

'Yes, what about him?'

'His wife told me that Eva liked the pool, but she'd never seen Sammy go near it. Well, according to Sally, Sammy hates the water. He's never learned to swim. He's terrified of it, and his son died of drowning.'

'Ah.'

'The one place Eva could be absolutely sure her husband would never go was the bottom of the pool. Unless they drained it first.'

Desai smiled. 'Why don't you tell McLarren the good news?'

'You do it, Leon.' She stopped herself saying, 'You probably want his approval more than me.' It was a mean thought, just because he seemed to have given up on Brock. 'You're in charge. I'll go and get changed.'

While she was in the little hut, changing back into her clothes, her mobile rang. 'Hello?'

'Hi, Kathy. Bren.'

'Bren! Thank goodness. What's going on?'

'We've been closed down, that's what's going on.' He sounded flat.

'What's been happening?'

'They've been searching Queen Anne's Gate for that bloody Canada Cover. And Brock's house. No success, naturally. Bloody idiots.'

'Where is he?'

'As far as I can make out, he spent today helping them with their enquiries. The word to Dot this evening was that he would be on stress leave for a while. None of us have seen him since first thing this morning.'

'What about you?'

'Remember that case a couple of days ago, about a tourist murdered in the Caribbean? I'm at home now, packing my hot-weather gear, what I've got of it. What do coppers in the West Indies *wear*, do you reckon?'

'They're sending you to the West Indies?'

'First available flight. Do you know how many headquarters' detectives are overseas at any particular time, giving advice to local forces? Twenty per cent. We've been missing out, Kathy.'

'Oh, Bren . . . This is terrible.'

'Yeah, well, never mind. At least you're still on the case. Got plenty of coverage in the papers this morning, I see. "Horror Find in Surrey Mansion", stuff like that. Concerning the case, I took a call this morning from the Farnham police, just before all hell broke loose. In the excitement I forgot about it. Seems the Starlings' milkman spoke to them. He'd heard the radio report that Mrs Starling had been missing since she went to London on the fourth. He wanted to tell them that he thinks she may have been there later than that.'

'He saw her?'

'No. Something about the stuff he delivered. Farnham police didn't think it amounted to much, but I thought I'd better pass it on.'

'Thanks, Bren.'

'How's McLarren?'

'Like he always is, only more so. He thinks his favourite character is behind all this.'

'Raphael the super-forger? You're joking!'

' 'Fraid not.'

'Bloody hell. That guy's amazing. Just keep your head down, Kathy, till this blows over. That's what we've all got to do, Brock included. Trust nobody. Especially Desai.'

Kathy felt chilled. 'Oh? How do you mean?'

'He's up to something.'

'Why do you say that?' Kathy glanced out of the doorway of the hut, checking that she was alone.

'I didn't like the way he was going on about Brock having a breakdown, for a start.'

'Well, he has been acting oddly, Bren.'

'It isn't just that . . . Leon's thick with McLarren.'

'Today, you mean? McLarren needs a lab liaison —'

'Not just today. Last week.'

'Last week?' Kathy felt a little jolt of alarm. 'You sure?'

'Last week, before any of us knew what was going on, Dot took a call from McLarren's office. Superintendent McLarren returning DS Desai's phone call. She mentioned it to me.'

'When was this? Saturday?'

'Saturday was the auction. No, it was before that. Friday. Brock had sent Leon off to work with the lab people on making the copy. Dot gave McLarren's office the lab number.'

Kathy was silent. She shivered, and ran her hand through her damp hair. They had first met with Sammy on Thursday. The third ransom note hadn't arrived until Friday morning. At that stage there was no conceivable reason why McLarren should have been aware of what was happening.

Desai found Kathy's silence on the journey back up to central London mystifying and rather intimidating. She merely nodded when he told her how pleased McLarren was with their find, and answered in monosyllables when he tried to make conversation. Trying to get some clue to her mood, he found himself struggling to make small-talk, something which, being no good at it, he normally despised. He would have been startled to know that her mind was preoccupied with calculations as to just how duplicitous he might be, and just how much allowance she should make for the fact that, as she was now prepared to admit to herself, she found him so attractive.

McLarren was waiting for them at the Broadway entrance of the New Scotland Yard building. As Kathy and Desai got into the back seat, McLarren's driver started the car and moved out into the traffic.

'Uxbridge,' McLarren told them. 'You weren't planning on an early dinner tonight, were you?' He chuckled. 'And is that the incriminating evidence?'

Desai reached forward and gave him the packages.

'Ah, yes. Excellent, excellent. This should put Mr Starling off his food for a wee while.'

'Expecting trouble, are we, sir?' Desai looked over his shoulder at the car following close behind, its windscreen filled by the silhouettes of large men.

'I'm very much afraid that we're going to cause Mr Starling some social embarrassment,' McLarren said. 'It's time we put some pressure on him. We understand that he and Mr and Mrs Cooper – the couple he's staying with in Uxbridge – have guests tonight. Two Malaysian property investors and their wives. They should just be getting tucked into the smoked salmon.'

'Do we know the Coopers?'

'No criminal record. They're both directors of a Portuguese time-share investment company in which Starling has – sorry, *had* – an interest, and they've a number of other business interests of their own. Younger than Starling. Sporty couple, by all accounts. Racehorses and ocean-going yachts.'

The house was a large neo-Georgian mansion, trying hard to look several hundred years old, but actually newer than the classic Aston Martin parked on the gravel drive in front of it. There was also a large white Mercedes and, tucked discreetly to one side, a van bearing the logo of a chef's hat and the name Lush Nosh. The front door was opened by a sleek tuxedo-clad youth, hired, so Kathy assumed from his look of confusion, for the evening. McLarren asked for Mr Cooper. After a moment a tall, tanned man in a cream suit came to the door. A third car had joined the two from the Yard, and Cooper looked alarmed at the invasion.

'May we come in, sir?' McLarren said, showing him his warrant card.

The hall was paved with squares of black and white marble, an archway leading directly off to one side to a room occupied by a long dining-table. The lingering summer evening light was supplemented by candles, their flames glittering on crystal and silver, casting a warm glow on the faces turned expectantly towards the visitors in the hall.

McLarren examined them in turn. 'Mr Starling with you, sir?'

'He . . . he's in his room.'

'What's he doing there?'

'Eh? He went to fetch something a couple of minutes ago. Why?'

'I have a warrant for his arrest,' McLarren said, loudly and distinctly enough for everyone to hear. At the dining-table, an athletic-looking blonde woman in a black cocktail dress sprang to her feet, and four pairs of Malaysian eyes widened in consternation.

'My God!' Mr Cooper said, in a whisper. 'You're wrong, you know. Quite wrong. He worshipped Eva. He wouldn't harm a hair —'

'Mr Starling is wanted on drugs-related charges, Mr Cooper. And we also have a warrant to search these premises, sir,' McLarren went on, in an official monotone, offering him a sheet of paper. 'We have reason to believe there are prohibited drugs on the premises, contrary to section one, paragraph four of the Misuse of Drugs Act, 1971.'

'Good grief!' Mr Cooper had turned much paler.

'Drugs?' one of the Malaysian men murmured anxiously across the table to the other. 'Drug squad?' They began talking rapidly in Malay, their wives joining in an agitated whisper.

'This is preposterous!' Mrs Cooper said loudly, bearing down on McLarren from her place at the head of the table. 'You've made some ridiculous cock-up!'

'I don't believe so, madam.' McLarren smiled benignly.

'But we've just served the salmon!' Mrs Cooper said, in a tone of outrage, then faltered at the absurdity of the whole thing.

'Well, I am extremely sorry about that. It's Mrs Cooper, is it? Superintendent McLarren.' He wiggled his bushy eyebrows and gave her a wolfish smile, which greatly increased her alarm. 'Please do continue with your dinner. We'll be as unobtrusive as we possibly can.'

She stared at him in disbelief, then turned back to try to calm her guests, who were rising to their feet. 'Please,' she said, the faintest note of hysteria detectable beneath the hockey-captain confidence of her voice, 'there's really no need to be concerned. There's been some incredibly stupid mistake. My husband will sort it all out. You read about this sort of thing in the papers all the time.'

Her four guests exchanged looks, trying to decide what was the socially acceptable thing to do.

'Mr Cooper,' McLarren went on, 'why don't you take us to see Mr Starling?'

Cooper led them along a short corridor to a door connecting to the self-contained granny-flat, which he referred to as the guests' wing. He knocked on the door, but there was no reply. He opened it and they went in. Across the sitting-room, the evening breeze stirred the curtains on each side of the open french windows leading out to the back garden. There was no sign of Sammy Starling, his scattered possessions suggesting a hurried departure.

While the others began their search for Starling, his records, and his prohibited substances, Kathy returned to the dining-room, where Mrs Cooper was sitting among the ruins of her dinner party.

'They've gone,' she said bitterly, waving at the empty seats of their guests. 'I just can't believe it. We've worked *so* hard for this, and we were *this* close, and this happens. It's all so . . . so . . . stupid!' She shook her head in despair.

Kathy took the seat beside her.

'I don't want to talk to that Scottish git!' Mrs Cooper continued, a flatter Midlands accent coming more strongly now through the home counties boarding-school vowels. 'Who does he think he is?' She reached into her small handbag and brought out a packet of cigarettes, one of which she lit aggressively from a candle. As she bent her face to the flame it illuminated the many little creases and wrinkles that long hours spent sailing and sunbathing had added to age and experience.

'It was Eva, wasn't it? The drugs thing,' she said, after drawing in a deep breath of smoke. 'Sammy wouldn't touch that stuff with a barge-pole. It terrified him.'

'He had a record in that area, at one time,' Kathy said gently.

'Oh, when he was a kid! God, we all do stupid things when we're kids. But not any more. Not for years. But I suppose your records are for ever, aren't they? God, it's so stupid! I've heard him talk about drugs, here, at this table, with Eva here too, and how it frightened him, the way things had become now.'

'How long have you known that Eva used drugs?'

'Oh . . . I suppose I've always suspected it, right from the beginning. She had these mood swings, and this way of being sort of abstracted sometimes, detached, her eyes and mind somewhere else. For Sammy it was part of her mystery and appeal, but I used to think, oho, this girl's on something.'

'This was right at the beginning, you say? When he first met her?'

Mrs Cooper sucked at her cigarette and breathed smoke out through both mouth and nose. 'In Portugal, yes. She and her family lived in this house on a block of land we wanted to make up a development site for a block of apartments. The house was nothing much, old and a bit run-down, but the site was spectacular, the best bit on a hillside overlooking the beach. We'd heard that the old man who owned the house was difficult, a crusty old bugger, the last in a long aristocratic line. When we eventually got an appointment to see him, Ivor didn't want to take Sammy. He thought it might put the old count off, Sammy being Chinese, but Sammy went anyway, and they got on quite well. Even more surprising, Sammy took a fancy to the old man's daughter. I remember Ivor talking about it afterwards. "Sammy's been smitten," he said, and he was right. I thought, when I heard how old she was, that he was a bloody fool, and he was just going to have to get over it, but he never did.'

The shock of the police raid had made Mrs Cooper talkative, and Kathy didn't want her to stop, but at that moment two detectives came into the dining-room and began opening the glass-fronted cabinets in which Mrs Cooper kept her crystal and glassware.

'Oh, hell! Be careful with that!' she cried, getting to her feet.

Kathy said, 'They will,' trying to sound completely confident. 'Let's go outside,' she suggested. 'Leave them to it. They will take care, I promise.'

Reluctantly the other woman picked up her cigarettes and let herself be led out to the back garden. They walked slowly over to a sundial, set on the edge of a bed of purple lavender. The evening sun had dropped below the surrounding houses and the garden was darkening in the twilight shadows.

'I have no difficulty with the idea of Sammy fancying Eva,' Kathy said. 'But what on earth did Eva see in him? Everyone assumes money. Was that it?'

'We talked about this endlessly,' Mrs Cooper said, looking anxiously back at the house, lights alive in every window. 'At first Sammy's infatuation was a bit of a joke, one that we were worried could backfire if the old count got to hear of it. But somehow Sammy seemed to charm them both. God knows how he did it – we couldn't work it out. Then, gradually, the idea of Sammy and Eva being a sort of item just seemed to become accepted.' She stubbed out her cigarette. 'I ought to be there, make sure they don't break anything.'

'Really, it's better not to watch. Let them do their job, Mrs Cooper. It'll soon be over. So, not money, then.'

'What?' She looked at Kathy, not comprehending.

'Eva and Sammy.'

'Oh . . . Well . . .' She returned to the subject. 'Yes, of course it was money, on one level. The family was broke, despite their blue blood, and a foreign millionaire must have had some appeal to Eva, and getting away from grumpy old Dad. But it was more complicated than that, more interesting. I mean, although Sammy is getting on, it's hard sometimes to know how old he is – You've met him, have you? With that round baby face and smooth skin, and his inscrutable smile, like a sort of doll. And sometimes I would think that she was older than him, less innocent in many ways. She would talk to him as if he was a little boy, playing with his stamps, and he would lap it up, and treat her like a precious bit of porcelain or something. For a while it seemed almost all right.'

She turned away and lit another cigarette. 'But, of course, it was doomed. She got bored with it before long. They should have sold the house in Surrey and bought somewhere new in town, but Sammy is so attached to it, his English country house . . .'

'They tried to make a fresh start, didn't they? I mean, they got rid of Sally.'

'Oh, yes. You've come across her, have you? Well, yes, obviously she had to go. Eva was quite firm about that. There was no way they could live under the same roof.'

'Did Sally go willingly, or was she pushed?'

'You should ask Sammy that.'

'I'd like to, but that may be difficult.' Kathy smiled.

'Oh . . . yes, of course.' Mrs Cooper gave a little grimace in response. 'Definitely pushed. She'd have clung on there in the hope that Sammy would see sense and kick Eva out one day, if Eva hadn't put an end to it.'

'How did she do that?'

'Oh, just put her foot down with Sammy, I suppose. Things got a bit touchy, we got the impression.'

'And then Eva persuaded Sammy to buy the London flat.'

'Mmm.' Mrs Cooper frowned. 'We never thought that was a good idea. I mean, in principle it seemed a good idea, but Sammy hardly went there, and pretty soon it became *her* pad.'

'What did she do there?'

'Well, I don't know. I mean, not directly. Sammy said she went shopping and watched movies, but I don't know.'

'Didn't she visit you when she was in town?'

'Look, we're closer to Farnham than to Canonbury. There wasn't much point her going there if she wanted to visit us. Same with Sammy. If he came here, he just wanted to go home to Farnham afterwards, not travel across town to the flat.'

'What other friends did she have in London, then?'

'Well, I don't know. I never met any of them. Unless you call the waiter at La Fortuna a friend.'

'Is that Tomaso?'

'Yes – you've met him, too, have you? I say, you're quite thorough, aren't you?'

'I just wish I could afford to eat there.'

Mrs Cooper laughed. 'Yes. Eva always did have expensive tastes, which Sammy indulged quite shamelessly.'

'I've seen her clothes.'

'Oh, yes, her clothes. And jewellery, holidays. Everything but cash.'

'Cash?'

'Yes. He explained it to Ivor once. Credit cards were OK, but not cash.'

'What did he say about it?'

'He said he was terrified that Eva would get robbed if she carried cash. But we thought it was something else. With the credit cards and accounts at the restaurants and stores he could check everything, and Ivor guessed that Sammy was afraid of her picking up some boy and indulging him. But now I think it was the drugs. I think he suspected.'

'Then why did he let her go off like that, for days on end, without contact?'

'I think he probably had little choice – she was pretty determined when she wanted to do something. And, anyway, I think you'll find he did try to keep a watchful eye on her, when she was away.'

'How?'

Mrs Cooper looked casually away, as if disclaiming any responsibility for what she was about to say. 'You've come across a Mr Wilkes, have you?'

'Wilkes?' Kathy recalled that Sally had also mentioned the private detective that Sammy had used to follow Marty Keller. 'Oh, yes, Sammy's private eye.'

'That's the one. Sammy used to get him to keep tabs on her whenever she was up in town on her own. He told us about it one evening, after he'd had a couple of drinks. Sammy was never a great drinker, and he got all gooey and confessed to us that he tried to look after Eva all the time, even when they were apart.'

'Did Eva know?'

'No! That was the embarrassing part. We had to swear not to

215

breathe a word to her. I found it kind of creepy, the next time we saw her in London, knowing that she was being followed, and knowing that she *didn't* know it.'

Kathy nodded. She saw Leon Desai approaching across the lawn, and thought, Duplicity everywhere. She turned back to the woman and said hurriedly, 'So, where has he gone now, Mrs Cooper? Any ideas?'

'Not a clue. Really.'

'Might he try to go overseas? To Portugal, perhaps?'

She thought. 'I suppose he might . . . But it's not as if he's got friends over there who would hide him or anything — I mean, if the police started calling. And he'd hardly go to Eva's family, not if he's suspected of killing her.'

'We never said that, Mrs Cooper, and yet it was the thing your husband assumed when we arrived.'

'Only because your man with the eyebrows said he wanted to arrest Sammy. It was the natural thing to think.'

'Was it?'

Mrs Cooper met Kathy's eye, then looked away. 'Look, he's the least violent of men . . .'

'Yes?'

'. . . normally,' the other woman added reluctantly.

Desai was waiting ten paces away, letting them finish their conversation. Kathy looked over at him and he came forward. 'Mrs Cooper, could you unlock your jewellery case for us, please?'

'Now I do want to be there,' she said determinedly, and marched off across the grass.

Kathy returned to the room where Sammy had been staying, and looked through the things he had left behind. Among them was a wallet of photographs, one of them showing Eva on a beach, wearing the yellow bikini Kathy had borrowed for her afternoon swim.

The light was fading when they returned to central London, McLarren's mood grim, as if some initial stage had now passed and the real work was about to begin. He and Hewitt were going to Cobalt Square, but Kathy, travelling now in the other car, had herself dropped on Victoria Street, outside New

Scotland Yard, so that she could catch a train home from St James's Park tube station. Once the cars had sped off into the night, however, she walked along Broadway until she came to the end of Queen Anne's Gate. As she approached the front door of Brock's annexe, she saw that a couple of lights were on in upper-floor windows. She still had her keys to the offices, although she half expected that the locks might have been changed.

They hadn't. She let herself in and made her way up through the maze of corridors and stairways to the level on which Brock's office was located. The main corridor lights were off, and in the subdued illumination of the emergency exit lighting, the glow beneath Brock's door was quite obvious. Kathy tapped softly on the door, and when there was no reply, she opened it.

Dot was alone in the room, standing behind Brock's desk.

'Dot, you're still here,' Kathy said.

'Hello, Kathy.' If Dot had been crying when Kathy had called her that morning, she had long since got over it. Now she looked sombre and not particularly pleased to see Kathy. 'I'm trying to put things to rights again after today. How are you?' She turned back to the pile of papers she had been sorting.

'Fine. You look tired.'

'Yes. What are you after?'

'I suppose I'd half hoped to find Brock.'

Dot looked up briefly at her over the top of her glasses. 'Not here you won't.'

'Where then?'

'I couldn't say, Kathy. Was there anything in particular?'

'I'm trying to understand what's going on.'

'Yes. Quite a few people are trying to do that.'

'And there have been some developments that I think he should know about.'

Dot put the papers down and stared fixedly at Kathy. 'If he hasn't been in touch with you, Kathy, I think you can assume that he feels it's best that way. Isn't that good enough?'

It seemed to Kathy that Dot was acting like a protective spouse, and she felt a surge of irritation. 'Are you in contact with him, Dot?' she asked, making an effort to keep her voice even.

'Not at present.'

'If you were, you might tell him that Sammy Starling has done a runner. And he's been told that Brock is effectively responsible for Eva's death, by switching the ransom stamp, presumably to steal it from Sammy. I think Brock might be in danger, if Sammy can find him.'

Dot nodded slowly. 'I understand.'

Kathy waited, hoping for more, but when none came she made to go.

Then Dot said, her voice softened, 'He has a very high regard for you, Kathy. You know that, don't you? Especially for your persistence. He always says that, in the end, that's what makes the difference.'

It occurred suddenly to Kathy that the room might be bugged, or Dot might think it was, so that she felt constrained to talk indirectly. Kathy said quietly, 'Is he all right, Dot? In himself, I mean?'

Dot gave Kathy a tight smile, then turned away.

When Kathy got home she threw a frozen meal in the microwave and sat at the window, staring out at the chains of lights twelve floors below, spreading out into the darkness. She jumped as the microwave and her mobile phone both began bleating at once, like a pair of pets competing for attention. The caller was one of those irritating people who don't say who they are straight away, expecting you to know their voice, and she couldn't place it although it was familiar.

'Hello? Kathy, is it?'

'That's right.'

'How are things going with you? Haven't caught you at an awkward moment, I hope?'

'Sorry, who is this?'

The voice chuckled. 'Oh, I'm sorry, Kathy. It's Peter White here. You called on me the other day.'

'Oh, yes.' Kathy's heart sank. 'Sorry, Peter, I didn't recognise your voice.'

'No, no, I should have said. I wondered if it might be a bit late to ring you, but then I thought, I'll bet Kathy doesn't go to bed early. Am I right?'

Kathy clenched her teeth and let a moment of silence pass

before she answered. 'Not usually, Peter, no. What can I do for you?'

'Well, it was more a matter of whether I could do anything for you, Kathy. I just thought, well, with all of these dramatic events I've been reading about in the papers, you might have thought of more questions for me, or something might have got you stumped that I could throw some light on.'

Kathy could hear the slur of whisky in his voice. She imagined him, sitting alone in his empty house, the TV channels exhausted, desperate to speak to someone, probably for the first time in days. She groaned inwardly and tried to think of something to talk about briefly before she could decently ring off – the press reports, the weather, his roses. And then a thought came to her.

'Well, there was something actually, Peter. Did you ever go and see Sammy's house?'

'Me, Kathy? How do you mean? I think I said that I refused his invitation.'

'No, not then. More recently. Within the last year or two. Perhaps you took a walk up there?'

There was a short silence, then a chuckle. 'You're right, Kathy! A couple of times I went for a walk up there on the Hog's Back, and just happened to go by Sammy's place, doing my nosy parker, not that I managed to see much, mind you. That would have been last summer, I suppose. We had a spell of lovely weather, and I made myself get out and about a bit. Well, well! And how did you track me down, eh?'

'Some people who live up there gave me a description that reminded me a little of you.'

'Really? Is that right? Well, I'll be blowed. That's bloody good detective work, Kathy. I take my hat off to you, I really do. How many young coppers these days would have had the patience and the wit to put that together, eh? I am impressed.'

Kathy's heart began sinking again beneath this effusive tide of bonhomie. 'Well, I wasn't sure . . .'

'You're checking up on any strangers in the area, are you? Of course you would. Kidnappers would have been bound to do a bit of a recce first. And this lot sounds very thorough from what I've been able to gather – thorough and bloody rough, eh? I must confess, I thought the whole thing might have been a bit of a joke at first, but not any more, eh? Not any more.'

'No.' Kathy felt suddenly very tired. Her meal was going cold in the microwave, and she didn't want to listen to this.

He seemed to read her mind. 'Anyway, you don't want to spend your precious leisure hours listening to a boring old fart like me, Kathy. I just wanted to let you know that I'm here to help if I can, in any way at all.'

'Thanks very much, Peter, I will remember that.' And remember not to give my number to people like this, she thought as she rang off.

She had just restarted the microwave when the phone rang again. She blinked in disbelief when she heard the same voice.

'Kathy! Sorry to bother you again so soon, but you know how it is – no sooner have you put the phone down than something jumps into your mind, and I wouldn't have been able to sleep without telling you.'

'Telling me what, Peter?'

'You asked me about when I went up by Sammy's, and it just occurred to me that I saw something a bit odd up there in the woods above his house one time.'

Kathy bit off the withering comment that came to her mind and instead said, in a calm voice, 'Really? What was that?'

'It was a man, watching the house – Sammy's house – through the trees.'

'Are you sure?'

'Oh, I'm positive. I was above him, on the ridge track, and he was crouching in the undergrowth, maybe twenty yards below me on the slope that encloses Sammy's place on the – which is it? The west, yes, the west. He had binoculars, and he was watching the house and the pool and the tennis court through the trees.'

'Could you describe him?'

'He had his back to me, I'm afraid, so I never saw his face. He was wearing a green jacket, and a green cap, so he was practically invisible in the bracken. I'd never have spotted him if it hadn't been for the dogs.'

'Dogs?'

'Yes, he had two dogs with him, Labradors or retrievers, sitting good as gold on each side of him. Gave me a start, I can

tell you. I thought at first I'd spotted a couple of young lions –
that's what they looked like. I did a year in Kenya in the Mau
Mau days, did I tell you that? Saw plenty of lions then . . .'

Kathy sighed and wondered what continuous sequential
reheating did to frozen Spicy Thai Chicken and Noodles. She
felt somehow that she knew, that it had been happening to her
for a couple of days now.

After she finally got White off the line, she sat down with her
meal and made a number of phone calls of her own. The last one
was to DS Bren Gurney's home number. It was now after
midnight, and she had to wait some time for the call to be
answered. Finally Bren's wife, Deanne, came on, sounding
sleepy.

'Deanne, I'm sorry to disturb you. It's Kathy Kolla here. Can I
talk to Bren?'

'What time is it? Oh . . . we were asleep, Kathy. Bren's going
abroad first thing tomorrow morning.'

Kathy thought that she caught something more in Deanne's
voice than irritation at being woken up, a residue of an old
suspicion that her husband was a bit too admiring of the
capabilities of the young female detective sergeant that Brock
had brought into their team. 'I'm sorry, I know it's a bad time to
call, but I just had to speak to him before he goes.'

'I see . . . Hang on.'

There was a delay, during which Kathy wondered what was
going on. Weren't they in the same room? Then Bren came on,
yawning. 'Hi, Kathy. What gives?'

'Sorry, Bren.'

'Yeah, yeah. What's the problem?'

'I need to get hold of Brock.'

Bren hesitated, then said, 'I'll give you his home number.'

'I've already tried that. There's no reply. And I've seen Dot,
and she won't, or can't, tell me where he is.'

'Well . . . then I don't think I can help. What's the
problem?'

'I need to talk to him about what he did yesterday – sacking
me, and the business with the Canada Cover.'

'Christ, Kathy.' Bren groaned. 'That's history. Things have
moved on.'

'I shouldn't have let it go at that,' Kathy persisted. 'I was just so taken by surprise. I need to hear him explain it to me.'

'Well, you can't!' Bren didn't try to hide the exasperation in his voice. 'Is that all? Can I go back to bed now?'

'You've been working with him for longer than anyone else on his team. You must have some idea where he is.'

'Kathy, I don't! You know what he's like. He's a secretive old bugger. He keeps his private life private. I've been working for him for eight years now, and I've seen the inside of his place maybe twice. He's been here for dinner with us a good few times, and each time he comes on his own and is excellent company and tells us next to nothing of his private life. Christ, do you think Deanne hasn't tried to get something out of him? I mean, that's a professional grilling, believe me, but he just smiles and tells a few yarns, and doesn't give an inch.'

Kathy could hear some smothered noises in the background, followed by Bren's chuckle.

'Anyway, the fact is, I don't know who his friends are, if he has any, and I haven't the faintest idea where he is, and even if I did, well, if he doesn't want to talk to you, why the hell should he?'

'Sammy's done a bunk, Bren,' Kathy said. 'McLarren told him, as clear as could be, that Brock switched the Canada Cover and so provoked the kidnappers into murdering Eva. Now Sammy's disappeared, and it seems that he owns a gun.'

'Christ. A pistol?'

'A Tikka M690 Deluxe hunting rifle, seven millimetre, with telescopic sight.'

'Bloody hell. Brock needs to know.'

'Yes.'

There was a silence as Bren thought. Kathy heard some murmur of discussion between him and Deanne, then, 'He had a wife, and a son, I think, but they were divorced decades ago. I think they're in Canada. As far as I know he hasn't been in touch with them for years. He used to fly gliders, belonged to a club on the North Downs somewhere . . . not far past Maidstone, I think. But I haven't heard him talk of it for several years . . . I don't know, Kathy. I'm stumped.'

'Do you remember, Bren, the first case I worked with you on, the murders in Jerusalem Lane?'

'The Marx sisters, yeah, what about it?'

'One morning I spotted Brock getting out of a red sports car, driven by a woman. I gave you the number, and you found out the name. Do you remember? We thought it was a hoot, him being so secretive.'

'Vaguely, yes, now you mention it. I'd forgotten about that. She never surfaced again, as far as I know.'

'Can you remember her name?'

'You're joking. Can you remember the car number?'

There was a long silence, then Kathy said, 'No, but the computer will.'

'Eh?'

'The vehicle registry computer will have a record of your enquiry. If you ask it, it'll tell you again.'

'What, now?' Bren said wearily.

'The computer never sleeps,' Kathy said. 'Thanks, Bren.'

Ten minutes later he called her back.

'A red Mercedes sports, registered to one Mrs Suzanne Chambers, then resident in Belgravia, a brisk walk from Queen Anne's Gate.'

'That's right, I remember it was a posh address.'

'Not any more.'

'Oh.' Kathy's heart sank. 'She's gone?'

'Now listed at 349A High Street, Battle, East Sussex.'

'Ah!'

'It's a long shot, Kathy.'

'I know.'

'Good luck. I mean it.'

'And you, Bren. See you when you get back.'

That night, lying alone in her narrow bed, the light of a full moon glowing through the curtains, Kathy suffered a feverish and fitful sleep, her mind filled by bizarre creations, like creatures escaped from a fairy-tale, or the inhabitants of some Hieronymus Bosch landscape of hell – a Chinese philatelist, a decapitated princess, Raphael and The Beast, Brock the thief – all impossible, surreal fictions. One part of her mind, a sceptical and practical part, told her that such creatures could not exist in the real world, while another part, equally insistent, reminded her that she had seen Eva's head with her own eyes, and heard Brock's dismissal of her with her own ears.

14

Acting Badly

She rose early, too early to go hunting Brock, she thought. Feeling agitated and impatient, she scribbled a list of notes while she nibbled some breakfast toast, then made a phone call to the duty officer in the Central File Office.

Half an hour later she found the address. The building was of the 1930s, and didn't look as if it had had much maintenance since, especially in recent years. The board of bell-pushes lay disconnected on the front step, and the front door opened on a shove. Kathy went up to the first floor, found the door she wanted and pressed a buzzer on the jamb. There was no reply. She tried again without success, and was about to give up when a door on the other side of the landing opened and a young man carrying a brightly coloured motorbike helmet came out.

'He's there,' he muttered, as he walked past. 'He just got back half an hour ago.'

Kathy nodded her thanks and pressed her thumb on the buzzer again, this time keeping it down, hearing the shrill noise muffled through the door.

After a minute the door was thrown open and a flabby figure dressed in sweatshirt, boxer shorts, feet bare, almost toppled out. 'Jesusfucking . . .' He stopped cursing and blinked at Kathy uncomprehendingly. He looked terrible, eyes bleary and bagged, stubble thick on his grey skin, hair standing upright in tufts.

'Morning, Mr Wilkes. DS Kolla, remember? The Eva Starling case?'

'Oh, Christ . . . yes, OK. Whassamatter?'

'Sorry to bother you. I needed to check a couple of things. Can I come in?'

'In?' He squeezed his eyes with the thumb and forefinger of his right hand, steadying himself against the door jamb with his left. 'What time is it?'

'Six thirty,' Kathy said brightly.

'A.M.? Bloody hell. I only just got to fucking sleep. I was on a job all last night.'

'Oh, I'm sorry. I thought I'd catch you before you went out. You want me to come back?'

'What? Oh, Christ, I'm awake now, aren't I? Better come in.'

He shuffled back inside and Kathy followed, closing the door quietly behind her.

It was pitch dark until he managed to stumble to the window and sweep the curtains back, letting sunshine flood in over a jumble of bedding, clothes and worn furniture.

'Don't mind this,' he mumbled, scratching and yawning. 'I'm between homes at the moment.'

It wasn't the mess Kathy minded but the smell, of sour damp cloth and pungent body odours, both very strong. She went over to the window. 'Mind if I . . . ?'

He shrugged and picked up a half full bottle of milk while she undid the catch and slid open the window. The sound and smell of passing traffic billowed in.

'It's about Eva, is it?' Wilkes said, voice hoarse. He took a pull at the milk and slumped onto a chair piled with discarded clothes. 'I read about it in the papers. Sick, innit. How's old Sammy taking it?'

'When was the last time you spoke to him?'

'On the phone, a week ago. When he asked me to look out for Eva. I told you lot.'

He caught the look on Kathy's face and straightened up slowly. 'Why? What's happened? He done a runner?'

'We need to speak to him urgently. If he contacts you, let us know straightaway, will you? Here's my number.'

'Yeah, Right. Will do.' Wilkes was alert now.

'You must know him pretty well. You've been working for him for a long time.'

'We weren't what you'd call friends. He'd just give us a bell if he needed some little job done, a bit of information, whatever.'

'You helped him when he first met Eva, didn't you? You went over to Portugal for him. Is that right?'

'That's ancient history, that is.'

'Tell me about it.'

'Oh . . .' Wilkes yawned elaborately. 'Sammy was doing some business over there, some development, and he wanted information on some people. He sent me over to do a bit of digging around for him.'

'You speak Portuguese?'

'Nah. I worked with a local guy. He speaks English pretty good.'

'What did you find out?'

'Sammy was interested in this old guy and his daughter. It wasn't too complicated. Financial information, mainly. The family had been rich once, but now they didn't have much more than their house, which Sammy and his partners wanted.'

'What about Eva? Didn't he want you to find out about her?'

Wilkes grinned slyly. 'Oh, yeah. You might say that. She'd been in a bit of trouble. Nothing you'll find in Interpol or whatever – her dad knew a lawyer who hushed it up. Teenage stuff, with drugs. Anyway, she was a real worry to her old man, and her auntie.'

'Auntie?'

'Yeah. Marianna. She calls her Auntie Marianna. Sort of mother figure, really. They were real keen to get her married off to someone solid with plenty of cash.'

'Yes, but not someone aged sixty, surely? What about all the rich young men down on the Algarve? She was very good-looking.'

'Oh, she was a right bloody cracker, I tell you, but the types she attracted weren't to Daddy's taste. She'd had a string of bad boys, and she was developing a reputation.'

'Go on.' Kathy gingerly removed a damp towel from the back of a chair facing Wilkes and sat down.

'Yeah. Only Sammy wasn't bothered. He just wanted her, and I reckon she just wanted out. Probably the idea of going off to London as the young wife of a rich, daft old sod didn't seem so bad. Even so,' Wilkes went on, warming to his story-telling, 'her dad wasn't having any of it, not at first. He's a man of principle, see, a gent of the old school. He couldn't come to terms with his daughter marrying Sammy.'

'So? How did Sammy persuade him?'

Wilkes gave a smug smile. 'Sammy sent me back a second time. He wanted me to find something on the old man that he could use, some kind of leverage. And I did.'

He sat back beaming, making Kathy ask, 'Yes? Go on.'

'While my off-sider went back through the paperwork, I followed the old geezer, see? For days and days, till I was sick to death of his routines – the bar, the quay, the park, the bar, the quay, the park, on and on. Then one day he stopped at a little shop in the old town. It sold antiques and gifts and coins and stamps. Old stamps. That's what he was interested in, just like Sammy. He went in and talked to the owner for ages about the stamps. Didn't buy anything.

'So then I got my off-sider to see what he could find out about that, and eventually he came up with a press report, fifteen years old, about the de Vasconcellos family selling their famous stamp collection to raise funds to send Eva's mother to Switzerland for a cure for her cancer. The collection had been in the family for three generations.

'Sammy was over the moon when I told him. He came up with this idea of a book on these special stamps that look like Eva, and dedicated it to her old man. I thought it was a bit loony myself, but it worked like a charm.'

'I see.'

'Yeah, well, Sammy presented him with the book, and an album of the same stamps that he put together for him, and the old geezer wept. Really, Sammy told me, he burst into tears. Apparently Eva's mother looked the spitting image. After that, Sammy could do no wrong. The old bloke sold him his house, gave him his blessing to marry his daughter, and then retired to an old folks' home, where he probably still is, dribbling on Sammy's stamp album.'

'Sammy bought her with stamps, you might say,' Kathy said.

'Well, yeah, I suppose you could put it like that.'

'Were they real, the stamps?'

'Real?'

'Yes. Or did he have copies made?'

'Copies? You mean forgeries?' Wilkes looked startled.

'Yes. Did Sammy have someone who made rare stamps for him?'

'Blimey. I never heard of anything like that. What makes you say that?'

'Did Sammy know anyone in that line of business, Ronnie?'

'A forger?'

'A good one.'

Wilkes gazed up at the ceiling, thinking. 'I've no idea. He never mentioned it to me.' He smiled at Kathy blandly.

'That sounds like a lie,' Kathy said, watching his expression carefully.

'Oi! I don't need to take this from you! I given you lots of help!'

Kathy shook her head dismissively. 'After they were married, you spied on her for him, didn't you?'

'I never!'

'I know, Ronnie. You reported on what she did in London, when she was at the flat in Canonbury.'

'Yeah,' he conceded. 'But it wasn't spying, just keeping an eye out for her, making sure she was all right. Sammy was concerned about her.'

'You gave him written reports?'

'Nah. I was never one for the paperwork.'

'That's why you haven't got anywhere, Ronnie. What about notebooks? You must have made notes of times and places?'

'It wasn't like that. I didn't follow her all the time. He didn't want me to do a proper surveillance job on her, just look in from time to time, to make sure she didn't get into trouble.'

'And did she?'

'Nah. Boring, really. Shopping, going to the movies, having a nosh. I sometimes felt tempted to tell her how to have a good time.'

'And did you?'

'Course not. Sammy'd have killed me.'

'Did she have a boyfriend?'

'No way.'

'What about the waiter at the Italian restaurant round the corner from her place?'

'You reckon?' He considered this for a moment, then dismissed it. 'Nah, I've watched them together in the restaurant. They were friends, like, sharing a joke, but nothing more, I'm sure.'

'Did you ever eat there with her?'

'I did once, matter of fact. She caught me out, getting out of a taxi, and I had to pretend it was a complete accident, me being there. She insisted on taking me in and giving me a nosh.'

'Did she get her drugs from the waiter?'

'Eh?' Wilkes raised his eyebrows in innocent surprise.

'Come on, Ronnie,' Kathy said wearily. 'Eva had a heavy coke habit.'

'No!' He expressed astonishment.

'I hope you're a better punter than an actor,' Kathy said, noticing the form guides and racing pages scattered among the debris on the table by the window. 'Drugs was the thing Sammy was most worried about, wasn't it? Come on, Ronnie, don't be stupid.'

'Yeah,' he conceded. 'He was worried about that. But if she was doing it, she was careful. I never saw her make a score, and I never saw her look as if she was under. Sammy got me to search the flat a couple of times, but I never found nothing. I reckon if she was getting stuff it was either from the restaurant or the cinema. Those were the two places she went regular, like.'

'Did he send you after her every time she went to London on her own?'

'Pretty much, I guess.'

'Tell me about this last time.'

'This last time?' Wilkes asked vaguely, wrinkling his brow in thought.

'Yes. Sammy rang you.'

'Oh, yeah.' His face cleared. 'Sammy rang me, that's right.'

'When?'

'Oh, well, Sunday night.'

'What did he say?'

'Just the usual. Eva was going up to the flat for a few days, and would I keep an eye out.'

'What time was this?'

'Latish. I dunno, ten, eleven, maybe.'

'At night? Was that usual? To phone you at that time?'

Wilkes shrugged.

'And you're certain it was Sunday?'

He looked at Kathy and hesitated. 'I think it was.'

'Don't you keep *any* records? A diary or something?'

'Nah. You reckon it was earlier?' he asked. 'Or later?'

'I want you to tell me, Ronnie. Think. Where were you when you took the call? It was your mobile, was it?'

'Cor . . .' He scratched his head. 'I was here, I reckon. But which day . . . I *think* it was Sunday.'

'You were positive the first time.'

'Was I? Well, I couldn't swear.'

'All right. What did you do then?'

'Nothing that evening. The next couple of days I called round to the flat, but there was no sign of her. I called Sammy, and at first he said to check on Marty Keller again, like I told you, then he changed his mind.'

That made sense, Kathy thought. By then Sammy would have received a ransom note and wouldn't have wanted Ronnie poking around, possibly alarming the kidnappers. But the timing of the earlier call to Ronnie puzzled her. Sammy had said that his wife had gone up to the flat on the previous Thursday. Surely he would have called Ronnie earlier than Sunday night.

'You said just now that Sammy phoned you on the Sunday night and said Eva was going up to the flat for a few days.'

'Yes.' Wilkes yawned and scratched, becoming bored with this.

'So she hadn't actually left then.'

'Eh? I dunno.'

'*Was going*. That means she hadn't yet gone.'

'Oh . . .' Vagueness filled Ronnie's face again. 'Well, I suppose you're right.'

Kathy sighed and got to her feet. 'I hope I never have to use you as a witness, Ronnie.'

He grinned. 'That's the general idea, innit?'

'What do you know about Sammy's gun?'

'Eh?' Ronnie's face dropped. 'Has he taken that bloody thing with 'im?' The idea seemed to worry him a good deal.

'I asked what you know about it.'

'Some prat, someone he'd done some business with, gave it to 'im for a present, several years ago. It was the most stupid bloody gift you could imagine for Sammy. He got all keen for a while, and joined this club. He took me there once, kind of showing off. Beautiful gun, mind, almost as big as 'im. Deadly accurate, except when he used it. Watching him blazing away on the firing range was the scariest thing I've ever seen. He hit everybody's target 'cept his own.'

'So he has ammunition?'

'Jesus, I don't know.' He looked pale.

At the door she stopped and said, 'What about Eva's mobile?'

'Eh?' He frowned. 'I don't remember her having one.'

Kathy looked hard at him, but his face expressed nothing but torpor.

When she got back to her car, she made a call to headquarters to have Sammy's phone records checked for his call to Ronnie, then headed south, driving against the incoming commuter flow, out towards the A21, the hop gardens and orchards of the Weald.

In Battle, 349A High Street turned out to be a shop, with the name Chambers Antiques over the window. Kathy watched lights come on, then someone reverse the sign hanging behind the door, from Closed to Open. She got out of the car, walked towards it and opened the door.

'Good morning.' A girl of about twenty seemed to be alone. She came round from behind the counter. 'Can I help?'

The interior of the shop glittered with the reflections of glass and crystal, the glow of polished wood and leather. Quality, Kathy thought, not tourist trash. The girl had a cloth in her hand, which she had been using on one of a number of ornate grandfather clocks ticking sumptuously in the background.

'I wondered if Mrs Chambers was in,' Kathy said.

'Oh, no, I'm afraid she isn't here at the moment. Can I give her a message?'

'Actually, it was Mr Brock I wanted.'

The girl looked at Kathy with a frown. 'Mr Brock?'

Kathy's hopes faded. 'David.'

'David?' The other woman smiled. 'Oh, yes?'

'It's rather urgent,' Kathy went on gamely, ready to give up. 'Very urgent, actually.'

'Oh dear.'

'Never mind. I'll try somewhere else.'

Kathy turned to the door and had her hand on the knob when the girl said, 'If it's really important, they've gone up to the Abbey.'

Kathy turned back, surprised. 'The Abbey?'

'Yes. You know, the site of the battle. They decided to go before all the tourists arrive, before it gets too busy.'

Kathy got directions and took the street towards the market-place, and behind it the battlemented mass of the gatehouse to the Benedictine abbey, now ruined on the hilltop beyond. There was already a short queue at the entry desk, people examining the souvenirs, reading the introductory notices. She paid her fee, took the handset offered her for the commentary, and set off along the marked trail.

She came to the terrace walk, a long, gravelled ridge on which the English army had been deployed on 14 October 1066, overlooking the boggy valley to her right, across which the Norman force had struggled for the best part of that day. There were a number of small groups of people on the walk, strolling slowly from one observation point to another, pausing to listen to their audio guides. Among them she saw a family, two small children, a woman and a man. The man was kneeling, tying the shoelace of the smaller child, a girl of three or four. It was only when he straightened upright that Kathy realised it was Brock.

The other child, a boy of perhaps eight, said something that made the woman laugh. She turned towards Brock, the sun on her face. Brock gestured to the boy, making big sweeping arcs with his hand, explaining the theory of trajectories. The boy listened carefully, then made him repeat part of it, enchanted by the notion that, through an empty sky, there are two alternative routes by which an arrow may arrive at precisely the same point. In this case, as he went on to demonstrate with his finger, in a manner that made the little girl go 'Yuck,' the eye of an English king.

Kathy held back, watching them, uncertain what to do. They appeared so enclosed in each other's company, like any ideal nuclear family, if somewhat extended in their age range. Grand-parents and grandchildren, perhaps. She frowned and turned away. Maybe later, she thought, she might catch him alone.

She retraced her steps, back to the end of the terrace walk, heading towards the entrance, when the phone in her shoulder-bag started ringing. She got it out and heard Brock's voice. 'I'm not sure that stalking is your forte, Kathy. Are you alone?'

'Hell,' she muttered. 'Yes . . . yes, Brock.'

'Well, if you've got this far, you'd better come and tell me what you've got to say.'

She turned back and found him sitting alone on a bench half-way along the terrace walk.

He was dressed in a light summer shirt and slacks, exactly like the tourist he was supposed to be, and seemed completely untroubled. He grinned at the slightly sheepish look on her face as she approached, and patted the seat beside him. 'Well, then?'

'Sorry,' she said. 'I tried every way to get a message to you.' She sat down.

'That's all right. I should have known that there was no way to elude Detective Kolla. Although I can't for the life of me think how you did manage to find me. It couldn't have been Dot?'

'She was most unhelpful.'

'Good. She was meant to be. Well, then, this message.'

Kathy described McLarren's interview with Starling, his disappearance, and his gun. 'McLarren made it sound as if you were directly responsible for Eva's death. Sammy seemed devastated. I think he may be trying to find you, Brock. I think you're in danger.'

'Mmm . . .' Brock considered this. 'Well, he won't find

234

me . . . Unless he's had the sense to tag along behind you, that is. He couldn't have done that, could he?'

Kathy blushed. 'No! No, of course not. I was very careful.'

'I hope so, Kathy. I'd hate to think that other innocent people were being put in danger.' He looked over his left shoulder towards the sound of a child's laughter among the ruined walls of the monks' dormitory, brooding over the old battlefield.

'Why don't I arrange protection?'

'Kathy,' he said gently. 'Do me a favour. Let me arrange things my own way. Please.'

She bit her lip. 'Sorry.'

'And what was the other thing?'

'The other thing?'

'That you wanted to see me about.' He considered her gravely as she met his eye.

'I . . . No, that was it, really.'

'You didn't want to ask me about my decision to kick you over to SO6?'

'Well, yes, I did, actually. I found that . . . quite hard to swallow, without explanation.'

Brock sighed. 'Yes. It was seeing what they'd done to Eva that really decided me, although I'd been uneasy from the beginning. You have to understand how it was the first time, with Sammy and Keller and the others. You know about Superintendent Tom Harley, do you? How he died?'

'Yes.'

Brock gazed out over the meadow, as if he might catch sight of the ghosts of ancient armies. 'That was one of the worst things I've had to work through. I'm not saying that Sammy deliberately framed him, but Sammy is a fighter – when it comes to the crunch, he'll use whatever he's got to hand, and Tom Harley's suicide certainly got him off the hook. Seeing Sammy again last week, grinning hopefully at me as if we were old pals setting out on a great new adventure, brought it all back. I wanted none of it.'

He sighed again and returned his attention to Kathy. 'And, as things developed, I liked it less and less. I could see things turning out badly, and I wanted you out of it. What they did to Eva, the business with the Canada Cover . . . These people are playing very rough. So I thought I would move you somewhere safer. When I became aware of Jock McLarren's interest, I thought that he might do very well. You would be removed, but still could keep a useful eye on the fringe. I didn't realise how quickly things would develop.'

'But couldn't you have explained all that?' Kathy protested. 'Couldn't you have taken me into your confidence a little?'

Brock shifted uncomfortably in his seat. 'Would that have been better? If I'd said, "Kathy, things are getting a bit rough around here, I think I'm about to be accused of theft, women are getting their heads cut off, and I want you to clear off somewhere a bit safer, out of the firing line," you would have said, "Yes, fine, whatever you say, Brock." Would you?'

Kathy chewed her lip but didn't reply.

'Now, with Bren it wouldn't have been a problem,' Brock continued. 'Tell Bren to bugger off to Barbados, and he packs his bag without a murmur. But you? Did you get him to help you find me, by the way?'

Kathy shook her head. 'I tried. He told me to leave you alone, like Dot.'

'Exactly! Everybody tells you to leave me alone, so what do you do? You track me down into the depths of darkest Sussex.' He snorted and added, 'Like Lassie.'

'*Lassie*?' Kathy flared.

'All right,' Brock relented. 'Not Lassie.' He smirked, and they both began to laugh.

When this passed, Kathy became serious again and said, 'Why does McLarren hate you, Brock? He seems to relish every chance to put you down.'

'I really don't know. I've never done anything to him, as far as I know. There's poison in this. The whole thing is poisoned.'

'Poor Eva,' Kathy whispered.

'Yes. Poor Eva. This is not a game.'

'That's what Peter White said last night.'

'Have you been talking to him again?'

'He rang me. He's desperate to help. Wanted to know what he could do.'

Brock groaned. 'Sorry. I should never have told you to see

him. It was part guilt, because I've never kept in touch, but I shouldn't have put it on to you. He was always a pain when you wanted a short answer — always wanting to give you more and more. Sometimes it was worthwhile, I suppose.'

'I think now he's just very sad and lonely. He needs something to think about, to be involved in.'

'And the last thing you need is to be his social worker.'

Kathy shrugged. 'I'd better let you get back to your, er, friends,' she said.

'Yes. My, er, friends have probably had enough history by now,' Brock said drily. 'If they haven't been bumped off by a lone sniper.'

'If it's any consolation, Sammy's a very bad shot, apparently.'

When she got back to her car, Kathy put a call through to the local police at Farnham, then headed north. When she reached the M25 she turned west, towards Surrey.

Sylvester's area was surprisingly large and dispersed, and it took Kathy the best part of an hour, driving slowly round the suburban streets and rural lanes around Farnham, before she finally spotted the electric milk float parked at the kerb. A big, ruddy-faced man was engrossed in his account book, trying to reconcile the figures with the fact that he'd run out of gold-topped dairy full cream before he rightfully should.

'Sylvester, is it?'

'Hello there,' he said cheerfully. 'Who wants him?'

Kathy showed him her ID.

'Ah, thought I'd hear from you lot again,' he said, putting down his book.

'What can you tell me?'

'Well, now, it was that report on the radio, the police asking for information from anyone who had seen Mrs Starling any time after Thursday morning, the third of July, when she had gone up to London.'

Kathy nodded. After Ronnie Wilkes, Sylvester made a gratifyingly confident and precise witness.

'But I didn't see how that could be, on account of the strawberry yoghurt.'

'The strawberry yoghurt?'

'That's right. Mrs Starling has a passion for it. Always has it for breakfast. And the point was, they didn't stop it till the following Tuesday, see? So she must have been there till then.'

'I see. Maybe they just forgot to cancel it.'

'Oh, no. They put out a fresh order each morning, see? Marianna does it. She writes it on an old envelope or the like, and sticks it in the neck of one of the empties. Her English isn't so hot, so she uses a code – M for milk, Y for yoghurt, DC for double cream, and so on. Last Monday week, for example . . .' He opened his book again and turned the pages back to 7 July, checking his record, '. . . here we are. It would have been, "2M, 1Y".'

'You know them, then? Mrs Starling and Marianna?'

'Oh, yes, and Mr S. We often say hello.'

'But all the same, maybe one of the others wanted some strawberry yoghurt.'

'No, no, no!' Sylvester dismissed the idea. 'People have their little ways. Marianna and Mr S hate strawberry yoghurt, think it's muck. We've had conversations about it. About Mrs S's tastes in dairy products.'

'Is that a fact? Did you speak to any of them around that time – on the Monday or Tuesday, for example?'

'I've been trying to recall that, but I can't say I did.'

Kathy thought. 'The order on the Monday morning included yoghurt, but I suppose she could have left on the Sunday evening, after Marianna had put out the order, and they forgot to change it.'

'Well, yes, I suppose that's possible. But I don't see how it could have been before that.'

'Thanks very much, Sylvester. You've been very helpful.' Kathy stood still for a moment, a wood pigeon cooing in the branches of a great oak, bees droning from a cascade of golden honeysuckle, sunlight dappling on a dusty lane. 'Don't want to swap jobs, do you?'

Sylvester chuckled. 'You wouldn't say that if you saw the paperwork, my dear, really you wouldn't.' Then he added, 'That Marianna. I reckon I saw her once with a black eye.'

'Really?'

'Might be nothing, mind you.'

It wasn't far to Poachers' Ease. Kathy stopped on the grass verge opposite the Fitzpatricks' cottage and walked across to the gate. The click and squeak brought the usual response from the Labradors, who escorted her enthusiastically up the path, although Kathy had difficulty looking Henrietta in the eye. Toby Fitzpatrick opened the front door. The sense of unease that she had noticed earlier seemed to have intensified. He looked grey, his smile tight and shallow, his voice tentative. If it is a marital thing, Kathy thought, it's more than a one-off row. And she thought of Peter White's information, and the look on Fitzpatrick's face when he had seen her by the pool. Did he spy on Eva in her pool, she wondered. Did he have a thing about her?

'Helen's out at the moment,' he said, peering round the half-open door at her. 'She'll be back in an hour.'

'I'd like to speak to you, Mr Fitzpatrick.'

'Oh.' He frowned, then reluctantly opened the door. 'Come in, then.'

He didn't invite her to sit down, and they stood awkwardly in the space just inside the house.

'I wanted to check one little detail in what you and your wife told us, Mr Fitzpatrick. About when Eva left to go up to London, remember? You told us that she went on the Thursday, which would be the third. Are you absolutely sure about that?'

'Oh.' Fitzpatrick swallowed. 'Yes, I think so.'

'How did you know? Did you see her leave?'

'Er, probably not, no. I suppose . . . I suppose Sammy told us.' He rubbed a hand across his face.

'Are you feeling all right? You don't look very well.'

'I'm all right. Was that all?'

'When would Sammy have told you this, about Eva leaving on Thursday?'

'Oh, God, I don't know, I – Oh, yes!' he said. 'He told Helen on the Sunday, when she and the other two went to play tennis. Didn't she tell you that?'

Kathy nodded. 'What about the Sunday evening? Where were you then?'

'What?' Fitzpatrick passed his hand over his face again, and Kathy thought he looked as if he were on the point of collapse.

'Please, sit down,' she said. 'What's the matter?'

'I'm sorry . . . I don't feel well. Maybe you should go.'

'Shall I get a doctor?'

'No, I just need to lie down.'

'I'll get you a glass of water.'

Kathy hurried through to the kitchen and found a glass, which she ran under the tap. The two glass vases she had noticed the first time she had come here were standing on the draining board beside the sink, one of them filled with flowers from the cottage garden, the other empty and turned upside down after being rinsed. It still had a small adhesive label on the base, *Made in Finland*.

When she returned to the front room with the glass of water, Toby Fitzpatrick seemed both more collected and more wan. He smiled faintly at her from the depths of the armchair and said, in a feeble voice, 'I'm so sorry. I have a slight heart condition . . . nothing serious, but I sometimes have a bit of a turn. I just need to stay calm for a while, then everything's all right.'

'Do you have medication I could fetch?'

'No, no. No need for that. Look, I really think it would be best if you come back when my wife is here — maybe tomorrow . . . if you still need to, that is.'

'OK, if you're sure you don't need help.'

She departed, thinking that there wasn't much to choose between the acting abilities of Toby Fitzpatrick and Ronnie Wilkes.

She left her car where it was, and began walking along the lane, trying to think. McLarren would want her back in London, she knew, following up leads on forged stamps. She could imagine him now, in his office in Cobalt Square, asking where the hell she was, and what the hell she thought she was doing, wandering through the bird-twittering woods on a beautiful sunny morning when there was real work to be done. Thinking of this, she was glad she had left her mobile in the car.

She came to the gates of the Crow's Nest, and it occurred to her that she still had the key to the house, and knew the code to deactivate the burglar alarm. There seemed no point in going in, when every inch had been covered twice by SOCO teams and forensic staff. But if Starling had lied about when Eva had left, there must have been a reason, and that reason must surely have occurred here.

Maybe. She thought of McLarren again, and walked to the front door feeling like a schoolkid playing truant.

Inside, the stillness of the house enveloped her once more. It was like the stillness of an extremely self-contained witness, which would only yield to an indirect form of interrogation.

She made her way to Starling's den. There was the green-baize-topped table where he had sat that night and wept over his stamps, just as Eva's father had wept over the copies Starling had given him. Did normal people do that? Did both men suffer from some kind of personality disorder, some obscure branch of kleptomania, perhaps, that they recognised in each other, and Eva recognised in both of them?

And there was Starling's wine rack against the end wall, an impressive collection of dozens of bottles, although he drank little according to Helen Cooper. Presumably another form of collecting for investment, for some of the bottles certainly looked old and dusty.

But why would they be dusty, Kathy wondered, in a room that was regularly cleaned? Come to that, why would they be kept on wooden racks in the den, when the house had a purpose-built wine cellar?

She went through to the kitchen, to the door that led to the cellar steps, and another question immediately faced her. The door had a lock, a Yale, the same kind as on the front door, and recently fitted by the look of it. Such locks had a knob on one side and a keyhole on the other, and were intended to prevent people on the keyhole side from coming through the door unless they had a key. Why would you put such a lock on a cellar door, with the knob on the kitchen side? To keep someone in the cellar, was the only answer that came to mind. It was so obvious that, once you'd spotted it, the lock might as well have had a flashing red light attached. And yet no one had noticed it during their searches.

Kathy turned the knob and went inside. She found the light switch and went down the cellar steps, breathing in the air, cool and fusty like a crypt. By the light of the naked electric bulb she went through the first cellar room, beneath the kitchen, to the second under the hall, where the old wine racks were formed beneath stone benches. When she examined them closely she found that a few of the apertures were thick with dust, while others, presumably recently occupied by bottles, had almost none. Not long ago someone had moved all the bottles to the new timber racks upstairs in the den. The SOCO team, looking for drugs, bloodstains, fibres, scratches or signs of violence, had paid no attention to the levels of dust inside the old wine racks. Why would they?

As a prison, the cellar was soundproof and secure. It was also spacious, clean and dry. Apart from the shelves of the wine racks, there was little dust, and the stone-flag floor was spotless. Frustratingly so. A Yale lock and some unused wine racks didn't necessarily amount to anything at all.

Kathy was searching for something more substantial when the floorboards above her head gave a creak. She froze. Another creak. A silence, and then another. Someone was walking across the hall, slowly.

This someone must have a key. Kathy had the only key given to the police, so it wasn't them. Who else? A neighbour? Could Toby Fitzpatrick have followed her to the house? Or someone closer to home? Sammy?

This someone would also presumably notice that the alarm had been switched off. Was this why they were moving so slowly across the hall? Kathy stepped silently back to the first cellar room, and almost immediately heard the muffled clump of a footstep on the polished floorboards of the kitchen directly over her head. They could hardly miss the open cellar door now, the glow of the cellar light within. Just as she was working on this thought, the cellar light clicked off and she heard the thump of the door being shut.

In the sudden total darkness Kathy swore to herself. In her mind the image was still fresh of the foot of the stairs, about fifteen feet in front of her and to the right. She walked forward towards it, banged her shin on the baluster post, grabbed the rail and sprinted up the steps. Without bothering to grope for the light switch she hammered on the door and called out.

She thought she heard a cry from the other side, stopped and listened. It seemed to take an age before the lock clicked and the door swung open, and she found herself facing Marianna, who had the knuckles of her left hand pressed to her mouth as if to stifle a scream. 'Oh, dear Mother of God,' she whimpered. 'You scare the living daylights from me.' Her English seemed to have become quite fluent. Kathy looked over her shoulder and saw the couple from the embassy with whom Marianna had been staying. Marianna turned to them and said a few words in Portuguese, at which they nodded and left, looking cautiously at Kathy.

'I come to check nothing smell in fridge,' she said, turning back to Kathy.

'I'm glad you did, Marianna. I wanted to talk to you.' Kathy tried to sound composed, although her heart was still hammering from her experience in the cellar.

Marianna looked anxious. Her eyes slipped past Kathy to the cellar door, then back to Kathy's face and, seeing the expression there, darted away. 'I make coffee,' she said.

'Never mind about coffee,' Kathy replied firmly. 'Sit down.' She sat opposite her, across the kitchen table. 'The last time we met, Marianna, you could hardly speak a word of English, and you told me a pack of lies about what an angel Eva was. Now I want the truth. I know about her drugs . . .' Marianna's bottom lip trembled, but there was no denial, '. . . and now I want some answers. OK?'

Marianna gave a deep sigh. 'OK.'

'Why did you tell me those lies? Were you afraid of Sammy? He beat you, didn't he?' Marianna looked startled, and Kathy saw she had got something wrong. 'He gave you a black eye, didn't he?'

Marianna's eyes widened, her bottom lip slowly pushed upward and she gave a sob. 'No, no,' she managed to say. 'Not Sammy. My little Eva gave me black eye. She is wicked girl, God rest her soul.'

'Tell me about it.'

Marianna sniffed. 'She was wild girl in Portugal. She worry

her daddy to death. Sammy was good man for her. At first they were happy. She is like little girl again. But then she grows bored.' Marianna pulled a tiny lace handkerchief from her sleeve and dabbed her nose, and began to twist the material in her fingers. 'She has secrets. I know this. She scream and fight with me, but she cannot fool her Auntie Marianna. I try to help Sammy. I say, "No cash, Sammy, give her no cash." But she is so *sneaky*. Sammy does not always believe me, but I know my Eva. She steals things, and sells her clothes and jewellery, and what else I don't know. I don't like to think what she do for drugs when she go to London. And all the time she get thinner and thinner, and then I start to find blood on her pillow. I tell Sammy, "We must do something, she is bleeding to death with drugs." He is very worried. He plead with her, he get angry, she cry and she promise, always false promises.'

She took another break to dab at her eyes and nose and take some deep breaths.

'Finally he say no more London, he sell flat. She scream and scream and scream. She go mad, and try to leave him. So we make her stay.'

Her eyes drifted over to the cellar door again.

'When was this, Marianna?'

'Two weeks ago, Thursday night. It is terrible. At first we lock her in her room upstairs. But then she begin to break things. We are frightened she will hurt herself. I say to Sammy, "We should get doctor," but Sammy is afraid. He want to keep her safe until she calm down, then he will send her to private clinic. We put bed downstairs in cellar for her. When her friends come, he say she is in London since Thursday.'

'Yes, I understand, Marianna. Go on.'

'On Sunday night she escape. At nine o'clock I go to see her, to say goodnight, and she pretend to sleep. I take all her clothes away to clean. While I do this, she steal my key to cellar door. I didn't know.' Marianna began to weep silently. 'She has nothing – no shoes, no money. She disappear into woods. Sammy go to her at eleven o'clock, and she is gone.'

'What was she wearing?'

'Her summer nightgown. Silk, almost nothing. She grab old

coat at the back door, we think, otherwise nothing. Near naked.'

'Surely she could have found something to wear when she left?'

'Sammy is moving about house. She don't stop. She go straight out. I check everywhere. She take nothing.'

'So she could have been gone, what, an hour? longer? before you discovered she was missing?'

Marianna nodded miserably.

'What did you do?'

'Sammy go out to look for her. He drive around, through the woods, down to Farnham, everywhere. Finally he come home, about midnight. He make phone calls. He say he think she will try to go to London, so he go there, to flat, to wait for her.'

'What about you? Did you stay here?'

'Yes. I wait in kitchen for her, all night, waiting for her to come home, like naughty little girl. But she not come.' She began to weep again, more deeply this time.

Kathy waited for her sobs to subside a little, then said, 'What happened next?'

'Sammy phone me from flat at dawn. She not come there. He say he stay there all day, and phone me every hour. Nothing.'

'Did Sammy say if he had contacted anyone else?'

Marianna shook her head.

'What about your neighbours, the Fitzpatricks? Wouldn't Sammy have spoken to them when he was searching for Eva in the woods?'

'I don't know. He is ashamed, and frightened.'

'Yes, I can see that. Marianna, I'm going to have to ask you to go over all this again, in a police station, and make a proper statement. But we can do that later, when you're feeling up to it. One last thing. Do you know where Sammy is now?'

Marianna looked at Kathy in surprise. 'Mr and Mrs Cooper?'

'No, he's left there, and no one knows where he's gone. We're worried for his safety. Where do you think he might be?'

Marianna's eyes widened in alarm. 'Oh, please God, no more death!'

15

An Orphan on our Doorstep

Kathy walked fast back along the lane towards her car and phone. But as she rehearsed in her mind what she had to say, she could hear McLarren reply, 'So what?' Starling and Marianna had covered up the real time at which Eva had left because of embarrassment, having already told the tennis players that she had gone the previous Thursday.

And it wasn't Sammy who was bothering Kathy now. She was thinking of Eva, fleeing down the lane, through the woods, barefoot, *almost naked*, as Marianna had said, and perhaps running into Toby Fitzpatrick in the twilight. Toby Fitzpatrick, who liked to watch her secretly from the woods through his binoculars, in her yellow bikini, in the pool; Toby Fitzpatrick who perhaps could lay his hands on a cardboard box of Finnish origin from the vases his wife had recently been given; Toby Fitzpatrick, whose dog had taken such a fancy to Eva's head, and who now seemed gripped by some sickness of spirit.

She stopped short of the Fitzpatricks' cottage and thought how much more compelling it would all be if she could find some physical evidence of a link to Eva's murder. And she thought again about the cardboard box in which her head had been delivered, and of the Iittala vases in the Fitzpatricks' house. Their label had looked fresh, the vases new. And there had been two of them, identical, bought in two identical Finnish cardboard boxes, perhaps. At least, the size seemed about right. And if one had been used to hold Eva's head a week ago, the other might still be around.

Above her on the slope she saw the chestnut tree beneath which Toby Fitzpatrick had stood silently watching her that first time she had come to the cottage. She made her way up through the bracken towards it, and found the path that led past the gate at the rear of the cottage garden.

There was a small covered area against the back wall of the cottage for the dustbins, a compost enclosure next to it, a bicycle wheel visible. The Fitzpatricks clearly liked to waste nothing. Old plant pots and lengths of rope and garden hose were neatly stacked. There were piles of old newspapers tied up with twine ready for recycling, and beside them cardboard boxes.

She opened the gate as silently as she could. There was no sign of the dogs as she walked down the brick path towards the cottage. The cardboard boxes were stacked, small within large, and when she reached them she began to pull them apart, looking for a partner for the pale grey box that was so vivid in her mind. She had barely begun when she was interrupted by the snout of a Labrador, pushing against her thigh. It gave a little yelp of pleasure, and she saw the other behind, equally eager.

She patted them. 'Good girls,' she whispered soothingly, until they were prepared to let her get back to her task. And suddenly there it was, identical to the one they had reconstructed from the debris on the road, and the sight of it gave her a jolt.

'What the hell are you doing?'

She swung round at the sound of Toby Fitzpatrick's voice. He was standing just a few paces behind her, and when he saw what she was holding he gave a stifled cry and turned as pale as he had when he had seen her at the pool in Eva's bikini. He was a picture of guilt, and Kathy said, spontaneously improvising, 'You saw her, didn't you? That night, a week last Sunday.'

'You know?' he said.

'Yes, Toby, I know.'

'Oh, God . . .' he muttered, and covered his face with his hand. 'The stamps and everything?'

'Yes,' Kathy said, trying not to look surprised. My God, she thought, he kidnapped Eva to get Sammy's stamps?

'It's all over, then.'

'It'll be a relief,' she said calmly, 'to talk about it.'

He stared at her in despair. 'Yes . . . I suppose it will, yes. It's been getting too much, worrying about it. I've been going off my head.'

'Why don't you tell me now? Get it off your chest.'

He hung his head in defeat. 'She was bleeding,' he began. 'Her feet were bleeding from running down the road in the dark. She was in such a state —'

'What's going on?' Helen Fitzpatrick's voice sounded sharply from the direction of the back door of the cottage. The dogs yelped in excitement and tore towards her as she stepped out into the sunlight. She was wearing a white plastic apron and yellow rubber gloves, both of which were smeared with blood, and in her right hand she was holding the broad-bladed cleaver she used to chop up the dogs' meat and bones. To Kathy she looked just like one of Dr Mehta's assistants.

'Darling . . .' Toby Fitzpatrick turned to her, his body bent in supplication.

'Toby, what is it?' Helen said. 'You look dreadful.' She glared at Kathy. 'What is it? What do you want?'

'It's all over, darling,' he replied, close to breaking. 'She knows everything.'

His wife's eyes narrowed at the sight of the cardboard box in Kathy's hands. 'What are you talking about, Toby?' she said softly. 'What does she know?'

'Mrs Fitzpatrick,' Kathy said quickly, 'I'm taking your husband to Farnham police station. You can come too, if you wish.'

Helen Fitzpatrick took a step towards her, then another. 'What for? We've told you everything we know several times over.'

'Mr Fitzpatrick wants to make a statement concerning the death of Eva Starling. Isn't that right, Mr Fitzpatrick?'

He looked from one woman to the other, then said, in a very small voice, 'Yes, yes. It's true.'

'Don't be stupid, Toby,' his wife said. 'You'll do no such thing.'

It was only at this point that Kathy realised, with a terrible clarity, that Helen Fitzpatrick knew every bit as much about what had happened as her husband. She was only a couple of paces away now, the cleaver raised to shoulder height, out of the way of the dogs with their thrashing tails. Like a manic chorus, they milled around Kathy, blocking her way back to the path. Beyond them Toby Fitzpatrick stood, looking wild and dazed.

'Mrs Fitzpatrick,' Kathy said, and thought, Is this how it was for Mary Martin? 'Helen, please think carefully. I'm a police officer, you know that.'

Helen Fitzpatrick stared at her for a long moment, then said, in a low voice, 'Oh, Toby. You bloody fool.' She turned on her heel and marched back into the cottage, followed by the dogs.

After a long silence, he said hoarsely, 'I could do with a drink.'

They went inside. As they went through the kitchen Kathy was relieved to see the cleaver abandoned beside a pile of ox hearts on the worktop. In the living-room they found Helen sitting rigidly on the sofa, still in her bloodstained plastic apron and gloves, staring at nothing.

'I – I'm getting myself a stiff brandy,' Fitzpatrick said. 'Anyone else?'

No one replied, and he went to a cupboard in the corner of the room and poured himself a drink with shaking hand.

'It must have been about ten o'clock that night,' he said. 'Sunday. We were about to go to bed when there was this frightful knocking on the front door, and there she was. I thought at first there must have been a sudden shower, because her hair was dripping wet. She had this old coat over her shoulders, and she was clutching her hands like this . . .' He held the glass of brandy in front of his chest as if he were praying with it. 'Helen wrapped her in a blanket, and sat her down over there, and she started talking. At first we couldn't make it out. She was quite wild, shaking and crying, and she was mixing up Portuguese with English words. Eventually she made us understand that Sammy had been keeping her locked up in their cellar. We couldn't believe it at first, it just seemed so bizarre. But there she was, in that state, when Sammy had told us she'd gone to London days before.

'I couldn't get her to explain why she was so wet. I said I'd fetch a doctor, or the police, but she wouldn't have it – she got really hysterical then, shrieking at me.' He looked around in dismay. 'Most of all she seemed terrified that Sammy would come to the cottage and find her, and she made us promise we wouldn't tell him she was there, and that we'd protect her.'

'I took her upstairs to the bathroom then,' Helen Fitzpatrick broke in dully. 'I tried to make out where she was hurt, but apart from some cuts to her feet, she didn't seem injured. She was thin as a rake, though, and shaking terribly, and she smelt of chlorine, as if she'd been in the swimming-pool. She was holding something between her hands, which I saw was a shiny metal tube, dark blue, and I thought . . . well, I had no idea what it was. I thought it might be something precious, jewellery or something, she was hanging on to it so tightly.

'I got her a dressing-gown and slippers to change into, and she calmed down a bit. She said that she would like a cup of tea, and I left her and came down to the kitchen to make it. When I returned with it, a few minutes later, the bathroom door was closed. There isn't a lock on it, and I knocked and went in. She was on her knees beside the bath, and I thought at first she must be being sick. But then she looked up at me with this funny smile, completely calm now. Beside her on the floor was the metal tube, in two pieces, and there were several little plastic bags, empty, lying around on the floor. I think I realised then what it was. The most weird thing, the thing that made me cross, was that I'd just received a letter from my sister, and I'd left it on the bathroom window-sill, and Eva had torn the page in two, and had rolled one half up into a sort of tube. And I thought, You bitch, I haven't finished reading that letter yet.

'We managed to get her downstairs again. She was calm, but not really with us, and she stumbled getting down the stairs. By this stage I was wondering whether we shouldn't ring Sammy and tell him to come and get her, but she seemed so genuinely frightened of him that I wasn't sure. When I mentioned Marianna, that seemed just as bad as Sammy. What she said she wanted was to go up to London. She said she had a friend there who would look after her.'

'Did she give a name?' Kathy said. 'Any indication at all of who it might be?'

'No, she was very secretive about it. Her manner was quite weird, playful one minute and paranoid the next. It was difficult to make sense of what she was saying half the time. She seemed to want us to take her to London straight away, but the thought of taking off in the middle of the night with her in such a state . . . Then . . .'

Helen paused and took a deep breath, as if coming to the difficult bit. 'Then she said she had a secret she would share with us, if we would take her to London. She said it was a very valuable secret, which Toby especially would be very interested in.' She turned her head away from her husband, who lowered his, his shoulders sagging visibly.

'She said that Sammy had been very mean to her – well, I had to laugh at that. It was incredible the clothes and things that Sammy showered on her. She was the most pampered wife I'd ever seen, and I told her so. But she got angry with me then. I think that was when I first realised that she didn't like me, probably never had. Anyway, I think that made it easier in a way for her to tell us her secret, because it was a punishment, not only for Sammy but also for us.

'She said that she'd found a way to get money from Sammy to buy things to make her happy – she meant her drugs, of course. She had a friend, she said, who sold expensive stamps to Sammy and gave her a commission on the sale. The reason she got the commission was that she had introduced Sammy to him, and also so that she would keep quiet about the fact that the stamps he was selling Sammy were worthless fakes. When she told us this, Toby made some strange sound, and I couldn't understand why he'd suddenly gone white. Then I guessed . . . Why don't you tell her, Toby?' she said, mouth tight.

He husband was crouched forward in his seat. He cleared his throat and muttered, 'Oh, God . . .'

'Go on!' she ordered him, and he straightened upright with an expressionless face and took up the story.

'Months ago, Sammy had shown me these stamps, Chalon Heads, which he'd been getting from a new source. They were of a much better quality, and a much better price, than he'd been able to obtain through the usual dealers and auction sales. They included some absolute corkers . . .

'Anyway, the story was that this dealer in London had a widow for a client, whose husband's family had been collecting stamps for generations. His father and grandfather had been colonial administrators in various places around the globe, and had built up a fabulous collection of Empire stamps, especially Chalon Heads. The old widow knew they had value, though not how much, but she didn't want to dispose of the lot because she hoped to leave most of them to her grandchildren one day. But in the meantime she had very little income, and there were living expenses and charities to support, so she was selling off her husband's legacy, a page at a time.

'According to Sammy, he had come to an agreement with the dealer to take all the old widow's stock, the minute it came through the door. Sammy was very excited about it, as if he'd found a hidden seam of gold, and I can remember how jealous I felt. Luck like that only came to people like Sammy, who didn't need it, I thought.

'From time to time he would show me his latest acquisitions from the widow's collection, as he called it. Part of him wanted to keep it a secret, but another part wanted to trumpet it from the rooftops, and I suppose I was the way he resolved it. I was the tame audience, appreciative and dependable, listening to him babbling on about the latest Head when he couldn't contain himself any more, and promising not to tell anyone else. He didn't realise that I was burning up inside with envy – they really were wonderful stamps.'

'He didn't tell you anything about the dealer?'

'Oh, no! Absolutely nothing. He was terrified others would get in and bump the prices up. It was only by accident that I discovered that the man was in London, when Sammy let drop one time that he'd been up to town again to buy more stamps. Come to think of it, he may have said that on purpose, as a false trail. Anyway, as it happened, he didn't need to tell me, because one time when I was coming away from a session with him, Eva met me in the garden. She teased me a bit, about playing with Sammy's stamps, like we were little boys. Then she asked me if I thought his latest purchases, from the widow, were any good, and I said, oh, gosh, yes, they were absolutely wonderful, and Sammy was so lucky to have found his source. Then she said that she knew where he got them from, "such a funny little man", she said. I asked if she'd met the dealer then, and she said she had. She knew where his shop was, and she said the man adored her, and would do anything for her. And I said something like, "Well, I wish you'd persuade him to sell some to me." It was a spontaneous remark, because I knew I didn't have any money to buy that sort of thing with. She just laughed.

'About a month later she phoned me, here, at home. I said that Helen was out at work, and she said she knew that, she wanted to talk to me. She said she'd been to see the dealer, and she had something I might be interested in. Well, it all sounded quite intriguing, and I agreed to walk the dogs past the end of her garden, and meet her. I wasn't really prepared for what she had to tell me.'

His wife gave a derisive snort.

'What it was,' Toby battled on, 'was that she had mentioned my interest to the dealer, and his response was that he wasn't prepared to put at risk his relationship with a dependable client like Sammy for the sake of one or two little sales on the side to me. Well, I felt a bit flattened, because I'd thought she'd got something positive to tell me, but I could understand his point of view.

'However, she said, the widow had just dropped in something big, a whole album. There was some story about her wanting to set up a trust fund for her grandchildren's education, or something. Sammy knew nothing of it yet, and the dealer might be prepared to sell it to me as a one-off, if I kept quiet about it to Sammy. He wouldn't split it up, I had to take the lot or nothing. I said, "What do you mean, big?" And she said, "Sixty thousand."

'I laughed, and told her that was way beyond my resources, and she seemed surprised, as if she couldn't imagine anyone not having sixty thousand quid to spend. Anyway, she had photocopies of the pages of the album, and I said I'd love to see them, and she gave them to me on the understanding that she had to give them back the following day to the dealer, who would then sell the album to Sammy.

'I took them home and had a close look at them, pages from a very old album, with this fabulous collection of mint Bahamas

Chalon Heads, all beautifully written up in an old-fashioned script. It was mouthwatering, it really was. So then I began checking the stamps against their market values in the Stanley Gibbons catalogue, and I soon realised that sixty thousand was an incredibly cheap price for them. There were individual items that alone were worth five thousand and more, and I calculated that, even discounting quite heavily, the album would fetch at least twice its price at auction.'

Fitzpatrick poured himself another brandy, his hand shaking as he held the bottle against the rim of the small glass. He took a sip, grimaced and coughed.

'So anyway,' he continued, 'I fell for it. I – I think you'd better tell them about the money, Helen. I feel rather sick.'

She looked at him coldly. 'We went through a bad patch, a few years back. Toby was made redundant, at the worst possible time in terms of our commitments. We'd got ourselves caught in the housing market, and ended up with a huge mortgage and negative equity. When we finally extracted ourselves, we'd lost most of our capital, and we couldn't get another mortgage to start again, what with Toby being out of work. I had this inspiration to come up here, as I told you before, to the Hog's Back, where I used to come as a little girl to stay with my aunt. It was running away, I suppose, and it seemed an impossible dream, until we came upon this place. It was exactly what I'd imagined, a little refuge in the woods. We couldn't afford to buy, of course, and we started renting, but we got to know the landlord, a retired judge, and he was really sweet, and after a while offered us an option to buy within five years, if we could raise enough, at a pretty reasonable price, which he would hold for us.

'Well, it seemed like a miracle, although we didn't have nearly enough. We had the remains of Toby's payout, and I started doing any kind of work I could get, and gradually we built it up. We had sixty thousand, amazingly enough.' Her eyes narrowed at her husband.

'I told you, darling,' he whispered, 'it was a pure coincidence she came up with that figure. I never told her or anyone else about our plan.' He turned to Kathy and said, with a pathetic sigh, 'I thought the stamps would double our money, you see.

We'd be able to buy the cottage, and everything would be all right.'

'But he didn't tell me,' Helen said.

'No. I didn't think Helen would agree to risk our money like that. Not on stamps. She's always thought they were a bit of a joke.'

'Didn't you get them checked by an expert?' Kathy said.

'Oh, I thought of that. They came with certificates of authentication, you see. Quite impeccable. And I had to act quickly, because the dealer was in two minds about selling to me rather than Sammy . . .'

He ran out of words. For a while nobody said anything, then his wife said, 'Yes, well, I knew none of this. So you can imagine how I felt when Eva, the poor orphan on our doorstep, revealed that the stamps were worthless, and that she'd ripped us off of our complete future. It wasn't helped by the fact that she seemed to think it was all a hilarious joke. She kept giggling, until I slapped her.'

Kathy nodded. 'What happened then?'

'She sobered up after that. When I'd finally understood the whole dreadful story, I said she would have to take us to the dealer, and he would have to give us our money back, but she refused. She said the money had all gone, and he would never pay. She said the only way we could get our money back would be to sell the stamps again, without letting on they were forgeries. After a while . . . I suppose I came to realise that that was the only way we would be able to hang on to the cottage. I knew it would be dishonest, a fraud, but the alternative was too much to bear, and it wasn't as if anyone would be really hurt by it, not if they never discovered that the stamps were fakes. I suppose the thing that decided it was when Eva suggested that the dealer could sell them to Sammy, and get our money back that way. She thought that was very funny. I thought . . .' she lifted her chin defiantly '. . . I thought that Sammy didn't really deserve his money and that house and everything else anyway. I mean, he made it in some sort of dodgy way, didn't he? He was nearly imprisoned for fraud some time ago, wasn't he? So I thought that it would be only fair if anyone had to lose by it he should. He could easily afford it, anyway . . .' Her defiance ran out of steam, and she went silent.

'So what did you decide to do?' Kathy asked.

'We decided that Toby would take Eva up to London, with the stamps, and she would arrange the sale through the dealer again. I would stay here in case Sammy came looking for Eva, and try to put him off the scent. I gave her some of my clothes, and they left, what, about eleven thirty, I suppose.'

Her husband nodded. 'She wanted to go to her flat, to get her own clothes and phone her dealer friend, she said. The plan was that we'd go to the dealer together that night, and I'd make sure there were no misunderstandings about us getting our money back. Anyway, by the time we got to Canonbury, she was asleep, and when I woke her up, she insisted she couldn't go on that night. She was in a pretty exhausted state. I had to practically carry her into the flat. I told her I'd call back in the morning, and we'd go to the dealer then.'

'You still had no idea where this man's shop was?'

'No, she wouldn't tell me anything. So I came home. Early next morning I went back up to town, and she was gone — at least, there was no reply at the flat. We've never heard from her again.'

Kathy looked from one to the other of the dejected pair. There was no doubt in her mind that they had told her the truth. 'I'm going to need a statement about Eva's visit that night,' she said, 'and all about the forged stamps, the dealer, and so on. You don't have the stamps any more, then?'

Fitzpatrick shook his head sadly. 'I can remember exactly what they were, though, and give you a full description.'

'What about the box?' Kathy asked. 'How did the killer get hold of that?'

'Helen put Eva's things in a paper carrier bag to take to London with her,' he explained. 'When we got there, the bag fell apart from the damp clothes, and I put them in the box which was on the back seat.' He looked at his wife. 'I used it to take your raspberry jam to the church fair the other week, do you remember?'

She nodded.

'I left the box in the flat.'

Kathy got to her feet.

'If you find the dealer,' Helen said, 'do you think there's any possibility that you could make him refund our money?'

'I don't know,' Kathy said. 'There's several people with that idea in their heads at present, I should think. Let's just hope we find him.'

McLarren's reaction, when Kathy reported to him later that afternoon, was much as she had anticipated. He was wearing a pair of vivid scarlet braces, his shirt-sleeves rolled up, and his mood was irritated, impatient and sarcastic. Hewitt was with him, and after she told them Marianna's story, McLarren looked pointedly at his assistant.

'Sergeant, I thought I had made it quite plain that, in my most *humble* opinion, the key to this case lies not in the marital problems of the Starlings, nor in Mrs Starling's penchant for prohibited substances, but in the forgeries. Those other matters are only likely to confuse our investigation and cause other branches of our fine service to interfere with its smooth progress, and I have to say that I do take a dim view of you gallivanting about the countryside while the rest of us have been fruitlessly attempting to track down Raphael's other victims in the great metropolis.' He brandished his eyebrows at her in his most intimidating manner, and Hewitt suppressed a smirk.

'That's what I'm coming to, sir. I've found another victim.'

'What? Explain yourself, lassie!'

Kathy did so, and McLarren's mood lifted. 'Well, now! That's splendid, Kathy, splendid!'

She made her escape before he changed his mind.

The front door of La Fortuna was locked – it was too early to be open for evening customers. The lights were off, and no one responded to Kathy's knock. She went round the corner and found a laneway that gave access to the back door. She could just faintly hear the sound of music from inside. She rapped on the door several times, and eventually it was opened by a young man wiping his hands on a white apron.

'Yeah?'

'Tomaso in?'

'Maybe. Who wants him?'

She showed her warrant card and followed him inside, through the kitchen to the dry store where Tomaso was checking cans of olive oil against a list on a clipboard.

'Hi, Inspector.' He looked at her briefly and went on with his task. 'Any developments?'

'Sergeant. Yes. I'd like a word.'

He caught the coolness in her voice and looked at her again. 'Sure.' He gave her a big smile and led her through into the dining-room.

'Want a drink?'

'A coffee would be good.'

'Sure. What you want?'

'Short black.'

Kathy watched him as he went to the machine in the corner of the bar and made the coffee. He brought over two tiny gold-rimmed cups and sat down opposite her. 'So, what's new?'

'Have you heard from Sammy Starling recently?'

'Mr Starling? No. Why?'

Kathy said nothing for a moment, then spoke more quietly, so that he had to lean forward to catch it. 'I'm not interested in what Eva put up her nose, Tomaso, except in so far as it leads to her killer. Understand?'

He met her gaze with a poker face, then gave a brief nod.

'She got her stuff here, didn't she?'

'No.' He shook his head decisively.

'But you knew about it.'

He waved a hand. 'I could make an informed guess, sure.'

'Tell me about it.'

He brought out a packet of cigarettes and offered her one. She refused and he lit up, considered her for a while as he smoked. Finally he seemed to come to a decision. 'OK. She needed cash. She didn't say what for, but I could guess. When she asked us, we would put extra on to her meal account, and give her the cash.' He spread his hands. 'It's no big deal. A customer needs some cash, no problem. Nothing wrong with that.'

'But you knew there was something funny about it.'

'Only because she asked us not to tell her husband. She said he was worried about her not eating, that she was anorexic, so she would come in and order maybe a salad, sometimes nothing at all, and we would make up a bill with the most expensive dishes on the menu, and she would take the difference in cash.'

'Why didn't you believe the anorexia story?'

He laughed. 'Because it was always the most expensive dishes that went on the bill, not the most nutritious. And wine, too, always the best. I don't know what gave her away.'

'Sammy found out?'

Tomaso raised the little cup to his lips. 'Sure. One lunch-time he came in here, by himself, and asked for me to serve him. He ordered a plate of pasta, then told me to stop playing games with his wife's account, or he would close us down. I didn't argue.'

'What did Eva make of that?'

'She must have made other arrangements, I don't know. She still came in here for a salad and a glass of wine.'

'Where did she get her drugs?'

'I don't know.'

'Yes, you do.'

He looked sulky, then smiled. 'I don't *know*, but I can guess. Sometimes she will come in here, and she's high, and I will say, "You're in a good mood tonight, Princess." Then she says, "Yes, I've been to the movies," or sometimes, "Yes, I've been to Hollywood." And I say, "Do you have a friend in Holly-wood, then, Princess?" And she says, "Sure, I have a very good friend in Hollywood." '

Tomaso paused to finish his coffee. 'There's a little cinema over in Camden Town shows foreign movies. Called Cinema Hollywood. I think that's where she met her friend.'

Kathy got to her feet.

'Satisfied?' Tomaso said.

'Yes. If you hear any word of Sammy, let me know, will you? He's dropped out of sight, and we're anxious to make contact with him. He may be trying to find Eva's murderer himself.'

A shadow of worry passed across Tomaso's face.

'There's nothing else I should know is there, Tomaso?' Kathy said.

'No, no. Say, you'd better give me your home phone number, just in case I need to reach you, eh?'

'I'm not often at home. This is my office number. There'll be someone there twenty-four hours. If I'm not there one of the other detectives will help you.'

He looked disappointed. 'Why don't you stay for a meal?'

She laughed. 'I couldn't even afford one of your salads, Tomaso.'

All the same, La Fortuna had put Kathy in the mood for Italian, and she stopped on the way home for some take-away lasagne at La Casa Romana, a little place not far from where she lived, and considerably closer to her budget.

After her meal and a bath, Kathy sat by the window of her small flat, looking at the street lights coming on below, sections at a time, across the hazy twilit city landscape. She had reconstructed several unexpected corners of the story — Eva's imprisonment and flight, her way of cheating Sammy and Toby, her source of drugs — but how much closer had she really got to the heart of it all?

Sammy must surely now be the prime suspect for Eva's murder. He had discovered Eva's escape at around eleven that night, and the fact that he had phoned Ronnie Wilkes soon after made it likely that he thought she was heading for Canonbury. He must have driven there after an abortive search along the woodland lanes around the Crow's Nest, and may well have been watching the flat when Fitzpatrick and Eva had arrived. He would have waited for the man to leave, then gone in and confronted his wife. Had she told him how she had been cheating him? The irony must have struck him very hard, that she had used the same thing, his beloved stamps, to cheat him that he had used to win her from her father. And if he then became enraged and killed her, how natural and appropriate to use them again in the story he concocted of a kidnapping revolving around the forthcoming stamp auction he would certainly have known all about. He would have needed help, a male, to telephone the instructions to Heathrow, and send the final message.

She turned these ideas round in her head, and felt they had a certain thematic consistency. But what had they to do with Raphael and the murder of Mary Martin? How would Eva have become involved with the stamp dealer and the forgery scheme in the first place? Through her drugs? And why had someone —

Sammy presumably – framed Brock over the disappearance of the Canada Cover?

To Kathy, this was the most worrying and puzzling thing. The meeting with him in Battle had been unsettling. It struck her how much she would miss him if he didn't come back. Not that she was dependent on him, but the thought that his disgrace might be irredeemable, that she would never be able to refer to him again, was like a death, the death of someone close.

She had been over those hours at Cabot's on the morning and afternoon of the auction again and again in her head, trying to fathom how it had been done. Now her mind began to replay it once again. At some point, when the sun finally dropped below the horizon and a green-orange glow in the sky was all that was left of the day, a thought began to form.

She made a call to the Fitzpatricks' cottage, and spoke for several minutes to Toby Fitzpatrick. He found her the information she wanted, and she rang off. The doodles on the writing pad in front of her formed a network of names, some linked and others, frustratingly, unconnected. She started again on a fresh sheet, then another and another until she gave up and went to bed.

16

The Moving Finger Writes

When the phone rang Kathy was in a deep sleep. As she fumbled for the light switch she registered the time on her bedside alarm as 1.16 a.m. She didn't immediately recognise the voice.

'Hewitt. Message from Superintendent McLarren for you. He says that you might care to join him at a crime scene.'

'Oh . . . right, fine. Where is it?'

'Shoreditch,' he said unenthusiastically. 'Eighteen Shepherd's Row.'

She dressed hurriedly and left. By the time she reached her car she was wide awake.

The area was mixed, commercial offices and warehouses spilling northwards from the City into areas of working-class housing spiked with larger Victorian institutional buildings. It had been a long time since this Shepherd's Row had seen any live sheep. It wriggled for just over a hundred yards in the general direction of Shepherdess Walk before coming to an end at an overscaled Edwardian pub, and it now housed a motley collection of low-cost service outlets – launderette, shoe repairs, shelving supplies, second-hand furniture, a pawn shop – as well as a street market three days a week. Tuesday had been one of those days, and the metal frameworks of the stalls stood deserted down the middle of the curving alley, sour smells of vegetable waste and burnt cardboard tainting the warm summer night.

Walter Pickering, dealer in stamps, banknotes and maps, occupied a small shop unit half-way along the alley, which was now the focus of attention. An ambulance had backed up the laneway left between market stalls and shop-fronts, and was standing by the open door of the shop. As Kathy arrived at the end of Shepherd's Row, its lights began flashing and it moved slowly forward. She drove on to the next corner, parked down a side-street and walked back.

A couple of uniformed men guarded the front shop area, with its counter, its shelves of old albums and reference books, and its displays of the products in which Walter Pickering traded. These looked, with their wrinkled plastic pouches and faded labels, remarkably drab and unappealing. The action had taken place in the office and store-room behind, now crammed with police, among whom she recognised Tony Hewitt and Leon Desai, who gave her a barely perceptible nod. This room was lined with industrial shelving on three sides, filled with card-board boxes. The fourth side was a bare wall. A naked fluores-cent strip-light was suspended over the centre of the room, directly above a single wooden chair with arms. This chair, a sturdy, blackened object, managed to convey, rather as electric chairs do, a strong sense of its recent occupant, for strips of elec-trical tape were still wrapped round each of its arms and bottom front legs, where he had been restrained, and his blood was splashed in spectacular patterns of splatters and spurts all round its focus. The bloody marks continued on to the bare wall facing the seat where, as if on a blackboard facing a single recalcitrant pupil, large letters of blood formed the single word, RAPHAEL.

'Jesus McTavish!' a voice murmured at Kathy's shoulder, as she stood taking this in. She turned to Superintendent McLarren in the doorway, newly arrived.

'Good evening, all,' he said briskly. 'Sorry I was delayed. Tony, fill us in, will you?'

'Sir. Local division alerted by neighbour's triple niner at 0018 reporting screams from the premises of Walter Pickering. Patrol officers discovered Mr Pickering here, alone, tied to this chair. He was semi-conscious. They called for medical assistance, and division called us on the strength of our recent warning regarding stamp dealers.'

'Good laddie.' McLarren said approvingly.

'I got here in time to interview Mr Pickering before the ambulance officers insisted on removing him to hospital. He was in very bad shape. He had been cut in a number of places by what he described as an old-fashioned, cut-throat razor. In particular, three of his fingers had been removed, and used by his assailant like marker pens, to write that name on the wall over there. Mr Pickering identified his assailant as "Sammy China".'

'Indeed. Our missing Mr Starling, I take it.'

'It was a nickname of his,' Kathy said.

McLarren nodded. 'Did you get out of Pickering what happened, Tony?'

'He lives above here, alone. He said that this Sammy called on him at about midnight, and insisted on seeing him in the shop. Sammy was a regular customer, and Pickering, of course, didn't know that he was on the run, though he had read about his wife's murder. Pickering is an old man, not very strong, and Sammy had no difficulty in overpowering him and taping him to the chair, where he proceeded to torture him in order to get information about forged stamps Pickering had been selling him.'

'Pickering admitted that to you, Tony?'

'Yes. He said that Sammy knew he had supplied them, and he was very angry about it. He wanted to know who else was involved, and eventually, with some persuasion, Pickering told him that his wife Eva had been a party from the beginning, and had taken a share of all proceeds.'

'How did Sammy take that, I wonder?'

'Not well, although Pickering said he thought Sammy already suspected, or half knew. Then Sammy wanted to know where the forgeries came from, and who had been behind it all. He demanded a name, but Pickering said he didn't know – he told me he was too scared to tell Sammy. So Sammy said they would discover the name one letter at a time. He cut off one of Pickering's fingers, and Pickering gave him the first letter, R. Sammy wrote it up, threw the finger away, and cut off another one. He said if the name was very long he'd have to go on and use other body parts, but if Pickering told him quickly, before the blood in the fingers dried up, he might get more than one letter out of each. I gather Pickering gave him the name pretty fast after that, sir.'

'Aye, no doubt,' McLarren said indifferently. 'What about an address, Tony? Did he tell him where he could find Raphael?' He leaned forward eagerly.

' 'Fraid not, sir. He said he passed out at that point, and I can believe it. He'd lost a bit of blood, apart from the shock. I'm surprised his ticker stood up to it.'

'Och, laddie!' McLarren said in disgust. 'You should have cut off a few more of his fingers yourself for it!'

'Yes, sir. I think the ambulance blokes might have objected.'

McLarren paced over to the wall and glared balefully at the large letters. 'Are you sure, Tony? Are you sure he didn't tell him?'

'Can't be certain. He was confused and pretty incoherent. But that was my impression. One thing I thought he did say was that Raphael and Eva were lovers.'

'Indeed!' McLarren's face lit up. 'How long before we can get to work on Mr Pickering ourselves, would you say?'

'Couldn't say. Days, most likely.'

'What about the house, upstairs?'

'Yeah. I haven't been up there yet, but the lads say it looks as if Sammy went upstairs after he'd done Pickering over down here – there's signs of bloody footprints on the landing, and some disturbance to drawers and things.'

'I wonder if he found it . . . Well, we must hope he did not, and that we shall! Full-scale alert for Mr Starling.'

'Done, sir.'

'And a complete search of this building, every floorboard and every inch of pipe it contains. We must have Raphael's location, ladies and gentlemen, before Sammy does, and before Raphael hears what's happened to his retail outlet.'

He turned to Kathy and added, 'Some people, you know, still doubt the very existence of Raphael. What will they make of this, I wonder?'

'It's a strong message, sir,' she said, unable to think of anything else to say.

'Aye, a strong message,' he repeated. 'A strong message.' And

265

then, in a melodramatic voice, with heightened rolling of his Rs, he intoned,

> 'The Moving Finger writes; and, having writ,
> Moves on: nor all thy Piety nor Wit
> Shall lure it back to cancel half a Line,
> Nor all thy Tears wash out a Word of it.

'Is that not very much the case, Kathy? The literal case.'

The house was not large, but its rooms were so crowded with years' accumulations of junk that they were extremely difficult to search. It was impossible for more than one or two people to get into each room at a time, and all of this slowed down the hunt for any secret records, correspondence or diaries that the dealer may have kept. A similar search was going on downstairs in the shop and store-rooms, but after several hours no reference had been turned up that could be linked to the name Raphael. New faces arrived, and McLarren, disappointed but even more determined, nominated a number of people to go home and get some sleep, Kathy and Desai among them.

They walked together down Shepherd's Row, and Desai said, 'I feel filthy after that.'

He did look crumpled, and weary, and not at all his usual smooth self. He looked as if he needed someone to say, 'Come on, I'll take you home with me and give you a nice bath and then we'll see . . .' She examined him out of the corner of her eye, his dark features shadowed in the light of the street lamps, and allowed herself a moment of fantasising. But something, the smell of burnt cardboard hanging in the air, perhaps, made it impossible to rid her mind of Pickering's store-room, so that the two thoughts – having her way with Desai, and Starling's handiwork with a razor – became unpleasantly mixed.

They stopped at the end of the lane, his car one way, hers the other.

'Well, take care, then,' he said gravely. 'I mean it.'

She smiled. 'You too, Leon,' and turned away.

It was only when she had reached the next block, and found herself quite alone, that the thought of walking up the dark side-street to her car made her hesitate. Somehow she had never quite believed that Starling had been capable of cutting off his wife's head, until tonight. She still found it difficult to reconcile the mental picture of someone deliberately removing an old man's fingers, one by one, and the chubby smiling face of Sammy Starling.

Desai had had similar misgivings. He slammed the car door shut, put the keys in the ignition and started up. Then he thought he would turn and drive back to check that Kathy had reached her car safely when some movement in his rear-view mirror caught his eye. He glanced at the wing mirror to get a better view back down the street, not realising that the movement had been inside the car. Then the glistening blade of an old-fashioned cut-throat razor passed in front of his eyes and he felt it come to a rest, cool, against his throat.

A voice close against his ear whispered. 'No sudden moves, copper, or I'll have your head off.'

Brock returned to his home in London early the following morning. Shortly after ten he took a call from McLarren.

'My dear chap,' the Scotsman declared jovially, as if the two of them were old golf-club pals. 'I wondered if we might meet?'

Brock mentally checked the immediate possessions he might need for a spell in interrogation. 'What had you in mind, Jock? Dinner at your club?'

McLarren chuckled. 'Something more immediate, I fear. You are at home?'

You know I am, Brock thought, glancing through the window at the car parked at the end of the street. 'Yes.'

'My lads will pick you up in, shall we say, one minute?'

He hung up, and Brock continued looking at the car, which showed a puff of white breath from its exhaust and began to move forward.

They took him, at what Brock considered quite unnecessary speed, not to Cobalt Square but to a run-down sixties office building half a mile away. The wood-grain laminate in the lift was chipped and scratched, the vinyl floors marked with black streaks, and the paint of the partition walls shabby with years of abuse from sticky tape, drawing-pins and fading sunlight.

'Dear Lord, how did we put up with places like this for so long?' McLarren sighed, offering Brock a worn metal chair at the table in the otherwise bare room. One wall was almost covered by a large, tattered map of London, the black congested pattern of its streets overprinted with another pattern, in red, of the boundaries of the eight police areas, and within those broad lines the finer pattern of the divisions, each with its two-letter code.

Brock sat down reluctantly. He was surprised – shocked – to see Kathy there, looking pale and tense, and he began to feel angry.

McLarren's crew withdrew, all except Tony Hewitt, leaving just the four of them.

'I can't offer you anything, Brock,' McLarren said. 'We have absolutely no facilities, I'm afraid. I wouldn't even know if the water in the toilets is turned on. But I thought this would be neutral and discreet, under the circumstances, and given the short notice –'

'What's this in aid of, Jock?' Brock said bluntly.

'Ah, well now . . .' McLarren spread his hands and examined them thoughtfully. 'We have a wee problem, Brock. And I would like to ask for your help.'

Brock assumed that this was his convoluted way of introducing a threat, one that presumably included Kathy in some way. 'What problem is that?'

McLarren checked his watch. 'Some fifty minutes ago, your friend Sammy Starling placed a triple-nine call on his mobile. He advised the police operator that he has DS Leon Desai as his prisoner. He further advised that he will cut off Desai's head at dawn tomorrow, unless you and the forger Raphael present yourselves, handcuffed together, at a location which he will nominate some time tonight.'

'Good grief,' Brock whispered. 'You said a *wee* problem.'

'Aye.' McLarren flexed his eyebrows and gave a grim smile. 'Several problems, in point of fact. One of which, of course, is that we still haven't the faintest idea who Raphael is or where we can find him. We've been hunting him for over two years now, and hardly seem likely to pin him down within the next eighteen hours for Mr Starling's benefit.'

McLarren sketched in the events of the previous night.

'Are you sure Sammy has got Leon?' Brock asked.

'We're checking, but he's not at his home. Kathy was the last person to see him, last night.'

'Sir. It would have been about four thirty a.m.,' Kathy said. 'We both left together. We walked to the bottom end of Shepherd's Row and then went in opposite directions to our cars. Leon said his was parked fifty yards to the east. That's the last I saw of him.'

'We're searching for his car now,' McLarren said. 'And I'm getting the tape of Starling's phone message brought here for us to listen to. They can't say at the moment what area the call came from, but they're working on it.'

Brock pondered. 'Presumably, if he wants us to bring Raphael in, he doesn't know his identity either.'

'Possibly. Maybe he just can't find him. Maybe he assumes that, with more time to work on Walter Pickering than he had, we may get more information out of him.'

'Yes, well, we should,' Brock said.

'Unfortunately, that's another of our wee problems, Brock. Pickering is in a coma, in intensive care. His condition is deteriorating, it seems, and it may be days or weeks before he can talk to us, if ever.'

'Grief . . . What exactly did he tell Sammy, do we know?'

'Tony's the only one can tell us that,' McLarren said cautiously. 'Eh, Tony?'

Hewitt straightened in his seat. He looked exhausted, eyes unnaturally bright. 'I can't say exactly. He was in a bad way, dopey one minute, crying the next. Half the time I had to get information from him by suggesting something, and him agreeing or disagreeing. He would be lucid for a bit, and say a few things, then he'd fade away. Then the ambulance guys arrived and started touching him, and that got him all upset and he wouldn't listen to me.'

He sighed and rubbed his face. 'I reckon he could have babbled anything at Starling at the end, and he'd have forgotten by the time I got to him. Just before they strapped the oxygen mask on him, I asked him who Raphael was, and he just stared up at me. I don't even know if he knows himself.'

Brock scratched at his beard distractedly. 'What's Pickering's background? Is he known to us?'

McLarren passed him a couple of sheets of paper. 'Small-time crookery — receiving, handling, offences under the Companies Act, tax evasion.'

Brock studied the record. 'Started out south of the river, like Sammy.'

Kathy said, 'Last night, Tony, you said he called his attacker Sammy China. Isn't that right?'

'Yeah, that's right.'

'Interesting,' Brock said. 'That's what they used to call Sammy way back. I haven't heard him called that in years.'

'Well, now, Brock,' McLarren said, 'that's the story. I'm going to make sure this has the very highest priority, of course. By midday every available officer in the Met will be out on the streets looking for Leon's car, and searching for Sammy's hideaway. We're questioning neighbours, tracking down Pickering's relatives and associates. So, have you any thoughts yourself? Any inspiration?'

'What about Pickering's records, Jock?' Brock said slowly. 'Surely there must be something there? Money, large amounts of it, changed hands.'

'Oh, aye, we're on to that all right. But remember, Brock,' he reached forward and tapped the paper in Brock's hands, 'tax evasion! This fellow had already had a taste of the Inland Revenue. If I know my man, he'll have gone to some trouble to hide his money trail, see?'

'Yes,' Brock agreed gloomily. 'Yes, you're right.'

There was a pause that became heavier as McLarren gave no sign of breaking it.

Then Kathy said, 'One thought, sir.'

'Aye, aye.' McLarren turned to her.

'There could have been others involved, couldn't there? In the fraud. Apart from Eva, Pickering and Raphael.'

McLarren frowned. 'We have no indication of it, as far as I know.'

Kathy hesitated, then said, 'Well, this is just a suggestion. I haven't been able to check it. But yesterday Toby Fitzpatrick mentioned that when he bought his forged stamps, they came with a certificate of authentication. I spoke to him again last night and asked him if he still had it, but he said he'd given it to Eva with the stamps. But he remembered the name of the expert who'd authenticated them. It was the same one we've been dealing with. Dr Waverley, Cabot's consultant.'

McLarren's frown deepened, 'Ye-es . . . And where does that take us, exactly?'

'So we know that Waverley certified at least one lot of fakes as genuine.'

'Aye, but we also know that Raphael's methods are extremely sophisticated, only detectable under laboratory conditions.'

'That's what Waverley told us, sir, yes.'

'He did freely admit to us that he'd been fooled by the ransom-note stamps,' McLarren went on. 'We can certainly call in other experts to confirm his opinion, but our lab people seemed convinced.'

Kathy glanced apprehensively at Brock. 'There is something else about Dr Waverley.'

'Really? Do go on.'

'Well, I've kept thinking about the day of the auction at Cabot's, and trying to work out how Brock could have been framed.'

She saw McLarren draw back a little in his chair, his eyes becoming guarded. She was almost sure he was going to challenge the word 'framed', but then he changed his mind and said, 'Yes, go on.'

'When we came to the end of the discussion about whether we should use the fake cover that the laboratory and Dr Waverley had made, he put it back into its envelope –'

'And offered it to Brock,' McLarren broke in. 'Yes, everyone who was there has agreed on that, including DCI Brock himself.' He deferred in Brock's general direction.

'But before he handed it to Brock,' Kathy went on carefully, 'he went to put it back into his briefcase, then changed his mind and handed it to Brock. I'm not sure, I wasn't paying close attention – nobody really was – but he might have switched the envelope with another in his bag, with a similar padding but no cover inside.'

She'd said it now, and immediately knew how half-baked it sounded.

McLarren was regarding her with astonishment. 'He'd planned the whole thing?'

'Yes.'

'But why, lassie?' McLarren sounded incredulous. 'Why steal a fake – his own fake? If he was working with the kidnappers, they were going to get the real stamp anyway.'

'I – I don't know. I think he might have been working with Sammy.'

'With Sammy?' McLarren's astonishment grew visibly. 'Whom he was also defrauding by authenticating his forged stamps?'

Kathy swallowed and remained silent. She briefly caught Tony Hewitt's look, bloodshot from lack of sleep, and contemptuous.

McLarren cleared his throat as if wanting rid of some embarrassing internal obstruction. Kathy knew that she had breached an undeclared convention of their meeting, by bringing up the matter about which Brock was being investigated. McLarren, as party to that investigation, did not want it confused with his present wee problem, and had not brought Brock there to hear theories of his innocence.

'I think,' McLarren declared firmly, 'that we'll stick to the suspects we have, until we have something a little more concrete.'

At that moment there was a knock at the door, and a man brought a message in for Hewitt, who ripped open the envelope and quickly read the contents. 'Starling's call came from south of the river,' he said. 'They doubt if they'll be able to pin it down closer than that.'

McLarren considered this. 'Would he have done that on purpose, Brock? Cross the river before making the call, to put us off the track?'

'I doubt it. I think he'll stay close to his prisoner.'

'And yet he's a canny wee bastard. What do you say, Tony?'

'Two thirds south, one third north.'

'Aye, that makes sense. It'll be clearer when we find Desai's car. Well, Brock, I'll not detain you further. If you have any more ideas, do please get in touch.'

He turned to Kathy, and it seemed to her that his manner towards her had changed. He seemed distant and slightly melancholy, as if saddened by the failure of a promising pupil. 'Why don't you run DCI Brock home now, Kathy, and then report to Cobalt Square for your assignment in the search?'

'Sir.'

McLarren turned his back on her with deliberation, and bent to consult with Hewitt, who didn't give either her or Brock a second glance.

As the lift doors closed behind them, Kathy let out a deep breath and said, 'Well, I blew that.'

'It was a good try, Kathy,' Brock murmured. 'Thanks, I appreciate it.'

'Don't you believe it possible either? About Waverley switching envelopes?'

'Actually, I do. But McLarren's objections are sound.'

Kathy said nothing more until they found the car in the car park behind the building. When she got behind the wheel she said, 'Why don't we pay him a visit?'

'Who?'

'Waverley. Test him, see how he reacts.'

'Your senior officer wouldn't approve.'

'We don't know that for a fact. It's just a matter of clearing up a loose end, that's all. Why don't you ring the manager at Cabot's and find out how we can reach Waverley?'

Brock smiled and took the phone she offered him.

James Melville was most helpful. 'Tim Waverley? Yes, I can tell you exactly where he is, as a matter of fact. He's upstairs in our stock-room at this moment. This is one of his days with us, going over some of the material for our next auction. Shall I warn him to expect you?'

They found Dr Waverley precisely where James Melville had directed them, deep in conversation with another member of Cabot's staff, who left as they approached. It was a high-ceilinged, cool room, lined with tall wooden cabinets of drawers, and a circular window high on one side throwing a disc of bright sunlight on to the floor. Waverley was dressed as he had been on each previous occasion, in cream summer suit, pale-blue shirt and navy blue bow-tie, and welcomed them with interest.

'Dreadful news of Mr Starling's wife, Chief Inspector. Has there been any progress?'

'Oh, yes.' Brock nodded grimly. 'There has indeed.'

'It was only a small point we wanted to check with you, Dr Waverley,' Kathy said, 'but we thought we'd better do it in person, to avoid any alarm.'

'Alarm?'

'Have you by any chance heard from Mr Starling in the past twenty-four hours?'

'Starling? No, I haven't.'

'Ah, good, that is a relief.'

'I'm not sure I follow. I wouldn't expect to hear from him. Is something wrong?'

'But you did know him quite well, didn't you? Before all this happened, I mean. You did checks for him, didn't you, to authenticate stamps he wanted to buy?'

'Occasionally, yes. Look, I explained all this to the super-intendent, McLarren. Hasn't he seen my report on the extent of the forgeries in the Starling collection yet?'

'Ah,' Brock said. 'We're working on different aspects of the case, Dr Waverley. He hasn't kept me up to date on that side of things.'

'Hasn't he?' Waverley looked doubtfully at Kathy, as at a slack student in a tutorial class.

'Could you give us a summary?' she asked.

'Oh, it's bad, I'm afraid. Very extensive range of forgeries, especially in the high-value categories. If it weren't so serious, financially, I mean, for Cabot's and Mr Starling, one would feel, well, elated perhaps – privileged certainly.'

'How do you mean?'

'This is one of the great forgery cases, that's all. Raphael is clearly up there with the greats – Spiro, Sperati and de Thuin.'

'Raphael, did you say?' Brock queried.

'Yes. Didn't the superintendent tell you that, either?'

Brock smiled. 'Oh, he told me, Dr Waverley. I just wondered how you came to know the name.'

'Because he told me too. How else?'

'Mr Starling never mentioned that name to you?'

'No, no, he didn't.'

'No one else? You'd never heard it before Superintendent McLarren told you?'

'Absolutely not. Why?'

'I'm just relieved, Dr Waverley, that's all.'

'You said that before. What is there to be relieved about, for God's sake?'

Brock looked at Kathy, as if not sure how much to say, then rubbed the side of his beard ruminatively and said, lowering his voice so that Waverley had to lean forward to hear, 'Well, we don't want to cause unnecessary alarm, sir, but the fact is that Mr Starling has . . .' He paused and looked again at Kathy, who looked grave, thinking that he was overplaying it a little.

'Has what?' Waverley demanded.

'Has gone missing. No, well, more than that, gone off the rails a bit.'

'A bit?'

'Last night he attacked a stamp dealer in Shoreditch.'

They both saw Waverley's face freeze instantaneously at the mention of the place.

'You're joking.'

'I'm afraid not. It was a very deliberate assault, sir. He cut off the fingers of his victim's right hand, one by one.'

Waverley's eyes goggled dramatically behind his glasses. 'No! For God's sake, why?'

'In order to make the man talk. He wanted information from him. Walter Pickering – know him do you, sir?'

'I – I don't think so. Dear God, cut off his fingers? That's – barbaric!'

'Indeed, but effective, up to a point. The point being that at which the victim passes out or dies of shock.'

'Pickering's dead?'

'No, but very poorly. In intensive care. He may not make it, and we haven't been able to determine how much he told Starling. That's the point, you see, Dr Waverley. We are concerned that Starling may have picked up information, wrongly, perhaps, about other people whom he may think cheated him.'

'Cheated?'

'The forged stamps were part of a systematic fraud to cheat Mr Starling. He is presently engaged in taking his own revenge on those concerned, and we are anxious to protect them. But we're hampered by lack of information. The person who might have helped us, Walter Pickering, is unable to communicate now, or probably for a number of days, by which time it may be too late for those whom Sammy Starling takes it into his head to punish.'

'Jesus Christ!'

'Quite. Are you sure you don't know Walter Pickering, Dr Waverley?'

'Pickering . . . Pickering . . .' Waverley gazed rather wildly up at the ocular window for inspiration. 'Hell . . . I'm not sure . . . Why? Do you have some reason to think . . .?'

'We think it likely that Raphael's product came to Starling by way of Pickering. You may have authenticated some of that material. You may therefore have come across Pickering, or be on his records.'

'His records?' Waverley swallowed hard. 'Yes, of course, he would have kept records, I suppose.'

'Very extensive records. But again, we have a difficulty, because Starling got to them before we did.'

'Did he? Good God.'

'Yes. His bloodstained footprints preceded us through Pickering's house, Dr Waverley. It was a fairly unsettling experience, following them. You can imagine . . . in every room, in every cupboard, in every filing cabinet.'

Take it easy, Brock, Kathy thought.

'Yes, I can imagine,' Waverley breathed.

'And you may be on his records in connection with other frauds, too,' Kathy added.

Waverley looked startled.

'We've found another customer of Pickering, a neighbour of Starling's called Fitzpatrick.'

'I've never heard of him.'

'But you provided a certificate of authentication for the

stamps he bought – Chalon Heads, similar to Starling's – which have also turned out to be forgeries.'

'Have they? Where are they? I haven't seen them, have I?'

'Not yet,' Kathy said. 'The point is, you do seem to have been quite extensively involved in Pickering's activities, and Starling may well take that as an indication –'

'Hang on!' Waverley got slowly to his feet, pushing the unruly lock of hair back from his brow angrily. 'I was not *extensively involved* in any fraud, if that's what you're implying. I am called upon to give an opinion on the authenticity of a great number of stamps, and I have made no bones about the fact that the work of your Raphael has indeed fooled me. He is extremely good at what he does, and I acknowledge my genuine error. But that does not make me a party to any fraud, and I am outraged that you should link my name with that of a dubious dealer.'

Brock held up his hand soothingly. 'No, no, no, Dr Waverley. That wasn't what Sergeant Kolla was trying to say. Perhaps she expressed herself badly.'

'Well . . .' Another flip of the hair, and he sat down again. 'All right, as long as that's clear.'

'That's fine. So we can be reassured, then, that Starling won't be coming after you. Do you have receipts, incidentally?'

'Receipts?'

'Yes, of your transactions with Pickering.'

'I told you, I don't recall any transactions with someone called Pickering.'

'Oh, I think you must have had some all the same. The stamps Mr Fitzpatrick bought from him came with your certificate. Surely Pickering would have paid you for providing that?'

'Perhaps the previous owner had me authenticate them.'

'There was no previous owner, though, Dr Waverley. Only Raphael, their maker.'

'Then maybe Raphael forged my certificate also!' Waverley said, with more than a touch of exasperation.

'Ah, good point,' Brock conceded. 'Look, I only mentioned this as something you might like to check from your files. Superintendent McLarren is particularly hot on these things, and if he comes across transactions with your name against them when he goes through Pickering's papers, he will naturally be checking them with you. You must have accurate records, I take it? For tax purposes, of course. Superintendent McLarren is very hot on the tax angle too.'

'Is he?' Waverley said hesitantly.

'We've taken up enough of your time.' Brock got to his feet. Kathy left Waverley her card, and he stared at it in a preoccupied sort of way as they turned to go.

When they got back into the car, Brock said, 'He didn't seem too much rattled, did he? After he'd recovered from the story of Pickering's fingers.'

'No. Maybe I was wrong. What now?' She looked at her watch. 'Midday. Seven and a half hours since Leon . . . I feel so helpless.'

'Yes, of course,' Brock murmured.

'You wouldn't believe the mess in Pickering's store-room, Brock. I didn't think Sammy would have been capable of it. It makes me feel sick, thinking of Leon . . .'

'Sammy has always been a cool thinker, Kathy.' Brock sounded reassuring. 'He never went in for unnecessary violence, and he has absolutely no reason to hurt Leon now.'

'But Eva affected him, didn't she? Made him act out of character. He used unnecessary violence on her, didn't he?'

'If it was him.'

'Who else? He's proved that now, hasn't he, with Pickering?'

'Sammy China . . .' Brock scratched his chin. 'I'd be interested in having a look at Pickering's file, see where he came from exactly. Do you think you could get it for me?'

'Sure.' Kathy sighed. Doing something was better than nothing, of course, but this seemed so futile. 'Do you want me to bring it to your home?'

'Somewhere more central, I think. I might reinstall myself at Queen Anne's Gate, if the coast is clear. I imagine the blood-hounds will have gone by now.'

'Isn't there anything else we can do?'

'We can do some thinking. And you can keep me up to date with McLarren's efforts. Let me know if they find Leon's car, or if anything else develops.'

Kathy dropped him at the offices at Queen Anne's Gate, now

closed up and deserted. She waited to see that they hadn't changed the locks, and watched him give a little wave as he stepped inside.

She was on Vauxhall Bridge when her phone started ringing. She pulled into the kerb and took the call, stifling a groan of frustration when she heard the hopeful voice.

'Sergeant Kolla? Kathy? Peter White here. Can you talk? I just wanted to see if my little clue had been of any help.'

For a moment Kathy couldn't think what he was talking about. Then she remembered his description of the man in the woods with the binoculars. 'Oh, yes, Peter,' she said reluctantly. 'Actually that was a great help. We tracked him down and we've now eliminated him from our enquiries.'

'Oh dear.' White sounded intensely disappointed.

'But he did provide us with further information, which was very helpful.' Kathy heard herself sounding like an official bulletin. 'Thanks to you.'

'Well, that's something, I suppose. You know, I've had a couple more bright ideas, Kathy. I'd like to discuss them with you.'

'Look, Peter,' Kathy said firmly, 'you've caught me right in the middle of something. I really haven't got time to talk. Sorry.'

'Oh. Is there a flap? Has there been a development?'

'I'm sorry, Peter, I must go.'

'Kathy!' His voice was tense with eager anxiety. 'Don't hang up. Please! I may be able to help, don't you see? I helped you once, I might be able to again! You must give me the chance! You must let me try!'

His appeal was so pathetic, so embarrassingly grovelling, that Kathy was tempted to press the button to kill the call. But then she thought, Why not? Maybe he does know Sammy better than anyone else.

'Peter . . . in confidence, all right?'

'Of course! Of course!'

'If Sammy were to go into hiding, have you any ideas where he might go?'

'He's done a runner!' Peter White was practically squealing with excitement. Kathy wondered if he took whisky in his cornflakes.

'*If* . . . if he did, Peter. What do you think?'

'Could he have left the country?'

'No. We think he's still in London.'

'In London . . . a bolt-hole . . . He's alone?'

'He has a hostage.'

'*A hostage!*'

'Calm down, Peter. An adult male. Which must make things more difficult for him.'

'Yes, yes . . .'

Kathy could hear White's heavy breathing in her ear as he tried to calm himself and think. 'Look . . . give me a minute, Kathy. Let me get my reference book, my index. I've got addresses there.'

There was a clunk as he put down the phone. In the background, faintly, she could hear a radio, and she pictured the view from his kitchen window, the garden of desperate roses, and shook her head sadly as she thought how she had made his day.

He came back on the line, breathless, and she wrote down the addresses he began to reel off. After a dozen he came to a halt. 'I think that's all I can suggest at this stage, Kathy. But let me think —'

'That's just great, Peter,' she said quickly. 'I'll get these checked straight away. If you have any more ideas, do let me know. But now I must go.'

'Of course, of course! Kathy, let me say thank you, thank you for letting me help.'

She stabbed her finger hurriedly at the button and put the car into gear.

17

Raphael

Soon after three that afternoon Desai's car was found in a car park in Whitechapel, just a mile to the south-east of Shepherd's Row. There were spots of blood on the driver's seat, and a bloodstained tissue on the floor between the pedals.

When Kathy phoned Brock with the news, she added, 'North of the river. McLarren and Hewitt are moving more people back across from the south. They think Sammy changed to his own car and continued east, to the areas he knew around West Ham.'

'That could be a mistake,' Brock said. 'Whitechapel is south from Shepherd's Row. He could have continued to the river, across Tower Bridge and into South London.'

'Yes.' Kathy sounded unconvinced and depressed. 'We just don't know, do we? And being forced to sit around waiting . . .'

'Any luck with Pickering's records?'

'I'm to pick them up in half an hour.'

'Good. Do you think you could bring us some food, while you're at it, Kathy? I'm starving.'

'What would you like?' she asked flatly.

'Doesn't matter. Maybe some Indian.'

'I don't know if he even liked curry. It would have been just like Leon to prefer kippers or something.'

'Yes, I know what you mean,' Brock said, worried by Kathy's

use of the past tense. 'And some coffee if you would. They've cleaned this place out. There's nothing else I should know, is there?'

'Not really. They've warned the hospitals, they've got ambulances ready, and blood of Leon's type, and a hostage negotiation team is being briefed. There's a story going round that McLarren has called for a volunteer to stand in as Raphael and be handcuffed to you.'

'Go on.'

'The story is that the volunteer's widow will get half a million compensation if things go wrong. It's bullshit, an office myth.'

'I'm sure it is.'

They were silent, then Kathy said, 'That's all I've got. I'll go and get the file now.'

She put down the phone and was on the point of leaving when it rang.

'Sergeant Kolla?' The voice was soft and tentative, and she didn't recognise it at first.

'Yes?'

'Tim Waverley. Have you a moment?'

'Of course, Dr Waverley.' Kathy sat down carefully, as if an abrupt movement might frighten him off. She reached for a pad and pen.

'Nothing significant, really,' he said, sounding very agreeable and smooth. 'I thought I'd better set the record straight, that's all.'

'What record is that, Dr Waverley?'

'Oh, Lord, you do sound so suspicious!' He laughed. 'And for God's sake call me Tim, won't you? No, look, I went away and checked my records after you called. Can I ask, the dealer in Shoreditch, is his shop in Shepherd's Row, by any chance?'

'Yes, it is.'

'Ah, well, that's it, then.'

'Sorry?'

'I believe his shop is called Shepherd's Stamps, and I've always assumed that his name must be Shepherd, like the street. I just call him Walter, so when your colleague was going on about somebody called Pickering, I didn't make the connection, you see? The point is, anyway, that I have had dealings with him, so

282

it is entirely possible that you might find my name in his address book or whatever.'

'Oh, I see. Have you ever been to the shop?'

'I have, actually. He got me to look at some stuff of his. The place doesn't look like much from the outside, but he had some very respectable wares. Perhaps respectable isn't quite the right word, in view of what you told me.' He chuckled, then became serious. 'But you don't think I'm in any danger from Mr Starling, do you?'

'I'm sure he's only going to be interested in people who conspired to cheat him.'

'Yes . . . Still, maybe I should go away for a few days until you catch him. What do you think?'

'We'd rather you didn't. We're likely to need you to examine any stamps we come up with, as evidence.'

'Oh, I see.' He sounded unhappy.

'What about the Fitzpatrick sale? Bahamas Chalon Heads, mostly mint with a number of fine covers. Did you recall anything about that?'

' 'Fraid not. Why don't you let me have a look at them?'

'Can't do that at the moment.'

'Oh. Well, send me a listing, and I'll try to rack my brains.'

'Yes, I will. Thanks. Was there anything else?'

'No, that was it. Just thought I'd clear that up.'

'Thank you.'

Kathy put down the phone and said softly to herself, 'That's crap, Tim old chap.'

She picked up Pickering's file from Cobalt Square, and continued on across the river to Queen Anne's Gate, detouring on the way to buy food from a corner take-away. Brock was alone in the building, its rambling corridors and offices eerily deserted. He led her to a small office she had never been in before, a clerk's room by the look of it, with filing cabinets and a couple of laser printers. Covering one wall was the same large map of London, its police areas and divisions, which had been in the room in which they had met with McLarren and Hewitt.

She gave Brock the carrier bag of food and coffee, and noticed some coloured-headed pins stuck into the map. 'Are those yours?' she asked.

He looked up briefly from unpacking the foil containers. 'Yes. What did you get?'

'Beef vindaloo. You like it hot, don't you?'

'Splendid. Did you get popadoms? Chutney?'

'No, sorry. I'll remember next time.'

'Never mind. I'll try to find plates.'

'You have it all. There's a plastic fork. You can eat it straight from the containers. I don't want any.'

'You sure? Need to eat, you know, especially when you're putting in long hours. It's a trap, to let yourself get run down.'

'I know. I'm fine. What about the pins?'

'Mmm . . .' He took a few mouthfuls before answering. 'OK. The pink pins are today's locations. Sammy's house, bottom left, outside the area; the flat at Canonbury, centre right; Cabot's, centre; Keller's brother, centre left; Heathrow, outer left; Sally's house and shop, lower centre; Wilkes's flat, bottom centre; the Coopers' house, outer left; Pickering's shop, upper centre.'

He paused and took some more food. 'Mmm. This isn't at all bad, Kathy. Sure you won't have some?' The curry was bringing a film of sweat out on Brock's forehead.

'No, thanks. I'll just have a coffee.' She reached for one of the polystyrene cups. 'Doesn't seem to amount to a pattern.'

'Quite. An arbitrary smattering of locations right across London.'

'What about the others?' Kathy looked at the cluster of blue pins, all together in a corner of South London.

'The blue ones are the old days, where people began. How about Pickering? Where did he grow up?'

Kathy thumbed through the file. 'Angell Town.'

'Quite, Brixton. Stick another blue pin in down there for him.'

'Who are the others for?'

'Sammy grew up there. So did Sally Malone, of course. And, just for good measure, so did Sammy's little helper, Ronnie Wilkes – well, Herne Hill, actually, bit to the south.'

'There's another one down there. Keller?'

'No, not Keller. He's the lone blue pin over in Essex, to the right.'

'Who, then?'

'Mmm . . .' Brock waved his fork vaguely in the air. 'We'll see.'

He carried on chewing.

Kathy stared at the map and thought to herself, So bloody what?

'Pickering called him Sammy China,' Brock said, as if answering her doubting thoughts. 'I thought that was interesting. After all, even if Pickering had known of Sammy in the old days, he'd been doing regular business with him in the present, when no one would dream of calling Sammy by his old nickname. Surely he would have referred to him as Starling, or Sammy Starling? And that made me wonder if there was something personal about all this. Something to do with the old days.'

Kathy felt despondent, but tried not to show it. Did Brock think that nobody else had thought of this? 'Tony Hewitt has had a couple of blokes working on a possible connection between Walter Pickering and Sammy Starling ever since we found Pickering last night, Brock. That's what held me up getting the file – they had it. I had to find someone else to borrow it for a couple of hours for me. Anyway, I understand that they've found at least three people – relatives and friends – who have known Pickering since he was a kid and who are convinced that he didn't know any Chinese lads as either friends or enemies. Pickering and Sammy didn't go to the same schools, work for the same people or support the same football teams. They grew up almost a mile apart, and there was no bus route between their homes.'

'Ah. They've done well to find that out in so short a time.' Brock took another mouthful of curry, drops of perspiration standing out on his brow. 'That certainly helps,' he added.

Kathy tried to work out how.

'Well, now,' Brock wiped his mouth and forehead with the paper napkins provided, took a gulp of coffee and got to his feet. 'It's been very frustrating sitting here. I feel the need of activity and fresh air. Let's take a drive, shall we?'

'Fine.' Kathy looked at him in surprise. 'Where to?'

Brock pointed to the one pink pin that touched the cluster of blue ones in South London. 'Sew Sally,' he said. 'Where else?'

Sally Malone was just turning the Open notice to Closed on the shop door when Brock and Kathy pulled up outside. She opened the door for them, looking apprehensive and combative.

'Is there news?' she asked, as they came in.

'Yes, Sally,' Brock said. 'There is. Lock up the shop and let's have a chat.'

She slid the bolts on the front door and led them through to the back.

'Bad, is it?'

As Brock told her briefly about Sammy's flight, his attack on Pickering and kidnapping of Leon Desai, she sank on to a chair, and the life seemed to ebb from her face.

'Oh . . .' was all she managed when he came to an end. She looked so devastated that Kathy got a glass of water from the sink and brought it to her.

'Now, Sally,' Brock said firmly, after a pause, 'I need some help from you before this gets any worse. Do you hear me, Sally?'

She didn't respond.

'Sally, have you ever heard of this Walter Pickering? I think he knew Sammy, from the old days. He came from around here. And he referred to Sammy as Sammy China.'

Sally looked up at Brock's face, but said nothing.

A movement at the door made Brock and Kathy both turn in that direction. Rudi Trakl was standing there, staring at them owlishly through his thick glasses. He gazed at the back of Sally's head for a moment, then came forward silently and stood behind her, putting his arms gently around her shoulders. He bent his head to her ear and whispered something. After a little while she blinked and seemed to come back to life again. She looked round and up at his face and whispered, 'It's Sammy, Rudi. He's —'

'I heard, *liebchen*, I heard.' He stroked her grey hair tenderly. 'Do you want to lie down? Have you taken your pills?'

Sally whispered, 'I don't feel well, Rudi.' She looked hopelessly at Brock and Kathy in turn.

'We must find Sammy,' Brock said softly, intently. 'We must find him soon, Sally.'

'Poor Sammy . . .' she whispered, and a tear trickled down her cheek.

Rudi patted her shoulder in mute sympathy. 'You must lie down now, *liebchen*.'

'Walter Pickering,' Brock tried again, but Sally lowered her head and began to shake it from side to side.

'Please,' Rudi said, holding up his hand. 'She is not well. You must let her lie down. She must take her pills.'

'We don't have much time,' Brock insisted.

The little wizened man looked up at his face gravely. 'All the same,' he said, 'you must wait until she is recovered. I know how this goes.'

'Who's her doctor, Mr Trakl?' Kathy said. 'I could call an ambulance.'

'No. Please, go down to the Prince of Wales on the corner. Wait for us there. I will bring her to you when she is ready.'

'I'm sorry,' Brock said. 'We're staying here.'

Rudi shook his head. His eyes looked large and extraordinarily compelling through the magnification of his lenses. 'No. Please do this. You must be patient. Otherwise she will not talk to you, believe me.'

Brock looked at him doubtfully, then said, 'Very well, Rudi. You understand how important this is, don't you?'

The other man nodded and began to lead Sally towards the door. She turned her head back after a moment, saw Brock and Kathy watching, and mumbled something. Brock moved forward and bent his head to hear. He noticed how blue Sally's lips had become.

'What was that, Sally?'

'I said, Sammy didn't know Walter.' Her voice was a croak. 'I did. I went out with Walter for over a year when I was seventeen. It was a secret. I never told my mum, or anyone.'

The effort of saying this seemed to finish her. She sagged in Rudi's arms and he turned to Brock. 'You must do as I say,' he pronounced firmly. 'Go now.'

They sat at a small corner table in the Prince of Wales. 'I haven't allowed myself a drink in over a week,' Brock grumbled, contemplating his third orange juice miserably. 'And they make us wait for them in a pub!' He looked at his watch yet again. Over an hour had passed, and the bar was filling up, the company becoming freer and more exuberant, the majority young and black, men and women in equal numbers.

'I'll go and check them again,' Kathy said, wanting some relief from sitting there, and slipped away. She returned five minutes later. 'No change. They're still there.'

'If they're not out by eight,' Brock growled, 'we'll sit on their doorstep and call an ambulance.'

At three minutes to eight, the pub door opened, and Sally came in on her own. Kathy pushed her way through the crowd and led her over to their table. She looked not much better in her colouring but her eyes were sharp, almost unblinking, as if she were holding herself together with will-power.

'All right, Sally?' Brock asked, as she sat down.

'I'm quite well now, Mr Brock. I'm ready.'

'Good. What can you tell us?'

'I want to help, if I can. I'm partly to blame, you see, for what's happened.'

'How is that?'

'Sammy and I didn't part on the best of terms, almost three years ago. I'd known him practically all his life, and worked for him and his family for thirty years, and I considered that he treated me quite shabby after all that. So, anyway, when Eva came to me one day, wanting money, instead of turning her away as I should . . .'

'Hang on, Sally,' Brock interrupted. 'Eva came here to see you? To get money from you?'

'I know, I couldn't believe it either, not after the way we'd parted. But that was her, wasn't it? She could call you all the names under the sun one day, then assume you loved her again the next, especially if she wanted something. And she didn't have too many people to go to for help.'

'I see. Go on, then.'

'Yes, well, I introduced her to Walter Pickering. I knew stamps was Sammy's weakness, and I'd heard that Walter had a sideline in supplying, well, specialist material in that area.'

'What do you mean, specialist? Stolen stuff, forgeries?'

Sally gave a little shrug. 'I suppose it was a spiteful thing to do, get back at Sammy like that, but there we are. I never intended for it to go so far.'

'Have you heard the name Raphael, Sally?'

She hesitated, then said, 'Yes, I heard it.'

'Do you know who he is?'

'Mr Brock, I told you I want to help. But I also have obligations, and friendships, and maybe only a little time left to share them.' She fixed Brock with sad, sharp eyes. 'Tell me what you most need to know, and I'll try to help. As for the rest . . .'

'Sally,' Brock's voice dropped to a whisper, 'I told you that Sammy had kidnapped a police officer. I didn't tell you why. Evidently he got the name Raphael from Walter, and he believes that Raphael is responsible not only for defrauding him with fake stamps but also for murdering Eva, and cutting off her head.'

Sally's jaw dropped, her eyes widened in horror. 'No! But I thought Sammy —'

'Killed Eva? Did you have any particular reason to think that?'

Sally seemed confused and agitated.

'Not only that. Sammy also believes that I tried to steal a valuable stamp from him while I was leading the investigation earlier on. So he's told us that he'll release his hostage only if both Raphael and I surrender to him by dawn tomorrow. If we fail to do this, he will cut off the officer's head.'

She gave a little cry, covering her mouth with her hand. 'What — what does he want you and Raphael for?'

'Well, I don't imagine it's to swap stamps, Sally,' Brock said, exasperation creeping into his voice. 'He's got a gun, and he's very disturbed. He almost killed Walter last night. He probably hasn't slept or eaten for days. He knows the whole of the Met is out there hunting for him. The strain of it must be driving him to the very edge. Some time tonight he's going to tell us where Raphael and I have to go. We can't afford to wait till then, Sally. I want to find him tonight, before he's wound himself up to that final scene. And I want to tell him that we have Raphael under lock and key, and charged with Eva's murder. Maybe then I can talk him into giving himself up.'

Sally gave a little moan of despair.

'Tell me where I can find Raphael, Sally. You may be the only one who can help us now.'

She wiped tears from both eyes with her fingers. 'I can't do that, Mr Brock. But maybe I can help you find Sammy.'

Brock took a deep breath, his hands balling into fists as if the effort of containing himself was becoming too much. 'How?' he said gruffly.

'Where have you been looking?'

Brock glanced across at Kathy, who brought her head closer to Sally and reeled off a list of locations. 'Business contacts he's had in the past twenty years, garages, workshops he's visited, empty premises advertised in recent weeks in the papers he reads, or on the routes he drives to Canonbury . . .' She went on for a while until she couldn't remember any more of the items on McLarren's schedule.

'Nothing around here, then?' Sally said.

'Around here?' Kathy looked across at Brock, who had a gleam in his eye.

'This is where he grew up. This is where we began,' she whispered. 'God help us.'

'Has he been here recently, then?' Kathy asked.

'Not to my knowledge. But he talked to Eva about it, not long ago . . . not more than a month ago. There was a bit in the property section of the Sunday papers. About how this old council-housing estate in Brixton that had been going to be demolished was going to be done up instead, turned into private flats. The picture in the paper made it look like somewhere on the Mediterranean, he said, all pink and yellow. The place was Myatts Grove, where we grew up.'

'How do you know this, Sally?' Brock asked quietly.

'She phoned me. Said she was coming up early in the month, to get her money from Walter. Raphael had been busy. I never saw her since.'

'I thought you two didn't get along?' Brock asked.

'Funny, innit? This brought us together, ripping Sammy off.' She raised weary eyes to Brock's and added, 'I'm not a very nice person, Mr Brock.'

He rubbed his chin and didn't reply. After some thought he

said, 'Sammy definitely mentioned this place to Eva? You're sure?'

'Yes. She said he told her he'd like to see it again, before they turned it into the Costa del Spade – that was his joke. She didn't get it. Sammy always enjoyed a little racist joke. He felt, being what he was, that he was entitled, like.'

'Let's go and take a look at it, then, Sally,' Brock said. 'Feel up to it, do you?'

'Don't worry about me. Tough as old boots, I am.'

She rose to her feet, tottered, and was caught by Kathy, to whom she felt as light as a bird.

They drove through the evening streets, low raking sunlight flattering the old brick terraces with a golden patina. It wasn't enough to make the Myatts Grove estate look good, however. They came upon it suddenly, turning a corner and being confronted by a wall of blackened brick with boarded window openings. A pioneering development of the London County Council in response to the housing crisis in London after the end of the First World War, its dark, abandoned five-storey bulk now looked grim, institutional and threatening. Graffiti sprayers had got to work on one end, but had lost heart and become dispirited with their task after fifty yards or so. Instead they'd turned to defacing the large advertisement board, which showed renderings of the block improbably transformed into a Mediterranean fishing village.

'Gawd. Don't look much now, does it?' Sally said.

It filled a city block in a U-shape plan, with a central court open at one end, and Sally directed them around the surrounding streets until they came to that end, and could look back through a high chain-link fence at the whole development, its access decks looking rather like the terraces of a stadium overlooking the central court, which had been originally intended as a landscaped park but had long since been paved over for car parking.

'Don't slow down, Kathy,' Brock murmured. 'Any guesses where he'd be, Sally?'

'Our flat was one level down from the top, near the north stair.' She pointed towards one of the internal corners of the building.

'Well, if he's there now he can get a clear view of the whole central court as well as this street, and across the road here to that wasteground.'

Kathy drove on to the next corner and slowed down beside a poster of a snarling dog's head and a security company's warning and phone number. Brock wrote it down and they continued, circling through the surrounding streets.

It was Sally who spotted the red sports car, conspicuously parked at the kerb two blocks away from Myatts Grove. 'That's Eva's. She hardly ever used it. That was one luxury she wasn't much interested in.'

Kathy pulled in and walked across to check it. It was locked, nothing apparent through the windows. She returned and pulled out her phone. 'That's it, all right. We call McLarren?'

Brock looked down the length of the street. 'Tell him to rendezvous in the car park behind those shops on the corner there. No sirens, and tell them to avoid the streets skirting the Myatts Grove estate. I'll call the security firm.'

Kathy was pacing in the car park, waiting impatiently for McLarren, when her phone went. She grimaced when she heard Peter White's voice. 'Peter, this is not a good time —'

'Have you found him, Kathy?'

'Not yet.'

'Don't ring off, Kathy. I've had another idea where he might be.'

'Peter, I really —'

'Kathy, listen! Have you thought what a hunted animal does when it goes to ground? It goes back to the safest place, the oldest place. I think that's where he might be. He was brought up on a council housing estate in Brixton, Myatts Grove. It's abandoned now . . .' White's voice trailed off as Kathy said nothing. 'It would be worth checking.'

Then Kathy said, 'I have to hand it to you, Peter . . .' The tension in her throat turned to a laugh. The old coot was amazing.

'What? What?' he was saying anxiously.

'Peter, you haven't lost your touch. I'm standing outside Myatts Grove now.'

'What? He is there? I'm right?'

'It's looking that way. Please, Peter, I must ring off. I promise I'll let you know when the dust has settled, OK?'

'Wonderful. Thank you, Kathy. Thank you!'

Twenty minutes later Brock and Kathy got into McLarren's car. The small car park was now jammed with unmarked cars as well as two armed-response vehicles.

'Well done indeed, Brock,' McLarren said, with fair grace. 'And you reckon he's somewhere in Myatts Grove, do you?'

'I've sent the security guard to check the perimeter. We didn't spot any signs of forced entry, but he may see something.'

'The sun sets in twenty-five minutes. I suggest we wait until it's completely dark before we move in. The negotiating team should be with us shortly.'

'Jock, it's your show, of course . . .'

McLarren eyed him. 'Aye, it is. And now you want to tell me how to run it, I suppose?'

Brock smiled. 'I was going to suggest that the first step will be to establish exactly where he is.'

'Of course. We've got the lads with the listening gear. They'll go into the floor below the one you think he's on. They'll find him, if he's there.'

'Fine, as long as they don't alarm him.'

'Brock! These laddies do this sort of thing every day.'

'Of course. I'm sorry. But they don't do it with one of my men on the end of a razor every day. Anyway, look, what I was going to suggest was that when they've finished, I go in –'

'*You* go in? Brock, my dear fellow! What are you dreaming of? Sending you in would be like pouring petrol on a fire! The man wants to kill you!'

And whose fault is that? Brock thought, but bit his tongue.

'Brock!' McLarren went on. 'Leave it all to the negotiating team. They've been preparing for this all day. They've got their psychological profiles of our Sammy all prepared, and their strategies all mapped out, and they are the experts at this particular part of the job. *You* find the wee bastard, and *they* talk him into coming quietly. Fair enough?'

'No, Jock, not in this case. I've known Sammy for a long

time, as you're aware. I'm quite certain he's come to the end of his tether, and that he'll go through with what he's got in mind.'

'And what's that, do you think?'

'I don't think he intends to come out of there alive, and if we don't give him what he wants, he'll take Leon with him – it's as simple as that. You can't develop a negotiating strategy for that – he doesn't want to negotiate. He just wants to wipe the slate clean before he goes.'

'And how would you overcome this death-wish?'

'You've got to give him something, and I'm all you've got that he wants. Once he's got me, I can talk him into releasing Leon because Leon will no longer be of any use to him.'

'And what then?'

'Then I talk to him, about Raphael, about what's really happened. He knows me, Jock. Face to face I can talk him round. Yelling at him through a loud-hailer isn't going to work.'

McLarren thought for a while. 'Good try, Brock, but I'm afraid not.'

'Why not?'

'Why not? Because people's lives are at risk, man, and that's no time to be improvising half-baked schemes, that's why not! It may make *you* feel better to exchange yourself for young Desai, but in my book it doesn't improve the situation one wee bit. I'd just exchange one hostage for another, and in the process lose the one bargaining chip I've got, namely your unworthy self. Sorry, Brock, we play this one exactly by the book.'

Brock returned to his seat in the front of Kathy's car. In response to her look he shook his head grimly.

'Hell!' Kathy swore softly, and smacked the steering wheel with the ball of her hand. 'Maybe he'd let me.'

'Don't waste your breath,' Brock murmured.

From the back of the car, Sally perked up. 'What's the matter?'

'Nothing, Sally. A technical matter. Everything's fine.'

'I asked what the matter was,' she said fiercely. 'I'm not a fool, Mr Brock. I deserve to be told what's going on.'

Brock looked back over his shoulder at her and smiled. 'Oh, I was trying to persuade Superintendent McLarren to let me negotiate personally with Sammy, but he won't allow it. He's right, I dare say.'

Sally frowned. 'You don't believe that, though, do you?'

'I think I could persuade Sammy to come out quietly, because I know him. But the superintendent rightly points out that we have experts who are very experienced at this sort of thing, negotiating with . . . with −'

'With what? Lunatics? Mass murderers?' Sally looked out of the car window at one of the ARVs and saw the men with rifles passing clips of ammunition between themselves. 'And if they fail, they'll kill him, won't they?'

'It won't come to that, Sally. The point is that he's probably in a frame of mind where he would welcome that. We have to give him something to want to live for.'

Sally looked him in the eye, then said, 'Come on, I'll talk to your superintendent.'

Brock raised an eyebrow at Kathy and jumped out after Sally. By the time he caught up with her she was rapping with her rings on McLarren's car window. He opened the door and stepped out.

'Dear lady . . .'

'I'd like a word, sir, if you don't mind,' she said firmly. 'In the car.'

He looked at her in astonishment, then at Brock. They got into McLarren's car.

'Superintendent,' Sally said, 'I'll come straight to the point. I believe you want to know the identity of Raphael, is that right?'

McLarren suddenly considered her very seriously. 'Yes, indeed. Can you help us, madam?'

'Yes, I can. I know Raphael's identity, and I suppose, looking around, there's not many left that do.'

'Well, now . . .' McLarren's face brightened in a rare smile of pure unmitigated joy. 'I'm absolutely delighted to hear it, Mrs Malone. Please, give me the name.'

'I will tell you, Superintendent, *after* you have allowed Mr Brock to meet with Sammy and try to bring him and the police officer out of there, but not before.'

'What?' McLarren's smile turned to something less pleasant.

He looked suspiciously at Brock, who said quickly, 'Sally, this isn't the way. If you know who Raphael is, you must tell us.'

'Thank you, Brock,' McLarren said, through clenched teeth. 'Come, Mrs Malone . . .'

'No, sorry. That's my deal. If you don't agree, I shan't tell you, not now and not ever.' She folded her arms determinedly.

'Mrs Malone,' McLarren said softly, in control again, 'let me assure you that if I thought for one moment that DCI Brock's way was best I would leap at it. But it is not. You don't realise what you're asking. To let Mr Brock go alone to speak to Sammy at this juncture would be tantamount to serving Brock a death sentence. Sammy would as like kill him, and DS Desai, and then himself.'

'No, he won't,' she replied firmly, 'because Mr Brock won't be alone. I'll be with him.'

'What?' McLarren and Brock spoke simultaneously.

Sally let them go on for a while, then she lifted a hand and they became quiet.

'There are certain things,' she said, 'which I know, and which nobody else knows. They are things that Sammy has to hear. He wants to hear them, because only that way can he start to live again. That's why I have to go with Mr Brock to speak to him, Superintendent. There's really no other way.'

McLarren stared at her, impressed despite himself. 'What are these things, Mrs Malone?'

'That's all I'm prepared to say.' She set her mouth in a firm line.

At 11.30 p.m., with police marksmen, floodlights and medical team in position, Brock and Sally climb up to the third floor and make their way along the access gallery. They walk carefully and slowly in the dark, for the route is littered with shards of bathroom fittings and glass from the period when the flats were trashed before being sealed up and sold to the developers. When they reach the flat from which the police team has heard the sounds of movement, Brock knocks on the plywood sheet that seals the door. He tries to make it sound neither frighteningly loud, nor timidly soft, but somehow confident and open. It is a lot to expect a knock to communicate, and for a full half-minute they wait in silence. Then he knocks again, and this time speaks. 'Sammy, it's David Brock. I have Sally Malone with me. She thought I might find you here. There's just the two of us on the walkway. The others are keeping their distance, so that we can talk.'

He says all this with his mouth close to the timber sheet, not sure how much will get through.

Then there is a sound of scraping, and the door to which the plywood has been nailed swings slowly open. In the darkness beyond, Brock can just make out the nose of a rifle barrel, pointing at his chest. The rifle recedes into the darkness, and Brock and Sally step cautiously inside. It waves them to the right, and they stumble through another doorway into a room.

'This was the living-room,' Sally whispers, and they hear the sound of the front door shutting and bolts being drawn into place. Then a battery camping light clicks on, filling the space with soft light. It illuminates a bare room, and the figure of Leon Desai crumpled in the corner, wide adhesive tape covering his eyes and mouth and binding his wrists and ankles.

Starling is standing by the door, covering them with his gun. He says, 'Sit down on the floor,' and they hear the agitation in his voice and also a hoarseness, perhaps through lack of fluids.

They obey, and then Brock says, 'Thanks for seeing us, Sammy. It's important that we talk.'

'No!' the voice is shrill. 'We've got nothing to talk about.'

'I'm your hostage now, Sammy,' Brock goes on, softly. 'Let the other fellow go, will you? He's got nothing –'

'*Shut up!*' Sammy screams, and it is a scream, so harsh and shocking that Brock and Sally flinch and go rigid where they sit. 'Don't you say one more word, or I'll kill you right there. I mean it!'

Clearly he does. Nobody says a word. It is impossible to tell what shape Desai is in. He is so still that he may be dead, suffocated by the tape, perhaps, or choked on his own vomit, without Starling even aware that he has killed his hostage.

'He wants to trick me, I know!' Starling goes on, talking to Sally. 'He steals Eva's ransom, and now he wants to trick me. I told them he must come with Raphael, but he brings you instead! Why did you come?'

'There were things I had to say to you, Sammy,' Sally says, very gently. 'Important things for you to understand.'

'If you've come here to soft-soap me, or tell me bad things about Eva . . .' He turns the gun towards her.

'I want to tell you some hard things, Sammy, some bad things, if you think you can cope with them. Bad things about me, as well as Eva.'

His mouth sets in a grim little line as he faces her.

'But perhaps I was wrong to come. I didn't realise how hard all this has been for you. You see, I'm sorry, but I really believed that it must have been you who killed Eva, until Mr Brock here told me I was wrong.'

Both of them on the floor watch Starling's face in the torchlight, trying to make out his reaction to this, but it remains inscrutable as ever. Then the light catches a glint of moisture at his eyes.

'I didn't kill Eva,' he says eventually.

'I know that, Sammy. I know that now.'

'Go away, Sally,' he said leadenly. 'I don't want to have to kill you too.'

She sighs, and her gaze moves slowly round the room. 'It's easy to imagine, in this light, how it used to be, isn't it, Sammy? Over there was Dad's chair, and over there was the table where Mum did her sewing. And where you are was where we kept your little chair. Do you remember that? You probably don't – you were too young to remember. You do remember our Mum sitting at the window, though, don't you? I can see her there now, Old Mother Hubbard . . .'

'Stop it, Sally,' he says, more sad than angry.

'You know, you were her favourite. Oh, I don't mean like Andy exactly – Mum worshipped Andy. But in another way. And you were my favourite too, my own little brother, my little Sammy China. I was so proud, taking you out with me, Sammy and Sally – I thought our mum had chosen your name special to be like mine. I didn't realise you already had it when you came.

'Isn't it funny how a place can bring it all back? That's why you came here, is it, Sammy? It's almost as if the memories have soaked into the walls, and when you sit here you can feel them oozing out again. Like you and your stamps – I'd forgotten you were collecting them even then. I can see you now, in your short trousers, at the table by the window, with Mum at one end doing her sewing and you at the other concentrating so hard on your stamps.'

'Andy collected stamps,' Starling says, in a whisper.

'So he did! That's how you got started, wasn't it? He came home on leave and talked you into it – gave you some stamps.'

'American stamps, air mail, with planes, 1941.'

'You do remember!'

'The best stamp in Andy's collection was a Great Britain 1929 Postal Union Congress, one pound black.' Starling's voice is oddly detached, unnaturally pitched, as if it really is a voice from the past, the voice of a small orphan boy. 'It was a wonderful stamp, big and black, with a picture of St George in armour on a horse killing the dragon with his lance. I loved it so much, I stole it. That was the first thing I ever stole. I couldn't help it. I don't know what I thought I would say when Andy came home and found it gone. Only Andy didn't come home . . .'

Sally purses her lips, and says softly to Brock, 'He was in bombers. Shot down over the North Sea.'

'He was a hero,' Starling says. 'Then you gave his whole collection to me. For a long time I couldn't bear to look at it. It was years before I started collecting again.'

'Is that right, Sammy? I never knew that.'

He looks at her with immense sadness and whispers, 'Please go now, Sally.'

'Sammy, you said you wanted Mr Brock to bring you Raphael. Well, he didn't cheat you. I'm sure he's never cheated you. He did exactly what you asked.'

'What?' Sammy looks at her, perplexed.

'I am Raphael, Sammy. At least, part of him. Me and Rudi Trakl, together we're Raphael.'

Starling looks at Brock as if this is his preposterous idea, but sees the same astonishment as he feels on Brock's face.

'You feel guilty about Andy's stamps, Sammy,' Sally goes on. 'Well, let me tell you something that I feel guilty about that's much worse than that. When you threw me out of your home – yes, you did, Sammy, as good as, accusing me of stealing Eva's jewellery – no!'

She holds up her index finger and Starling's attempt to argue this point dies away.

'I couldn't stay there after that, you knew that very well, and I was angry. I thought, my mum took little Sammy into our home when he was an orphan, and now he kicks me out in my old age without a penny.'

Starling makes another attempt to protest, but she waves it aside. 'All right, yes, it was all her doing, but you believed every word she told you, and wouldn't listen when I tried to warn you, right? Right. Anyway, I came back to this part of town, where we all grew up, and the council gave me a little place, temporary, like, and I took up again with some old friends who'd stayed hereabouts, like Rudi Trakl, who worked for a time for my dad. Poor Rudi was going blind, cataracts in both eyes, at the wrong end of a long hospital waiting list, and drinking every penny he could get because of it. I looked after him, poor old bugger, and tried to work out how we could get enough money to live better and get his eyes fixed.

'Now, I'd left you my forwarding address, as you know, and one day, bright as a button, who should turn up on my doorstep but Eva. I couldn't believe the gall of the girl, even less when she got round to telling me what she wanted. She was in a right pickle, she said, going mad with worry. You remember that beautiful gold and emerald necklace you gave her?'

Starling's eyes widen and he becomes very still.

'Yes, well, she said she'd been very stupid and lost it, and I knew what that meant, of course – sold it for drug money. She said you'd been asking where it was, and she'd told you it was having the clasp repaired, but sooner or later she knew you were going to find out the truth, unless she could replace it. She'd found another identical one in the shop you bought it from, and she needed ten thousand quid to buy it. Unfortunately she had no cash, but she was sure that I must have squirrelled a bit away over the years, and would I lend it to her?'

Starling leans back against the wall, looking more ashen than before, but he doesn't challenge Sally's story.

'I blew my flippin' lid, believe me. I told her everything I knew and suspected about her, and told her to eff off in no uncertain terms. She scarpered with a flea in her ear, but later

300

on, when I'd calmed down and was telling Rudi about it, another thought came into my head. I thought, here's Sammy wants to spend all his money on bloody stamps, and here's Eva, Rudi and me all needing that money in our different ways. Why can't we all be happy? Tell the truth, I didn't care whether Eva was happy or not, but I figured she'd have to be part of it. The key was Rudi. He'd always been a brilliant copier. I remember him in our dad's shop when I started work there, copying the drawings for the latest fashions so you couldn't tell the difference between Dior and Hubbard. And he'd told me he'd made copies of etchings for this bent art dealer he knew up West. Only that was before his eyes got bad, and I wasn't sure he could still do it. But he knew about stamps, and when I told him what was in my mind he said he'd give it a try.

'That first one was the most difficult. We used your book, of course, Sammy. We picked a nice one from your book . . .'

'Nova Scotia, 1853, one penny brown, block of twenty, mint.' Sammy recites dully.

'I daresay you're right. Rudi's a perfectionist, and it was agony to watch him, his nose almost touching the surface of the plate, working away all hours, week after week. But it did take his mind off the booze.

'While he was working at that, I found Walter. We needed someone in the business, see, to make it look convincing. I would have preferred someone else, someone more dependable, who looked more respectable, but Walter was the only one I could find. And that was when we decided that we would have to invent Raphael.

'I didn't really trust Walter, you see. I knew him of old, and I knew he had a reputation as a grass. I was bothered that he might decide one day to shop us, either to the Old Bill or to you, and so I didn't want him to know where the stamps would be coming from, and who would really be involved. Raphael was Eva's idea. She invented him, like one of the characters in those movies she was always going to see. I never thought Walter would swallow it, but she believed in Raphael, and she could make other people believe in him too.

'When the stamps were finished, Eva took them to Walter's shop in Shepherd's Row. She told him that she had a rich husband who was mad keen on stamps. She said she also had a lover, a young penniless art student, who was very clever at copying things. She and her lover wanted to steal money from her husband by selling him fake stamps that the lover would make. But they needed a proper stamp dealer to act as middle man, to convince the husband that it was all above board. Was he interested?

'She made it sound like a fairy story, you know the way she could tell you something in that accent of hers, and Walter was fascinated, but of course he wanted nothing to do with it. Not until she showed him Rudi's work. He told her it was so good that he couldn't believe it wasn't the real thing, and she told him things about Raphael, about the etchings he had been doing for the art market, and other things. And then he realised that this could be a serious proposition.

'Eva told him that this was the bait, a free sample to get her old man hooked. She would give this to him, and say she had sold one of her necklaces to buy it for him from this funny little shop she'd found. Then her husband would come to the shop, and they would begin to sell him other high-value stamps that her lover, Raphael, would make for them, and then they would all be rich.

'I'm sorry, Sammy,' she says, and falls silent.

'He told me they were lovers,' Sammy whispers, 'Eva and Raphael. That's why I cut off his fingers. He told me the name straight away, but I cut them off anyway. I was very upset.'

'Of course you were,' Sally says consolingly. 'Considering everything that had happened.'

'Hang on,' Brock says. 'What about the murder of Mary Martin?'

Sally hangs her head. 'When everything worked so well, Walter wanted to know more about Raphael, and Eva obliged. She created little stories for him, like instalments of a movie serial. As well as Raphael, there was this friend of his that they called The Beast, because he was so scary and nobody knew his name. She invented him to frighten Walter, in case he turned difficult.

'One day Walter told Eva that he'd heard about a new machine that a forger like Raphael would be interested in. He showed her a photocopy of the specifications that he'd come across, and told her some details of when and where it would be kept in London, on its way to a printer up north. He said he'd heard all this on the grapevine. When Eva told us, we all thought what a joke it was that he was taking Raphael so seriously, wanting to help him. Of course, there was no way we could try to steal the machine, although we wished we could.

'Then we read in the papers what had happened to the lady copper in the warehouse, and the joke wasn't funny any more. But the thing was, it impressed Walter no end. He was convinced Raphael had killed the copper, and from then on he treated Eva with a kind of dread, as if she might set The Beast on him if he didn't behave. She lapped it up.'

Brock shakes his head, perplexed. 'And Walter knew nothing about you and Rudi?'

'Nothing. Eva would take him fresh stamps that Raphael had given her, and collect the money in return. They made up the story of the widow and her family heirloom collection together, she and Walter.'

Starling looks devastated as the full extent of their betrayal sinks in. 'I got expert opinion,' he whispers. 'I had the first few lots checked, to make sure . . .'

'Dr Waverley?' Sally says.

'You know him?' Brock asks.

'Oh, yes. He was a smart one. He came to Walter's shop one day and said that he'd been checking some of the stamps that Sammy had bought from him. He didn't come right out and say they were forgeries, and Walter got the impression he wasn't absolutely sure. He was fishing, probing Walter's story, letting him know he had doubts about the whole thing. He certainly got Walter worried. Finally he said, "Tell you what, Mr Pickering, why don't you suggest to your seller that they might like to pay me a fee to authenticate the stamps before they come to Mr Starling, so as to avoid the embarrassment that might arise if I were to find that some of them weren't quite right?" Walter agreed to put the proposal to his client, and we decided we had to go along with it. Ten per cent, he took. That's what we called him, Dr Ten Per Cent. The rest was divided equally between Walter, Eva, Rudi and me.'

'Do you have records of what was paid to Waverley?' Brock asks.

'Walter kept a book of all Raphael's transactions, money in and money out.'

'I've got it,' Starling says, pulling a small notebook from his hip pocket. 'He gave it to me. But I can't make out who the people are.'

'He gave them nicknames. Waverley is Afghan, because Walter said he reminded him of an Afghan hound, tall and thin and over-bred.'

Sally gets slowly to her feet, goes over to Starling, puts her arms round him and draws him to her, so tiny and frail that she makes him look ungainly large, and he sags and begins sobbing in her arms.

'Poor Sammy,' she whispers. 'Poor Sammy . . .'

Eventually he lifts his head to Brock and says, 'Who killed her, Mr Brock? Who killed my Eva?'

'Someone who hates us both, Sammy. They took everything from you and made you look like a murderer, and for good measure they made me look like a thief. I think it's time we sat down together and put an end to it, don't you?'

Starling nods, and wipes the back of his hand across his eyes. Brock gets stiffly to his feet and goes over to Desai. 'Leon, old chap,' he whispers anxiously, 'can you hear me?'

The head stirs and gives a little nod. Thankfully Brock takes hold of the tape and peels it off, layer by layer, until Desai is blinking up at him ruefully. He has a large bruise on his left temple, and he winces with pain as Brock frees his wrists and ankles, so that Brock tells him to stay on the floor and wait for help.

Brock is the first through the front door, waving into the darkness, then shading his eyes when the floodlights come on, and holding Starling's rifle up for them to see. He turns back to the doorway, and Starling comes through, blinking tentatively, hands in the air.

He points down into the darkness of the central courtyard towards the streetlights at the far end, illuminating the waste-ground which they had driven past earlier that evening. 'That's where I was going to get you and Raphael to come, Mr Brock,' he says. 'One bullet each for you, I had. Then one for me.' He sighs hopelessly. 'I couldn't have got things more wrong, could I?'

'It hasn't been your week, Sammy.'

'You can say that again. I reckon I must have killed a Chinaman.'

He grins weakly at Brock, who smiles back encouragingly, and is then startled to see a small black hole appear in the centre of Starling's forehead, followed a moment later by the ringing smack of a gunshot. Without changing his expression, Starling drops like a sack of potatoes to the floor.

There are sudden shouts, cries from the darkness. Brock drops to his knees, pulling Sally down with him, calling to Desai to stay inside. Sally is wiping stuff from her eyes, spray from the exit wound in the back of Starling's head.

18

The Source

Tim Waverley objected strenuously to being roused at dawn. As he was brought down to the interview room he didn't shrink from making comparisons between the Metropolitan Police and the KGB to the silent officers who accompanied him. He became quiet, however, when he saw the grim-faced pair waiting for him, Brock meeting his eyes without acknowledgement, and McLarren with eyebrows bristling furiously at the sheet of paper clutched in his hands.

'Sit down,' McLarren said, without preliminaries, and immediately cautioned him.

Waverley looked from one to the other without replying, now very alert. He tried to make out what was written on the paper McLarren had set aside on the table. It appeared to be a list of some kind.

'Dr Waverley, we require you to make a full statement of your involvement in the events which have led to the death of Eva Starling,' McLarren went on.

Waverley paled a little. He took his time replying, sweeping the errant lock of hair back from his forehead. 'I've had no involvement in Eva Starling's death, Superintendent. Perhaps I should say no more until I get legal advice.'

'As you wish,' McLarren said.

'What exactly am I suspected of?'

'Suspected is no longer the relevant word, Dr Waverley. You are known to have been a party to a fraud involving the sale of forged stamps to Mr Sammy Starling.'

'Oh, really?' Waverley said carefully. He was momentarily disconcerted to notice a black stain on the sleeve of Brock's blue shirt – blood, surely – as if the man has been bleeding profusely. 'Have you found Mr Starling then?' he asked, tearing his eyes away from it. 'The last time we spoke he was on the run. Has he accused me of something?'

'This,' said McLarren, sliding the sheet of paper across the table, 'is a full schedule of payments you received from Mr Walter Pickering in respect of the sale of forged stamps to Mr Starling.'

Waverley flushed. 'I certainly carried out inspections for Pickering, authenticating new material – I've already stated that.'

'Most of these stamps you never saw. You simply took ten per cent from the seller in order to keep quiet about their dubious quality when you reported to the buyer, from whom you also took a fee. Dr Ten Per Cent, they called you. Did you know that?'

Waverley, who had been about to make some other point, stopped short and his colour deepened. He took the sheet of paper cautiously and examined it.

'How much, exactly, do you know?' he said at last. 'I mean, if you already know it all, there's not a lot of point in my saying anything, is there?'

'We want your version. And your co-operation will be noted and the court advised accordingly. That is likely to be especially important when it comes to the murder charge.'

'What murder charge?' Waverley jerked up straight, sending his hair flopping forward again. He adjusted hair and spectacles in one fluid movement. 'You don't imagine that I was involved in any murder?'

'You were a party to the kidnapping of Mrs Starling.'

'No!'

'What about the business of switching envelopes that morning at Cabot's, before the auction?'

'Oh – you know about that? You have found Starling, then, haven't you? He's told you.'

McLarren gave no response. Waverley took a deep breath before continuing. Again he blinked at the sleeve of Brock's shirt, trying to make out if he was hurt.

'I have the greatest admiration for Raphael, you know,' he said, with some little defiance. 'Whatever else he may have done, he is an absolute angel when it comes to forging postage stamps. I think I would have kept quiet even if they hadn't offered me money, just to see what else he'd come up with. And I just loved the story, didn't you? The love affair, and all that. And everything was going along just fine, until, what, a week, ten days ago? Is that all it was? It seems so much longer.

'Anyway, I got a phone call from this character, who said he was representing somebody who wanted me to authenticate a stamp for them. I said fine, and asked who had recommended me, and he said Mr Raphael. That stopped me short, as you can imagine. Then he mentioned one or two names, Pickering and Starling and Chalon Heads, and the way he said these things was quite intimidating. The nub of it was that he knew exactly what was going on, and the price of his silence was my co-operation and confidentiality in the matter of his client's business.

'At the end of last week, Friday it would have been, I think, he contacted me again, and asked if I'd had anything to do with Mr Starling recently. I was very surprised, because I'd just spent the morning talking with you and Mr Starling about the third ransom note, and about the possibility of making a copy of the Canada Cover. I mentioned something of this to him, and he was extremely interested. He insisted on our meeting, which we did later that afternoon, at a place in Hyde Park which he nominated.

'He made me go through everything again, every detail. He wasn't a very impressive character, yet he was extremely intimidating, mainly because he knew so much about me and about the business with Pickering.'

'What was his name?'

'He said just to call him Ronnie. He gave me the number of his mobile.' Waverley took his wallet from his pocket and handed over a card on which a number had been written.

'His phone rang, actually, when I was there, and he told whoever it was on the other end what I'd been telling him. At the end of it he told me that his client would require my services on the following afternoon, to authenticate a special stamp, and that's when I realised that he must be referring to the Canada Cover, and that these must be the kidnappers.' He shook his head. 'That scared me stiff, I can tell you. He saw that, and he threatened me, said that his client wouldn't hesitate to kill me if I messed it up or breathed a word to anyone. I had no choice, you see. I had to co-operate.'

Waverley paused for a drink of water, his hand shaking as he lifted it to his mouth.

'That night he phoned me again. I was at the forensic science laboratories at the time, and I was terrified, taking his call there of all places. He asked me how the copy was going, and I said it looked as if we could have something good enough by the next day, in time for the auction. Then he said he had two instructions for me. The first was that I had to make sure that the copy wasn't used, by throwing doubt on its quality when we met to make the final decision next day. The other, which terrified me even more, was that I had to make sure that Chief Inspector Brock took charge of the copy, and to exchange it at the last minute for an identical but empty packet. When I asked why, he said they were going to make it look as if he had stolen the real stamp, and that would take the heat off them.'

'It had to be Chief Inspector Brock?' McLarren asked.

'Yes, no one else.'

'And presumably they paid you for this little service.'

'They . . . promised me payment, yes. But I never received it, under the circumstances.'

'How much?'

'Fifty thousand, once they had sold the Canada Cover on to this buyer they had lined up.'

'Well, that must have made you feel a wee bit braver. What do you mean, under the circumstances?'

'Well, because of what happened – I mean, it all went so amazingly well, at first. I was absolutely petrified, in a room full of police, that someone would see me switching the packages, but they didn't. I gave Chief Inspector Brock the empty packet and kept the copy to hand over to Ronnie later that afternoon, when I had to meet him to authenticate the Canada Cover that Mr Starling had delivered to the airport. But later, at lunchtime, when I looked in my bag, I was stunned to find that the envelope had gone.'

'Oh, yes?' McLarren said, keeping his voice neutral. 'And how did you account for that?'

'I couldn't! I was absolutely dumbfounded. And frightened, too, about what Ronnie's client would say. It was only when I met Ronnie later that afternoon that I realised what had happened.'

He took another gulp of water.

'Go on,' McLarren urged impatiently.

Waverley glanced nervously at Brock, who had said nothing at all, had just sat there observing him balefully, like Moses in a bloodstained shirt. 'Er . . . Yes, that afternoon, I met Ronnie in a quiet back-street in Southall. I had some portable equipment in the car – a small microscope. I got a shock when I studied the cover and realised that it was the copy that had gone missing from my bag. And then I understood what must have happened. It was obvious. When we met that morning at Cabot's, there had been an expectation that we would use the copy to fool the kidnappers. Sammy was keen on the idea. But after I'd given my opinion on the copy, that all changed and the police wouldn't agree to it. Sammy left the room at that point, and he didn't see me hand the package over to Chief Inspector Brock. When he returned, we broke up to get coffee, and he, assuming the copy was in my bag, must have taken it. Then later, on the way to the airport, he exchanged it for the real cover, hoping the kidnappers wouldn't be able to tell.'

He shook his head. 'It was a tragic miscalculation. Ronnie was beside himself when I told him. He went off in a fury, warning me to keep everything to myself. Later, when I heard what had happened to Mrs Starling, I realised just how savagely they had reacted to Sammy's attempt to cheat them. My God, I had no idea things would go so far. But I couldn't say anything, could I? I was implicated by then, wasn't I?'

He stared at them both, vainly seeking some kind of sympathy, the limp lock of hair over his right eye left untouched.

'You were indeed,' McLarren said grimly. 'So where is the real Canada Cover now, Dr Waverley?'

'Why, Sammy Starling has it, doesn't he? He never handed it over.'

Later that morning they pulled Ronnie Wilkes off a flight bound for New Zealand, where his sister lived. He had turned up at Heathrow not long after the morning news bulletin broke the story about the murder of Sammy Starling, and booked the first available flight. The plane had already taxied to the end of the runway, and Ronnie was safely strapped in his seat, relief soaking through him, when the main cabin door was reopened and the detectives came aboard and arrested him. The anticlimax at the end of all that nervous strain made him throw up as soon as his feet touched the ground, and he made little attempt to deny the accusations that McLarren levelled against him in the Heathrow police station.

Ronnie had been approached, he said, a couple of years ago, by someone acting for a former police officer, who had a grudge against Sammy Starling. This man knew that he worked for Sammy, and also knew about Ronnie's gambling, and that he had been lately getting badly into debt. He had offered money, a little to be going on with, and the promise of a lot later, if Ronnie would give him information about Sammy. It had been innocuous at first: the man, who called himself Mr K, would ring him up every few weeks, they would chat about the details of Sammy's life, and a few days later an envelope would arrive for Ronnie with some money.

Then gradually Mr K began to focus on Eva's trips to town. He insisted that Ronnie clear with him what he would report to Sammy about Eva's movements, and when he discovered her association with the stamp dealer Walter Pickering, and began to suspect her drug habit fed through the Cinema Hollywood, Mr K had instructed him to say nothing of these things to his employer. He had never been entirely sure what Eva, Pickering and Waverley were up to, but from the way Mr K spoke about it he began to feel that he knew more, and was following up these leads himself, letting Ronnie know only what he thought necessary.

Several times he had thought of telling Sammy what was going on, but he'd needed the cash, and the longer it went on the more difficult it was to come clean. The crunch came when Mr K instructed him to steal three stamps from Sammy's collection. He had been very particular as to which ones he wanted, from some country Ronnie had never heard of. He'd had to wait several weeks before the opportunity presented itself, with Mr K phoning him up every other night, ranting away at him to do what he was told or else. That's when he'd first begun to realise that Mr K was a nutter, and that it might be dangerous to cross him.

'So who was this Mr K?' McLarren demanded.

Ronnie had never met him face to face, and was never given a phone number or address. But when Sammy told him one day that he wanted him to follow an ex-copper whose name was Keller, he'd put two and two together. When he'd reported this to Mr K, the man had laughed, and told him what to tell Sammy, and not to bother following Keller.

'But Marty Keller didn't get out of jail until this last April,' McLarren objected.

'Yeah, well, it was his brother, Barney, wasn't it? Getting things ready for when Marty came out. Stands to reason. Must have been him.'

'And where is Marty Keller now, Ronnie? Where can we find him? He's not been seen at his flat in days.'

'He rents a mechanic's workshop in Wembley. That's where he keeps his gear. There's a bed there, and a toilet. It's where he kept Eva. That's where he'll go to ground. Only you won't take him. He told me he wouldn't go back to jail again.'

Ronnie was right. Marty Keller fired just one shot when armed police surrounded the workshop. The police doctor pronounced him dead at 1307 hours, killed with the same rifle and in the same manner as Sammy Starling.

Once he was certain that Keller was dead, Ronnie Wilkes informed police that Keller had told him that he had buried Eva's body somewhere in the woods above Sammy's house, the Crow's Nest.

Jock McLarren felt ambivalent about his triumph. On the one

hand he had solved both the most notorious murder of the year and the most significant philatelic fraud of the decade. On the other, his famous Raphael had turned out to be a risible opponent, and the prosecution of the pathetic figures of Sally and Rudi was going to provide plenty of opportunities for snide jokes at his expense within the corridors of Cobalt Square and New Scotland Yard. Of their surviving victims, Cabot's, as inheritors of one of the finest collections of classic stamp forgeries, were inclined to play down the affair, leaving only the Fitzpatricks. Their best interests seemed to lie in some form of private reimbursement of their lost funds by the forgers. So many key witnesses were dead, or, in the case of Walter Pickering, unlikely to survive a trial. On balance, McLarren thought he might use every bit of his influence to encourage the Crown Prosecution Service to the view that the case against Sally and Rudi might be difficult to pursue. In the public interest, of course.

Having come to this decision, McLarren was persuaded that they had won, on the whole, a glorious victory, and he told his secretary to round up a few of the key players for celebratory drinks in his office at seven that evening, and especially those, like Brock and to a lesser extent Kathy, towards whom he had an uneasy sense that he had behaved badly.

Brock spent most of the afternoon fussing over Leon Desai's accommodation in hospital, and the prognosis for his severe concussion, suffered, like the broken jaw and cracked ribs, when Starling had inadvertently pushed him down a flight of stairs during their forced entry at Myatts Grove. Kathy passed her time following up a number of loose ends in the case to be mounted against the surviving perpetrators.

At 7.10 p.m., Kathy opened the door to McLarren's office. The men were in shirt-sleeves, McLarren, Brock, Hewitt standing by the windows looking out over Vauxhall station, drinks in hand. A knot of others from McLarren's team stood on the other side of the room. There was a companionable murmur of relaxed conversation, of tension easing away.

'Come in! Come in, lassie!' McLarren waved a hand at her. 'What are you drink—?' He stopped in mid-sentence and stared in surprise at the person Kathy was leading into the room.

'Sir, I hope you don't mind, but Peter White has been helping us, and I thought it might be appropriate if he joined us.'

'Well . . .' McLarren recovered quickly. 'Why, certainly, of course! Come away in, Peter, old friend.'

White ducked his head in an embarrassed little bob. 'I really didn't think it proper for me to be here, Jock, but Kathy insisted . . .'

'Of course you should be here! She was quite right. What's your poison, eh? As if we didn't know.' He clapped White on the arm and led him to the drinks. It was apparent to everyone that the retired chief inspector couldn't hide his pleasure at being there. His face glowed pink and freshly shaved, and he had dressed carefully, a little too formally, his best suit and best tie, now five or six years out of fashion.

Kathy went over to the group of lower-ranking staff on the other side of the room and spoke for a while to DC Colleen Murchison, with whom she had spent part of the afternoon.

Conversation became louder as the drink flowed, and then McLarren's voice rose above the hubbub to make a short and good-humoured speech, thanking them all, and most particularly their comrades from SO1 and laboratory liaison. Toasts were proposed, a couple of jokey remarks tossed around, and conversations resumed. Kathy watched the triumvirate across the room: Brock, White and the ebullient McLarren, three old hands congratulating each other, yarning about old times, and felt profoundly depressed. Something made McLarren look up at that point and he caught the expression on her face, and thought that, despite his generous words of thanks, he had perhaps failed to please her, although God knows he had tried. And so, with a little spurt of gallantry he called to her across the room, rather too loudly, so that conversations died away again, 'Kathy! You look low in spirits, lassie. Come and let me replenish you!'

The room went silent, and someone sniggered.

Kathy didn't stir, then replied, 'I was thinking of Mary Martin, sir.'

'Oh, Lord, yes.' McLarren's face darkened. That was the black thought that he had been avoiding all day – that they had discovered Raphael but failed to find Mary's killer. And at that moment he did not appreciate Kathy bringing it up, in such a way, at their triumph. The rest of the room didn't like it either. She hadn't even known Mary Martin, as they all had.

'After all our hard work, it turns out that poor Mary was the victim of a random act,' McLarren said heavily. 'The sort of thing that could happen to any of us, at any time, when our luck runs out.'

There was a murmur of assent. Someone muttered a toast to Mary's memory. Glasses were raised awkwardly, the drinks no longer quite as palatable.

'I don't think so,' Kathy said quietly, looking down at the empty glass in her hand, feeling the pressure of their attention turn on her again.

'I beg your pardon?' McLarren said. 'You'll have to explain that remark for us, lassie. What has Mary's murder to do with Eva Starling's?'

'I think it has everything to do with it, sir. Mary Martin's death was the thing that kept the Raphael investigation going, without which none of this would have happened. Everything changed with Mary's death. It was the time that Marty Keller had a breakdown in prison, the time when Cabot's published their programme of auctions for the following twelve months, leading up to the auction for which Eva died . . .'

Voices came from around the room, puzzled, some angry. McLarren cut across them: 'What the hell are you talking about, Sergeant?'

Kathy was very pale. She took a deep breath and gripped the edge of the table behind her to stop herself shaking. 'And it was the shocking way that Mary was killed that galvanised everyone, wasn't it? I looked at the photographs this afternoon. The terrible wounds, like the way the Mau Mau used to hack people to death with machetes . . . Peter White was in Kenya at that time, weren't you, Peter? You mentioned it to me. You must have seen wounds like that?'

White seemed rather startled to be singled out in this way. He looked at Kathy as if she were mad, then gave a modest little bow to the others and retired again behind his glass of whisky.

'Kathy,' McLarren was looking with concern at her now, 'I think that's enough, lassie.' His voice was conciliatory. 'We've all put in some very long, hard hours. You need some rest. You've earned it.' At his elbow White leaned over and whispered something in McLarren's ear.

'Sir, I've referred the photographs and reports of Mary Martin's death to Dr Mehta,' Kathy said. 'I've asked him to establish if the same weapon may have been used to decapitate Eva Starling.'

'What!' The room erupted now with noise. Only Kathy was silent and still, and Brock. She looked over at him and he gave her a little nod, his face as masked and expressionless as Sammy Starling's would have been.

As the noise subsided, McLarren said angrily, 'There is no connection between the murder of the two women, Sergeant. Dammit! Eva Starling's killer was in a maximum-security prison at the time of Mary Martin's death!'

'Was he? The plan to kidnap Eva and fix Sammy was begun long before Marty Keller got out of prison. Ronnie Wilkes was recruited a couple of years ago.'

'By someone acting on Marty's instructions – his brother Barney.' McLarren sounded exasperated.

'We've been interviewing Barney all afternoon. He denies it.'

'Of course he does!'

'And he wasn't in London at the time Mary Martin was killed. I've checked. On the morning of the eighth of July last year he was in Durham, visiting his brother in jail.'

'But that's what I'm telling you!' McLarren spluttered, astounded at the insolent persistence of the woman facing him. 'They had nothing to do with Mary's death!'

Kathy said, 'Why –' The syllable caught in her throat, so dry, and she coughed and started again, making her voice big enough to command their attention. 'Why was SO6 fed material on Raphael for a full year before Mary died?'

The question brought instant silence. This was home ground. McLarren stared at her.

'Now that we know that Raphael was simply a private fairy-tale, a family rip-off played by Sally and Rudi and Eva and Walter Pickering on Sammy Starling, why would they want anyone else to get a whiff of it, let alone set off a full-scale investigation by SO6?'

People were exchanging glances, shaking their heads.

'Can I ask, sir, who your sources were for the stories about Raphael?' Kathy persisted.

At first McLarren seemed inclined to tell her to go to hell, but then decided that humouring her might be easier. 'We had information coming in from all over,' he said gruffly. 'Why,' he smiled, trying to lighten the mood, 'even Peter here had his ear to the ground for us, didn't you, Peter?'

White shrugged noncommittally.

'Peter White was a Raphael source?' Kathy asked.

'Aye.'

'And in exchange you gave him information, and kept him involved in things.'

'Aye.' Jock McLarren glared at Kathy, beginning to feel really quite irritated. The damn woman was standing there, in his office, in front of his colleagues, drinking his booze, and *interrogating* him.

'Did you wonder . . .' Kathy stopped and rephrased it. 'Weren't there questions about why this information was being leaked? I mean, surely a super-forger would want to be invisible, especially when there was so little physical evidence that he existed?'

'All right! That's enough, Sergeant!' McLarren exploded. 'You go home now and get some rest, and first thing tomorrow morning you report to my office and tell me what's on your damned mind.'

Kathy didn't move. She saw Peter White staring at her with something like fascination, eyes glittering bright, a tight little smile playing on the mouth beneath the precisely clipped moustache.

'Sir,' Kathy persisted, 'I'd like to say what I think happened to Mary Martin.'

Someone put down their drink too heavily on a glass-topped table, with a bang. Someone else muttered 'Jesus!'

White turned to McLarren and said in a low voice, which everyone clearly heard, 'I warned you, Jock. I told you she was a bloody menace.'

But Jock McLarren couldn't send her away now, when the whole room was straining to hear what she had to say about Mary's death.

'Go on, then,' he said ominously. 'One minute, then you leave.'

'I think the source of the Raphael information came upon it accidentally, while he was digging for something to damage Sammy Starling. He gave it to you as a trade, to keep himself in touch with things inside the force. In a way it was quite innocent – he believed the stories to be true. He just embellished them a bit, to make them irresistible. And he genuinely hoped you would catch Raphael, so that Sammy would suffer by being confronted with his wife's betrayal. But not too soon, because he wanted to continue being your source.

'Then you decided to set a trap for Raphael. You gave your informants details of the new copying machine, of course, so that the word would get back to Raphael. The source was as interested as anyone to see what would happen. He had a real dilemma – if Raphael was caught, he would lose his information to trade with you, but if Raphael didn't show up there was a danger that the whole investigation would be abandoned as a waste of time. I imagine the source was there, in Kilburn, watching and waiting with the rest of you, although you didn't see him. As time passed and Raphael didn't appear, he probably realised that there could be another way, one that would keep the Raphael story alive. He got some hired help, and when the stake-out at the warehouse was finally abandoned, he went in himself, to remove the copier as if Raphael had outsmarted you all.

'But unfortunately Mary Martin returned. I imagine she confronted the hired help because her gun was drawn. The source was behind her, although she didn't know it. He had brought something – a machete, perhaps – to open the packing cases. She heard him, and began to turn, and he realised that he knew her, and realised, too, that she would recognise him if she saw him. I suppose he had only a split second to decide what to do. He killed her.'

Kathy looked across at Peter White. 'You knew Mary, didn't you, Peter? I saw on her record that she worked in your section for six months, before you had her transferred somewhere else. You said that *she* was a menace too, I recall. You wrote it on her file.'

White's jaw dropped. He lowered his glass and was about to utter some oath or protest but Kathy ploughed on.

'Everything changed after that. What had been almost a game became, for the killer, a very serious and deadly thing. From that moment, Sammy and Eva were doomed. I don't think you did it to avenge Tom Harley, really, Peter. Nor Marty Keller. I think you drew Keller into it like you did the others, thinking they were serving their own ends when really they were only serving yours, as you brought them all, Sammy and Eva, Pickering, Waverley and Keller, crashing down in flames. And Brock too – why not contaminate him in the general collapse?'

White put down his glass very deliberately and stepped forward, fists clenched so tight that his arms shook with the tension, at first unable to speak with rage.

'You mad, stupid bitch,' he finally spat at her. 'I knew from the first that you were a waste of space.'

He lifted his right arm slowly up to shoulder height, as if it held the handle of an invisible weapon which he would bring down on Kathy's head. Jock McLarren, looking shocked, jumped forward and took his arm. 'Easy, Peter!'

White was shaking. He turned his face to McLarren's and said, 'Does she think anyone would believe this? I tell you, Jock, she's lost it! I warned you! They can't cope with the pressure.'

'How did Keller find Sammy last night, Peter?' Kathy cut in, her voice angry and harsh. 'How did he know to come to Myatts Grove to shoot Sammy? He knew because I told you we were there and you told him. You'd recruited me, just as you'd once recruited Superintendent McLarren. You phoned me to give me your helpful ideas, and I was so sorry for this lonely old bastard, and so impressed when you finally got something right, that I laughed and told you where Sammy was, and as good as put a bullet through his head.'

She turned to McLarren and said, 'That's why I'm *low in spirits*, sir. I killed Sammy Starling.'

19

A Chalon Head

Kathy sat on the edge of Leon Desai's bed, eating the grapes she'd brought for him. He watched her, his head bandaged, jaw wired.

'I'm sorry you can't eat these,' Kathy said. 'I should have realised.'

'Never mind,' he mumbled through clenched teeth. 'Thanks for the book.'

He lifted the paperback she'd brought and read the title again thoughtfully, *The God of Small Things*.

'This isn't some kind of ironic comment on my personal attributes, is it?' he asked.

She laughed. 'Of course not.'

'They say I'll have a scar on my left temple.'

'Oh dear. So you won't be perfect any more.'

'Only on the outside. How are you getting on with White?'

Kathy shrugged. 'He's enjoying himself. This is much better than pruning roses. He's the unrivalled centre of attention. There's no chance that he'll do himself in with a bottle of pills. Not for a while, anyway.'

She munched another few grapes. 'The psychologist has come up with a preliminary diagnosis. Narcissistic Personality Disorder, he reckons.'

'What's that?'

Kathy took a pad from her bag and consulted her notes. ' "A personality disorder is where the subject displays normal reasoning processes and mental state, but nevertheless exhibits bizarre or otherwise unacceptable behaviour." '

'That covers everyone.'

Kathy nodded. 'The point is that they are responsible for their actions. Narcissistic Personality Disorder is . . .' she searched through her notes and quoted ' ". . . a pervasive pattern of inflated self-importance, lack of empathy with others, and at the same time hypersensitivity to their evaluation." '

'That's everybody again,' Leon mumbled, through his swollen mouth.

'White exhibits classic symptoms, apparently. He has features of a "craving personality", a "manipulative personality" and a "paranoid personality".'

'That's what I said – perfectly normal.'

'He demands to be seen as someone special, entitled to special treatment, he reacts to criticism with feelings of rage, and he has chronic feelings of envy for those he perceives as more successful. Apparently that's the root of his hatred of Brock. Even though they reached the same rank, he always felt that others looked up to Brock more. It was he who convinced McLarren that Brock was corrupt. Similarly he was enraged by Sammy's wealth and marriage to a young, attractive woman, and he has a special dislike of young women whom he suspects of being more successful than he was at their age. As for being manipulative . . .'

Kathy put her her notes away and took a few more grapes. 'He's not a nice man. While he was within the discipline of the force, and had a wife to temper his behaviour, he was probably not too bad. It was the stress of loneliness and isolation after his retirement and his wife's death that made it all spiral out of control.'

'Never mind about him, Kathy,' Desai said. 'Indulge my personality disorder, will you? Do you think that I'm not a nice man? I thought we were getting along OK, and then suddenly the shutters came down. It was at Sammy's house that day, after you found Eva's stuff. You've hardly spoken a word to me since, until now.'

Kathy lowered her eyes. 'You're asking me this, when you're lying there in that state, and I can't possibly give you a hard time.'

'That's right. It's characteristic of my manipulative, craving, paranoid personality.'

Kathy gave a tight little smile and raised her eyes to his. 'When I was getting changed that afternoon, while you made the call to McLarren, it suddenly occurred to me that you must have betrayed Brock to McLarren in the first place – that you'd been passing everything on to him.'

Desai stared at her for a moment before saying, very softly, 'Go on. What else?'

'I thought . . . I thought it possible that McLarren had told you to confront Brock the previous evening, to see what he would do, to bring matters to a head and let McLarren take over Brock's investigation . . . which is exactly what happened.'

Kathy looked away, unable to hold the gaze of those dark, unblinking eyes gazing up at her from the frame of white bandage.

She was aware of Leon shifting himself beneath the tight fold of the bedcovers, turning away from her.

'Was I wrong?' she asked.

He took a long time to make a reply, and when it came his voice was soft and angry. 'You jump so easily to conclusions, Kathy. You're so bloody determined to trust nobody.'

She looked down at him, staring away to the far end of the ward where an old man with a walking-frame was making imperceptible progress towards a toilet door. 'Tell me, then. Please.'

He shook his head angrily. 'McLarren didn't need me to betray Brock to him, Kathy. McLarren has had a need-to-know notice on the central computer for months. As soon as the tests on the ransom-note stamps were completed, and the clerk at the lab entered the word "forgery" on her machine, McLarren's office was informed – it was automatic. But yes, I answered his questions when he asked. I didn't hide anything from him to protect Brock. Why should I have done? I work as laboratory liaison for a number of teams, I would have done the same with any of them. And no, McLarren didn't ask me to confront Brock with what we knew about the Canada Cover. I did that myself. I wanted Brock to tell us what was going on, and put a stop to it.'

He rolled back and stared at her. 'This is a matter of loyalty, is it, Kathy? You think I should have behaved differently?'

Kathy felt sick. 'No. I'm sorry, Leon. You were right. You couldn't have done anything else. I suppose . . . I suppose the difference between us was that I knew Brock better. I *knew* that he couldn't have taken the Canada Cover.'

'A matter of trust, then. You trusted Brock, but not me.'

She sighed. 'I'd better go. Can I just tell you that –'

Her words were cut off by the sound of Brock's voice. 'There you two are! I've been half-way round the hospital trying to find you. When did they move you up here, Leon?'

He looked at them, straightening upright as he came to the side of the bed, fixing smiles on their faces. 'What's up? You look down in the dumps, old chap. Kathy depressing you, talking shop, is she? Here, I brought you something to read.'

'Thanks, Brock.' He frowned as he saw the title. '*Shame* . . .'

'Haven't read it, have you?'

'Er . . . no.'

'Has Kathy told you about her performance in McLarren's office last night?'

'I heard about it. I think the whole Met has.'

'It was gripping stuff.' Brock shot Kathy a smile. 'Very impressive. McLarren is a changed man. And as for White . . .' Brock shook his head as if still having trouble with the idea. 'A very evil old man. I'm beginning to feel that all the old men in this force should be put down humanely.'

'It was you who convinced me about him, Brock,' Kathy said quietly.

'Me? How come?'

'Your extra blue pin on the London map, remember? I couldn't figure out who it was, and then I remembered that White had used the nickname Sammy China when I talked to him that first time. So I looked up White's file and found he grew up on the Myatts Grove estate too. His hatred of Sammy must have been a very long-term one.'

'Did he?' Brock said in astonishment. 'I didn't know that. My extra pin was Rudi Trakl – at that stage I wasn't sure if he was involved.'

Desai tried to laugh, but could only wince. 'So this is detective work. I think I'll stick to forensics.'

'Don't mock,' Kathy said. 'We got it all worked out in the end. Except for the Canada Cover. I checked with Cobalt Square. They've searched everywhere. No luck. It looks as if Sammy will take his million to the grave.'

Brock was looking uncomfortable. 'Kathy, one thing I do appreciate is the way you stood up for me against McLarren and the others, over that missing Canada Cover.'

'It wasn't that hard,' Kathy said, feeling Desai look away, and the heavy lump in the pit of her throat growing again. 'I knew you couldn't possibly have taken it, so then it was a matter of working out how it was switched, and Waverley was the only possibility.'

'Yes, I'd hoped you'd come to that conclusion. I knew I could rely on you.'

'Hoped?' Kathy looked puzzled, Brock even more uneasy. 'How do you mean? You already knew he'd done that?'

'I'm afraid so, Kathy. I saw him do it. The fact is,' Brock drew an envelope from his jacket pocket and laid it on the bedclothes between the three of them, 'your faith in me was somewhat misplaced. But I knew I could rely on that, too.'

Kathy looked at him in astonishment, then down at the envelope. She reached across and cautiously picked it up. When she opened the flap she saw the corner of a familiar Chalon Head inside. She drew out the cover carefully and recognised the flamboyant copperplate writing addressed to Mrs Sandford Fleming beneath the black stamp.

'Is this it?' she asked finally.

Brock nodded.

Kathy felt, rather than saw, Desai's eyes burning into her; she kept hers focused on the little stamp, unable to look back at him.

Brock said, 'When I saw Waverley switch the envelopes, I couldn't make out what was going on. At that stage I believed Sammy had staged his wife's disappearance, and the only thing I could think was that Waverley must be working for him, and that they hoped to substitute the copy for the real stamp, and steal it. So when the chance presented itself, I took the other envelope from Waverley's bag, and later that afternoon, when they brought the original upstairs after the auction, I exchanged it for the copy. I thought that would sow a bit of confusion in the enemy camp, although I didn't appreciate then quite how much.'

'But,' Desai's voice was tight, 'why didn t you produce it when they started accusing you of stealing it? And why didn't you tell *us*, last Monday night?'

'I'm sorry, Leon. By then I realised that I was a target as well as Sammy, and I wanted to find out who was behind this, who would benefit and how. And I didn't want you to lie for me – I wanted you to play it absolutely straight, as of course you did.'

Kathy winced and looked away.

Brock shifted on the edge of the bed and added, 'Of course, the longer it went on, the more difficult it became to find the right occasion to produce the damn thing. The thing that haunts me is that if I'd just let things be Eva would still be alive. You said yesterday, Kathy, that you felt responsible for Sammy's death, which is nonsense, of course, but what I did was much worse. They killed Eva because they thought Sammy had cheated them.'

Kathy shook her head. 'No. The head was cold, remember? Frozen. She was already dead by the day of the auction.'

'The forensic evidence isn't conclusive,' Brock objected.

'I'm sure of it, Brock. Beheading Eva was central to Sammy's punishment, a sick joke, a play on Sammy's obsession with Chalon Heads, and a repetition of what White had done to Mary Martin. That's what kept White going, the thought of Sammy opening that box.'

Brock rubbed his face wearily. 'Maybe. Anyway, now I just don't know what the hell to do. I'm walking around with a million quid in my pocket, and I don't know how to give it back.'

Finally Kathy managed to look Desai in the face. He stared at her in silence, his expression neutral and distant, the old Desai, cool and detached.

Then he cleared his throat and turned his attention to Brock.

'My head still hurts,' he murmured. 'And my memory of the time I spent in the Myatts Grove flat with Sammy is pretty hazy after that fall. I couldn't see anything, of course, with the tape over my eyes, but he talked, to me and to himself, quite a bit. I have this feeling that he mentioned something about hiding the Canada Cover.'

Brock looked at him with surprise.

Kathy said, 'Oh, Leon . . .' Then she stopped whatever it was she had been about to say and instead added, 'Yes, that's quite possible, I should think.'

'You might be able to jog my memory,' Desai said to her. 'Maybe if you could lay your hands on a copy of the report describing where they searched, it might come back to me.'

She looked away as she felt a tear coming into her eye.

Brock broke in, 'I couldn't possibly ask you to do that. It's my own damned fault. I should have been more open with you both from the beginning.'

'Yes, well, it's a matter of trust,' Desai said. 'And it'll cost you another slap-up meal at La Fortuna, Brock.'

He added this lightly, and Brock laughed ruefully, but Kathy could hear the edge in Desai's voice, and knew she wasn't forgiven. She got to her feet and looked down at the little portrait on the envelope.

'A female head of the greatest beauty . . .' she said sadly. 'And it all began so innocently, in the days before I knew a cottonreel from a woodblock . . .'

She turned and walked away.